Darlene

PRAISE FOR
DEBBIE MACOMBER

Macomber "tells the parable of women's age-old
concerns with gentle humor and charm."
—*Publishers Weekly*

"Debbie Macomber is one of the few true originals in
women's fiction… Her books are touching and
marvelous and not to be missed."
—Anne Stuart

"Macomber knows what she is doing;
she is no stranger to the *New York Times* bestseller list.
She knows how to please her audience."
—*The Statesman Journal*

New York Times bestselling author Debbie Macomber always enjoyed telling stories—first to her baby-sitting clients, and then to her own four children. As a full-time wife and mother and an avid romance reader, she dreamed of one day sharing her stories with a wider audience. In the autumn of 1982 she sold her first book, and then began making regular appearances on the *USA Today* bestseller list. Now her heartwarming stories have conquered the *New York Times* bestseller list, and there are over forty million copies of her books in print worldwide!

DEBBIE MACOMBER

AN IDEAL MARRIAGE?

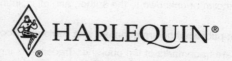

HARLEQUIN®

TORONTO • NEW YORK • LONDON
AMSTERDAM • PARIS • SYDNEY • HAMBURG
STOCKHOLM • ATHENS • TOKYO • MILAN • MADRID
PRAGUE • WARSAW • BUDAPEST • AUCKLAND

ISBN 0-373-83480-2

AN IDEAL MARRIAGE?

Copyright © 2001 by Harlequin Books S.A.

The publisher acknowledges the copyright holder of the individual works as follows:

FATHER'S DAY
Copyright © 1991 by Debbie Macomber

FIRST COMES MARRIAGE
Copyright © 1991 by Debbie Macomber

HERE COMES TROUBLE
Copyright © 1991 by Debbie Macomber

Printed in Canada

CONTENTS

FATHER'S DAY

CHAPTER ONE

"I CAN'T BELIEVE I'm doing this," Robin Masterson muttered as she crawled into the makeshift tent pitched over the clothesline in the backyard of her new home.

"Come on, Mom," ten-year-old Jeff urged, shifting to make room for her. "It's warm as toast in here."

Down on all fours, a flashlight in one hand, Robin squeezed her way inside. Jeff had constructed the flimsy tent using clothespegs to hold up the blankets and rocks to secure the base. The space was tight, but she managed to manoeuvre her slim body into the sleeping bag.

"Isn't this great?" Jeff asked. He stuck his head out of the front opening and gazed at the dark sky and the spattering of stars that winked back at them. On second thought Robin decided they were laughing at her, those stars. And with good reason. There probably wasn't another thirty-year-old woman in the entire state of California who would agree to this craziness.

It was the first night in their new house and Robin was exhausted to the bone. They'd started moving out of the apartment before five that morning and she'd just finished unpacking the last box. The beds were assembled, but Jeff wouldn't hear of doing anything as mundane as sleeping on a real mattress. After waiting years to camp out in his own backyard, her son wasn't about to delay the adventure by even one night.

Robin couldn't let him sleep outside alone, and, since he hadn't met any neighbours yet, there was only one option left. Surely there would be a Mother of the Year award in this for her.

"You want to hear a joke?" Jeff asked, rolling on to his back and nudging her.

"Sure." She swallowed a yawn, hoping she could stay awake long enough to laugh at the appropriate time. She needn't have worried.

For the next half-hour, Robin was entertained with a series of riddles, nonsense rhymes and off-key renditions of Jeff's favourite songs from summer camp.

"Knock knock," she said when it appeared her son had run through his repertoire.

"Who's there?"

"Wanda."

"Wanda who?"

"Wanda who thinks up these silly jokes?"

Jeff laughed as though she'd come up with the funniest line ever devised. Her son's enthusiasm couldn't help but rub off on Robin and some of her weariness eased. Camping was fun—sort of. But it had been years since she'd slept on the ground and, frankly, she couldn't remember it being quite this hard.

"Do you think we'll be warm enough?" she teased. Jeff had used every blanket they owned, first to construct the tent and then to pad it. To be on the safe side, two or three more were piled on top of their sleeping bags on the off-chance an Arctic frost descended upon them. It was spring, but a San Francisco spring could be chilly.

"Sure," he answered, missing the kidding note in her voice. "But if you get cold, you can have one of mine."

"I'm fine," she assured him.

"You hungry?"

Now that she thought about it, she was. "Sure. Whatcha got?"

Jeff disappeared into his sleeping bag and returned a moment later with a limp package of licorice, a small plastic bag full of squashed marshmallows and a flattened box of raisins. Robin decided to forgo the snack.

"When are we going to buy me my dog?" Jeff asked, chewing loudly on the raisins.

Robin listened to the sound and said nothing.

"Mom...the dog?" he repeated after a few moments.

Robin had been dreading the question most of the day. She'd managed to forestall Jeff for the past month by telling him they'd discuss getting a dog after they were settled in their house.

"I thought we'd start looking for ads in the paper first thing tomorrow," Jeff said, still munching.

"I'm not sure when we'll start the search for the right dog." She was a coward, Robin freely admitted, but she so hated to disappoint Jeff. He had his heart set on a dog. How like his father he was, in his love for animals.

"I want a big one, you know. None of those fancy little poodles or anything."

"A collie would be nice, don't you think?"

"Or a German shepherd," Jeff added.

"Your father loved dogs," she whispered, although she'd told Jeff that countless times. Lonny had been gone for so many years, she had trouble remembering what their lives had been like together. They'd been crazy in love with each other and married shortly after their high-school graduation. A year later, Robin became pregnant. Jeff had been barely six months old when Lonny was killed in a freak car accident on his way home from work. In the span of a few short moments, Robin's comfortable cosy world had been sent into a tailspin, and ten years later it was still whirling.

With her family's help, she'd gone back to school and obtained her degree. She was now a certified public accountant working for a large San Francisco insurance firm. Over the years she'd dated a number of men, but none she'd ever seriously consider marrying. She wasn't a high-school kid any longer and her life was far more complicated now than it had been at eighteen. The thought of falling in love again terrified her.

"What kind of dog did Dad have when he was a kid?" Jeff asked.

"I don't think Rover was any particular breed," Robin answered, then paused to recall exactly what Lonny's childhood dog had looked like. "I think he was mostly...Labrador."

"Was he black?"

"And brown."

"Did Dad keep any other animals?"

Robin smiled at the warm memory of her late husband. She enjoyed the way Jeff loved hearing stories about his father. No matter how many times he'd heard them. "He collected three more pets the first year we were married. It seemed he was always bringing home a stray cat or lost dog. We couldn't keep them, of course, because we weren't allowed pets in the apartment complex. We went to great lengths to hide them for a few days until we could locate their owners or find them a good home. For our first wedding anniversary, he bought me a goldfish. Your father really loved animals."

Jeff beamed and planted his chin on top of his folded arms.

"We dreamed of buying a farm someday and raising chickens and pigs and maybe a cow or two. Your father even talked of buying a pony for you." Hard as she might try, she couldn't quite hide the pain in her voice. Even after all these years, the memory of Lonny's sudden death still hurt. Looking at her son, so eager for a dog of his own, Robin missed her husband more than ever.

"You and Dad were going to buy a farm?" Jeff cried, his young voice ebullient. "A pony for me? Really? Do you think we'll ever be able to afford one? Look how long it took to save enough to buy the house."

Robin smiled. "I think we'll have to give up on the idea of you and me owning a farm, at least in the near future."

When they'd first married, Robin and Lonny had talked for hours about their dreams. They'd charted their lives, confident that nothing would ever separate them. Their love had been far too strong. Robin had never told Jeff about buying a farm. Nor had she told him how they'd planned to name it Paradise. Paradise, because that was what the farm would be to them. In retrospect, not telling Jeff was a way of protecting him. He'd lost so much—not only the guidance and love of his father but all the things they could have had as a family. She'd never mentioned the pony before, or the fact that Lonny had always longed for a horse of his own, too....

Jeff yawned loudly and Robin marvelled at his endurance. He'd carted in as many boxes as the movers had, racing up and down the stairs with an energy Robin could only envy. He'd unpacked the upstairs bathroom, as well as his own bedroom and had helped her organise the kitchen.

"I can hardly wait to get my dog," Jeff said, his voice tapering to a murmur. Within minutes he was sound asleep.

"A dog," Robin said softly as her eyes closed. She didn't know how she was going to break the bad news to Jeff. They couldn't get a dog—at least not right away. She was unwilling to leave a large dog locked indoors all day while she went off to work and Jeff was in school. Tying one up in the backyard was equally unappealing, and she couldn't afford to build a fence. Not this year, anyway. Then there was the cost of feeding a dog and paying the vet's bills. With this new home, Robin's budget was already stretched to the limit.

ROBIN AWOKE FEELING chilled and warm at the same time. In the gray dawn, she glanced at her watch. Six-thirty. At some point during the night, the old sleeping bag that dated back to her high-school days had come unzipped and the cool morning air had chilled her arms and legs. Yet her back was warm and cozy. Jeff had probably snuggled up to her during the night. She sighed, determined to go back to sleep for another half-hour or so. With that thought in mind, she reached for a blanket to wrap around her shoulders and met with some resistance. She tugged and pulled, but to no avail. It was then that she felt something wet and warm close to her neck. Her eyes shot open. Very slowly, she turned her head until she came eyeball to eyeball with a big black dog.

Robin gasped loudly and struggled into a sitting position, which was difficult with the sleeping bag and several blankets wrapped around her legs, imprisoning her.

"Where did you come from?" she demanded, edging away from the dog. The Labrador had eased himself between her and Jeff and made himself right at home. His head rested on his paws and he looked perfectly content, if a bit disgruntled to have his nap interrupted. He didn't seem at all interested in vacating the premises.

Jeff rolled over and opened his eyes. Immediately, he bolted upright. "Mom," he cried excitedly. "You got me a dog!"

"No—he isn't ours. I don't know who he belongs to."

"Me!" Jeff's voice was triumphant. "He belongs to me." His thin arms hugged the animal's neck. "You really got me a dog! It was supposed to be a surprise, wasn't it?"

"Jeff," she said firmly. "I don't know where this animal came from, but he isn't ours."

"He isn't?" His voice sagged in disappointment. "But who owns him then? And how did he get inside the tent with us?"

"Heavens, I don't know." Robin rubbed the sleep from her eyes while she attempted to put her garbled thoughts in some kind of order. "He looks too well fed and groomed to be a stray. He must belong to someone in the neighborhood. Maybe he—"

"Blackie!" As if in reply, she was interrupted by a crisp male voice. "Blackie. Here, boy."

The Labrador lifted his head, but stayed where he was. Robin didn't blame him. Jeff was stroking his back with one hand and rubbing his ears with the other, all the while crooning to him softly.

With some effort, Robin managed to divest herself of the sleeping bag. She reached for her tennis shoes and crawled out of the tent. No sooner was she on her feet than she turned to find a lanky man standing not more than a few yards from her, just on the other side of the hedge that separated the two properties. Obviously he was her neighbour. Robin smiled, but the friendly gesture was not returned. In fact, the man looked downright unfriendly.

Her neighbour was also an imposing man, at least six feet tall. Since Robin was only five-three, he towered head and shoulders above her. Instinctively, she stiffened her back, meeting his dark eyes. "Good morning," she said coolly.

He barely looked in her direction, and when he did, he dismissed her with little more than a nod. After a night on the ground, with her son and a dog for bedmates, Robin realised she wasn't going to win any beauty pageants, but she resented the way his eyes flickered disinterestedly over her.

Robin usually gave people the benefit of the doubt, but towards this man, she felt an immediate antipathy. His face was completely emotionless, which gave him an intimidating air. He was clearly aware of that and used it to his advantage.

"Good morning," she said again, clasping her hands tightly. She drew herself to her full height and lifted her chin. "I believe your dog is in the tent with my son."

Her news appeared to surprise him; his face softened. Robin was struck by the change. When his face relaxed, he was actually a very attractive man. For the most part, Robin barely noticed how good-looking a man was or wasn't, but this time...she noticed. Perhaps because of the contrast with his forbidding demeanor of only a moment before.

"Blackie knows better than to leave the yard. Here, boy!" He shouted for the Labrador again, this time including a sharp whistle loud enough to pierce Robin's eardrums. Almost immediately the dog emerged from the tent and reluctantly approached the hedge.

"Is that your dog?" Jeff asked, dashing out right behind Blackie. "He's great. How long have you had him?"

"I'll make sure he doesn't bother you again," the man said, ignoring Jeff's question. Robin supposed his words were meant to be an apology. "He's well trained—he's never left my yard before. I'll make sure it doesn't happen again."

"Blackie wasn't any bother," Jeff hurried to explain, racing forward. "He crawled into the tent with us and made himself at home, which was all right with us, wasn't it, Mom?"

"Sure," Robin answered, flipping her shoulder-length auburn hair away from her face. She'd had it tied at the nape when she'd gone to bed, but it had pulled free during the night. Robin could well imagine how it looked now. Most mornings it tended to resemble foam on a newly poured mug of beer.

"We're friends, aren't we, Blackie?" Jeff knelt, and without hesitation the dog came to him, eagerly licking his face.

The man's eyes revealed fleeting surprise, and his dark brows drew together over his high-bridged nose. "Blackie," he snapped. "Heel."

The Labrador squeezed between two overgrown laurel bushes and returned to his master, who didn't look any too pleased at his dog's affection for Jeff.

"My son has a way with animals," Robin explained.

"Do you live here?" Jeff asked next. He seemed completely unaware of their new neighbour's unfriendliness.

"Next door."

"Oh, good," Jeff returned with a wide grin. He placed his right hand on his chest. "I'm Jeff Masterson and this is my mom, Robin. We moved in yesterday."

"I'm Cole Camden. Welcome to the neighbourhood."

Although his words were cordial, his tone wasn't. Nor the look on his face. Robin felt about as welcome as a punk-rock band at a retirees' picnic.

"I'm getting a dog myself soon," Jeff went on affably. "That's why we moved out of the apartment building—I couldn't have a pet there except my goldfish."

Cole nodded without comment.

Oh, great, Robin thought. After years of scrimping and saving to buy a house, they were going to be stuck with an ill-tempered next-door neighbour. His house was older than the others on the block. Much bigger, too. Robin guessed that his home, a sprawling three-storey structure, had been built in the early thirties. She knew that at one time this neighbourhood had been filled with large opulent homes like Cole Camden's. Gradually, over the years, the older homes had been torn down and a series of two-storey houses and trendy ramblers built in their place. Her neighbour's house was the last vestige of an era long past.

"Have you got any kids?" Jeff could hardly keep the eagerness out of his voice. In the apartment complex there had always been plenty of playmates around, and the ten-year-old was eager to make new friends, especially before he started classes in an unfamiliar school on Monday morning.

Cole's face hardened and Robin could have sworn the question had angered him. An uncomfortable moment passed before he answered. "No, I don't have any kids." His voice held a rough undertone, and for a split second Robin was sure she saw a flash of pain in his eyes.

"Would it be all right if I played with Blackie sometimes? Just until I got my own dog?"

"No." Cole's response was sharp, but, when Jeff flinched at the vehemence with which he spoke, Cole appeared to regret his harsh tone. "I don't mean to be rude, but it would probably be best if you stayed in your own yard."

"That's all right," Jeff said. "You can send Blackie over here to visit any time you want. I like dogs."

"I can see that." A hint of a smile lifted the corners of his mouth. Then his cool gaze moved from Jeff to Robin, his face again expressionless, but she sensed that in some way he'd made up his mind about them, categorised them and come to his own conclusions.

If Cole Camden thought he could intimidate her, Robin had news for him. He'd broadcast his message loud and clear. He didn't want to be bothered by her or her son, and in return he'd stay out of her way. That was fine with her. Terrific, in fact. She didn't have time for humouring grouches.

Without another word, Cole turned and strode toward his house with Blackie at his heels.

"Goodbye, Mr Camden," Jeff called, raising his hand.

Robin wasn't surprised when their neighbour didn't give them the courtesy of a reply.

In an effort to distract Jeff from Cole Camden's unfriendliness, she said brightly, "Hey, I'm starving. How about you?"

Jeff didn't answer right away. "Do you think he'll let me play with Blackie?"

Robin sighed, thinking about the dilemma that faced her. She didn't want Cole to hurt Jeff's feelings, but it wasn't likely their neighbour would appreciate her son's affinity with his Labrador. By the same token, a neighbour's dog, even one that belonged to a grouch, would ease her guilt over not being able to provide Jeff with the dog she'd promised him.

"What do you think, Mom?" Jeff prompted. "He'll probably let me play with Blackie sometimes, don't you think?"

"I don't know, honey," she whispered. "I just don't know."

LATER THE SAME DAY, after buying groceries to stock their bare kitchen shelves and picking up several other necessities, Robin counted the change at the bottom of her purse to be sure she had enough money for the subway on Monday morning. Luckily she had enough spare change for BART—Bay Area Rapid Transit—for the week, but it was packed lunches for her and Jeff until payday, which was two weeks away.

Her finances would have been in better shape if they could have waited another year to move out of the apartment, but at the rate property values were rising Robin couldn't possibly have saved to keep pace with inflation. The interest rates were at a two-year low and she'd decided soon after the first of the year that if she was ever going to move out of the apartment this was the time.

"Mom!" Jeff crashed through the back door, breathless. "We're in trouble."

"Oh?" Robin glanced up from the salad she was mixing. A completely disgusted look on his face, her son flung himself into a chair and plopped his elbows on the table. Then he let out a forceful sigh.

"What's wrong, Jeff?"

"I'm afraid we made a bad mistake."

"How's that?"

"There're nothing but girls in this neighbourhood." He made it sound as though they'd unexpectedly landed in enemy territory. "I rode my bike up and down the street and all I saw were girls." He wrinkled his nose with aversion.

"Don't worry, you'll be meeting lots of boys in school Monday."

"You aren't taking this seriously!" Jeff cried. "I don't even think you fully understand what this means. There are seven houses on this block. Six of them have kids and only one has a boy, and that's me. I'm surrounded by women!"

"How'd you find all this out?"

"I asked, of course." He sighed again. "What are you going to do about it, Mom?"

"Me?" Robin asked, somewhat taken aback. "Are you suggesting we move back to the apartment?"

Jeff considered this for only a moment. "I'd think we should if it weren't for two things. We can't have a dog there. And I found a fort."

"A fort?"

"Yes," he said solemnly. "It's hidden way back in Mr Camden's yard and covered by a bunch of brush. It's real neat there. I don't think he knows about it, because the word on the street is he doesn't like kids. Someone must have built it and I'm going to find out who. If there's a club going, I want in. I've got the right—I live closer to Mr Camden than anyone else does."

"Agreed." Robin munched on a slice of green pepper and handed one to Jeff. "So you think it would be all right if we stayed?"

"I guess so," Jeff conceded, "at least until I find out more about the fort."

Robin was about to say something else when the doorbell chimed.

Jeff's blue eyes met hers. "I bet it's one of those pesky girls," he said in disgust.

"Do you want me to get rid of her?"

Jeff nodded emphatically. "Please."

Robin was smiling when she answered the front door. Jeff was right about one thing—it was a girl, and one who, she guessed, was a couple of years younger than her son. She hadn't come alone, though. Standing with the youngster was an adult.

"Hi," the woman said cheerfully, flashing Robin a warm smile. "I know you've barely had a chance to get settled in, but I wanted to introduce myself. I'm Heather Lawrence and this is my daughter, Kelly. We live next door, and we'd like to welcome you to the neighbourhood."

Robin introduced herself as she opened the door and invited them in. Heather was cute and perky. Her hair was cut in a short bob that bounced when she spoke. Robin knew right away she was going to like her neighbour. Heather's warm reception was a pleasant change from the way Cole Camden had welcomed her.

"Would you like some coffee?" Robin asked.

"If you're sure I'm not interrupting anything."

"I'm sure." Robin led the way into the kitchen where Jeff sat waiting. He cast her a look that suggested she should be shot for treason, then muttered something about forgetting that mothers were really *girls* in disguise and headed out the front door.

Robin reached for two matching ceramic mugs and poured a cup of coffee for her new friend. She offered Kelly a glass of juice, then slid into the chair across the table from the girl and her mother. "I'm sorry about Jeff." She felt obliged to apologise. "He's at the age where he thinks girls are a plague to society."

"Don't worry about it," Heather said, smiling. "Kelly isn't keen on boys herself."

"They're creeps. I'd rather ride my bicycle than visit with a boy, anyway," the girl announced. "But Mom wanted me to come over here with her so she didn't look like a busybody. Right, Mom?"

Heather blushed and cast her daughter a murderous glance.

Robin laughed. "I thought it would take several weeks to get to know my neighbours and I've met two in one day."

"Someone else has already been over?"

"Cole Camden introduced himself this morning," she explained, keeping her eyes averted to hide the resentment she felt toward her unfriendly neighbour. Even now, hours later, she couldn't help thinking about the way he'd reacted to her and Jeff.

"Cole Camden introduced himself?" Heather repeated, sounding shocked. She frowned, staring into space as though digesting the fact.

"To be honest, I think he would have preferred to avoid me until the next Ice Age, but his dog wanted to make friends with Jeff."

Heather's mouth opened and closed twice. "Blackie did?"

"Is there something strange about that?"

"Frankly, yes. To say Cole keeps to himself is an understatement. I don't think he's said more than a handful of words to me in the entire two years since Kelly and I moved here. I don't know why he continues to live in the neighbourhood." She paused to respond to her daughter, who was asking permission to go back home. "Thank Robin for the juice, honey. Anyway," she went on, turning back to Robin when her daughter skipped out of the door, "he's all alone in that huge house and it's ridiculous, really. Can you imagine what his heating bills must be? Although, personally, I don't think money is much of a problem for him. But then, that's something I wouldn't know."

It didn't surprise Robin to learn Cole lived alone. She'd barely met the man, but guessed that life held little joy for him. It was as though love, warmth and friendship had all been found lacking and had therefore been systematically dismissed.

"Apparently, he was married once. At least that's what I've heard, but he was divorced long before I moved here."

Robin had dealt with unfriendly men before, but something about Cole struck her hard and deep, and she wasn't sure what it was or why he would evoke such a strong feeling within her.

"He and his dog are inseparable," Heather added.

Robin nodded, barely listening. He'd intimidated her at first, but when she'd pulled herself together and faced him squarely he'd loosened up a bit and, later, even seemed amused. But then Jeff had asked him about children, and Robin had witnessed the flash of pain in his eyes.

As if by magic, her son's face appeared around the door. When he saw that Kelly was gone, he walked into the room, hands buried in his back pockets.

"Do you have a dog?" he asked Heather.

"Unfortunately, no. Kelly's allergic to animal fur."

Jeff nodded as though to say that was exactly the kind of thing he expected from a girl. "We're getting a German shepherd soon, aren't we, Mom?"

"Soon," Robin responded, feeling wretched. After Heather left, she was going to tell Jeff the truth. She fully intended to let him have his dog, but he'd have to wait a while. For a good part of the day, she'd been practicing what to say. She'd even come up with a compromise idea. They could get a cat. Cats didn't seem to mind being left on their own, and they didn't need the same kind of exercise. Although she wasn't crazy about keeping a litter box in the house, Robin was willing to put up with that inconvenience until she could afford to have a fence built. She planned to be positive and direct with Jeff. He'd understand. At least she hoped he would.

Heather stayed only a few minutes more, and the visit was a fruitful one. Robin learned that Heather was divorced, worked mornings in an office, and provided after-school day care in an effort to spend more time with Kelly. This information was good news to Robin and the two women agreed that Jeff would go to the Lawrence house before and after school, instead of the community centre several blocks away. The arrangement suited them both; even Jeff shrugged his agreement.

Robin would have liked to ask her new friend more about Cole, but his name didn't come up again, and she didn't want to seem too curious about him.

After Heather left, Robin braced herself for the talk with Jeff about getting a dog. Unfortunately, it didn't go well. It seemed that after waiting nearly ten years, a few more months was completely unacceptable.

"You promised!" he shouted. "You said I could have a dog when we moved into the house!"

"You can, sweetheart, but not right away."

Unusual for Jeff, tears gathered in his eyes, and he struggled to hold them back. Soon Robin felt moisture filling her own eyes. She hated disappointing Jeff more than anything. His heart was set on getting a dog right away, and he considered the offer of a cat a poor substitute.

He left the house soon afterward. In an effort to soothe his hurt feelings, Robin cooked her son's favorite meal—macaroni cheese with sliced sausages and lots of ketchup.

She didn't see him on the pavement or the street when she went to check half an hour later. She stood on the porch, wondering where he'd gone. His bike was parked inside the garage, and he'd already aired his views about playing with any of the girls in the neighbourhood.

It would be just like him to storm into his room in a fit of indignation and promptly fall asleep. Robin hurried upstairs to his bedroom, which was across the hall from her own.

His bed was made and his clothes hung neatly in the cupboard. Robin decided that in another day or two, everything would be back to normal.

It wasn't until she turned to leave that she saw the note on his desk. Picking it up, Robin read the first line. Immediately, she felt a swirling sense of panic.

Dear Mom,
You broke your promise. You said I could have a dog and now you say I have to wait. If I can't have a dog, then I don't want to live with you any more. This is goodbye forever.

Love, Jeff

CHAPTER TWO

FOR A MOMENT, Robin was too stunned to react. Her heart was pounding so hard that it echoed in her ears like thunder, so loud it seemed to knock her off balance.

Rushing down the stairs, she stood on the porch, cupped her hands over her mouth and screamed frantically. "Jeff!"

Cole Camden was standing on his front porch, too. He released a shrill whistle and stood waiting expectantly. When nothing happened, he called, "Blackie!"

"Jeff!" Robin tried again.

"Blackie!"

Robin called for Jeff once more, but her voice cracked as the panic engulfed her. She paused, placed her hand over her mouth and closed her eyes in an effort to gather her composure, which was crumbling more every minute.

"Blackie!" Cole yelled. He looked furious about his dog's disappearance.

It took Robin only a moment to put two and two together. "Cole," she cried, running across the lawn toward him, "I think Jeff and Blackie might have run away together."

Cole looked at her as though she were deranged, and Robin couldn't really blame him. "Jeff left me a note. He wants a dog so badly and we can't get one right away because...well, because we can't, and I had to tell him, and he was terribly disappointed and he decided to run away."

Cole's mouth thinned. "The whole idea is ridiculous. Even if Jeff did run away, Blackie would never go with him."

"Do you honestly think I'd make something like this up?" she shrieked. "The last time I saw Jeff was around four-thirty, and I'd bet cold cash that's about the same time Blackie disappeared."

Cole's gaze narrowed. "Then where are they?"

"If I knew that, do you think I'd be standing around here arguing with you?"

"Listen, lady, I don't know your son, but I know my dog and—"

"My name's not lady," Robin flared, clenching her hands into tight fists at her sides. He was looking at her as though she were a madwoman on the loose—which she was where her son was concerned. "I'm sorry to have troubled you. When I find Jeff, I'll see to it that your dog finds his way home."

Cole's eyes shot sparks in her direction, but she ignored them. Turning abruptly, she ran back to her own house. Halfway there, she stopped dead, and whirled around to face Cole again. "The fort."

"What fort?" Cole demanded.

"The one that's back in the furthest corner of your yard. It's covered with brush.... Jeff found it earlier today. He wouldn't know anywhere to go and that would be the perfect hiding place."

"No one's been there in years," Cole said, discounting her suggestion.

"The least we can do is look."

Cole's nod was reluctant. He led the way to his backyard, which was much larger than hers. There was a small grove of oak trees at the rear of the property and beyond that a high fence. Apparently the fort was situated between the trees and the fence. A few minutes later, in the most remote corner of the yard, nestled between two trees, Robin spied the small wooden structure, which blended into the terrain. If Robin hadn't been looking for the hideaway, she'd never have seen it.

It was obvious when they neared the space that someone had taken up residence. Cole lowered himself on to all fours, peered inside, then looked back at Robin with a nod. He breathed in sharply, apparently irritated by this turn of events, and agilely crawled through the narrow entrance.

Not about to be left standing by herself, Robin got down on her knees and followed him in.

Just as she'd suspected, Jeff and Blackie were huddled together in a corner. Jeff was sound asleep and Blackie was curled up at his side, guarding him. When Cole and Robin entered, the Labrador lifted his head and wagged his tail in greeting.

The fort wasn't much bigger than the tent Jeff had constructed the night before, and Robin was forced to pull her knees close and loop her arms around them. Cole's larger body seemed to fill every available bit of space.

Jeff must have sensed that his newfound home had been invaded because his eyes fluttered open and he gazed at Robin, then twisted his head to stare at Cole.

"Hi, Mom," he said sheepishly. "I bet I'm in trouble, aren't I?"

Robin was so grateful to find him that all she could do was nod. If she'd tried to speak, her voice would have wobbled and heaved with emotion, which would only have embarrassed them both.

"So, Jeff," Cole said sternly. "You were going to run away from home. I see you brought everything you needed with you." He pushed the frying pan and atlas into the middle of their cramped quarters. "What I want to know is how you convinced Blackie to join you."

"He came all on his own. He just sort of followed me," Jeff murmured, but his eyes avoided Cole's. "I wouldn't have taken him on purpose—he's your dog."

"I'm glad you didn't…coerce him."

"All you took was a frying pan and an atlas!" Robin cried, staring at the cast-iron skillet and the atlas with its dog-eared pages.

Cole and Jeff both ignored her outburst.

"I take it you don't like living around here?" Cole asked.

Jeff stiffened, then vigorously shook his head. "Mom told me when we moved I could have a dog and now I can't, and worse than that she dragged me into a neighbourhood filled with girls. That would have been all right if I had a dog, but then she broke her promise. A promise is a promise and it's sacred. A guy would never do that."

"So you can't have the dog until later?"

"And all because of a stupid fence."

Cole nodded. "Fences are important, you know. You know what else? Your mom was worried about you."

Jeff looked at Robin, who was blinking furiously to keep the tears from dripping down her face. The upheaval and stress of the move had drained her emotionally and she was an unmitigated mess. Normally, she was a calm, controlled person, but this whole thing with Jeff was her undoing. That and the fact she'd hardly slept the night before in the makeshift tent.

"Mom," Jeff said, studying her anxiously, "are you all right?"

She covered her face with both hands. "I slept with a dog and you ran away and all you took was a frying pan and an atlas." That made no sense whatsoever. Robin felt as if she'd been run over by a steamroller, and once the tears started they wouldn't stop. Her shoulders shook jerkily.

"I'm sorry, Mom," Jeff said softly. "I didn't mean to make you cry."

"I know," she whimpered. "I want you to have a dog, I really do, but we can't keep one locked up in a house all day and we don't have a fence and...and you looked at me and I swear it was Lonny all over again."

"Who's Lonny?" Cole cocked his head toward Jeff, speaking in a whisper.

"Lonny was my dad. He died when I was real little. I don't even remember him."

Cole shared a knowing look with her son. "It might be a good idea if we got your mother inside the house."

"You think I'm getting hysterical, don't you?" Robin cried. "I want you both to know I'm in perfect control. A woman can cry every now and again if she wants. Venting your emotions is healthy—all those books say so."

"Right, Mom." Jeff gently patted her shoulder, then crawled out of the fort. He waited for Robin, who emerged after him, and offered her a hand. Cole and Blackie followed.

Jeff took Robin's arm, cupping her elbow as he led her toward the back door of their house, as if he suspected she couldn't find her way without his guidance.

Once inside, Robin reached for a tissue and loudly blew her nose.

Her composure was shaky, but when she turned to Cole, she intended to be as reasonable as a judge. As polite as a preacher.

"Have you got any aspirin?" Cole asked Jeff.

Jeff nodded, and dashed up the stairs to the bathroom, returning in thirty seconds flat with the bottle. Cole filled a glass with water and delivered both to Robin. How he knew she had a fierce headache she could only guess.

"Why don't you lie down for a couple of minutes? I'm sure you'll feel better."

"I feel just fine, thank you," she snapped, more angry with herself for over-reacting than with him for taking charge.

"Do you have family close by?" Again Cole directed the question to Jeff, which only served to further infuriate Robin. Jeff was ten years old! She, on the other hand, was the adult. If this man had questions they should be directed to her, not her son.

"Not any more," Jeff answered in an anxious whisper. "Grandma and Grandpa moved to Arizona last year, and my uncle lives in L.A."

"I don't need to lie down," Robin said forcefully. "I'm perfectly fine."

"Mom," Jeff countered, his voice troubled, "you don't look so good."

"You were talking about frying pans and sleeping with dogs in the same breath," Cole elaborated, his eyebrows raised.

"I think Mr Camden's right," Jeff concurred. "You need rest— lots of rest."

Her own son had turned traitor on her. Robin couldn't believe it. Jeff took her hand gently and led her into the family room, which was directly off the kitchen. He patted the quilted pillow on the sofa, wordlessly suggesting she place her head there. When she resisted, he pulled the rug from the chair and draped it around her, securely tucking the ends behind her shoulders, as though she were in imminent danger of freezing to death.

Robin couldn't believe she was allowing herself to be led around like a...like a puppy. As if reading her thoughts, Blackie wandered over to her side and lowered his bulk on to the carpet beside the sofa.

"That's a neat fort you've got there," Jeff told Cole once he'd finished tucking in the blanket. Robin watched him hurry back to the kitchen, grab a plate, then load it with macaroni cheese and hand it to Cole, apparently wanting to share his favourite meal with their neighbor.

Cole set the plate on the counter. "Thanks anyway, Jeff, but I've got to get back to the house. In the future, if you're thinking about running away—don't."

"Yeah, I guess you're right," Jeff said with a mildly guilty look. "My mom turned into a basket case."

Cole smiled—at least, it was as close to a smile as Robin had seen. "You're both going to be all right. She intends to get you that dog, you know. Just hang on, it'll be sooner than you think."

Jeff walked to the sliding glass door with Cole. "Mr Camden, can I ask you something important?"

"Sure." He stood just inside the house.

"Is anyone using the fort?"

"Not that I know of."

Jeff looked hopeful. "It didn't look like anyone had been inside for a long time."

"Six years," Cole murmured absently.

"That long? How come?" Jeff asked. "It's a great fort. If it's all right with you I'd like to go over there sometimes. I promise not to walk in any flower beds or anything, and I won't leave a mess. I'll take real good care of everything."

Cole hesitated only for a moment. He looked at Jeff, and Robin held her breath as his expression softened. Then he shook his head. "Maybe sometime in the future, but not now."

Jeff's deep blue eyes brightened; apparently the refusal didn't trouble him. "That's great. When I can use the fort, would it be all right if I took Blackie with me? He followed me today, you know. I didn't have to do anything to get him to tag along." Jeff paused and lowered his eyes. "Well, hardly anything."

"I thought as much. As your mom said, you have a way with animals."

"My dad did, too. If he hadn't died he would have gotten me a pony and everything."

There was such pride in Jeff's voice that Robin bit her bottom lip to keep from crying all over again. Jeff and Lonny were so much alike. What she'd said to her son earlier had been true. More and more, Jeff was starting to take on his father's looks and personality.

Cole hesitated, gazing down at Jeff. An emotion flashed in his eyes, so transient Robin couldn't name it. He laid his hand on Jeff's thin shoulder. "Since your mother explained there's going to be a delay in getting you a dog, it'd be all right to borrow Blackie every now and then. As long as you stay in your own yard. I don't want him running in the neighbourhood unless he's on a leash."

"Do you really mean it? Gee, thanks, Mr Camden. I'll do everything you ask."

Robin had the feeling Jeff would have agreed to just about any terms as long as he could see Blackie. It wasn't a dog of his own, but it was as close as he was going to get for the next few months.

Once Cole had left, Jeff joined her on the sofa, his hands folded together on his lap. "I'm sorry, Mom," he muttered, his chin buried in his chest. "I promise I'll never run away again."

"I should hope not," she said. Wrapping her arms around him, she hugged him close, kissing his cheek.

"Gee whiz," Jeff grumbled, rubbing his face. "I'd never have apologised if I'd known you were going to kiss me."

A WEEK PASSED. Jeff liked his new school and, as Robin had predicted, he found his class contained an equal number of boys and girls. With his outgoing personality, he quickly collected a handful of new friends.

On Sunday afternoon, Robin was in the family room reading the newspaper when Jeff ambled in and sat down across the room from her. He took the baseball cap from his head and studied it for several moments.

"Something bothering you?" she asked, lowering the paper to get a better view of her son.

He shrugged. "Did you know Mr Camden used to be married?"

"I heard something along those lines," Robin said absently. But other than Heather's remarks the previous week, she hadn't learned anything else. In fact, she'd spoken to her neighbour only when she went to pick Jeff up every afternoon. The child-care arrangement with Heather was working beautifully, but there had been little opportunity to chat.

As for Cole, Robin hadn't seen him at all. Since he'd been so kind and helpful in the situation with Jeff, Robin had revised her opinion of him. He liked his privacy and that was fine by her; she had no intention of interrupting his serene existence. The memory of their first meeting still rankled, but she was willing to overlook that shaky beginning.

"Mr Camden had a son who died."

Robin's heart constricted. It made sense: the flash of pain she'd seen when Jeff had asked him about children, the word on the street that Cole didn't like kids, the abandoned fort. "I... How did you find that out?"

"Jimmy Wallach. He lives two streets over and has an older brother who used to play with Bobby Camden. Jimmy told me about him."

"I didn't know," Robin murmured, saddened by the information. She couldn't imagine her life without Jeff—the mere thought of losing him was enough to tear her apart.

"Mrs Wallach heard Jimmy talking about Bobby Camden and she said that Mr. Camden got divorced and it was real bad, and then a year or so later Bobby died. She said he's never been the same since. Like someone else took over his mind and body."

Robin ached for Cole, and she regretted all the uncharitable thoughts she'd had that first morning.

"I feel sad," Jeff whispered, frowning. His young face was as intent as she'd ever seen it.

"I do, too," Robin returned softly.

"Mrs Wallach seemed real surprised when I told her Mr Camden said I could play in Bobby's fort some day. Ever since his son died, he hasn't let any kids in the yard or anything. She said he hardly talks to anyone in the neighbourhood anymore."

Heather Lawrence had said basically the same thing, but not the reason for it. Probably because she didn't know.

"Are you still going to barbecue hamburgers tonight for dinner?"

Robin nodded, surprised by the abrupt way Jeff had changed the subject. "If you want." Next to macaroni cheese, grilled burgers were Jeff's all-time favourite food.

"Would it be all right if I invited Mr Camden over to eat with us?"

Robin hated to refuse her son, but she wasn't sure a dinner invitation was a good idea. She didn't know Cole very well, but from what she'd learned he wasn't one to socialise with the neighbours. In addition, Jeff might blurt out questions about Cole's dead son that would be terribly painful for him.

"Mom," Jeff pleaded, "I bet no one ever invites him to dinner and he's all alone."

"Sweetheart, I don't know if that would be the right thing to do."

"But we owe him, Mom," Jeff implored. "He let me throw sticks for Blackie twice this week."

"I don't think Mr Camden's home," Robin said, picking up the newspaper while she weighed the pros and cons of Jeff's suggestion. Since last Sunday, Robin hadn't spoken to Cole once, and she wasn't eager to initiate a conversation. He might read something into it.

"I'll go check and see if he's home." Before she could react, Jeff was out the front door, letting the screen door slam in his wake.

He returned a couple of minutes later breathless and excited. "Mr Camden's home and he said he appreciated the invitation, but he had other plans for tonight."

"That's too bad," Robin murmured, hoping she sounded sincere.

"I told him we were having strawberry shortcake for dessert and he said that was his favourite."

Robin hated to admit it, but she was relieved Cole wouldn't be showing up for dinner. The man made her feel nervous and uncertain. She didn't know why that should be, only that it was a new and unfamiliar sensation.

"Thanks, Mom."

Robin jerked her head up from the newspaper. "Thanks for

what?'' She hadn't read a word in five minutes. Her thoughts had been dominated by her neighbour.

Jeff rolled his eyes. "For letting me take a piece of strawberry shortcake over to Mr Camden.''

"I said you could do that?''

"Just now.'' He walked over to her and playfully tested her forehead with the back of his hand. "You don't feel hot, but then, with brain fever you never know.''

Robin swatted playfully at her son's backside.

Laughing, Jeff raced outdoors, where his bicycle was waiting. A half-hour later, he was back in the house. "Mom! Mom!'' he cried, racing into the kitchen. "Did you know Mr Camden owns a black Porsche?''

"I can't say I did.'' She was more interested in peeling potatoes for the salad than discussing fancy cars. She didn't know enough about sports cars to get excited about them.

Jeff jerked open the bottom drawer and rooted through the rag bag until he found what he was looking for. He pulled out a large square that had once been part of his flannel pyjamas, then started back outside. "He has another car too, a big four-wheel drive.''

"Just where are you going, young man?'' Robin demanded.

"Mr Camden's waxing his car and I thought I'd go help him.''

"Did he ask for your help?''

"No,'' Jeff said impatiently.

"He may not want you to.''

"Mom!'' Jeff rolled his eyes as if to suggest she was overdoing this mothering thing. "Can I go now?''

"Ah...I suppose,'' she agreed, but her heart was in her throat. She moved into the living-room and watched as Jeff strolled across the lawn to the driveway where Cole was busy rubbing liquid wax on the gleaming surface of his Porsche. Without a word, Jeff started polishing the dried wax with his rag. Cole straightened and stopped smearing on the wax, obviously surprised to see Jeff. Robin bit her lower lip, not knowing how her neighbour would react to Jeff's willingness to help. Apparently he said something, because Jeff nodded, then walked over and sat cross-legged on the lawn. They didn't seem to be carrying on a conversation and Robin couldn't help wondering what Cole had said to her son.

Robin returned to the kitchen, grateful that Cole's rejection had apparently been gentle. At least he hadn't sent Jeff away. She peeled another potato, then walked back into the living-room and glanced out the window again. This time she discovered Jeff standing next to Cole, who was, it seemed, demonstrating the right way to polish a car. He made wide circular motions with his arms, then stepped aside to let Jeff tackle the Porsche again. Cole nodded and smiled, then patted him on the head before walking around to the other side of the car.

Once the salad was ready, Robin decided to venture outside.

Jeff paused and waved enthusiastically when he caught sight of her on the porch. "Isn't she a beaut?" he yelled.

It looked like an ordinary car to Robin, but she nodded enthusiastically. "Wonderful," she answered. "Afternoon, Cole."

"Robin." He returned her greeting absently.

He wore a sleeveless grey sweatshirt and she was surprised by how muscular and tanned his arms were. From her conversation with Heather Lawrence, Robin had learned Cole was a prominent attorney. And he'd seemed to fit the lawyer image to a T. Not any more. The lawyer was gone and the *man* was there, bold as could be. Her awareness of him as an attractive virile male was shockingly intense.

The problem, she decided, lay in the fact that she hadn't expected Cole to look so...fit. The sight of all that lean muscle came as a pleasant surprise. Cole's aggressive unfriendly expression had been softened as he bantered teasingly with Jeff.

Blackie ambled to her side and Robin leaned over to scratch the dog's ears while she continued to study his master. Cole's hair was dark and grew away from his brow, but a single lock flopped stubbornly over his forehead and he had to toss it back from his face every once in a while. It was funny how she'd never noticed that about him until now.

Jeff must have said something humorous because Cole threw back his head and chuckled loudly. It was the first time she'd ever heard him laugh. She suspected he didn't often give in to the impulse. A smile crowded Robin's face as Jeff started laughing, too.

In that moment the oddest thing happened. Robin felt something catch in her heart. The tug was almost physical, and she experienced a completely unfamiliar feeling of vulnerability....

"Do you need me to roll out the barbecue for you?" Jeff shouted when he noticed she was still on the porch. He'd turned his baseball cap around so that the bill faced backward. While he spoke, his arm continued to work feverishly, buffing the passenger door with his rag.

"Not...yet."

"Good, 'cause Mr. Camden needs me to finish up this side for him. We're on a tight schedule here, and I don't really have time. Cole's got a dinner date at five-thirty."

"I see." Standing on the porch, dressed in her old faded jeans, with a mustard-spotted terry-cloth hand towel tucked in the waistband, Robin felt as appealing as Ma Kettle. "Any time you're finished is fine."

So Cole Camden's got a date, Robin mused. *Of course he's got a date,* she told herself. Why should she care? And if watching Jeff and Cole together was going to affect her like this, it would be best to go back into the house now.

Over dinner, all Jeff could talk about was Cole Camden. Every other sentence was Cole this and Cole that, until Robin was ready to slam her fist on the table and demand Jeff never mention their neighbour's name again.

"And the best part is, he paid me for helping him wax his car for him," Jeff continued, then stuffed the hamburger into his mouth, chewing a mile a minute in his enthusiasm.

"That was more than generous of him."

Jeff nodded enthusiastically. "Be sure and save some shortcake for him. He said not to bring it over 'cause he didn't know exactly when he'd get home. He'll stop by," he said.

"I will." Robin sincerely doubted her neighbour would. Jeff seemed to be under the impression Cole would show up at any time; Robin knew better. If Cole had a dinner date, he wasn't going to rush back just to taste her home-made dessert, though she did have to admit she made an excellent shortcake.

As she suspected, Cole didn't come by. Jeff grumbled about it the next morning. He was convinced Cole would have if Robin hadn't insisted Jeff go to bed at his regular time.

"I'll make shortcake again soon," Robin promised, hurrying to pack their lunches. "When I do, you can take a piece over to him."

"All right," Jeff muttered.

That evening, when Robin returned home from work, she found Jeff playing with Blackie in Cole's backyard.

"Jeff," she cried, alarmed that Cole might discover her son on his property. He'd made it clear Jeff wasn't to go into his yard. "What are you doing at Mr. Camden's? And why aren't you at Heather's?" She walked over to the hedge and placed her hands on her hips, frustrated with her ten-year-old.

"Blackie's chain got all tangled up," Jeff explained, looking sheepish. "He needed my help. I told Heather it would be OK with you and…" His voice trailed off.

"He's untangled now," Robin pointed out.

"I know, but since I was here it seemed like a good time for the two of us to—"

"Play," Robin completed for him.

"Yeah," her son said, nodding eagerly. Jeff was well aware he'd done wrong, but had difficulty admitting it.

"Mr Camden doesn't want you in his yard, and we both know it." Standing next to the thick laurel hedge, Robin watched with dismay as Cole opened his back door and stepped outside. Blackie barked in greeting, and his tail swung with enough force to knock Jeff off balance.

When Cole noticed Jeff in his yard, he frowned and cast an accusing glare in Robin's direction.

"Jeff said Blackie's chain was tangled," she rushed to explain.

"How'd you get over here?" Cole asked her son, and although he didn't raise his voice it was clear he was displeased. "The gate's locked and the hedge is too high to leap over."

Jeff stared down at the lawn. "I came through the gap in the hedge—the same one Blackie uses. I crawled through it."

"Was his chain really tangled?"

"No, sir," Jeff said in a voice so low that Robin had to strain to hear him. "At least not much. He could have straightened it out himself…. I just thought, you know, that maybe he'd like the company."

"I see."

"He was all alone and so was I." Jeff lifted his eyes defiantly to his mother's, as if to suggest the fault was entirely hers. "I go to Mrs. Lawrence's after school, but it's all girls there, and I'd rather be shot than play with dolls."

"Don't you remember what I said about your coming into my yard?" Cole asked him.

Jeff nod was sluggish. "Yes. You said maybe I could sometime, but not now. I thought…I hoped that since you let me help you wax your car you wouldn't mind so much."

"I mind," Cole said flatly.

"He won't do it again," Robin promised, "will you, Jeff?"

"No," he murmured. "I'm sorry, Mr Camden."

For an entire week Jeff kept his word. The following Monday, however, when Robin returned from the BART station, Heather explained that Jeff had mysteriously disappeared about a half hour earlier. She assumed he'd gone home; he'd said something about expecting a call.

Unfortunately, Robin knew exactly where to look for him, and it wasn't at home. Even more unfortunate was the fact that Cole's car pulled into the driveway just as she was opening her door. Throwing aside her briefcase and bag, she rushed through the house, jerked open the sliding glass door at the back and raced across her yard.

Her son was nowhere to be seen, but she immediately realised he'd been with Blackie. The dog wasn't in evidence, and she could see Jeff's favorite baseball cap on the lawn.

"Jeff," she called, afraid to raise her voice. She sounded as though she was suffering from a bad case of laryngitis.

Neither boy nor dog appeared.

She tried again, taking the risk of shouting for Jeff in a normal tone, praying it wouldn't attract Cole's attention. No response. Since Jeff and Blackie didn't seem to be within earshot, she guessed they were in the fort. There was no help for it; she'd have to go after him herself. Her only hope was that she could hurry over to the fort, get Jeff and return to her own yard, all without being detected by Cole.

Finding the hole in the laurel proved difficult enough. The space was little more than a narrow gap between two thick plants, and for a distressing moment, Robin doubted she was slim enough to squeeze through. Finally, she lowered herself to the ground, hunched her shoulders and managed to push her way between the shrubs. Her head had just emerged when she noticed a pair of polished men's shoes on the other side. Slowly, reluctantly, she glanced up to find Cole towering above her, eyes narrowed with suspicion.

"Oh, hi," she said, striving to sound as though it was perfectly normal for her to be crawling into his yard on her hands and knees. "I suppose you're wondering exactly what I'm doing here...."

"The question did cross my mind."

CHAPTER THREE

"IT WAS THE MOST embarrassing moment of my entire life," Robin repeated for the third time. She was sitting at the kitchen table, resisting the urge to bury her face in her hands and weep.

"You've already said that," Jeff grumbled.

"What possessed you to even think about going into Mr Camden's yard again? Honestly, Jeff, you've been warned not to at least half a dozen times. What do I have to do? String barbed wire between our yards?"

Although he'd thoroughly disgraced himself, Jeff casually rotated the rim of his baseball cap between his fingers. "I said I was sorry."

A mere apology in no way compensated for the humiliation Robin had suffered when Cole had found her down on all fours, crawling through his laurel hedge. If she lived to be an old woman, she would never forget the look on his face.

"You put me on television and phone restriction already," her son reminded her.

The punishment could be another mistake to add to her growing list. At times like this, she wished Lonny were there to advise her. She needed him, and even after all these years, still missed him. Often, when there wasn't anyone else around, Robin found herself talking to Lonny, discussing things. Without television and the phone, the most attractive form of entertainment left open to her son was playing with Blackie, which was what had got him into trouble in the first place.

"Blackie belongs to Mr Camden," Robin felt obliged to tell him. Again.

"I know," Jeff said, "but he likes me. When I come home from school, he goes crazy. He's real glad to see me, and since there aren't a whole lot of boys in this neighborhood—" he paused as if she were to blame for that ""—Blackie and I have this understanding. We're buds.''

"That's all fine and dandy, but you seem to be forgetting that Blackie doesn't belong to you." Robin stood and opened the refrigerator, taking out a package of chicken breasts.

"I wish he was my dog," Jeff grumbled. In an apparent effort to make peace, her son walked over to the cupboard, removed two plates and proceeded to set the table.

After dinner, while Robin was doing the dishes, the doorbell chimed. Jeff raced down the hallway to answer it even before Robin could dry her hands. Her son returned a moment later with Cole Camden at his side.

Her neighbour was the last person Robin had expected to see— and the last person she *wanted* to see.

"Mom," Jeff said, nodding toward Cole, "it's Mr Camden."

"Hello, again," she managed, striving for a light tone, and realizing even as she spoke that she'd failed. "Would you like a cup of coffee?"

"No, thanks. I'd like to talk to both of you about—"

Not giving him the opportunity to continue, Robin nodded so hard and fast she nearly dislocated her neck. "I really am sorry about what happened. I've had a good long talk with Jeff and, frankly, I understand why you're upset and I don't blame you in the least. You've been more than understanding about this whole unfortunate episode and I want you to know there won't be a repeat performance of what happened today."

"From either of you?"

"Absolutely," she said, knowing her cheeks were as red as her fingernail polish. Did he have to remind her of the humiliating position he'd found her in earlier?

"Mom put me on television and phone restriction for an entire week," Jeff explained sheepishly. "I promise not to go into your fort again, Mr Camden. And I promise not to go in my backyard after school, either, because Blackie sees me and gets all happy and excited—and I guess I get all happy and excited, too—and that's when I do what I'm not supposed to do."

"I see." Cole smiled down at Jeff. Robin found it a rather unusual smile. It didn't come from his lips so much as his eyes. Once more she witnessed a flash of pain, and another emotion she could only describe as longing. Slowly his gaze drifted to Robin. When his dark eyes met hers, she suddenly found herself short of breath.

"Actually I didn't come here to talk to you about what happened earlier this afternoon," Cole explained. "I'm going to be out of town for the next couple of days, and since Jeff and Blackie seem to get along so well I thought Jeff might be willing to look after him. That way I won't have to put him in the kennel. Naturally I'm prepared to pay your son for his time and effort. If he'll agree, I'll let him play in the fort while I'm away."

Jeff's eyes grew rounder than Robin could ever remember seeing them. "You want me to watch Blackie?" he asked, his voice incredulous. "And you're going to *pay* me? Can Blackie spend the night here? Please?"

"I guess that answers your question," Robin said, smiling.

"Blackie can stay here if it's OK with your mom," Cole told Jeff. Then he turned to her. "Would that create a problem for you?"

Once more his gaze held hers, and once more she experienced that odd breathless sensation.

"I... No problem whatsoever."

Cole smiled then, and this time it was a smile so potent, so compelling, that it sailed straight through Robin's heart.

"MOM," JEFF HOLLERED as he burst through the front door late Thursday afternoon. "Kelly and Blackie and I are going to the fort."

"Kelly? Surely this isn't the *girl* named Kelly, is it? Not the one who lives next door?" Robin couldn't resist teasing her son. Apparently Jeff was willing to have a "pesky" girl for a friend, after all.

Jeff shrugged as he opened the cookie jar and groped inside. He frowned, not finding any cookies left and removed his hand, his fingertips covered with crumbs that he promptly licked off. "I found out Kelly isn't so bad."

"Have you got Blackie's leash?"

"We aren't going to need it. We're playing Sam Houston and

Daniel Boone, and the Mexican army is attacking. I'm going to smuggle Blackie out and go for help. I can't use a leash for that.''

"All right, just don't go any farther than the Alamo and be back by dinnertime.''

"But that's less than an hour!'' Jeff protested.

Robin gave him one of her don't-argue-with-me looks.

"But I'm not hungry and—''

"Jeff,'' Robin said softly, widening her eyes just a bit, increasing the intensity of her look.

"You know, Mom,'' Jeff said with a cry of undisguised disgust, "you don't fight fair.'' He hurried out the front door with Blackie trotting faithfully behind.

Smiling to herself, Robin placed the meat loaf in the oven and carried her coffee into the backyard. The early evening air was filled with the scent of spring flowers. A gentle breeze wafted over the budding trees. How peaceful it seemed. How serene. All the years of pinching pennies in order to save for a house of their own seemed worth it now.

Her gaze wandered toward Cole Camden's yard. Jeff, Kelly and Blackie were inside the fort, and she could hear their raised voices every now and again.

Cole had been on her mind a great deal during the past couple of days; she'd spent far too much time dwelling on thoughts of her neighbour—about his reputation in the neighbourhood and the son he'd lost.

The tranquillity of the moment was shattered by the insistent ringing of the phone. Robin walked briskly to the kitchen, set her coffee on the counter and reached for the receiver.

"Hello.''

"Robin, it's Angela. I'm not catching you at a bad time, am I?''

"No,'' Robin assured her. Angela worked in the same department as Robin, and over the years the two had become good friends. "What can I do for you?'' she asked, as if she didn't already know.

"I'm calling to invite you to dinner—''

"On Saturday so I can meet your cousin Frank,'' Robin finished, rolling her eyes. Years before, Angela had taken on the task of finding

Robin a husband. Never mind that Robin wasn't interested in meeting strangers! Angela couldn't seem to bear the thought of anyone spending her life alone and had appointed herself Robin's personal matchmaker.

"Frank's a really nice guy," Angela insisted. "I wouldn't steer you wrong, you know I wouldn't."

Robin restrained herself from reminding her friend of the disastrous date she'd arranged several weeks earlier.

"I've known Frank all my life," Angela said. "He's decent and nice."

"Decent" and "nice" were two words Robin had come to hate. Every man she'd ever met in this kind of arrangement was either decent or nice. Or both. Robin had come to think the two words were synonymous with dull, unattractive and emotionally manipulative. Generally these were recently divorced men who'd willingly placed themselves in the hands of family and friends to get them back into circulation.

"Didn't you tell me that Frank was recently divorced?" Robin asked.

"Yes, about six months ago now."

"Not interested."

"What do you mean you're not interested?" Angela demanded.

"I don't want to meet him. Angela, I know you mean well, and I apologise if I sound like a spoilsport, but I can't tell you the number of times I've had to nurse the fragile egos of recently divorced men. Most of the time they're emotional wrecks."

"But Frank's divorce was final months ago."

"If you still want me to meet him in a year, I'll be more than happy to have you arrange a dinner date."

Angela released a ragged sigh. "You're sure?"

"More than sure. Positive."

A short disappointed silence followed. "All right," Angela murmured in obvious frustration. "I'll see you in the morning."

"Right," Robin said, and because she felt guilty, she added, "I'll bring the coffee."

"OK."

Robin lingered in the kitchen, frowning. She hated it when her friends put her on the spot this way. It was difficult enough to say no, but knowing that Angela's intentions were genuine made it even worse. Just as she was struggling with an attack of guilt, the phone rang again. Angela! Her friend must have suspected that Robin's offer to buy the coffee was a sign that she was weakening.

Gathering her fortitude, Robin seized the receiver and said firmly, "I'm not interested in dating Frank. I don't want to be rude, but that's final!"

Her abrupt words were followed by a short shocked silence, and then, "Robin, hello, this is Cole Camden."

"Cole," she gasped, closing her eyes. "Uh, I'm sorry, I thought you were someone else. A friend." She slumped against the wall and covered her face with one hand. "I have this friend who's keen on arranging dates for me, and she doesn't take no for an answer," Robin quickly explained. "I suppose you have friends wanting to arrange dates for you, too."

"Actually, I don't."

Of course he didn't. No doubt there were women all over San Francisco who longed to date Cole. He didn't require a personal matchmaker. All someone like him had to do was look interested and women would flock to his side.

Her hand tightened around the receiver and a sick weightless feeling attacked the pit of her stomach. "I apologise. I didn't mean to shout in your ear."

"You didn't."

"I suppose you called to talk to Jeff," she said. "He's with Blackie and Kelly—Kelly Lawrence, the little girl who lives on the other side of us."

"I see."

"He'll be back in a few minutes, if you'd like to call then. Or if you prefer, I could run and get him, but he said something about sneaking out and going for help and—"

"I beg your pardon? What's Jeff doing?"

"Oh, they're playing in the fort, pretending they're Houston and Daniel Boone. The fort is now the Alamo."

He chuckled. "I see. No, don't worry about chasing after him. I'd hate to see you waylaid by the Mexican army."

"I don't think I'd care for that myself."

"How's everything going?"

"Fine," she assured him.

She must have sounded rushed because he added, "You're sure this isn't a bad time? If you have company..."

"No, I'm here alone."

The short silence was broken by Cole. "So everything's going all right with Blackie? He isn't causing you any problems, is he?"

"Oh, no, everything's great. Jeff lavishes him with attention. The two of them are together practically every minute. Blackie even sleeps beside his bed."

"As you said, Jeff has a way with animals," Cole murmured.

His laugh, so tender and warm, was enough to jolt her equilibrium. She had to pinch herself to remember that Cole was a prominent attorney, wealthy and respected. She was an accountant. A junior accountant at that.

The only thing they had in common was the fact that they lived next door to each other and her son was crazy about his dog.

The silence returned, only this time it had a relaxed, almost comfortable quality, as though neither wanted the conversation to end.

"Since Jeff isn't around," Cole said reluctantly, "I'll let you go."

"I'll tell him you phoned."

"It wasn't anything important," Cole said. "Just wanted to let you know when I'll be back—late Friday afternoon. Will you be home?"

"Of course."

"You never know, your friend might talk you into going out with Fred after all."

"It's Frank, and there isn't a snowball's chance in hell."

"Famous last words!"

"See you Friday," she said with a short laugh.

"Right. Goodbye, Robin."

"Goodbye, Cole."

Long after the connection had been broken, Robin stood with her hand on the receiver, a smile touching her eyes and her heart.

"MOM, I NEED my lunch money," Jeff called impatiently from the bottom of the stairs.

"I'll be down in a minute," she answered. Mornings were crazy and always had been. In order to get to the Glen Park BART station on time, Robin had to leave the house half an hour before Jeff left for school.

"What did you have for breakfast?" she hollered down as she put the finishing touches on her makeup.

"Frozen waffles," Jeff shouted back. "And don't worry, I didn't drown them in syrup and I rinsed off the plate before I put it in the dishwasher."

"Rinsed it off or let Blackie lick it clean for you?" she asked, as she hurried down the stairs. Her son was busy at the sink and didn't turn around to look at her.

"Blackie, honestly, is that maple syrup on your nose?"

At the sound of his name, the Labrador trotted over to her. Robin took a moment to stroke his thick fur, before fumbling for her wallet to give Jeff his lunch money.

"Hey, Mom, you look nice."

"Don't sound so surprised," she grumbled. "I'm leaving now."

"OK," Jeff said without the slightest bit of concern. "You won't be late tonight, will you? Remember Mr Camden's due back."

"I remember, and no, I won't be late." She grabbed her packed lunch and headed for the front door.

Even before Robin arrived at the subway station, she knew the day would drag. Fridays always did.

She was right. At six, when the subway pulled into the station, Robin felt as though she'd been away forty hours instead of the usual nine. She found herself hurrying and didn't fully understand why. Cole was scheduled to return, but that didn't have anything to do with her, did it? His homecoming wasn't anything to feel nervous about, nor any reason to be pleased. He was her neighbour, and more Jeff's friend than hers.

The first thing Robin noticed when she arrived on Orchard Street was Cole's Porsche parked in the driveway of his house.

"Hi, Mom," Jeff called as he raced across the lawn between the two houses. "Mr Camden's back."

"So I see." She removed her keys from her purse and opened the front door.

Jeff followed her inside. "He said he'd square up with me later. I wanted to invite him to dinner, but I didn't think I should without asking you first."

"That was smart," she said, depositing her jacket in the cupboard on her way into the kitchen. She opened the refrigerator and took out the thawed hamburger and salad makings.

"How was your day?" she asked.

Jeff sat down at the table and propped his elbows on it. "All right, I guess. What are you making for dinner?"

"Taco salad."

"How about just tacos? I don't understand why you want to ruin a perfectly good dinner by mixing green stuff with it."

Robin paused. "I thought you liked my taco salad."

Jeff shrugged. "It's all right, but I'd rather have just tacos." Once that was made clear, he cupped his chin in his hands. "Can we rent a video tonight?"

"I suppose," Robin returned absently as she added the meat to the onions browning in the skillet.

"But I get to choose this time," Jeff murmured. "Last week you picked out a musical." He wrinkled his nose as if to suggest being forced to watch men and women sing and dance was the most disgusting thing he'd ever had to endure.

"Perhaps we can find a compromise," she suggested.

Jeff nodded. "As long as it doesn't have a silly love story in it."

"OK," Robin said, doing her best not to betray her amusement. Their difference in taste when it came to movies was legendary. Like most boys his age Jeff preferred gory thrillers, while Robin couldn't bear to rent anything violent. Unfortunately, her son was equally offended by the sight of men and women staring longingly into each other's eyes.

The meat was simmering in the skillet when Robin glanced up and noted that her son's look was surprisingly thoughtful. "Is something troubling you?'' she asked, and popped a thin tomato slice into her mouth.

"Have you ever noticed that Mr. Camden never mentions he had a son?''

Robin set the paring knife against the cutting board. "It's probably painful for him to talk about.''

Jeff nodded, and, with the innocent wisdom of youth, he whispered, "That man needs someone.''

THE MEAL WAS FINISHED, and Robin was standing in front of the sink rinsing off the dinner plates when the doorbell rang. Robin knew it had to be Cole.

"I'll get it,'' Jeff cried as he raced past her at breakneck speed. He threw open the door with enough enthusiasm to tear it from its hinges. "Hi, Mr Camden!'' he said eagerly.

By this time Robin had smoothed her peach-coloured sweater over her slim hips and placed a friendly—but not too friendly—smile on her face. At the last second, she ran her fingers through her hair, striving for the casual I-didn't-go-to-any-trouble look, then wondered at her irrational behaviour. Cole wasn't coming over to see *her*.

Robin could hear Jeff chatting away at ninety miles an hour, telling Cole they were renting a movie and how Robin insisted that every show he saw had to have the proper rating, which he claimed was totally ridiculous. He went on to explain that she considered choosing the film a mother's job and apparently a mere kid didn't have rights. When there was a pause in the conversation, she could envision Jeff rolling his eyes dramatically.

Taking a deep breath, she stepped into the entryway and smiled. "Hello, Cole.''

"Robin.''

Their eyes met instantly. Dark brown sought out light blue. Robin's first coherent thought was that a woman could get lost in eyes that dark and not even care. She swallowed tightly and lowered her gaze.

"Would you care for a cup of coffee?'' she asked, having difficulty dragging the words out of her mouth.

"If it isn't too much trouble.''

"It isn't." At least it wouldn't be if she could stop her heart from pounding so furiously.

"Where's Blackie?" Jeff demanded, opening the screen door and glancing outside.

"I didn't bring him over. I thought you'd be thoroughly tired of him by now."

"Tired of Blackie?" Jeff cried. "You've got to be kidding!"

"I take it I should have known better," Cole teased.

Robin returned to the kitchen and took mugs from the cupboard, using these few moments to compose herself.

The screen door slammed, and a moment later Cole appeared in her kitchen. "Jeff went over to my house to get Blackie."

She smiled and nodded. "Do you take cream or sugar?" she asked, tossing the question over her shoulder.

"Just black, thanks."

Robin normally drank hers the same way. But for some reason she couldn't begin to fathom, she added a generous teaspoonful of sugar to her own, stirring briskly as though she feared it wouldn't dissolve.

"I hope your trip went well," she said, carrying both mugs into the family room where Cole had chosen to sit.

"Very well."

"Good." She sat a safe distance from him, across the room in a wooden rocker, and balanced her mug on her knee. "Everything went without a hitch around here, but I fear Jeff may have spoiled Blackie a bit."

"From what he said, they did everything but attend school together."

"Having the dog around has been wonderful for him. I appreciate your giving Jeff this opportunity. Not only does it satisfy his need for a dog, but it's taught him about responsibility."

The front door opened and the canine subject of their conversation shot into the room, followed by Jeff, who was grinning from ear to ear. "Mom, would it be all right if Mr Camden stayed and watched the movie with us?"

"Ah…" Caught off guard, Robin didn't know what to say. After being away from home several days, watching a move with his neigh-bours probably held a low position on Cole's list of priorities.

To Robin's surprise, Cole's eyes searched hers as though seeking her approval.

"You'd be welcome...I mean, you can stay if you'd like, unless there's something else you'd rather do. I mean, I'd...we'd like it if you did, but..." She let whatever else she might have said fade away. She was making a mess of this, and every time she tried to smooth it over, she only stuck her foot further down her throat.

"What movie have you rented?"

"We haven't yet," Jeff explained. "Mom and me had to come to an understanding first. She likes the mushy stuff and gets all bent out of shape if there's a little blood. You wouldn't believe the love story she forced me to watch last Friday night." His voice dipped with renewed disgust.

"How about if you and I go rent the movie while your mother and Blackie make the popcorn?"

Jeff's blue eyes brightened immediately. "That'd be great, wouldn't it, Mom?"

"Sure," she agreed, and was rewarded by Jeff's eager smile.

Jeff and Cole left a few minutes later. It was on the tip of her tongue to give Cole instructions on the type of movie appropriate for a ten-year-old boy, but she swallowed her concerns, willing to trust his judgement. Standing on the porch, she watched as the two climbed inside Cole's expensive sports car. She pressed her hand to her throat, grateful when Cole leaned over the front seat and snapped Jeff's seat belt snugly in place. Her son must have commented on how Robin made him wear a seat belt, too, because Cole's gaze flew to her. She raised her hand in farewell, and Cole did the same. It was a simple gesture, yet Robin felt as if they'd communicated so much more than a simple farewell.

"Come on, Blackie," Robin said, "let's go start the popcorn." The devoted Lab trailed behind her as she returned to the kitchen. She set the old battered pot on the stove and turned on the burner, heating a generous amount of vegetable oil, then adding kernels. It was while she was waiting for the first few to pop that the words slipped from her mouth.

"Well, Lonny, what do you think?" Talking to her dead husband came without conscious thought. It certainly wasn't that she expected him to answer. Whenever she spoke to him, the words came spontaneously from the deep well of love they'd once shared. She supposed she should feel foolish doing it, but so many times over the long years since he'd died she had felt his presence and his love. Robin assumed that the reason she talked to him was born out of a need to discuss things with the one other person who'd loved her son as much as she did. In the beginning she was sure she needed to visit a psychiatrist or arrange for grief counselling, but later she convinced herself that every widow went through this in one form or another.

"He's grown so much the past year, hasn't he?" she asked, and smiled. "Meeting Cole has been good for Jeff. He lost a child, you know, and I suppose having Jeff move in next door answers a need for him, too."

The first kernels of corn popped and Robin transferred her attention to the pot, gripping its faded black handle and shaking it gently.

A couple of minutes later, Jeff and Cole returned with a movie that turned out to be an excellent compromise—a teenage comedy that was surprisingly witty and entertaining.

Jeff sprawled on the carpet munching popcorn with Blackie by his side. Cole sat on the sofa and Robin chose the rocking chair. She removed her shoes and tucked her feet beneath her. She was enjoying the movie; in fact, several times she found herself laughing outright.

Cole and Jeff laughed, too. The sounds were contrasting—one deep and masculine, the other young and pleasantly boyish—yet they harmonised, blending with perfect naturalness.

Soon Robin found herself watching Jeff and Cole more than the movie. The two...no, the three of them were comfortable together. Robin didn't try to read any significance into that. Doing so could prove emotionally dangerous, but the thought flew into her mind and refused to leave.

The credits were rolling when Cole pointed to Jeff, whose head was resting on his arms. For the first time, Robin noted that her son's eyes were closed.

"He's asleep," Cole said softly.

Robin smiled and nodded. She got up to carry the empty popcorn bowls into the kitchen. Cole stood, too, taking their glasses to the sink, then returned to the family room to rewind the movie.

"Do you want me to carry him upstairs for you?" he asked, glancing down on the slumbering Jeff.

"No," she whispered. "When he wakes up in the morning, he'll think you treated him like a little kid. Egos are surprisingly fragile at ten."

"I suppose you're right."

The silence felt as loud as thunder to Robin. Without Jeff, awake and chattering, as a buffer between them, she felt clumsy and self-conscious around Cole.

"It was nice of you to stay," she said, more to fill the quiet than because she had anything important to communicate. "It meant a lot to Jeff."

Jeff had mentioned that Cole had an active social life. Heather Lawrence had confirmed it by casually letting it drop that Cole was often away on weekends. Robin wasn't entirely sure what to think about it all. If there was a woman in his life, that was his business, not hers.

"It meant a lot to me, too," he said, standing in front of the VCR while he waited for the movie to finish rewinding.

The kitchen and family room, actually quite spacious, felt close and intimate with Cole standing only a few feet away.

Robin's fingers were shaking as she stacked the bowls and soda glasses in the dishwasher. She tried to think of some bright and witty comment to make, but her mind was blank.

"I should be going."

Was that reluctance she heard in his voice? Somehow Robin doubted it; probably wishful thinking on her part. Half of her wanted to push him out the door and the other half didn't want him to leave so early. But there really wasn't any reason for him to stay. "I'll walk you to the door."

"Blackie." Cole called for his dog. "It's time to go."

The Lab didn't look pleased with this turn of events. He took his own sweet time lumbering to his feet and stretching his long sleek body before trotting to Cole's side.

Robin was about to open the door when she realised she hadn't thanked Cole for getting the movie. She turned, and his dark eyes delved into hers. Whatever thoughts had been taking shape in her mind fled like leaves scattering in the wind. She tried to smile, however weakly, but it was difficult when he was looking at her so intently. His gaze slipped to her mouth, and in a nervous movement, she moistened her lips. Before she was fully aware of how it had happened, Cole's fingers were in her hair and he was lifting her mouth to meet his.

His eyes held hers, as if he expected her to stop him, then they slowly closed and his mouth grazed hers. Robin's eyes drifted shut, but that was the only response she made.

He kissed her again, even more gently than the first time. His lips were tender, and Robin moaned softly, not in protest, but in wonder and surprise. It had been so long since a man had kissed her like this. So long that Robin had forgotten the wealth of sensations a mere kiss could evoke. Her hands crept to his chest, and her fingers curled into the soft wool of his sweater. Hesitantly, timidly, her lips trembled beneath his, parting as the kiss blossomed. Cole sighed and took full possession of her mouth.

Robin sighed, too. The tears that welled in her eyes were a shock. She was at a loss to explain where they came from or why. They silently slipped down her face, and it wasn't until she felt the moisture that she realized she was crying.

Cole must have felt the tears at the same moment as she had, because he abruptly broke off the kiss and raised his head. His eyes searched hers as his thumb brushed the moisture from her cheek.

"Did I hurt you?" The question was whispered.

She shook her head vehemently.

"Then why...?"

"I don't know." She couldn't explain something she didn't understand herself. Rubbing the heels of her hands across her eyes, she attempted to wipe away the evidence. She forced a smile and looked up at him. "I'm nothing if not novel," she said with brittle cheerfulness. "I don't imagine many women break into tears when you kiss them."

Cole looked as confused as Robin felt.

"Don't worry about it. I'm fine." She wanted to reassure him, but was having too much trouble analyzing her own reactions to answer his doubts.

"Let's sit down and talk about this."

"No," she said quietly. Adamantly. That was the last thing she wanted. "I'm sorry, Cole. I really am. This has never happened before and I'm at as much of a loss to understand it as you are."

"But…"

"The best thing we can do is chalk it up to a long tiring work week."

"It's not that simple."

"Probably, but I'd prefer to just forget it. Please?"

"Are you all right?"

"Emotionally or physically?" She tried to joke, but didn't succeed. "Both."

He was so serious, so concerned, that it was all Robin could do not to dissolve into a fit of fresh tears. She'd made a world-class fool of herself with this man, not once but twice.

This man, who had suffered such a tremendous loss himself, was so gentle, so tender with her, and instead of helping it only made matters worse. "I'm sorry, really I am," she said raggedly, "but I think you should go home now."

CHAPTER FOUR

"You know what I'm in the mood for?" Angela Lansky said as she sat on the edge of Robin's desk early Monday afternoon.

"I certainly hope you're going to say food," Robin teased. The two shared the same lunch hour and were celebrating a cost-of-living raise by eating out.

"A shrimp salad," Angela elaborated. "Heaped six inches high with big fresh shrimp."

"I was thinking Chinese food myself," Robin said, "but, now that you mention it, shrimp salad sounds good." She opened her bottom drawer and withdrew her purse.

Angela was short and enviably thin with thick brown hair that fell in natural waves over her slim shoulders. She used clips to hold the abundant curls away from her face and looked closer to twenty than the thirty-five Robin knew her to be.

"I know just the place," Angela insisted. "The Blue Crab. It's on the wharf and worth the trouble of getting there."

"I'm game," Robin said.

They stopped at the bank to deposit their cheques, and then headed for the restaurant. They decided to catch the Market Street cable car to Fisherman's Wharf. After purchasing their tokens they joined the quickly growing line.

"So how's the kid doing?" Angela asked. She and her salesman husband didn't plan to have children themselves, but Angela enjoyed hearing about Jeff.

"He signed up for baseball through the park program and starts practice this week. I think it'll be good for him. He was terribly lonely this weekend now that Blackie's back with Cole."

"But isn't Blackie over at your place as much as he was before?" Angela asked.

Robin shook her head. "Cole left early Saturday morning and apparently took his dog with him. Jeff moped around for most of the weekend like a lost puppy, so to speak."

"Where'd your handsome neighbour go?"

"Good grief, how am I supposed to know that?" Robin countered with a soft laugh, hiding her disappointment at his disappearance. "Cole doesn't clear his schedule with me."

The way he'd left—without a word of farewell or explanation—still hurt. It was the kind of hurt that came from realising what a complete fool she'd made of herself with this worldly, sophisticated man. He'd kissed her and she'd started weeping. Good lord, he was probably doing back flips in order to avoid seeing her again, and she couldn't blame him.

"Do you think Cole was with a woman?"

"That's none of my business!"

"But I thought your neighbour said Cole spent his weekends with a woman friend."

Robin didn't remember mentioning that to Angela, but she obviously had, along with practically everything else. Robin had tried to convince herself that confiding in Angela about Cole was a clever way of thwarting her friend's matchmaking efforts. Unfortunately, the whole thing had backfired in her face. In the end the last person she wanted to talk about was Cole, but of course Angela persisted in questioning her.

"Well?" Angela demanded. "Did he spend his weekend with a woman or not?"

"What he does with his time is his business, not mine," Robin reiterated. She pretended not to care. But she did. Too damn much. She'd promised herself she wasn't going to put any stock in the kiss or the powerful attraction she felt for Cole. Within the space of one evening, she'd wiped out every pledge she'd made to herself. She hadn't said anything to Jeff—how could she?—but she was just as disappointed as he was that Cole had left for the weekend.

"I was hoping something might develop between the two of you," Angela murmured. "Since you're obviously not interested in meeting

Frank, it would be great if you got something going with your neigh-bour.''

Robin cast her a plaintive look that suggested otherwise. "Cole Camden lives in the fanciest house in the neighbourhood. He's a partner in the law firm of Blackwell, Burns and Dailey, which we both know is one of the most prestigious in San Francisco. And he drives a car with a name I can barely pronounce. Now what would someone like that see in me?''

"Lots of things," Angela countered.

Robin snickered. "I hate to disillusion you, my friend, but the only thing Cole Camden and I have in common is the fact that my small yard borders his massive one.''

"Maybe," Angela agreed, raising her eyebrows. "But I noticed something different about you from the first time you mentioned him.''

"That's ridiculous.''

"It isn't," Angela insisted. "I've watched you with other men over the past few years. A guy will show some interest, and at first everything looks peachy-keen. You'll go out with him a couple of times, maybe even more, but before anything serious can develop you've broken off the relationship without ever really giving it a chance.''

Robin didn't have much of an argument, since that was true, but she made a token protest just the same. "I can't help it if I have high standards.''

"High standards!" Angela choked back a laugh. "That's got to be the understatement of the century. You'd find fault with Prince Charming.''

Robin rolled her eyes, but couldn't hold back a smile. Angela was right, although that certainly hadn't slowed her matchmaking efforts.

"From the time you first mentioned your neighbour," Angela went on, "I noticed something different about you, and frankly I'm thrilled. In all the years we've known each other, this is the first time I can remember you giving a man this much attention. Until now, it's always been the other way around.''

"I'm not interested in Cole," she mumbled. "Oh, honestly, Angela, I can't imagine where you come up with these ideas. I think you've been reading too many romance novels.''

Angela waved her index finger under Robin's nose. "Listen, my friend, I'm on to you. You're not going to divert me with humour, or weasel your way out of admitting it. You can't fool me—you're attracted to this guy and it's frightening you to death. Right?''

The two women gazed solemnly at each other, both too stubborn to admit defeat. Under the force of her friend's unyielding determination, Robin was the one who finally gave in.

"All right!" she cried, causing the other people waiting for the cable car to turn and stare. "All right," she repeated in a whisper. "I like Cole, but for the life of me I don't understand it."

Angela's winged brows arched speculatively. "He's attractive and wealthy, crazy about your son, generous and kind, and you haven't figured it out yet?"

"He's also way out of my league."

"I wish you'd quit categorising yourself. You make it sound as though you aren't good enough for him, and that's ridiculous."

Robin just sighed.

The cable car appeared then, its bell clanging as it drew to a stop. Robin and Angela boarded and held on tightly.

Jeff loved hearing about the history of the cable cars, and Robin loved telling him the story. Andrew Hallidie had designed them because of his deep love for horses. Day after day, Hallidie had watched them struggling up and down the treacherous hills of the city, carting heavy burdens. Prompted by his concern for the animals, he'd invented the cable cars that are pulled by a continuously moving underground cable. To Jeff and to many others, Andrew Hallidie was a hero.

Robin and Angela were immediately caught up by the festive atmosphere of Fisherman's Wharf. The rows of fishing boats along the dock bobbed gently with the tide, and although Robin had never been to the Mediterranean the view reminded her of pictures she'd seen of French and Italian harbours.

The day was beautiful, the sky blue and cloudless, the ocean sparkling the way it did on a summer day. The entire spring had been exceptionally warm. It wasn't uncommon for Robin to wear a winter coat in the middle of July, especially in the mornings when there was often a heavy fog accompanied by a cool mist from the Bay. But this spring, they'd experienced some lovely weather, including today's.

"Let's eat alfresco," Angela suggested, spying a free table outside the restaurant.

"All right," Robin agreed cheerfully. The Blue Crab was a popular restaurant and one of several in a long row that lined the wharf. More elegant dining took place inside, but the pavement was crowded with diners interested in a less formal meal.

Once they were seated, Robin and Angela were waited on quickly, and they promptly ordered their shrimp salads.

"So," Angela murmured, spreading her napkin over her lap while closely studying Robin. "Tell me more about your neighbour."

Robin froze. "I thought we were finished with this subject. In case you hadn't noticed, I'd prefer not to discuss Cole."

"I noticed, but unfortunately I was just getting started. It's a novelty for you to be so keen on a man, and I know hardly anything about him. It's time, Robin Masterson, to tell all."

"There's nothing to talk about. I already told you everything I care to," Robin answered crossly. She briefly wondered if Angela had guessed that Cole had kissed her. At the rate things were going, she was probably going to drag it out of her before lunch was over. Robin sincerely wished she could think of some clever way to change the subject.

Tall glasses of iced tea arrived and Robin was reaching for a packet of sugar when she heard a masculine chuckle that reminded her instantly of Cole. She paused, savouring the husky sound. Without really meaning to, she found herself scanning the tables, certain Cole was seated only a short distance away.

"He's here," she whispered before she could guard her tongue.

"Who?"

"Cole. I just heard him laugh."

Pushing back her chair in order to get a fuller view of the inside dining area, Robin searched through a sea of faces, but didn't find her neighbor's.

"What's he look like?" Angela whispered.

Ten different ways to describe him shot through her mind. To say he had brown hair, neatly trimmed, coffee-coloured eyes and was about six foot two seemed inadequate. To add that he was strikingly attractive in ways she didn't know how to explain further complicated the problem.

"Tell me what to look for," Angela insisted. "Come on, Robin, this is a golden opportunity. I want to get a good look at this guy. I'm not about to let a chance like this slip through my fingers. I bet he's gorgeous."

Reluctantly, Robin continued to scan the diners, but she didn't see anyone who remotely resembled Cole. Even if she did see him, she wasn't completely sure she'd point him out to Angela, although she hated to lie. Perhaps she wouldn't have to. Perhaps she'd imagined the whole thing. It would have been easy enough to do. Angela's questions had brought Cole to the forefront of her mind; they'd just been discussing him and it was only natural for her to—

Her heart pounded against her rib cage with the force of a wrecking ball as Cole walked out of the restaurant foyer. He wasn't alone. A tall, slender woman with legs that seemed to go all the way to her neck and a figure as shapely and athletic as a dancer's was standing at his side. She was blond and, in a word, gorgeous. Robin felt as appealing as milk weed in comparison. The woman's arm was delicately tucked in Cole's, and she was smiling up at him with eyes big and blue enough to turn heads.

Robin's stomach tightened into a hard knot.

"Robin," Angela said anxiously, leaning toward her, "what is it?"

Cole was strolling past them, and in an effort not to be seen, Robin quickly stuck her head under the table pretending to search for her purse.

"Robin," Angela muttered, lowering her own head and peeking under the linen tablecloth, "what's the matter with you?"

"Nothing." Other than the fact that she was going to be ill. Other than the fact that she'd never been more outclassed in her life. "I'm fine, really." A smile trembled on her pale lips.

"Then what are you doing with your head under the table?"

"I don't suppose you'd believe my napkin fell off my lap?"

"No."

A pair of shiny black shoes appeared. Slowly, reluctantly, Robin twisted her head and glanced upward, squinting at the flash of sunlight that nearly blinded her. It was their waiter. Heaving a giant sigh of relief, Robin straightened. The first thing she noticed was that Cole had left.

The huge shrimp salads were all but forgotten as Angela, eyes narrowed and elbows braced on the table, confronted her. "You saw him, didn't you?"

It wouldn't do any good to pretend otherwise, so Robin nodded.

"I take it he was with someone?"

"Not just someone! Miss Universe was draped all over his arm."

"That doesn't mean anything," Angela said. "Don't you think you're jumping to conclusions? Honestly, she could have been anyone."

"Right." Any fight left in Robin had long since evaporated. There was nothing like seeing Cole with another woman to bring her firmly back to earth—which was right where she belonged.

"She could have been a client."

"She probably was," Robin concurred, reaching for her fork. She didn't know how she was going to manage one shrimp, let alone a whole plate of them. Heaving another huge sigh, she plowed her fork into the heap of plump pink darlings. It was then that she happened to glance across the street. Cole and Miss Universe were walking along the sidewalk, gazing intently at each other. For some reason, known only to the fates, Cole looked across the street at that very moment. His gaze instantly narrowed in on her. He stopped midstride as though shocked to have seen her.

Doing her best to pretend she hadn't seen *him*, Robin took another bite of her salad and chewed vigorously. When she glanced up again, Cole was gone.

"MOM, I NEED SOMEONE to practise with," Jeff pleaded. He stood forlornly in front of her, a baseball mitt in one hand, a ball in the other.

"I thought Jimmy was practising with you."

"He had to go home and then Kelly tossed me a few pitches, but she had to go home, too. Besides, she's a girl."

"What am I?" Robin muttered. "Chopped liver?"

"You're a mom," Jeff answered, clearly not understanding her question. "Don't you see? I've got a chance of making pitcher for our team if I can get someone to practise with me."

"All right," Robin agreed, grumbling a bit. She set aside her needlepoint and followed her son into the backyard. He handed her his old catcher's mitt, which barely fit her hand, and positioned her with her back to Cole's yard.

Robin hadn't been able to completely avoid her neighbour in the past week, but she'd managed to keep her distance. For that matter, he didn't seem all that eager to run into her, either. Just as well, she supposed.

He stayed on his side of the hedge. She stayed on hers.

If he passed her on his way to work, he gave an absent wave. She returned the gesture.

If they happened to be outside at the same time, they exchanged smiles and a polite greeting, but nothing more. It seemed, although Robin couldn't be sure, that Cole spent less time outside than usual. For that matter so did she.

"OK," Jeff called, running to the end of their yard. "Squat down."

"I beg your pardon?" Robin shouted indignantly. "I agreed to play catch with you. You didn't say anything about having to squat!"

"Mom," Jeff said impatiently, "think about it. If I'm going to be the pitcher, you've got to be the catcher, and all catchers have to be low to the ground."

Muttering complaints under her breath, Robin sank to her knees, worried the grass would stain her jeans.

Jeff tossed his arms into the air in abject frustration. "Not like that!" He said something more that Robin couldn't quite make out—something about why couldn't moms be guys.

Reluctantly, Robin assumed the posture he wanted, but she didn't know how long her knees would hold out. Jeff wound up his arm and let loose with a fastball. Robin closed her eyes, stuck out the mitt and was so shocked when she caught the ball that she toppled backward into the wet grass.

"You all right?" Jeff yelled, racing toward her.

"I'm fine, I'm fine," she shouted back, discounting his concern as she brushed the dampness from the seat of her jeans. She righted herself, assumed the position and waited for the second ball.

Jeff raced back to his mock pitcher's mound, gripped both hands behind his back and stepped forward. Robin closed her eyes again. Nothing happened. She opened her eyes cautiously, puzzled about the delay. Then she recalled the hand movements she'd seen pitchers make in the movies and flexed her fingers a few times.

Jeff straightened, placed his hand on his hip and stared at her. "What was that for?"

"It's a signal…I think. I saw the guy in the movie *Bull Durham* do it."

"Mom, leave that kind of stuff to the guys in the movies. All I want you to do is catch my pitches and throw them back. It might help if you kept your eyes open, too."

"I'll try."

"Thank you, I appreciate that."

Robin suspected she heard a tinge of sarcasm in her son's voice. She didn't know what he was getting so riled up about; she was doing her best. It was times such as these that she most longed for Lonny. When her parents had still lived in the area, Jeff's grandfather had stepped in whenever her son needed a father's guiding hand, but they'd moved to Arizona a couple of years ago. Lonny's family had been in Texas since just before his death. Robin hadn't seen them since the funeral, although Lonny's mother faithfully sent Jeff birthday and Christmas gifts.

"You ready?" Jeff shouted.

"Ready." Squinting, Robin stuck out the mitt, prepared to do her best to catch the silly ball, since it seemed so important to her son. Once more he swung his arms behind him and stepped forward. Then he stood there, poised to throw, for what seemed an eternity. Her knees were beginning to ache.

"Are you going to throw the ball, or are you going to stare at me all night?" she asked after a long moment had passed.

"That does it," Jeff shouted, tossing his mitt to the ground. "You just broke my concentration."

"Well, for crying out loud, what's there to concentrate about?" Robin muttered, rising awkwardly to her feet. Her legs had started to lose feeling, the way she'd crouched there, balanced on her toes.

"This isn't working," Jeff cried, stalking toward her. "Kelly's only in third grade and she does a better job than you do."

Robin decided to let that comment pass. She pressed her hand to the small of her back, hoping to ease the ache she was beginning to feel.

"Hello, Robin. Jeff."

Cole's voice came at her like a hangman's noose. She straightened abruptly and winced at the sharp pain that shot through her back.

"Hi, Mr Camden!" Jeff shouted as though Cole was a conquering hero returned from the war. He raced across the yard, past Robin and straight to the hedge. "Where have you been all week? I've hardly seen you."

"I've been busy." He might have been talking to Jeff, but his eyes were holding Robin's. She tried to look away—but she couldn't.

His eyes told her she was avoiding him.

Hers answered that he'd been avoiding her.

His said it was time for things to change.

Her eyes suggested she'd rather things continue as they were.

"I guess you *have* been busy," Jeff was saying. "I haven't seen you in days and days and days." Blackie squeezed through the hedge and Jeff fell to his knees, his arms circling the dog's neck lovingly.

"So how's the baseball going?" Cole asked.

Jeff sent his mother a disgusted look, then shrugged. "All right, I guess."

"What position are you playing?"

"Probably outfield. I had a chance to make pitcher, but I can't seem to get anyone who knows how to catch a baseball to work with me. Kelly tries, but she's a girl and I hate to say it, but my own mother is worthless."

"I did my best," Robin felt obliged to remind him.

"She catches with her eyes closed," Jeff said.

"How about if you toss a few balls at me?" Cole offered.

Jeff blinked as if he thought he'd misunderstood their neighbour. "You want me to throw you a few pitches? You're sure?"

"Positive."

The look on her son's face defied description as Cole hopped over the hedge. Jeff's smile stretched from one side of his face to the other as he tore to the opposite side of the yard, unwilling to question Cole's generosity a second time.

For an awkward moment, Robin stayed where she was, not knowing what to say. Her heart was full of gratitude, as full as Jeff's smile. She looked up at Cole, her emotions soaring—and tangling like kite strings in a brisk wind. She was deeply grateful for his offer, but also confused. Thrilled by his presence, but also frightened.

"Mom?" Jeff muttered. "In case you hadn't noticed, you're in the way."

"Are you going to make coffee and invite me in for a chat later?" Cole asked quietly.

Her heart sank to the pit of her stomach. "I have some things that need to be done, and...and..."

"Mom?" Jeff shouted a second time.

"I think it's time you and I talked," Cole said, staring straight into her eyes.

"Mom, are you moving or not?"

She tossed a frantic look over her shoulder. "Oh...oh, sorry," she whispered, blushing. Robin hurried away, then stood on the patio watching as the ball flew across the yard a couple of times with a speed that amazed her.

After catching a dozen of Jeff's pitches, Cole got up and walked over to her son. They spoke for several minutes. Reluctantly, Robin decided it was time to go back in.

It astonished her how hard and loud her heart was pounding. She busied herself wiping counters that were already perfectly clean and tried to stop thinking about the beautiful woman she'd seen with Cole on the Wharf.

Jeff stormed into the house fifteen minutes later. "Mom, would it be all right if Mr Camden strings up an old tyre from the apple tree?"

"I suppose. Why?"

"He said I can use it to practise pitching, and I wouldn't need to trouble you or Kelly."

"I don't think I have an old tyre."

"Don't worry, Mr Camden has one." He ran outside again before she could comment.

Jeff was back in the yard with Cole a few minutes later, far too soon to suit Robin. She forced a weak smile to her lips. That other woman was a perfect damsel to his knight in shining armour, she thought wryly. Robin, on the other hand, considered herself more of a court jester.

Her musings were abruptly halted when Cole walked into the kitchen, trailed by her son.

"Isn't it time for you to take your bath, Jeff?" Cole asked pointedly.

It looked for a minute as though the boy was going to argue. For the first time in recent memory, Robin would have welcomed some resistance from him.

"I guess," he said. Bathing was about as popular as homework.

"I didn't make any coffee," Robin said in a small voice. She simply couldn't look at Cole and not see the beautiful blonde on his arm.

"That's fine. I'm more interested in talking than drinking coffee, anyway," he said. He walked purposefully to the table and pulled out a chair. He gestured for her to sit down.

Robin didn't. Instead, she examined her watch. "My goodness, will you look at the time?"

"No." Cole headed towards her, and Robin backed slowly into the counter.

He should never have kissed her. She should never have allowed it.

"We're going talk about that kiss," Cole warned her.

"Please, don't," she whispered. "It meant nothing! We'd both had a hectic week. We were tired.... I wasn't myself."

Cole's eyes burned into hers. "Then why did you cry?"

"I...don't know. Believe me, if I knew I'd tell you, but I don't. Can't we just forget it ever happened?"

His shoulders heaved once in a silent sigh as he threaded his long fingers through his hair. "That's exactly what I've tried to do all week. Unfortunately it didn't work."

CHAPTER FIVE

"I'VE PUT IT COMPLETELY out of my mind," Robin said, continuing her string of untruths. "I wish you'd do the same."

"I can't. Trust me, I've tried," Cole told her softly. He smiled and his sensuous mouth widened as his eyes continued to hold hers. The messages were back. Less than subtle messages. *You can't fool me,* they said, and *I didn't want to admit it either.*

"I..."

The sense of expectancy was written in clean, clear strokes across his face. For the life of her, Robin couldn't tear her eyes from him.

She didn't remember stepping into his arms, but suddenly she was there, encompassed by his warmth, feeling more sheltered and protected than she had since her husband's death. This comforting sensation spun itself around her as he wove his fingers into her hair, cradling her head. He hadn't kissed her yet, but Robin felt the promise of it in every part of her.

Deny it though she might, she knew in her heart how badly she wanted Cole to hold her, to kiss her. He must have read the longing in her eyes, because he lowered his mouth to hers, stopping a fraction of an inch from her parted lips. She could feel warm moist breath, could feel a desire so powerful that she wanted to drown in his kiss.

From a reservoir of strength she didn't know she possessed, Robin managed to shake her head. "No...please."

"Yes...please," he whispered just before his mouth settled firmly over hers.

His kiss was the same as it had been before, only more intense. More potent. Robin felt rocked to the very core of her being. Against every dictate of her will, she felt herself surrendering to him. She felt herself forgetting to breathe. She felt herself weakening.

His mouth moved to the delicate line of her jaw, spreading small, soft kisses there. She sighed. She couldn't help it. Cole's touch was magic, and the walls guarding her heart were threatened for the first time in almost ten years. Unable to stop herself, she turned her head to the other side, yearning for him to trace a row of kisses there, as well. He complied.

Once more, Robin sighed, her mind filled with traitorous, sensuous thoughts. It felt so good in his arms, so warm and safe...but she knew the feeling was deceptive. She'd seen him with another woman, one far better suited to him than she could ever be. For days she'd been tormented by the realisation that the woman in the restaurant was probably the one he spent his weekends with.

"No, please don't." Once more she pleaded, but even to her own ears the words held little conviction.

In response, Cole delivered a long slow series of feather-light kisses to her lips, effectively silencing any protest. Robin trembled, breathless.

"Why are you fighting me so hard?" Cole whispered. His hands framed her face, his thumbs stroking her cheeks. They were damp and she hadn't even realised she was crying.

She heard the sudden sound of footsteps bounding down the stairs. At the thought of Jeff finding her in Cole's arms, she abruptly broke away and turned to stare out the darkened window, hoping for a moment to compose herself.

Jeff burst into the room. "Did you kiss her yet?" he demanded of Cole. Not waiting for an answer, Jeff raced toward Robin and grabbed her by the hand. "Well, Mom, what do you think?"

"About what?"

"Mr Camden kissing you. He did, didn't he?"

It was on the tip of her tongue to deny the whole thing, but she decided to brazen it out. "You want me to rate him? Like on a scale of one to ten?"

Jeff blinked, uncertain. His questioning glance flew to Cole.

"She was a ten," Cole said out of the corner of his mouth.

"A...high seven," Robin returned.

"A high seven!" Jeff cried, casting her a disparaging look. He shook his head and walked over to Cole. "She's out of practice,"

he said confidingly. "Doesn't know how to rate guys. Give her a
little time and she'll come around."

"Jeff," Robin gasped, thoroughly amazed to be having this type
of discussion with her son, let alone Cole, who was looking all too
smug.

"She hardly goes out at all," Jeff added. "My mom's got this
friend who arranges dates for her, and you wouldn't believe some of
the guys she's been stuck with. One of them came to the door—"

"Jeff," Robin said sharply, "that's enough!"

"But one of us needs to explain."

"Mr Camden was just leaving," Robin said, glaring at her neighbour, daring him to contradict her.

"I was? Oh, yeah. Your mom was just about to walk me to the
door, isn't that right, Robin?"

She gaped at Cole as he reached for her hand and gently led her
in the direction of the front door. Meekly she submitted, but not
before she saw Jeff give Cole a thumbs-up.

"All right," Cole said, standing in the entryway, his hands heavy
on her shoulders. "I want to know what's wrong."

"Wrong? Nothing's wrong."

"It's because of Victoria, isn't it?"

"Victoria?" she asked, already knowing that had to be the woman
with him the day she'd seen him at the Blue Crab.

"Yes. Victoria. I saw you practically hiding under your table, pretending you didn't notice me."

"I... Why should I care?" She hated the way her voice shook.

"Yes, why should you?"

She didn't answer him. Couldn't answer him. She told herself it
didn't matter that he was with another woman. Then again, it mattered more than she dared admit.

"Tell me," he insisted.

Robin lowered her gaze. If only he'd stop holding her, stop touching her. Then she might be able to think clearly. "You looked right
together. She was a perfect complement to you. She's tall and blonde
and—"

"Cold as an iceberg. Victoria's a business associate—we had lunch together. Nothing more. I find her as appealing as…as dirty laundry.''

"Please, don't explain. It's none of my business who you have lunch with or who you date or where you go every weekend or who you're with. Really. I shouldn't have said anything. I don't know why I did. It was wrong of me—very wrong. I can't believe we're even talking about this.''

Jeff's head shot out from the kitchen. "How are things going in here?"

"Good," Robin said. "I was just telling Cole how much we both appreciated his help with your pitching.''

"I was having real problems until Cole came along," Jeff confirmed. "Girls are good for some things, but serious baseball isn't one of them.''

Robin opened the front door. "Thanks," she whispered, her eyes avoiding Cole's, "for everything.''

"Everything?"

She blushed, remembering the kisses they'd shared. But before she could think of a witty reply, Cole brushed his lips across hers.

"Hey, Cole," Jeff cried, running to the front door. "I've got a baseball game Thursday night. Can you come?"

"I'd love to," Cole answered, his eyes holding Robin's. Then he turned abruptly and strode out the door.

"JEFF, WE'RE GOING TO BE LATE for the game if we don't leave now.''

"But Cole isn't home yet," Jeff protested. "He said he'd be here.''

"There's probably a very good explanation," Robin stated calmly, although she was as disappointed as Jeff. "He could be tied up in traffic, or delayed at the office, or any one of a thousand other things. He wouldn't purposely not come.''

"Do you think he forgot?"

"I'm sure he didn't. Come on, sweetheart, let's get a move on. You've got a game to pitch." The emphasis came on the last word. The first game of the season and Jeff had won the coveted position of first-string pitcher. Whether it was true or not, Jeff believed Cole's tutoring had given him the advantage over the competition. Jeff hadn't told him the news yet, keeping it a surprise for today.

"When you do see Cole, don't say anything, all right?" Jeff pleaded as they headed toward the car. "I want to be the one who tells him."

"My lips are sealed," she said, holding up her right hand. For good measure, she pantomimed zipping her mouth closed. She slid into the car and started the engine, but she glanced in the rearview mirror several times, hoping Cole would somehow miraculously appear.

He didn't.

The game was scheduled for the baseball diamond in Balboa Park, which was less than two miles from Robin's house. A set of bleachers had been arranged around the diamonds, and Robin climbed to the top. It gave her an excellent view of the field—and of the parking area.

Cole knew the game was at Balboa Park, but he didn't know which diamond and there were several. Depending on how late he was, he could waste valuable time looking for the right field.

The second inning had just begun when Heather Lawrence joined Robin. Robin smiled at her.

"Hi," Heather returned. "What's the score?"

"Nothing nothing. It's the top of the second inning."

"How's the neighbourhood Orel Hershiser doing?"

"Jeff's doing great. Terrific. He managed to keep his poise when the first batter got a hit off his second pitch. I think I took it worse than Jeff did."

Heather grinned and nodded. "It's the same way with me. Kelly played goalie for her soccer team last year, and every time the opposing team scored on her I took it like a bullet to the chest."

"Where's Kelly now?"

Heather motioned toward the other side of the field. The eight-year-old was leaning casually against a tall fir tree. "She didn't want Jeff to know she'd come to watch him. Her game was over a few minutes ago. They lost, but this is her first year and just about everyone else's, too. The game was more a comedy of errors than anything.''

Robin laughed. It was thoughtful of her neighbour to stop by and see how Jeff's team was doing.

Heather laced her fingers over her knees. "Jeff's been talking quite a bit about Cole Camden." She made the statement sound more like a question and kept her gaze focused on the playing field.

"Oh?" Robin wasn't sure how to answer. "Cole was kind enough to give Jeff a few pointers about pitching techniques."

"Speaking of pitching techniques, you two certainly seem to be hitting it off."

Heather was beginning to sound a lot like Angela, who drilled her daily about her relationship with Cole, offering advice and unsolicited suggestions.

"I can't tell you how surprised I am at the changes I've seen in Cole since you two moved in. Kelly's been wanting to play in that fort from the moment she heard about it, but it's only since Jeff moved in that she was allowed in Cole's yard."

"He's been good for Jeff," Robin said, training her eyes on the game. Cole's relationship with her son forced Robin to examine his motives. He'd lost a son, and there was bound to be a gaping hole in his heart. At first he hadn't allowed Jeff in his yard, or even approved of Blackie and Jeff's becoming friends. But without anything ever being said, all that had fallen to the wayside. Jeff played continually in Cole's yard, and with their neighbour's blessing. Jeff now had free access to the fort and often brought other neighbourhood kids along with him. Apparently Cole had given permission. Did he consider Jeff a sort of substitute son? Robin shook off the thought.

"Jeff talks about Cole constantly," Heather said. "In fact, he told me this morning that Cole was coming to see him pitch. What happened? Did he get hung up at the office?"

"I don't know. He must have been delayed, but—"

"There he is! Over there." Heather broke in excitedly. "You know, in the two years we've lived on Orchard Street, I can only recall talking to Cole a handful of times. He was always so standoffish. Except when we were both doing yard work, I never saw him, and if we did happen to meet we said hello and that was about it. The other day we bumped into each other at the grocery store and he actually smiled at me. I was stunned. I swear that's the first time I've ever seen that man smile. I honestly think you and Jeff are responsible for the change in him.''

''I think you're crediting me with more than my due,'' Robin said, craning her head to look for Cole.

''No, I'm not,'' Heather argued. ''You can't see the difference in him because you're new to the neighbourhood, but everyone who's known him for any length of time will tell you he's like a different person.''

Jeff was sitting on the bench while his team was up at bat. Suddenly he leapt to his feet and waved energetically several times, as though he was flagging down a rescue helicopter. His face broke into a wide, eager smile. His coach must have said something to him because Jeff nodded and took off running toward the parking area.

Robin's gaze followed her son. Cole had indeed arrived. The tension eased out of her in a single breath. She hadn't realised how edgy she'd been. In her heart she realised Cole would never purposely disappoint Jeff, but her son's anxiety had been as keen as her own.

''Listen,'' Heather said, standing, ''I'll talk to you later.''

''Thanks for stopping by.''

''Glad to,'' Heather said, climbing down the bleachers. She paused at the bottom and wiggled her eyebrows expressively, then laughed merrily at Robin's frown.

Heather must have passed Cole on her way out, but Robin lost sight of them as Jeff raced on to the pitcher's mound for the bottom of the second inning. Even from this distance Robin could see that his eyes were full of happy excitement. He discreetly shot her a look and Robin made a V-for-victory sign, smiling broadly.

Cole leapt up the bleachers and sat down beside her. ''Sorry I'm late. I was trapped in a meeting, and by the time I could get out to phone you you'd already left for the field.''

''Jeff and I knew it was something like that.''

''So he's pitching!'' Cole's voice rang with pride.

"He claims it's all due to you."

"I'll let him believe that," Cole said, grinning, "but he's a natural athlete. All I did was teach him a little discipline and give him a means of practising on his own."

"According to Jeff you taught him everything he knows."

He shook his head. "I'm glad I didn't miss the whole game."

"There'll be others," she said, but she was grateful he'd come when he had. From the moment they'd left the house, Robin had been tense and guarded. Cole could stand *her* up for any date, but disappointing Jeff was more than she could bear. Rarely had she felt this emotionally unsettled. And all because Cole had been late for a Balboa Park Baseball League game. It frightened her to realise how much Jeff was beginning to depend on him. And not just Jeff, either....

"This is important to Jeff," Cole said as if reading her mind, "and I couldn't disappoint him. If it had been anyone else it wouldn't have been nearly as important. But Jeff matters—" he paused and his eyes locked with hers "—and so do you."

Robin felt almost giddy with a flood of relief. For the first time since Lonny's tragic death, she understood how carefully, how completely, she'd anesthetised her life, refusing to admit anyone or anything into it that might cause her or Jeff more pain. For years she'd been drifting in a haze of denial and grief, refusing to acknowledge or deal with either. What Angela had said was true. Robin had dated infrequently and haphazardly, and kept any suitors at a safe and comfortable distance.

For some reason, she hadn't been able to do that with Cole. Robin couldn't understand what was different or why; all she knew was that she was in serious danger of falling for this man, and falling hard. It terrified her....

"Have you and Jeff had dinner?" Cole asked.

Robin turned to face him, but it was a long moment before she realised he'd asked her a question. He repeated it and she shook her head. "Jeff was too excited to eat."

"Good. There's an excellent Chinese restaurant close by. The three of us can celebrate after the game."

"That'd be nice," she whispered, thinking she should make some excuse to avoid this, and realising almost immediately that she didn't want to avoid it at all.

"CAN I HAVE some more pork-fried rice?" Jeff asked.

Cole passed him the dish and Robin watched as her son heaped his plate high with a third helping.

"You won," she said wistfully.

"Mom, I wish you'd stop saying that. It's the fourth time you've said it. I know we won, you don't need to remind me," Jeff muttered, glancing at Cole as if to beg forgiveness for his mother, who was obviously suffering from an overdose of maternal pride.

"But Jeff, you were fantastic."

"The whole team was fantastic." Jeff reached for what was left of the egg rolls and added a dollop of plum sauce to his plate.

"I had no idea you were such a good hitter," Robin said, still amazed at her son's athletic ability. "I knew you could pitch—I'd seen that myself. But two home runs! Oh, Jeff, I'm so proud of you— and everyone else." It was difficult to remember that Jeff was only one member of a team, and that his success was part of a larger effort.

"I wanted to make sure I played well, especially 'cause you were there, Cole." Once more Jeff stretched his arm across the table, this time reaching for the nearly empty platter of almond chicken.

As for herself, Robin couldn't down another bite. Cole had said the food at the Golden Wok was good, and he hadn't exaggerated. It was probably the best Chinese meal she'd ever tasted. Jeff apparently thought so, too. The boy couldn't seem to stop eating.

It was while they were laughing over their fortune cookies that Robin heard bits and pieces of the conversation from the booth behind them.

"I bet they're celebrating something special," an elderly gentleman commented.

"I think their little boy must have done well at the baseball game," his wife said softly.

Their little boy, Robin mused. The older couple dining directly behind them thought Cole and Jeff were father and son.

Robin's eyes flew to Cole, but if he had heard the comment he didn't give any sign.

"His mother and father are certainly proud of him."

"It's such a delight to see these young people so happy. A family should spend time together."

A family. The three of them looked like a family.

Once more Robin glanced at Cole, but once again he seemed not to hear the comments. Or if he had, he ignored them.

But Cole must have sensed her scrutiny because his gaze found hers just then. Their eyes lingered without a hint of the awkwardness Robin had felt so often before.

Jeff chatted constantly on the ride home with Robin. Since they'd both brought their cars, they drove home separately. They exchanged good-nights in the driveway and entered their own houses.

Jeff had some homework to finish and Robin ran a load of clothes through the washing machine. An hour later, after a little television and quick baths, they were both ready for bed. Robin tucked the blankets around Jeff's shoulders, although he protested he was much too old for her to do that. But he didn't complain too loudly or too long.

"Night, Jeff."

"Night, Mom. Don't let the bedbugs bite."

"Don't go all sentimental on me, all right?" she teased, as she turned off his light. She was convinced he fell asleep the instant she left the room. She returned downstairs to secure the house for the night, then headed up to her own bedroom. Once upstairs, she paused in her son's doorway and smiled gently. They'd both had quite a day.

At about ten o'clock, she was sitting up in bed reading an Anne Perry mystery when the phone rang. She reached for it quickly, always anxious about late calls. "Hello."

"You're still awake." It was Cole, and his voice affected her like a surge of electricity.

"I...was reading," she said.

"It suddenly occurred to me that we never had the chance to finish our conversation the other night."

"What conversation?" Robin asked.

"The one at the front door...that Jeff interrupted. Remind me to give that boy lessons in timing, by the way."

"I don't even remember what we were talking about." She settled back against the pillows, savouring the sound of his voice, enjoying the small intimacy of lying in bed, listening to him. Her eyes drifted shut.

"As I recall you'd just said something about how it isn't any of your business who I lunch with or who I spend my weekends with. I assume you think I'm with a woman."

Robin's eyes shot open. "I can assure you, I don't think anything of the sort."

"I guess I should explain about the weekends."

"No. I mean, Cole, it really isn't my business. I can't believe I even suggested anything remotely like that. It doesn't matter. Really."

"I have some property north of here, about forty acres," he explained gently, despite her protests. "The land once belonged to my grandfather, and he willed it to me when he passed away a couple of years back. This house was part of the estate, as well. My father was born and raised here. I've been spending a good deal of my free time remodelling the old farmhouse. Sometime in the future, I might move out there."

"I see." She didn't want to think about Cole leaving the neighbourhood, ever.

"The place still needs a lot of work, and I've enjoyed doing it on my own. It's coming along well."

She nodded and a second later realised he couldn't see the action. "It sounds lovely."

"Are there any other questions you'd like to ask me?" His voice was low and teasing.

"Of course not," she denied immediately.

"Then would you be willing to admit you enjoy it when I kiss you? A high seven? Really? I think Jeff's right—we need more practise.''

''Uh...'' Robin didn't know how to answer that.

''I'm willing,'' he said, and she could almost hear him smile.

Robin lifted the hair from her brow. ''I can't believe we're having this discussion. I really can't.''

''You said that before. Would it help if I told you how much I enjoy kissing you?''

''Please...don't,'' she whispered. She didn't want him to tell her that. Every time he kissed her, it confused her more. Despite the sheltered feeling she experienced in his arms, something deep and fundamental inside her was afraid of loving again. No, terrified. She was terrified of coming to care for Cole. Terrified of what the future might hold.

''The first time shook me more than I care to admit. Remember that Friday night we rented the movie?''

''I remember.''

''I tried to stay away from you afterwards. For an entire week I avoided you.''

Robin didn't answer. She couldn't. Lying back against the pillows, she stared at the ceiling as a sense of warmth enveloped her. A feeling of comfort...of unfamiliar happiness.

There was a short silence, and in an effort to bring their discussion back to a less intimate—less risky—level, she said, ''Thank you for dinner. Jeff had the time of his life.'' She had, too, but she couldn't find the courage to admit it.

''You're welcome.''

''Are you going away this weekend to work on the property?''

She had no right to ask him that, and was shocked at how easily the question emerged.

''I don't think so.'' After another brief pause, he murmured, ''When was the last time you went on a picnic and flew a kite?''

''I don't remember,'' she admitted.

''Would you consider going with me Saturday afternoon? You and Jeff. The three of us together.''

''Yes...Jeff would love it.''

"How about you? Would you love it?"

"Yes," she whispered.

There didn't seem to be anything more to say, and Robin ended the conversation. "I'll tell Jeff in the morning. He'll be thrilled. Thank you."

"I'll talk to you tomorrow, then."

"Right. Tomorrow."

"Good night, Robin."

She smiled softly. He said her name the way she'd always dreamed a man would, softly, with a mixture of excitement and need. "Good night, Cole."

For a long time after they'd hung up Robin lay staring at her bedroom walls. When she did turn off her light, she fell asleep as quickly as Jeff seemed to have. She woke about midnight, surprised to find the sheets all twisted as if she'd tossed and turned frantically. The bedspread had slipped onto the floor, and the top sheet was wound around her legs, trapping her.

Sitting up, she untangled her legs and brushed the curls from her face, and wondered what had caused her restlessness. She didn't usually wake abruptly like this.

She slid off the bed, found her slippers and went downstairs for a glass of milk.

It was while she was sitting at the table that it came to her. Her hand stilled. Her heartbeat accelerated. The couple in the Chinese restaurant. Robin had overheard them and she was certain Cole must have, too.

Their little boy. A family.

Cole had lost a son. From what little Robin had learned, Cole's son had been about the same age as Jeff was now when he'd died. First divorce, and then death.

Suddenly it all made sense. A painful kind of sense. A panicky kind of sense. The common ground between them wasn't their back-yards, but the fact that they were both victims.

Cole was trying to replace the family that had been so cruelly taken from him.

Robin was just as guilty. She had been so caught up in the tide of emotion and attraction that she'd refused to recognise what was staring her in the face. She'd ignored her own suspicions and fears, brushing them aside.

She and Cole were both hurting, needy people.

But once the hurt was assuaged, once the need had been satisfied, Cole would discover what Robin had known from the beginning. They were completely different people with little, if anything, in common.

CHAPTER SIX

"WHAT DO YOU MEAN you want to meet my cousin?" Angela demanded, glancing up from her desk, a shocked disbelieving look on her face.

"You've been after me for weeks to date Fred."

"Frank. Yes, I have, but that was B.C."

"B.C.?"

"Before Cole. What happened with you two?"

"Nothing!"

"And pigs have wings," Angela said with more than a trace of sarcasm. She stood up and walked around to the front of her desk, leaning against one corner while she folded her arms and stared unblinkingly at Robin.

Robin knew it would do little good to try to disguise her feelings. She'd had a restless night and was convinced it showed. No doubt her eyes were glazed; they ached. Her bones ached. But mostly her heart ached. Arranging a date with Angela's cousin was a sure indication of her distress.

"The last thing I heard, Cole was supposed to attend Jeff's baseball game with you."

"He did." Robin walked to her own desk and reached for the cup of coffee she'd brought upstairs with her. Peeling off the plastic lid, she cautiously took a sip.

"And?"

"Jeff pitched and he played a fabulous game," Robin supplied, hoping her friend wouldn't quiz her further.

Angela continued to stare at Robin. Good grief, Robin thought, the woman had eyes that could cut through solid rock. Superman should have eyes like this.

"What?" Robin demanded when she couldn't stand her friend's

scrutiny any longer. She took another sip of her coffee and nearly scalded her lips. If the rest of her day followed the pattern set that morning, she might as well head home now. The temptation to climb back into bed and hide her head under the pillow was growing stronger every minute.

"Tell me what happened with Cole," Angela demanded.

"Nothing. I already told you he was at Jeff's baseball game. What more do you want?"

"The least you can do is tell me what went on last night," Angela said slowly, carefully enunciating each word as though speaking to someone who was hard of hearing.

"Before or after Jeff's baseball game?" Robin pulled out her chair and plopped herself down.

"Both."

Robin gave up. Gesturing weakly with her hands, she shrugged, took a deep breath and poured out the whole story in one huge rush. "Cole was held up at the office in a meeting, so we didn't meet at the house the way we'd planned. Naturally Jeff was disappointed, but we decided that whatever was keeping Cole wasn't his fault, and we left for Balboa Park without him. Cole arrived just as Jeff was ready to pitch the bottom of the second inning. Jeff only allowed three hits the entire game, and scored two home runs himself. Afterward Cole took us all out for Chinese food at a fabulous restaurant I've never heard of but one you and I will have to try sometime. Our next raise, OK? Later Cole phoned and asked to take Jeff and me on a picnic Saturday. I think we're going to Golden Gate Park because he also mentioned something about flying kites." She paused, dragged in a fresh gulp of air and gave Angela a look that said "try and make something out of that!"

"I see," Angela said after a lengthy pause.

"Good."

Robin wasn't up to explaining things, so if Angela really *didn't* understand, that was just too bad. She only knew that she was dangerously close to letting her emotions take charge of her life. She was becoming increasingly attracted to a man who could well be looking to replace the son he'd lost. Robin needed to find a way to keep from following her heart, which was moving at breakneck speed straight into Cole's arms.

"Will you introduce me to Frank or not?" she demanded a second time, strengthening her voice and her conviction.

Angela continued to stare at her with those diamond-cutting eyes while she rubbed the sides of her jaw with her thumb and index finger. "I'm not sure yet."

"You're not sure!" Robin echoed, dismayed. "For weeks you've been spouting his virtues. According to you, this cousin is as near a god as a human being can get. He works hard, buys municipal bonds, attends church regularly and flosses his teeth."

"I said all that?"

"Close enough," Robin muttered. "I made up the part about flossing his teeth. Yet when I ask to meet this paragon of limitless virtue, you say you're not sure you want to introduce me. I would have thought you'd be pleased."

"I am pleased," Angela said, frowning, "but I'm also concerned."

"It's not your job to be concerned. All you have to do is call Fred and let him know I'm available Saturday evening for drinks or dinner or a movie or whatever. I'll let him decide what he's most comfortable with."

"It's Frank, and I thought you just said you were going on a picnic with Cole on Saturday."

Robin unfolded a computer printout, prepared to check a long row of figures. If she looked busy and suitably nonchalant, it might prompt Angela into agreeing. "Jeff and I will be with Cole earlier in the day. I'll simply make sure we're back before late afternoon, so there's no reason to worry."

Robin's forehead puckered gently. "I am worried, I can't help being worried. Honestly, Robin, I've never seen you like this. You're so...so determined."

"I've always been determined," Robin countered, glancing up from the computer sheet.

"Oh, I agree one hundred per cent," Angela said with a heavy sigh, "but not when it comes to anything that has to do with men.

My thirteen-year-old niece has more savvy with the opposite sex than you do!''

"MOM, LOOK HOW HIGH my kite is," Jeff hollered as his box kite soared toward the heavens.

"It's touching the sky!" Robin shouted, and laughed with her son as he tugged and twisted the string. Despite all her misgivings about her relationship with Cole, she was thoroughly enjoying the afternoon. At first, she'd been convinced the day would turn into a disaster. She was sure Cole would take one look at her and know she was going out with another man that evening. She was equally sure she'd blurt it out if he didn't immediately guess.

Cole had been as excited as Jeff about the picnic and kite-flying expedition. The two of them had been fussing with the kites for hours—buying, building and now flying them. For her part, Robin was content to soak up the sunshine.

The weather couldn't have been more co-operative. The sky was as blue as she'd ever seen it and the wind was perfect. Sailboats scudding on the choppy green waters added dashes of bright colour.

In contrast to all the beauty surrounding her, Robin's heart was troubled. Watching Cole, so patient and gentle with her son, filled her with contradictory emotions. Part of her wanted to thank him. Thank him for the smile that lit up Jeff's young face. Thank him for throwing open the shades and gently easing her toward the light. And part of her wanted to shut her eyes and run for cover.

"Mom, look!" Jeff cried as the kite whipped and kicked in the wind. Blackie raced at his side, as the sleek red and blue kite sliced through the sky, then dipped sharply and crashed towards the ground at heart-stopping speed, only to be caught at what seemed the last second and lifted higher and higher.

"I'm looking, I'm looking!" Robin shouted back. She'd never seen Jeff happier. Pride and joy shone from his face, and Robin was moved almost to tears.

Cole stood behind Jeff, watching the kite. One hand rested on the boy's shoulder, the other shaded his eyes as he gazed toward the sky. The two laughed, and once more Robin was struck by the mingling of their voices. One mature and measured, the other young and excited. Both happy.

A few moments later, Cole jogged over to Robin's blanket and sat down beside her. He did nothing more than smile at her, but she felt an almost physical jolt.

Cole stretched out and leaned back on his elbows, grinning at the sun. "I can't remember the last time I laughed so much."

"You two certainly seem to be enjoying this," Robin said.

If Cole noticed anything awry with her, he didn't comment. She'd managed not to tell him about the date with Angela's cousin; she certainly didn't want him to think she was trying to make him jealous. That wasn't the evening's purpose at all. Actually she wasn't sure she fully understood *what* she hoped to accomplish by dating Fred...Frank. She mentally shouted the name five times. Why ever did she keep calling him Fred? She didn't know that any more than she knew why she was going out with him. On the morning she'd talked Angela into making the arrangements for her, it had seemed a matter of life and death. Now she only felt confused and regretful.

"Jeff says you've got a date this evening."

So much for her worry that she might blurt it out herself, Robin thought. She glanced at Cole. He might have been referring to a minor rise in stock prices for all the emotion revealed in his voice.

"A cousin of a good friend. She's been after me for months to meet Frank—we're having dinner."

"Could this be the Frank you weren't going out with and that was final?"

Robin stared at him blankly.

"You answered the phone with that when I called to inquire about Blackie. Remember?"

"Oh, yes," she muttered. Suddenly she felt an intense need to justify her actions. "It's just that Angela's been talking about him for so long and it seemed like the right thing to do. He's apparently very nice and Angela's been telling me that he's a lot of fun and I didn't think it would hurt to meet him...." Once she got started, Robin couldn't seem to stop explaining.

"Robin," Cole said gently, his eyes tender. "You don't owe me any explanations."

She instantly grew silent. He was right, she knew that, yet she couldn't help feeling guilty and confused. She was making a terrible mess of this.

"I'm not the jealous type," Cole informed her matter-of-factly.

"I'm not trying to make you jealous," she returned stiffly.

"Good," Cole said and shrugged. His gaze moved from her to Jeff, who was jogging across the grass. Blackie was at his side, barking excitedly.

He hadn't asked, but she felt obliged to explain who would be watching her son while she was out. "Jeff's going to the movies with Heather and Kelly Lawrence while I'm out."

Cole didn't say anything. All he did was smile. It was the same smile he'd flashed at her earlier. The same devastating, wickedly charming smile.

He seemed to be telling her that she could dine with a thousand different men and it wouldn't disturb him in the least. As he said, he wasn't the jealous type. Great. This was exactly the way she'd wanted him to respond, wasn't it? She could date a thousand different men, because Cole didn't care about her. He cared about her son.

"Let me know when you want to leave," he said with infuriating self-assurance. "I wouldn't want you to be late."

On that cue, Robin checked her watch and was surprised to note that it was well past four. They'd been having so much fun, the day had simply slipped away. When she looked up, she found Cole watching her expectantly. "It's...I'm not meeting Frank until later," she said, answering his unspoken question evasively while she gathered up the remains of their picnic.

It was an hour later when they decided to leave Golden Gate Park. Jeff and Cole loaded up the kites, as well as the picnic cooler, and placed them in the back of Cole's car. It took them nearly an hour to get back to Glen Park because of the heavy traffic, which pinched Robin's schedule even more tightly. But that was hardly Cole's fault—it wasn't as if he'd *arranged* for an accident on the freeway.

Cole and Jeff chatted easily for most of the ride home. Sitting in the back, Jeff leaned so far forward that his face was poised directly between Robin and Cole.

When they arrived at the house, both Robin and Jeff helped Cole unload the car. Blackie's barking only added to the confusion.

"I suppose I'd better get into the house," Robin said, her eyes briefly meeting Cole's. She felt awkward all of a sudden, wishing Jeff was there as a barrier, instead of carting things on to Cole's porch.

"We had a great time," she added self-consciously. She couldn't really blame her nervousness on Cole; he'd been the perfect companion all day. "Thank you for the picnic."

Jeff joined them, his eyes narrowing as he looked at Cole. "Are you honestly going to let her do it?"

"Do what?" Robin demanded of her son.

"Go out with that other man," Jeff said righteously, inviting Cole to leap into the argument. "I can't believe you're going to let her get away with this."

"Jeff. This isn't something we should be discussing with Mr Camden."

"All right," he murmured with an expressive sigh. "But I think you're making a mistake." He cast a speculative glance in Cole's direction. "Both of you," he mumbled under his breath and headed for the house.

"Thanks for the wonderful afternoon, Cole," Robin said again.

"No problem," he answered, hands in his pockets, his stance relaxed. "Have a good time with Frank."

"Thanks, I will," she muttered, squinting at him suspiciously just before she turned toward the house. Darn it, she actually felt guilty! There wasn't a single solitary reason she should feel guilty for agreeing to this dinner date with Angela's cousin, yet she did. Cole must have known it, too, otherwise he wouldn't have made that remark about having a good time. Oh, he knew all right.

As ROBIN WAS RUNNING the bath, Jeff raced up the stairs. "Mom, I need money for the movie." He thrust her purse into her hands. "How much are you going to give me for goodies?"

"Goodies?"

"You know popcorn, pop, a couple of candy bars. I'm starving."

"Jeff, you haven't stopped eating all day. What about the two hot dogs I just fixed you?"

"I ate them, but that was ten or fifteen minutes ago. I'm hungry again."

Robin handed him seven dollars, prepared for an argument. That amount was enough to pay his way into the movie and supply him with popcorn and a soda. Anything beyond that he could do without.

Jeff took the money from her and slowly shook his head, as though she'd intentionally slighted him. "That's it, kid," she said in a firm voice.

"Did I complain?" Bright blue eyes stared back at her innocently.

"You didn't have to. I could see the rebellion in your face."

Jeff was ready to leave a few minutes later, just as Robin was getting dressed. He stood outside her bedroom door and shouted that Kelly and her mom were there to pick him up.

"Have a good time. I won't be later than ten-thirty," she assured him.

"Can't I wait for you over at Cole's after the movie?"

"Absolutely not!" Robin's heart skidded to a dead stop at the suggestion. The last person she wanted to face at the end of this evening was Cole Camden. "You didn't ask him, did you?"

"No...but I'm not all that excited about going to Kelly's afterward. I'm there every day, you know."

"Sweetie, I'm sorry. I promise I won't be late."

"You're sure I can't go over to Cole's?"

"Jeffrey Leonard Masterson, don't you dare bother Cole, do you understand me?"

He blinked a couple of times. She rarely used that tone of voice with him, but she didn't have the time or energy to argue about this.

"I guess," he said with an exaggerated sigh. "But could you make it home closer to ten?"

"Why ten?"

"Because I don't want to do anything stupid like fall asleep in front of Kelly," he whispered heatedly.

"I'll be back as soon as I can," Robin promised.

Glancing at her clock radio, she gasped at the time. She was running late. From the moment she'd made the arrangements to meet Frank, she hadn't given the reality of this evening much thought. Just forcing herself to go through with it had depleted her of energy.

Robin had always hated situations like this. Always. She was going to a strange restaurant, meeting a strange man, and for what? She didn't know.

Tucking her feet into her pumps, Robin hurried to the bathroom to spray on a little cologne. Not much, just enough to give herself some confidence. She rushed down the stairs and reached for her purse.

Her hand was on the doorknob when the phone rang. For a moment, Robin intended to ignore it. It was probably for Jeff. But what if the call was from her parents? Or Frank—calling to cancel? Ridiculous though it was, each ring sounded more urgent than the last. She'd just have to answer, or she'd wonder who it was all evening. Muttering under her breath, she dashed into the kitchen.

"Hello," she said impatiently.

For a moment there was no response. "Robin, it's Cole." He sounded nothing like himself. "I lied." With that the line was abruptly disconnected.

Robin held the receiver away from her ear and stared at it for several seconds. He'd lied? About what? Good heavens, why had he even phoned? To tell her he'd lied.

There wasn't time to phone him back and ask what he meant.

"WOULD YOU CARE for something to drink?" Frank Eberle asked, glancing over the wine list.

"Nothing, thanks," Robin said. Frank had turned out to be a congenial sort, which was a pleasant surprise. He was quite attractive, with light blue eyes and a thick head of distinguished-looking salt-and-pepper hair. Angela had once mentioned he was "a little bit" shy, which had panicked Robin since she was a whole lot shy, at least around men. The way she'd figured it, they'd stare at each other most of the night, not knowing what to say. At least they had Angela in common. Whereas with Cole, all they shared was—

Her thoughts came to an abrupt stop. She refused to think about her neighbor or his last-minute phone call. She balked at the idea of dining with one man and wistfully longing for another—which was exactly what she was doing.

Robin studied the menu, pretending to decide between the prime-rib special and the fresh halibut. But the entire time she gazed at the menu, she was racking her brain for a topic of conversation.

Frank saved her the trouble. "For once," he said, "Angela didn't exaggerate. You're something of a surprise."

"I am?" It was amusing to hear him echo her own reaction.

Frank nodded, his smile gentle and reserved. "When Angie phoned earlier in the week, I wasn't sure what to expect. She keeps wanting me to date her friends. And to hear her talk, she's close friends with dozens of gorgeous women all interested in meeting me."

Robin grinned. "She should run a dating service. I can't tell you the number of times she's matched me up with someone, or at least tried to."

"But you're a comfortable kind of person to be around. I could sense that right away."

"Thank you. I...wasn't sure what to expect, either. Angela's raved about you for weeks, wanting to get the two of us together." Robin glanced from the menu to her companion, then back again. She felt the same misgivings every time she agreed to one of these arranged dates.

"I've been divorced six months now," Frank volunteered, "but after fourteen years of married life, I don't think I'll ever get accustomed to dating again."

Robin found herself agreeing. "I know what you mean. It all seems so awkward, doesn't it? When Lonny and I were dating I was in high school, and there was so little to consider. We knew what we wanted and knew what we had to do to get there."

Frank gave her a small smile. "Now that we're older and—" he paused "—I hesitate to use the word wiser...."

"More sophisticated?"

"Right, more sophisticated," Frank repeated. His hand closed around the water glass. "Life is so complicated now. I'd been out of the swing of things for so long, I hadn't realised that the role men played in relationships had changed. Women aren't the fragile creatures they used to be, if you know what I mean."

Robin had certainly been feeling fragile and artless and incredibly naïve, but she nodded. "Men aren't the same, either."

"You're right about that," Frank said with an abrupt nod of his head.

The waitress came for their order, and from then on the evening went smoothly. The sense of kinship she felt with Frank surprised Robin. He was obviously at ease, too. Before she knew how it happened, Robin found herself telling him about Cole.

"He sounds like the kind of guy most women would leap off a bridge to meet."

Robin nodded. "He's wonderful to Jeff, too."

"Then what's the problem."

"His wife and son."

Frank's mouth sagged open. "He's married?"

"Was," she rushed to explain. "From what I understand his wife left him and sometime later his son died."

"That's tough," Frank said, reaching for his coffee. "But that was years ago, right?"

"I...don't know. Cole's never told me these things himself. In fact, he's never mentioned either his wife or his son."

"He's never mentioned them?"

"Never," she confirmed. "I heard it from a neighbour."

"That's what's bothering you, isn't it?"

The question was sobering. Subconsciously, from the moment Robin had learned of Cole's loss, she'd been waiting for him to tell her. Waiting for him to trust her enough. Waiting for him to share his pain.

Frank and Robin lingered over coffee, chatting about politics and the economy and several other stimulating topics. But the question about Cole refused to fade from her mind.

They parted outside the restaurant and Frank kissed her cheek, but they were both well aware they wouldn't be seeing each other again.

Their time together had been a brief respite. It had helped Frank deal with his loneliness and helped Robin understand what was troubling her about Cole.

The first thing Robin noticed when she pulled into her driveway was that Cole's house was dark. Dark and silent. Silent and lonely. So much of her life had been those things—before she'd met him.

She needed to talk to him. She wanted to ask him about his phone call. She longed to ask him about his wife and the son he'd lost. But the timing was all wrong.

For a long moment Robin sat alone in her car feeling both disappointed and sad.

Heather greeted her with a smile and a finger pressed to her lips. "Both kids were exhausted. They fell asleep in the living room almost as soon as we got back."

After Jeff's busy day, it was astonishing that he'd lasted through the movie. "I hope he wasn't cranky."

"Not in the least," Heather assured her.

Robin yawned, and realised how exhausted she was. She wanted nothing more than to escape to her room and sleep until noon the following day.

"Would you like a cup of coffee before you go?" Heather asked.

"No, thanks." Robin had been blessed with good neighbours. Heather on her right and Cole on her left.

Together Robin and Heather woke Jeff, who grumbled about his mother being late. He was too drowsy to realise it was only nine-thirty, or that she'd returned ahead of schedule.

After telling Heather a little about her evening, Robin guided her son across the yard and into the house. She walked upstairs with him and answered the slurred questions he struggled to ask between wide, mouth-stretching yawns.

Tugging back his quilt, Robin gently urged him into his bed. Jeff kicked off his shoes and reached for the quilt. It wasn't the first time he'd slept in his clothes and it probably wouldn't be the last.

Smiling to herself, Robin quietly moved down the stairs.

On impulse, she paused in the kitchen and reached for the phone.

When Cole answered on the first ring, she swallowed a gasp of surprise.

"Hello," he said a second time.

"What did you lie about?" she asked softly.

"Where are you?"

"Home."

"I'll be right there." Without a further word, he hung up.

A minute later, Cole was standing at her front door, hands in his back pockets. He stared at her as if it had been months since they'd last seen each other.

"All right, you win," he said, edging his way in.

"Win what? The door prize?" she asked, controlling her amusement with difficulty.

Not bothering to answer her, Cole headed for the kitchen, where he sank down in one of the pine chairs. "Did you have a good time?"

She sat down across from him. "I really did. Frank's a gentle, caring man. We met at the Higher Ground—that's a cute little restaurant close to the BART station and—"

"I know where it is."

"About your phone call earlier. You said—"

"What's he like?"

"Who? Frank?"

Cole gave her a look that suggested she have her intelligence tested.

"He's very nice. Divorced and lonely."

"What's he do for a living?"

"He works for the city, I think. We didn't get around to talking about our careers." No doubt Cole would be shocked if he knew she'd spent the greater part of the evening discussing her relationship with him!

"What did you talk about then?"

"Cole, honestly, I don't think we should discuss my evening with Frank. Would you like some coffee?"

"Are you going to see him again?"

Robin ignored the question. Instead she left the table and began to make coffee. She was concentrating so carefully on her task that she didn't notice Cole was directly behind her. She turned—and found herself gazing into the darkest, most confused and frustrated pair of eyes she'd ever seen.

"Oh," she gasped. "I didn't realise you were so close."

His hands gripped her shoulders. "Why did you go out with him?"

Surely that wasn't distress she heard in Cole's voice. Not after all that casual indifference this afternoon. She frowned, bewildered by the weary pain she saw in his eyes. And she finally realised: contrary to everything he'd claimed, Cole was jealous. Really truly jealous.

"Did he kiss you?" He asked the question with an urgency, an intensity, she'd never heard in his voice before.

Robin blinked, frozen by the stark need she read in him.

Cole's finger rested on her mouth. "Did Frank kiss you?" he repeated.

She shook her head and the motion brushed his finger across the fullness of her bottom lip.

"He wanted to, though, didn't he?" Cole asked with a brooding frown.

"He didn't kiss me." She was finally able to say the words. She couldn't kiss Frank, or anyone else. The only man she wanted to be kissed and held by was the man looking down at her now. The man whose lips were descending on hers...

CHAPTER SEVEN

"SO, DID YOU LIKE this guy you had dinner with last night?" Jeff asked, keeping his eyes on his bowl of cold cereal.

"He was nice," Robin answered, pouring herself a cup of coffee and joining him at the table. They'd slept late and were spending a lazy Sunday morning enjoying their breakfast before heading for the eleven o'clock service at church.

Jeff hesitated, his spoon poised above the bowl. "Is he nicer than Cole?"

"Cole's...nicer," Robin admitted reluctantly. "Nice" and "nicer" weren't terms she would have used to describe the differences between Frank and Cole, but in her son's ten-year-old mind they made perfect sense.

A smile quivered at the edges of Jeff's mouth. "I saw you two smooching last night," he said, grinning broadly.

"When?" Robin demanded—a ridiculous question. It could only have been when Cole had come over to talk to her. He'd admitted how jealous he'd been of Frank and how he'd struggled with the emotion and felt like a fool. Robin had been convinced she was the one who'd behaved like a dolt. Before either of them could prevent it, they were in each other's arms, seeking and granting reassurance.

"You thought I was asleep, but I heard Cole talking and I wanted to ask him what he was going to do about you dating this other guy; so I came downstairs and saw you two with your faces stuck together."

The boy certainly had a way with words.

"You didn't look like you minded, either. Cole and me talked about girls once and he said they aren't much when they're ten or so, but they get a whole lot more interesting later on. He said girls are like green apples. At first they're all sour and make your lips pucker, but a little while later they're real good.''

"I see," Robin muttered, not at all certain she liked being compared to an apple.

"But when I got down the stairs I didn't say anything," Jeff said, "because, well, you know."

Robin nodded and sipped her coffee in an effort to disguise her discomfort.

Jeff picked up his cereal bowl and drank the remainder of the milk in loud gulps. He wiped the back of his hand across his lips. "I suppose this means you're going to have a baby now."

Robin was too horrified to speak. The swallow of coffee caught halfway down her throat and she started choking. In an effort to help her breathe, Jeff started pounding her back with his fist, which only added to her misery.

By the time she caught her breath, the tears were streaking down her face.

"You all right, Mom?" Jeff asked, his eyes wide with concern. He rushed into the bathroom and returned with a wad of tissue.

"Thanks," she whispered, wiping her face. It took her a moment or two to regain her composure. This was a talk she'd planned on having with her son a few years down the road. "Jeff, listen...kissing doesn't make babies."

"It doesn't? But I thought... I'd hoped... You mean you won't be having a baby?"

"I... Not from kissing," she whispered, taking in deep breaths to stabilise her pulse.

"I suppose the next thing you're going to tell me is that we'll have to save up for a baby the way we did for the house and now the fence before we get me a dog."

This conversation was growing more complicated by the moment. "No, we wouldn't have to save for a baby."

"Then what's the holdup?" her son demanded. "I like the idea of being a big brother. I didn't think much about it until we moved here. Then when we were having dinner at the Chinese restaurant I heard this grandma and grandpa couple in the booth next to us talking, and they were saying neat things about us being a family. That was when I started thinking real serious about babies and stuff.''

"Jeff," Robin said, rubbing her hands together as she gathered her thoughts. "It isn't as simple as that. Before there's a baby, there should be a husband."

"Well, of course," Jeff returned, looking at her as if she'd insulted his intelligence. "You'd have to marry Cole first, but that would be all right with me. You like him, don't you? You must, otherwise you wouldn't be kissing him that way."

Robin sighed. Of course she *liked* Cole, but it wasn't that simple. Unfortunately she wasn't sure she could explain it in terms a ten-year-old could understand. "I—"

"I can't remember ever seeing you kiss a guy like that. You looked real serious. And when I was sneaking back up the stairs I heard him ask you to have dinner alone with him tonight and that seemed like a real good sign, if you know what I mean."

The next time Cole kissed her, Robin thought wryly, they'd have to scurry to a cupboard out of Jeff's view. The things that child came up with...

"You are going to dinner with him, aren't you?"

"Yes, but—"

"Then what's the problem? I'll ask him to marry you if you want."

"Jeff!" she cried, leaping to her feet. "Absolutely not. That's something between Cole and me, and neither of us would appreciate any assistance from you. Is that clearly understood?"

"All right," he muttered, but he didn't look too pleased. He reached for a piece of toast, shredding it into thirds. "But you're going to marry him, aren't you?"

"I don't know."

"Why not? Cole's the best thing that's happened to us."

Her son was staring at her intently, his baseball cap twisted around to the back of his head. Now that she had his full attention, Robin couldn't find the words to explain. "There's more to it than you realise, sweetie." She made a show of glancing at the clock. "It's time to change and get ready for church."

Jeff nodded and rushed up the stairs. Robin followed at a much slower pace, grateful to put an end to this complicated and embarrassing subject.

The minute they were home from the service, Jeff reached for his baseball mitt. "Jimmy Wallach and I are going to the school yard to practice hitting balls. OK?"

"OK," Robin said absently. "How long will you be gone?"

"An hour."

"I'm going grocery shopping, so if I'm not home when you get back you know what to do?"

"Of course," he muttered.

"YOU'RE ROBIN MASTERSON, aren't you?" a tall middle-aged woman asked as she manipulated her grocery cart alongside of Robin's.

"Yes," Robin said expectantly. The other woman's eyes were warm and her smile friendly.

"I thought you must be—I've seen you from a distance. I'm Joyce Wallach. Jimmy and Jeff are good friends. In fact they're at the school yard now, hitting baseballs."

"Of course," Robin said, pleased to make the other woman's acquaintance. They'd talked on the phone several times, and she'd met Joyce's husband once, when Jimmy had spent the night. The boys had wanted to play on the same baseball team and were keenly disappointed when they'd been assigned to different teams. It had been Jimmy who'd told Jeff about the death of Cole's son.

"I've been meaning to invite you to the house for coffee," Joyce went on to say, "but I started working part-time and I can't seem to get myself organised."

"I know what you mean." Working full-time, keeping up with Jeff and her home was about all Robin could manage herself. She didn't know how other mothers were able to accomplish so much.

"There's a place to sit down here," Joyce said, and her eyes brightened with the idea. "Do you have time to chat now?"

Robin agreed, delighted. "Sure. I've been wanting to meet you, too." The Wallachs lived two streets over, and Robin fully approved of Jimmy as a friend for Jeff. He and Kelly had become friends, too, but her ten-year-old son wasn't as eager to admit being buddies with a girl. Kelly was still a green apple in Jeff's eye, but the time would come when he'd appreciate having her next door.

"I understand Jeff's quite the baseball player," Joyce said at the self-service counter.

Robin nodded. She poured herself a plastic cup of iced tea and paid for it. "Jeff really loves baseball. He was disappointed he couldn't play with Jimmy."

"They separate the teams according to the year of birth. Jimmy's birthday is in January so he's with another group." She frowned. "That doesn't really make much sense, does it?" She chuckled, and Robin couldn't help responding to the soft infectious sound of Joyce's laughter. She found herself laughing, too.

They pulled out chairs at one of the small tables in the supermarket's deli section.

"I feel like throwing my arms around you," Joyce said, grinning broadly. "I happened to see Cole Camden the other day and I couldn't believe my eyes. It was like seeing him ten years ago, the way he used to be. I thought I saw Jeff with him. Did the two of them happen to be at Balboa Park recently?"

"Cole came to Jeff's first game."

"Ah." She nodded, as if that explained it. "I don't know if anyone's told you, but there's been a marked difference in Cole lately. I can't tell you how happy I am to see it. Cole's gone through so much heartache."

"Cole's been wonderful for Jeff," Robin said, then swallowed tightly. She felt a renewed stab of fear that Cole was more attracted to the idea of having a son than he was in a relationship with her.

"I have the feeling you've *both* been wonderful for him," Joyce added.

Robin's smile was losing its conviction. She lowered her gaze and studied the lemon slice floating on top of her tea.

"My husband and I knew Cole quite well before the divorce," Joyce went on to explain. "Larry, that's my husband, and Cole played golf every Saturday afternoon. Then Janice decided she wanted out of the marriage, left him and took Bobby. Cole really tried to save that marriage, but the relationship had been in trouble for a good long while. Cole doted on his son, though—he would have done anything to spare Bobby the trauma of a divorce. Janice, however—'' Joyce halted abruptly, apparently realising how much she'd said. ''I didn't mean to launch into all this—it's ancient history. I just wanted you to know how pleased I am to meet you at last.''

Since Cole had told her shockingly little of his past, Robin had to bite her tongue not to plead with Joyce to continue. Instead, she bowed her head and said, ''I'm pleased to meet you, too.''

Then she looked up with a smile. ''Jimmy's finally got the friend he's always wanted. There are so few boys his age around here. I swear my son was ready to set off firecrackers the day Jeff registered at the school and he learned you lived only two blocks away.''

''Jeff claimed he couldn't live in a house that's surrounded by girls.'' Robin shook her head with a mock grimace. ''If he hadn't met Jimmy, I might have had a mutiny on my hands.''

Joyce's face relaxed into a warm smile. She was energetic, animated and fun, gesturing freely with her hands as she spoke. Robin felt as if she'd known and liked Jimmy's mother for years.

''There hasn't been much turnover in this neighborhood over the years. We're a close-knit group, as I'm sure you've discovered. Heather Lawrence is a real sweetie. I wish I had more time to get to know her. And Cole, well... I realise that huge house has been in his family for years, but I half expected him to move out after Janice and Bobby were killed.''

The silence that followed was punctuated by Robin's soft involuntary gasp. ''What did you just say?''

''That I couldn't understand why Cole continued living in the house on Orchard Street. Is that what you mean?''

''No, after that—about Janice and Bobby.'' It was difficult for Robin to speak. Her tongue was desert dry and each word felt as if it had been scraped from the roof of her mouth.

''I assumed you knew they'd both been killed,'' Joyce said, her eyes full of concern. ''I didn't realise, I mean, I thought for sure that Cole had told you.''

"I knew about Bobby. Jimmy said something to Jeff, and Jeff told me, but I hadn't any idea that Janice had died, too. Heather Lawrence told me about the divorce, but she didn't say anything about Cole's wife dying."

"I don't think Heather knows. She moved into the neighbourhood long after the divorce, and lord knows Cole's close-mouthed enough about it."

"When did all this happen?"

"Several years ago now. It was all terribly tragic," Joyce said. "Just thinking about it makes my heart ache all over again. I don't mean to be telling tales, but frankly if there's any blame to be placed I'm afraid it would fall on Janice. She wasn't the kind of woman who's easy to know or like. I shouldn't speak ill of the dead, and I don't mean to be catty, but Janice did Cole a favour when she left him. Naturally, he didn't see it that way—he was in love with his wife and crazy about his son. Frankly, I think Cole turned a blind eye to his wife's faults because of Bobby."

"What happened?" Perhaps having a neighbour fill in the details of Cole's life was the wrong thing to do; Robin no longer knew. Cole had never said a word to her about Janice or Bobby, and she didn't know if he ever would.

"Janice was never satisfied with Cole's position as a city attorney," Joyce explained. "We'd have coffee together every now and then, and all she'd do was complain how Cole was wasting his talents and that he could be making big money and wasn't. She had bigger plans for him. But Cole loved his job and felt an obligation to follow through with his commitments. Janice never understood that. She didn't even try to sympathise with Cole's point of view. She constantly wanted more, better, newer things. She didn't work herself, you know.

"Janice was never happy, never satisfied. She hated the house and the neighbourhood, but she soon realised all the whining and manipulating in the world wasn't going to do one bit of good. Cole fully intended to finish out his responsibilities to the city, so she played her ace. She left him, taking Bobby with her."

"But didn't Cole try to gain custody of Bobby?"

"Of course. He knew, and so did everyone else, that Janice was using their son as a pawn. She was never the motherly type, if you know what I mean. If you want the truth, Janice was an alcoholic. There were several times I dropped Bobby off at the house and suspected Janice had been drinking heavily. I was willing to testify on Cole's behalf, and I told him so. He was grateful, but then the accident happened and it was too late."

"The accident?" A huge heaviness settled in her chest. Each breath pained her and brought with it the memories she longed to forget, memories of another accident—the one that had taken her husband from her.

"It was Janice's fault—the accident, I mean. She'd been drinking and should never have been behind the wheel of a car. The day before, Cole had been in to see his attorneys, pleading with them to move quickly because he feared Janice was becoming more and more irresponsible. But it wasn't until after Janice moved out that Cole realised how sick she'd become, how dependent she was on alcohol to make it through the day."

"Dear lord," Robin whispered. "Cole must have felt so guilty."

"It was terrible," Joyce returned, her voice quavering. "I didn't know if Cole would survive that first year. He holed up inside the house and severed relationships with everyone in the neighbourhood. He was consumed by his grief. Later he seemed to come out of it a little, but he's never been the same.

"The irony of all this is that eventually Janice would have got all she wanted, had she been more patient. A couple of years ago, Cole accepted a partnership in one of the most important law firms in the city. He's made a real name for himself, but money and position don't seem to mean much to him—they never have. I wouldn't be surprised if he walked away from the whole thing someday."

"I think you're right. Cole told me not long ago that he has some property north of here that he inherited from his grandfather. He's restoring the house, and he said something about moving there. It's where he spends most of his weekends."

"I wondered if it was something like that," Joyce said, nodding. "There were rumours floating around the neighbourhood that he spent his weekends with a woman. Anyone who knew Cole would realise what a crock that is. Cole isn't the type to have a secret affair.''

Robin felt ashamed, remembering how she'd been tempted to believe the rumour herself.

"For a long time," Joyce went on, "I wondered if Cole was ever going to recover from Janice and Bobby's deaths, but now I believe he has. I can't help thinking you and Jeff have had a lot to do with that.''

"I...think he would have come out of his shell eventually.''

"Perhaps, but the changes in him lately have been the most encouraging things so far. I don't know how you feel about Cole or if there's anything between you, but you couldn't find a better man.''

"I...I'm falling in love with him,'' Robin whispered, voicing her feelings for the first time. The words hung in the air like a dark, heavy cloud.

"But I think that's absolutely wonderful, I really do!'' Joyce said enthusiastically.

"I don't.'' Now that the shock had worn off, Robin was forced to confront her anger. Cole had told her none of this. Not a single word. That hurt. Hurt more than she could have expected. But the ache she felt was nothing compared to the grief Cole must face each morning, the pain that weighed down his life.

"Oh, dear,'' Joyce said. "I've really done it now, haven't I? I knew I should have kept my mouth shut. You're upset and it's my fault.''

"Nonsense,'' Robin whispered, making an effort to bring a smile to her dry lips and not succeeding. "I'm grateful we met, and more than grateful you told me about Janice, and about Cole's son.'' The knowledge produced a dull ache in Robin's heart. She felt grief for Cole and a less worthy emotion, too—a sense of being slighted by his lack of trust in her.

She was so upset on the short drive home that she missed the turn on to Orchard Street and had to take a side street and double back.

As she neared the house, she saw that Cole was outside watering his lawn. He waved, but she pretended not to notice and pulled into the driveway. Desperate for some time alone before facing Cole, Robin did her best to ignore him as she climbed out of the car. She needed a few more minutes to gather her thoughts and tutor her emotions.

She was almost safe, almost at the house, when Cole stopped her.

"Robin," he called, jogging toward her. "Hold on a minute, would you?"

She managed to compose herself, squaring her shoulders and drawing on her dignity.

His wonderful eyes were smiling as he hurried across over, fast approaching her. Obviously he hadn't realised there was anything wrong. "Did Jeff happen to say anything to you about seeing us kiss last night?" he asked.

Her mouth was so dry that she had to swallow a couple of times before she could utter a single syllable. "Yes, but don't worry, I think I've got him squared away."

"Drat!" he teased, snapping his fingers. "I suppose this means I don't have to go through with the shotgun wedding?"

She nodded, keeping her eyes lowered, fearing he would be able to read all the emotion churning inside her.

"You have nothing to fear but fear itself," she said, forcing a lightness into her tone.

"Robin?" He made her name a question and a caress. "Is something wrong?"

She shook her head, shifting the bag of groceries from one arm to the other. "Of course not," she said with the same feigned cheerfulness.

Cole lifted the bag from her arms. Robin knew she should have resisted, but she couldn't; she felt drained of strength. She headed for the house, knowing Cole would follow her inside.

"What's wrong?" he asked a second time, setting the groceries on the kitchen counter.

It was still difficult to speak and even more difficult, more exhausting, to find the words that would explain what she'd learned.

"Nothing. It's just that I've got a lot to do if we're going out for dinner tonight."

"Wear something fancy. I'm taking you to a four-star restaurant."

"Something fancy?" Mentally she reviewed the contents of her cupboard, which was rather lacking in fancy.

"I'm not about to be outclassed by Frank," Cole teased. "I'm going to wine and dine you and turn your head with sweet nothings."

He didn't need to do any of those things to turn her head. She was already dangerously close to being in love with him, so close that she'd blurted it out to a woman she'd known for a grand total of twelve minutes.

Abruptly switching her attention to the bag of groceries, Robin set several packages on the counter. When Cole's hands settled over her shoulders, her eyes drifted shut. "It isn't necessary," she found herself admitting.

Cole turned her around to face him. "What isn't?"

"The dinner, the wine, the sweet nothings."

Their gazes held. As if choreographed, they moved into each other's arms. With a groan that came deep from in his throat, Cole kissed her. His hands tangled in the auburn thickness of her hair. His lips closed over hers with fierce protectiveness.

Robin curled her arms tightly around his neck as her own world started to dip and spin and whirl. She was standing on her tiptoes, her heart in her throat, when she heard the front door open.

Moaning, she dragged her mouth from Cole's and broke away just as Jeff strolled into the kitchen.

The ten-year-old stopped, his brow furrowed, when he saw the two of them in what must surely look like suspicious circumstances.

"Hi, Mom. Hi, Cole." He strolled casually to the refrigerator and yanked open the door. "Is there anything decent to drink around this place?"

"Water?" Robin suggested.

Jeff rolled his eyes. "Funny, Mom, real funny."

"There are a few more sacks of groceries in the car. Would you get them for me?" He tossed her a look that suggested the child-labour laws needed reviewing, until Robin added, "You'll find a six-pack of soda in there."

"OK." He raced out of the house and returned a minute later, carrying one sack and sorting through its contents as he walked slowly into the kitchen.

"I'll lend you a hand, sport," Cole said, placing his hand on Jeff's shoulder. He glanced at Robin and his eyes told her they'd continue their discussion at a more opportune moment.

Robin started emptying the sacks, hardly paying attention as Jeff and Cole brought in the last couple of bags. Cole told her he'd pick her up at six, then left.

"Can I play with Blackie for a while?" Jeff asked, a can of cold soda clenched in his hand.

"All right," Robin answered, grateful to have a few minutes alone.

Robin cleared the countertops and made Jeff a sandwich for his lunch. He must have become involved in his game with Cole's dog because he didn't rush in announcing he was hungry.

She went outside to stand on the small front porch and smiled as she watched Jeff and Blackie. Her son really had a way with animals—like his father. Every time Robin saw him play with Cole's Labrador, she marveled at how attuned to each other they were.

She smiled when she realised Cole was outside, too; he'd just finished watering his lawn.

"Jeff, I made a sandwich for you," she called.

"In a minute. Hey, Mom, watch," he yelled as he tossed a ball across the lawn. Blackie chased after it, skidding to a stop as he caught the bright red ball in his mouth.

"Come on, Blackie," Jeff urged. "Throw me the ball."

"He can't do that," Robin said in astonishment.

"Sure, he can. Just watch."

And just as Jeff had claimed, Blackie leapt into the air on all fours, tossed his head and sent the ball shooting into the street.

"I'll get it," Jeff hollered.

It was Cole's reaction that Robin noticed first. A horrified look came over his face and he threw down the hose. He was shouting even as he ran.

Like her son, Robin had been so caught up in Blackie's antics that she hadn't noticed the car barrelling down the street, directly in Jeff's path.

CHAPTER EIGHT

"JEFF!" ROBIN SCREAMED, fear and panic choking her. Her hands flew to her mouth in relief as Cole grabbed Jeff around the waist and swept him out of the path of the speeding car. Together the two fell backward on to the wet grass. Robin raced over to them.

"Jeff, how many times have I told you to look before you run into the street? How many times?" Her voice was high and hysterical. "You deserve the spanking of your life for that stunt!"

"I saw the car," Jeff protested loudly. "I did! I was going to wait for it. Honest." He struggled to his feet, looking insulted at what he obviously considered an over-reaction.

"Get into the house and wait for me there," Robin demanded, pointing furiously. She was trembling so badly that she could barely speak.

Jeff brushed the grass from his jeans and lifted his head to a dignified angle, then casually walked toward the house. Not understanding, Blackie followed him, the rubber ball in his mouth, wanting to resume their play.

"I can't, boy," Jeff mumbled just loud enough for her to hear. "My mother just had some kind of anxiety attack that I'm gonna get punished for."

Cole's recovery was slower than Jeff's. He sat up and rubbed a hand across his eyes. His face was ashen, his expression stark with terror.

"Everything's all right. Jeff isn't hurt," Robin hurried to assure him. She slipped to her knees in front of him.

Cole nodded without looking at her. His eyes went blank and he slowly shook his head, as if to clear his mind.

"Cole," Robin said softly, "are you all right?"

"I...I don't know." He gave her a faint smile, but his eyes remained glazed and distant. He placed one hand over his heart and shook his head. "For a minute there I thought Jeff hadn't seen that car and...dear lord, I don't know...if that boy had been hurt..."

"Thank you for acting so quickly," Robin whispered, gratitude and relief filling her heart. She ran her hands down the sides of his face, needing to touch him, seeking a way to comfort him, although her heart ached at his words. So many times over the past few weeks, she'd suspected—and feared—that Cole's feelings had more to do with replacing the family he'd lost than love for her and Jeff.

With a shudder, Cole locked his arms around her waist and pulled her close, burying his face in the gentle curve of her neck as he dragged deep gulps of air into his lungs.

"Come inside and I'll get us some coffee," Robin suggested.

Cole murmured agreement, but he didn't seem in any rush to release her. Nor she him. Her hands were in his hair and she rested her cheek against his, savouring these moments of closeness now that the panic was gone.

"I lost my son," Cole whispered and the words seemed to be wrenched from the deepest part of his soul. His voice held an agony only those who have suffered such a loss could understand. "In a car accident six years ago."

Robin kissed the crown of his head. "I know."

Cole broke away from her, slowly raising his eyes to meet hers. Mingled with profound grief was confusion. "Who told you?"

"Joyce Wallach."

Cole closed his eyes. "I could use that coffee."

They both stood, and when Cole wrapped his arm around her waist Robin couldn't be sure it was to lend support or to offer it.

Inside the house, Jeff was sitting at the bottom of the stairs, his knees pressed under his chin. Ever loyal, Blackie lay beside him.

Jeff raised his head when Robin opened the front door, his round eyes following her. "I saw the car," he repeated. "You're getting upset over nothing. I hope you realise that. Hey, what's wrong with Cole?" he asked abruptly. He glanced from Robin to their neighbor and then back to his mother. "He looks like he's seen a ghost."

In some way, Robin supposed, Cole had.

"You all right, sport?" Cole asked. "I didn't hurt you when we fell, did I?"

"Naw." He bit his lip, eyes lowered.

Cole frowned. "You don't sound all that certain. Are you sure you're OK?"

Jeff nodded reluctantly. "I will be once I find out what my mother intends to do to me. I really was going to stop at the kerb. Honest."

The kid would make an excellent attorney, Robin decided.

"I think I might have over-reacted," Cole said. He held open his arms and Jeff flew into them without a second's hesitation. Briefly Cole's eyes drifted shut, as though in silent thanksgiving for Jeff's safety.

"I didn't mean to frighten you," Jeff murmured. "I would have stopped."

"I know."

"I promise to be more careful."

"I certainly hope so," Robin said.

Cole released Jeff and sighed deeply, then looked at Robin. "You said something about coffee?"

She smiled and nodded. "I'll get it in a minute. All right, Jeff, you can go outside, but from now on if you're playing ball with Blackie, do it in the backyard. Understand?"

"Sure, Mom," her son said eagerly. "But—" he paused "—you mean that's it? You aren't going to ground me or anything? I mean, of course you aren't going to because I did everything I was supposed to—well, almost everything. Thanks, Mom." He tossed the red ball into the air and deftly caught it with one hand. "Come on, Blackie, we just got a pardon from the governor."

Robin followed the pair into the kitchen and watched as Jeff opened the sliding glass door and raced into the backyard with Blackie in hot pursuit. Reassured, she poured them each a mug of coffee while Cole pulled out one of the kitchen chairs. She carried the mugs to the table, then sat down across from him.

Cole immediately reached for her hand, lacing her fingers with his own. He focused his concentration on their linked hands. "Bobby was my son. He died when he was ten."

"Jeff's age," Robin said as a chill surrounded her heart.

"Bobby was so full of laughter and life I couldn't be around him and not smile."

Talking about Bobby was clearly difficult for Cole, and Robin longed to do or say something that would help. But she could think of nothing to ease the agony etched so deeply on his handsome face.

"He was the kind of boy every father dreams of having. Inquisitive, sensitive, full of mischief. Gifted with a vivid imagination."

"A lot like Jeff," she murmured, and her hands tightened around the mug.

Cole nodded. "Bobby used to tell me that I shouldn't worry about Janice—she was my wife—because *he,* my ten-year-old son, was taking care of her."

Robin held her breath as she watched the fierce pain in his eyes. "You don't need to tell me this." Not if it was going to rip open wounds that weren't properly healed yet.

"I should have told you long before this," he said, frowning slightly. "It's just that even now, after all these years, it's still difficult to talk about my son. For a good many years, I felt as though a part of me had died with Bobby. The very best part of me. I don't believe that any more."

"Jeff reminds you a lot of Bobby, doesn't he?" Robin doubted Cole fully understood that he was transferring his love from one boy to the other.

A reluctant smile tugged at the corners of his mouth. "Bobby had a huskier build and was taller than Jeff. His sport was basketball, but he was more of a spectator than a participant. His real love was computers. Had he lived, I think Bobby would have gone into that field. Janice never understood that. She wanted him to be more athletic, and he tried to please her." Cole's gaze dropped to his hands. "Janice and I were divorced before the accident happened. She died with him. If there's anything to be grateful for in their deaths, it's the knowledge that they both went instantly. I couldn't have stood knowing that they'd suffered." He paused long enough to take a sip of the coffee, and grimaced once. "You added sugar?"

"I thought you might need it."

He chuckled. "I have so much to thank you for."

"Me?"

"Do you remember the afternoon Jeff ran away?"

She wasn't likely to forget it. With Jeff around, Robin always figured she didn't need to do aerobic exercise to keep her heart in shape. Her son managed to do it with his antics.

"I left on a business trip to Seattle soon afterward," he reminded her.

"I remember." That was when Jeff had watched Blackie for him.

"Late one afternoon, when the meeting was over and dinner wasn't scheduled for another couple of hours, I went for a stroll," Cole said. "It was still light and I found myself on the waterfront. The sky was a vivid blue and the waters green and clear. It's funny I would remember that, but it's all so distinct in my memory. I stood alone on the pier and watched as a ferry headed for one of the islands, cutting a path through the waves. Something brought Bobby to my mind, although he's never far from my thoughts, even now. The most amazing thing happened that afternoon. It's difficult to find the words to explain." He hesitated, as though searching for a way to make Robin understand. Then apparently he gave up the effort and slowly shook his head.

"Tell me about it," Robin suggested in a quiet voice.

"Well, standing there at the end of the pier...I don't know. For the first time since I lost my son, I felt his presence more than I did his absence. It was as if he was there at my side, pointing out the Olympic Mountains to me and asking questions. Bobby was always full of questions. My heart felt lighter than it had in years—as though the heavy burden of pain and grief had been lifted from my shoulders. For no reason whatsoever, I started to smile. I think I've been smiling ever since. And laughing. And feeling.

"When I got back to the hotel, I had the sudden urge to hear your voice. I didn't have any excuse to call you, so I phoned on the pretense of talking to Jeff and checking up on Blackie. But it was your voice I wanted to hear."

Robin smiled through the unexpected rush of tears that clouded her eyes, wondering if Cole realised what he was saying. It might have been her voice he thought he wanted to hear, but it was Jeff he'd called.

"I found a new freedom on that Seattle pier. It was as if, in that moment, I was released from the past. I can't say exactly what it was that changed. Meeting you and Jeff played a big role in it, I recognise that much, but it was more than that. It was as if something deep inside me was willing to admit that it was finally time to let go."

"I'm glad for you," Robin whispered, not knowing what else to say.

"The problem is, I never allowed myself to properly grieve or deal with the anger I felt towards Janice. She was driving at the time and the accident was her fault. Yet deep in my heart I know she would never purposely have done anything to injure Bobby. She loved him as much as I did. He was her son, too.

"It wasn't until I met you that I realised I had to forgive Janice. I was never the kind of husband she needed and I'm afraid I was a disappointment to her. Only in the last couple of years of our marriage was I willing to accept that she suffered from a serious emotional and mental illness. Her addiction to alcohol was as much a disease as cancer. I didn't understand or accept her weakness, and because of that we all suffered."

"You're being too hard on yourself," Robin said, but she doubted Cole even heard her.

"The anger and the grief were a constant gnawing pain. I refused to acknowledge or deal with either emotion. Over the years, instead of healing, the agony of my loss grew more intense. I closed myself off from friends and colleagues and threw myself into my work, spending far more time in the office than I did at home. Blackie was virtually my only companion. And then a few years ago I started working on my place in the country. But the pleasure that gave me came from hard physical work, the kind that leaves you too tired to think." His features softened and he smiled at her. "I'd forgotten what it was to fly a kite or laze in the sunshine."

"That was why you suggested the picnic with Jeff and me?"

He grinned and his dark eyes seemed almost boyish. "The last time I was in Golden Gate Park was with Bobby, shortly before the accident. Deciding to have a picnic there was a giant step for me. I half expected to feel some pangs of grief, if not a full-blown assault. Instead I experienced a joy and appreciation for the renewal I felt. Laughter is a gift I'd forgotten. You and Jeff helped me realise that, as well."

Everything Cole was saying confirmed her worst fears.

"Mom!" Jeff roared into the kitchen with Blackie at his heels. "Is there anything decent to eat around here? Are you guys still going out to dinner? I don't suppose you'd consider bringing me, would you?"

Cole chuckled, then leapt to his feet to playfully muss Jeff's hair. "Not this time, sport. Tonight is for your mother and me."

TWO HOURS LATER, as Robin stood in front of the bathroom mirror, she had her doubts about agreeing to this dinner date. She was falling in love with a man who hadn't fully dealt with the pain of losing his son and his wife. Perhaps she recognised it in Cole because she saw the same things in herself. She loved Lonny and always would. He'd died years earlier and she still found herself talking to him, refusing to involve herself in another relationship. A part of her continued to grieve and seemed it always would.

Examining herself in the mirror, Robin surveyed her calf-length skirt of soft blue velvet, and white silk blouse with a large teardrop pearl pin tucked at the neck.

She was fussing with her hair, pinning one side back with combs and studying the effect, when Jeff strolled into her room. He leaned casually against the doorway, a bag of potato chips in his hand.

"Hey, you look nice."

"Don't sound so surprised." She decided she'd spent enough time on her hair and fastened her pearl earrings. Jeff was disappointed about not joining them, but he'd been a good sport—especially after Cole promised him lunch at a special fish-and-chip place on the Wharf the following Saturday.

"You're wearing your pearls?" Jeff mumbled, mouth full of potato chips.

"Yes," Robin said, turning to face him. "Do they look all right?"

Jeff's halfhearted shrug didn't do a lot to boost Robin's confidence. "I suppose. I don't know about stuff like that. Mrs. Lawrence could probably tell you." He popped another potato chip into his mouth and munched loudly. "My dad gave you those earrings, didn't he?"

"For our first wedding anniversary."

Jeff nodded. "I thought so." His look grew reflective. "When I grow up and get married, will I do mushy stuff like that?"

"Like what?"

"Waste a bunch of money on something that dangles from a woman's ear?"

"Probably," Robin said, not bothering to disguise her amusement. "And lots of other things, too. Like taking your wife to dinner and telling her how beautiful she is and how much you love her."

"Yuck!" Jeff wrinkled his nose. "You really know how to ruin a guy's appetite." With that he turned to march down the stairs, taking his potato chips with him.

Robin stood at the top of the staircase. "Cole will be here any minute, so you can go over to Kelly's now," she called down.

"All right. I put my plate in the dishwasher. Is there anything you want me to tell Kelly's mom?"

"Just that I won't be too late."

"You're sure I can't come with you?" Jeff tried one more time.

Robin didn't give him an answer, knowing he didn't honestly expect one. After a moment, Jeff grumbled for show, then headed out the front door for the neighbour's.

Robin returned to the bathroom and smiled into the mirror, picturing Jeff several years into the future and seeing Lonny's handsome face smiling back at her. She was warmed by the image, certain that her son would grow into as fine a young man as his father had been. Robin couldn't ask for anything more.

"You don't mind that I'm wearing the pearls for Cole, do you?" she asked her dead husband, although she knew he would never have objected. She ran the tips of her fingers over them, feeling reassured.

The doorbell chimed just as Robin dabbed perfume to the pulse points at her neck and wrists. She drew in a calming breath, glanced quickly at her reflection once again, then walked down the stairs to answer the door.

Cole was dressed in a black pin-striped suit and looked so handsome that her breath caught. He smiled as she let him in, but for the life of her she couldn't think of a solitary thing to say.

His eyes held hers as he reached for her hands. Slowly, he lowered his gaze, taking in the way she'd styled her hair, the pearl pin and the outfit she'd chosen with such care.

"You are so beautiful," he said.

"I was just thinking the same about you," she confessed.

His mouth tilted in a grin. "If I kiss you, will it ruin your lipstick?"

"Probably."

"I'm going to kiss you, anyway," he said in a husky murmur that tugged at her heart. Tenderly he fit his mouth to hers, weaving his fingers through her hair. The kiss was gentle and slow and thorough. A single kiss, and she was clay ready to be moulded. The realisation struck her hard. When Cole touched her, Robin felt alive all the way to the soles of her feet. *Alive.* Healthy. A red-blooded woman. When he released her, she was shocked to find that she was trembling. From the inside out.

"I've mussed your hair," he apologised. His hands found her nape under the soft cloud of hair.

"And you've got lipstick on your mouth," she managed quaveringly, reaching up to wipe it away with her fingers. "There. It'll only take me a moment to fix my hair," she said, picking up her purse and moving to the hallway mirror.

He stood behind her, his hands on her shoulders as she brushed her hair, then carefully tucked the loose curls back into place with the tortoiseshell combs.

"Are you ready?" he asked when she'd finished.

Robin nodded, unable to find her voice.

Cole led her outside to his car and held open the passenger door. He glanced around, then dropped a quick kiss on her unsuspecting lips. He chuckled at her look of surprise as he hurried around the car, his movements lighthearted, and slipped into the driver's seat.

"You didn't tell me where we're having dinner."

"I told Heather Lawrence in case she needs to get hold of you for anything, but otherwise it's a surprise."

Robin wasn't sure what to think. A number of San Francisco's restaurants were famous internationally, but her knowledge of fancy dining places was limited. She assumed this one was somewhere in the heart of the city, until he exited from the freeway heading south along Highway 101 toward the ocean.

"Cole?" she asked hesitantly.

"Don't worry," he said, casting her a swift glance that didn't conceal the mischievous twinkle in his eyes. "I promise you dinner will be worth the drive."

The restaurant sat high on a cliff, with a stunning view of the surf battering against jagged rocks below.

Cole parked the Porsche, then came around to help her out, taking the opportunity to steal another kiss. It was with obvious reluctance that he released her. His arm found her waist as he directed her towards the doors leading into the elegant restaurant. The maître d' escorted them to a table that overlooked the water and with a flourish presented them with elaborate menus.

Robin scanned the list of entrées, impressed with the interesting variations on basic themes. She was less impressed with the prices— a single dinner cost as much as an entire week's worth of lunches. For her *and* Jeff.

"When you said fancy you weren't joking, were you?" she whispered, biting her lip.

Cole lowered his menu and sent her a vibrant smile. "Tonight is special," he said simply.

"You're telling me. If I wasn't having dinner with you, I'd probably have eaten a toasted cheese sandwich and a bowl of tomato soup with Jeff."

Their waiter appeared and both ordered one of the restaurant's specialties—a scallop and shrimp sauté—which proved as succulent and spicy as the menu had promised.

They talked through dinner and afterward, over steaming cups of Irish coffee. It amazed Robin that they had so much to say to one another, although they hadn't touched on the issue closest to her heart. But she hesitated to broach the subject of Cole's relationship with Jeff. She didn't want to risk the delightful camaraderie they were sharing tonight. Their conversation could have gone on for hours and in fact did. They talked about the books they'd read, recent movies they'd seen, records they liked. It came as a pleasant surprise to discover that their tastes in music were similar. And they preferred many of the same authors.

All evening they laughed, they argued, they talked, as if they'd been friends most of their lives. Cole grinned so often that it was hard for Robin to remember that she'd once actually wondered if the man ever smiled.

Robin told Cole about her job and how much she enjoyed accounting. She voiced her fears about not being the kind of mother she wanted to be for Jeff. "There are so many things I want to share with Jeff that I don't have time for. There just aren't enough hours in a day."

Cole talked about his career goals and his dreams. He spoke of the forty acres willed to him by his grandfather and how he'd once longed to close himself off from the world by moving there.

"But you aren't going to now?" Robin asked.

"No. I no longer have any reason to hide. The house is nearly finished and I may still move there, but I'll maintain my work schedule." He stared down into his steaming coffee. "I was approached last week about running for the state senate."

Robin's heart swelled with pride. "Are you going to do it?"

"No. I'm not the right man for politics. I'll support someone else, but a political career doesn't interest me. It never has, although I admit to being flattered."

A band started playing then, and several couples took to the dance floor.

"Shall we?" Cole asked, nodding in that direction.

"Oh, Cole, I don't know. The last time I danced was at my cousin's wedding ten years ago. I'm afraid I'll step all over your feet."

"I'm game if you are."

She was reluctant but agreed to try. They stood, and she moved naturally into his embrace, as if they'd been partners for years. Robin's eyes slowly closed when Cole folded her in his arms, tucking her head against the side of his chin. In that moment she experienced a surge of joy that surprised her with its intensity.

The dance ended, but they didn't leave the floor.

"Have I told you how lovely you are?" Cole asked, his mouth close to her ear.

Robin grinned and nodded. "Twice. Once when you picked me up at the house and once during the meal. I know you're exaggerating, but..." She hesitated, then added, "When I'm with you, I feel beautiful."

"I don't think a woman's ever paid me a higher compliment."

She raised her eyes and was shocked by the powerful emotions in his.

"Do you mind if we leave now?" he surprised her by asking.

"No, of course not, if that's what you want."

He frowned. "If it were up to me I'd spend the rest of the night right here with you in my arms, but I have this sudden need to kiss you, and if I do it here and do it properly we're going to attract a lot of attention.''

Cole quickly paid the bill and he hurried Robin to the car. The minute they were settled inside, he reached for her. He did as he'd promised, kissing her until she was breathless and weak. Her arms clung to him and his mouth sought hers once more.

''At least I'm not making you cry this time,'' he said softly.

''That still embarrasses me,'' she admitted. ''It's never happened with anyone. Ever. I still don't understand it. I don't know if I ever will.''

''I don't think I'll ever forget it.''

''Please do.''

''No,'' he said, shaking his head. ''It touched me in a way I can't explain. It helped me realise that I was going to love you. After Janice and Bobby, I doubted there was any love left in me to give. You taught me otherwise. Jeff taught me otherwise. My heart is full and has been almost from the moment we met.'' He took her hand and pressed her palm to his heart. ''Do you feel it?''

Robin nodded. ''It's beating so hard,'' she whispered.

''That's because I'm nervous.''

''Nervous? About what?''

Cole slid a hand into his pocket and brought out a small black velvet box.

Robin's heart started to pound in double time. ''Cole?'' she said anxiously, not sure what she should think or how she should act.

''I love you, Robin.'' His voice was hoarse. ''I realised it the moment I heard your voice when I called from Seattle. And every moment since has convinced me how right it is to love you.'' He opened the box and revealed the largest diamond Robin had ever seen. Slowly he raised his eyes to hers. ''I'm asking you to be my wife.''

CHAPTER NINE

"YOU MEAN THIS WHOLE evening...you arranged this because you intended to ask me to marry you?" Robin asked, pressing the tips of her fingers to her trembling lips. Despite her fears a gentle gladness suffused in her heart.

"Surely it isn't that much of a surprise?" he murmured. "I've never made an effort to hide the way I feel about you or how much I enjoy Jeff."

Contrary to what Cole might think, his proposal *did* come as a surprise. "I...I don't know what to say."

"A simple yes would suit me," Cole urged warmly.

"But... Oh, Cole, it would be so easy to marry you, so easy to link my life and Jeff's to yours and never look back, but I don't know if it would be right for us or for you. There's so much to consider, so many factors to weigh in a decision this important. I'd like nothing better than to say yes, but I just can't do it."

"Are you asking for time?" Cole's eyes seemed to penetrate hers, even in the dark.

"Please." For now, that seemed the simplest thing to say, although her hesitation was based on something much deeper. Cole had found a peace within himself since meeting her and Jeff; he'd told her so that very afternoon. She was tempted to say yes, to turn away from her doubts and agree to marry him. Cole had been so good for Jeff, so wonderful to her.

"I hate to disappoint you," she murmured, sadness weighing down her voice.

"I know exactly what you're thinking, exactly how you're feeling."

"You do?" Somehow she doubted it. But knowing she couldn't delay it any longer, she jumped in with both feet. "I was...just thinking about what you told me this afternoon. How you'd recently dealt with the loss of Janice and Bobby. While you were talking, I couldn't help feeling your exhilaration. You've obviously found a newborn sense of freedom. I think the question you need to ask yourself is if this rebirth you've experienced is what prompted the idea of marrying again.''

"No," he said flatly. "Falling in love with you did."

"Oh, Cole," she whispered. "It must seem like fate to have Jeff and me move in next door, and it gets more complicated with Jeff being the same age as Bobby...."

"Maybe it does all appear too convenient, but if I was just looking for a woman and a child, then Heather Lawrence would have filled the bill. It's you I fell in love with."

"But how can you be so sure?" she countered quickly. "We barely know each other."

Cole smiled at her doubts. "The first time we kissed was enough to convince me I was going to love you. It was the Friday night after I returned from Seattle, remember?"

Robin nodded, wincing a little.

"I was so stunned by the powerful effect that kiss had on me that I avoided you for an entire week afterward. If you want the truth, I was terrified. You'll have to remember, up until that time I was convinced I was incapable of ever falling in love again. One kiss and I felt jolted to the core. You hit me hard, Robin, right between the eyes, and I needed time to step back and analyse what was happening. That's the reason I don't have any qualms now about giving you however long you need to sort out what you're feeling. I want you to be very sure."

Robin released a pent-up sigh and her shoulders heaved. Cole folded her in his arms and his chin brushed against the crown of her head while his hands roved in wide circles across her back. The action was soothing and gentle. She was beginning to feel more confident in his love, but she had to be careful. She *wanted* him to love her, because she was so much in love with him.

Cole tucked a finger under her chin and lifted her face to his. As their eyes met, he slanted his mouth over hers in a wildly possessive kiss, a kiss filled with undisguised need.

When he broke away, Robin was trembling. She buried her face in his neck and drew several deep breaths.

"If you're going to take some time to think about things," Cole whispered against her hair, "then I wanted to give you something more to think about."

"HAVE YOU HAD A CHANCE to check those figures on—" Angela began, then stopped abruptly, waving her hand in front of Robin's face.

"A chance to check what figures?" Robin asked, making a determined effort to focus. She knew she'd been behaving like a sleepwalker most of the morning, but she couldn't stop thinking about Cole's marriage proposal.

"What's with you today?" Angela demanded. "Every time I look over here, I find you staring into space with this perplexed expression on your face."

"I was...just thinking," Robin muttered.

"About what?"

"Nothing," Robin insisted.

"Come on, girl, you know better than that. You can't fool me." Angela leaned her hip against the edge of Robin's desk and crossed her arms, taking her usual aggressive stance. "I've known you far too long, and from everything you *haven't* said, I'd guess your handsome neighbour's involved. What's he done now?"

"Cole? What makes you ask anything so ridiculous?"

Angela frowned, shaking her head slowly. Then she stretched out her hands and made a come-hither motion. "Tell Mama everything," she intoned. "You might as well get it over with and tell me now, because you know that sooner or later I'm going to drag it out of you. I always do. What kind of friend would I be if I didn't extract your deepest darkest secrets?"

"He took me to dinner," Robin admitted, knowing that Angela was right. Sooner or later, she'd wheedle it out of her.

"Where'd he take you?"

She shrugged, wanting to keep that to herself. "It was outside the city."

"*Where* outside the city?" Angela pressed.

"Heavens, I don't know. Somewhere along the coast on Highway 101."

Angela uncrossed her arms and started pacing in front of Robin's desk. "It wasn't the Cliffhouse, was it?"

"I...I think it might have been," Robin murmured, concentrating on the task in front of her. The one she should have finished several hours earlier, but hadn't. The one she couldn't seem to focus on, even now.

"Aha!" Angela cried, pointing her index finger toward the ceiling, like the detective in a comic spoof.

"What?" Robin cried.

"If Cole took you to the Cliffhouse, he did it for a reason."

"Of course he did. The food was fabulous. By the way, you were right about Frank, he's exceptionally nice," Robin said hurriedly, in an effort to interrupt her friend's line of thought before she inadvertently stumbled on the reason for Robin's pensive mood.

"You already told me what you think of Frank, remember?" Angela muttered, tapping her finger against her lips. "Cole took you to dinner at the Cliffhouse," she repeated slowly, as though reviewing a vital clue in a puzzling murder mystery.

"To be honest, I think his choice of restaurant had something to do with Frank," Robin inserted, tossing her sleuth friend a red herring.

"So Cole was jealous?"

"Not exactly," Robin said, leaning back in her chair. "Well, maybe a little," she amended, knowing Angela would never believe her if she denied it completely. "I mean, Cole did invite me to dinner as soon as he learned I was dining with Frank, so I guess you could say he was a little jealous. But not much. Cole's not the jealous type—he told me that himself."

"I see." Angela was frowning as she walked back to her desk. Her look remained thoughtful for the rest of the morning, though she didn't question Robin again. But when they left for lunch, she showed a renewed interest in the subject of Cole.

"How's Jeff?" she began as they stood in line in the employees' cafeteria.

"Fine," Robin said as she reached for a plastic tray.

"That's all you're going to say?"

"What more do you want to know?"

"I ask about Jeff once a week or so, then sit back and listen for the next fifteen minutes while you tell me about the latest craziness he's led you into," Angela said heatedly. "It never fails. You've told me about him running away with a frying pan and an atlas. You've bragged about what a fabulous pitcher he's turning out to be, and you list a multitude of details about every game he's played. After you tell me all about his athletic ability, you generally mention how good he is with animals and all the tricks he's taught Blackie in the past week or so.

"Today I innocently ask how Jeff is, and what do I get? *Fine.* All right, Robin, tell me what happened with Cole Camden before I go loony trying to figure it out."

"It's something I need to figure out myself," Robin insisted. She paused to study the salads before selecting a mound of cottage cheese and setting it on her tray.

"What are you doing now?" Angela cried, throwing her arms in the air. "You hate cottage cheese. You never eat it unless you're upset about something and looking for ways to punish yourself." She lifted the small bowl from Robin's tray and replaced it with a fresh fruit salad, shaking her head the entire time.

The problem with Angela was that she knew Robin all too well.

They progressed a little farther down the line. Robin stood in front of the entrées, but before she chose one, she glanced at her friend. "You want to pick one out for me here, too?" she asked drily.

"Yes, I do, before you end up requesting liver and onions."

Angela picked the lasagne, thick with melted cheese and spicy Italian sauce. "If you're looking for ways to punish yourself, girl, there are tastier methods."

Despite her thoughtful mood, Robin found herself smiling.

Once they'd paid for their lunches, Angela led her to a window table that offered a certain amount of privacy. Robin busied herself arranging her dishes on the table and set the tray aside.

Angela sat directly across from her, elbows braced on either side of her lunch. "Are you sure there isn't anything more you'd care to tell me?"

"About what?"

"About you and Cole. I can't remember the last time I saw you like this. It's as if you're trapped in some kind of maze and can't find your way out."

The description was so apt that Robin felt a tingling sensation along her spine. She did feel hopelessly lost. Her mind was cluttered, her emotions confused. She had one foot in the present, one foot in the past, and didn't know which way to turn.

"I talked to Frank on Sunday afternoon," Angela continued, dipping her fork into a crisp green salad. "He said he enjoyed the evening you spent with him, too, but doubted you'd be seeing each other again because it was obvious to him you were in love with Cole Camden. In fact, Frank said you talked about little else the entire evening."

"He said all that, did he?"

Angela nodded. "He's right, isn't he? You are in love with Cole, aren't you?"

"I...I don't know."

"What do you mean you don't know?" Angela persisted. "It's written all over you. You've got that glazed look and you walk around in a trance, practically bumping into walls."

"You make it sound like I need an ambulance."

"Or a doctor," Angela whispered, leaning across the table as far as possible. "Or maybe a lawyer... That's it!" she said loud enough to attract the attention of several people at nearby tables. "Cole took you to bed, and now you're so confused you don't know what to do. I told you I'd stumble on the answer sooner or later." Her eyes flashed triumphantly.

"That's not it," Robin declared, half rising from the table in hot denial. She could feel the colour crowding into her cheeks as she glanced around the cafeteria. When she sat back down, she covered her face with both hands. "If you must know, Cole asked me to marry him."

A moment of shocked silence followed before Angela shrieked with pure delight. "That's fabulous! Wonderful! Good grief, woman, what's wrong with you? You should be in seventh heaven. It isn't every day a handsome, wealthy, wonderful man extends a proposal of marriage. I hope to high heaven you leapt at the chance." She hesitated, growing suddenly still. "Robin? You did tell him you'd marry him, didn't you?"

Robin swallowed and slowly shook her head. "No. I asked him for some time to think things through."

"Think things through?" Angela squealed. "What is there to think through? He's rich. He's handsome. He's in love with you and crazy about Jeff. What more could you possibly want from the man?"

Tears brimmed in Robin's eyes as she looked up to meet her friend's avid gaze. "I think he's more in love with the idea of having a family than he's interested in me."

"Is Cole coming?" Jeff asked, working the stiffness out of his baseball mitt by slamming his fist into the middle of it several times.

"I don't know," Robin said, glancing toward their neighbour's house as they walked to the car. "I haven't talked to him in the last few days."

"I noticed. You're not mad at him, are you?"

"Of course not," Robin said, sliding into the driver's seat of her compact. "We've both been busy."

Jeff fingered the bill of his baseball cap, then secured the cap to his head. "I saw him yesterday and told him about the game, and he said he might come. I hope he does."

Secretly Robin hoped Cole would be there, too. Over the past five days, she'd discovered she missed not talking to him. She hadn't come to any decision, but he hadn't pressed her to make one, willing to offer her all the time she needed. Robin hadn't realised how accustomed she'd grown to his presence. How much she needed to see him and talk to him. Exchange smiles and glances. Touch him...

When she was married to Lonny, they were two people very much in love, two people who'd linked their lives to form one whole. But Lonny had been taken from her, and for a long time afterwards Robin had stumbled through life with a huge part of her missing.

All week she'd swayed back and forth over Cole's proposal, wondering if she should ignore her doubts. Wondering if she *could* ignore them. Sleepless nights hadn't yielded the answer. Neither had long solitary walks in Balboa Park while Jeff practiced with his baseball team.

"Cole said—" Jeff started to say, then stopped abruptly as his hands flew to his head. A panicky look broke out on his face and he stared at Robin.

"What's wrong? Did you forget something?"

"My lucky hat!" Jeff cried. "It's on my dresser. We have to go back."

"For a baseball cap?" Robin didn't bother to disguise how silly she considered that idea. "You're wearing a baseball cap. What's wrong with that one?"

"It won't work. You have to understand, Mom, it's my *lucky* hat. Not an ordinary one. I've been wearing it every since we played our first game. I had that very same hat when I hit my first two home runs. I can't play without it," he explained frantically. "We have to go back. Hurry, or we'll be late for the game. Turn here," he cried, pointing at the closest intersection.

"Jeff," she said, hoping to reason with her son. "It isn't the hat that makes you play well."

"I knew you were going to say something like that," he muttered, "and deep down I know it's probably true, but I want to be on the safe side, just in case. We've got to go back and get that hat!"

Knowing it would only waste valuable time and effort to argue, Robin did as he requested. After all, his entire career as a major-league pitcher hung in the balance!

She was smiling as she entered her driveway. Sitting in the car while Jeff ran inside for his lucky cap, Robin glanced over at Cole's place. His car was gone. It had been since early that morning, and she suspected he was at the property, working on his house. Jeff would be disappointed about Co.. missing his game, but he'd understand.

Jeff came barrelling out of the house, slamming the front door. He leapt into the car and fastened his seat belt. "Come on, Mom," he said anxiously, "let's get this show on the road." As if she'd caused the delay, Robin thought to herself, amused by her son's sudden impatience.

By the time they arrived at Balboa Park, the car park was filled to overflowing. Robin was fortunate enough to find a space on the street, a minor miracle in itself. Perhaps there was something to this magic-cap business after all.

Jeff ran across the grass, hurrying toward his teammates, leaving Robin to fend for herself, which was fine. He had his precious cap and was content.

The bleachers were crowded with parents. Robin found a seat close to the top and had just settled into place when she saw Cole making his way towards her. Her heart did an immediate flip-flop before righting itself. It wasn't until he sat next to her that she found her tongue.

"I thought you were working up on the property this weekend."

"And miss seeing Jeff pitch? Wild horses couldn't have kept me away." He was smiling at her with that cocky heart-stopping smile of his.

"How have you been?" she asked, unable to keep her eyes off him. He looked too good to be true, and his dark gaze was filled with warmth and tenderness. How could she help getting lost in eyes that generous? It seemed impossible to fight him any longer.

"I've missed you like crazy," he whispered, and the humour seemed to drain out of him as his eyes searched hers. "I didn't think it was possible to feel this alone. Not any more."

"I've missed you, too."

He seemed to relax once she'd said that. "Thank you," he said quietly. "Have you been thinking about what I said last weekend?"

She lowered her head. "I haven't thought of anything else."

"Then you've made up your mind?"

"No." She kept her face lowered, not wanting him to read her confusion.

He tilted her chin with one finger, forcing her to meet his eyes. "I promised myself I wouldn't ask you and then I couldn't seem to stop myself. I won't again."

She offered him a weak smile, and Cole looked around him, clearly wanting to kiss her, but not in front of such a large gathering. The funny part was, Robin didn't care about being seen. She was so hungry for the reassurance of his touch that it didn't matter to her that they were in the middle of a crowded park.

"I see Jeff's wearing his lucky hat," Cole said, clasping her hand and giving her fingers a comforting squeeze.

"You know all about that?"

"Of course. Jeff tells me everything."

"He panicked when he realised he was wearing the wrong one, and I had to make a U-turn in the middle of the street because he'd left the guaranteed-to-pitch-well baseball cap on his dresser."

"You can't blame him. The luck has lasted through five games now."

"I wonder if it'll last until he reaches the pros," Robin said, sharing a smile with him.

"You're doing all right?" Cole asked unexpectedly.

She nodded, although it wasn't entirely true. Now that she was with Cole, every doubt she'd struggled with all week vanished like fog under an afternoon sun. Only when they were apart was she forced to confront her fears.

"After Jeff's finished here, let's do something together," Cole suggested. "The three of us."

She nodded, unable to refuse him anything.

"Come to think of it, didn't I promise Jeff lunch? I seem to recall making a rash pledge to buy him fish-and-chips because we were leaving him with Heather and Kelly Lawrence when we went to dinner last week."

Robin grinned. "It seems to me he said something about that."

They went to a cheerful little fish-and-chip restaurant down by the Wharf. The weather had been chilly all morning, but the sun was out in full force by early afternoon. Jeff was excited about his team's latest win and attributed it all to the luck brought to them by his cap.

After a leisurely lunch, the three of them strolled along the busy waterfront. Robin bought a loaf of fresh sourdough bread and a small bouquet of spring flowers. Jeff found a plastic snake he couldn't bear to live without and paid for it with his allowance.

"Just wait till Jimmy Wallach sees this!" he crowed.

"I'm more curious to see how Kelly Lawrence reacts," Robin said.

"Oh, Kelly likes snakes," Jeff told them cheerfully. "Jimmy was over one day and I thought I'd scare Kelly with a live garden snake, but it was Jimmy who started screaming. Kelly said snakes were just one of God's creatures and there was nothing to be afraid of. Isn't it just like a girl to get religious about a snake?"

Jeff raced down the sidewalk while Cole and Robin stood at the end of the pier.

"You look tired," Cole said, as his fingers gently touched her forehead, brushing back the thick curls.

"I'm fine," she insisted, gazing out at the cool green waters of San Francisco Bay. But Cole was right; she hadn't been sleeping well.

"I see so much of myself in you," Cole said softly.

His words surprised her. "How's that?"

"The pain mostly. How many years has Lonny been dead?"

"Ten. In some ways I'm still grieving for him." She couldn't be less than honest with Cole.

"You're not sure if you can love another man, are you? At least not with the same intensity that you loved Jeff's father."

"That's not it at all. I...I just don't know if I can stop loving him."

Cole went very still. "I never intended to take Lonny away from you or Jeff. He's a part of your past, an important part. Being married to Lonny, giving birth to Jeff, contributed to making you what you are." He paused, and they both remained silent.

"Bobby had been buried for six years before I had the courage to face the future. I hung on to my grief, carried it with me everywhere

I went, dragging it like a heavy piece of luggage I couldn't travel without.''

"I'm not that way about Lonny," she countered, ready to argue, not heatedly or vehemently, but logically, because what he was saying simply wasn't true. She grieved for her dead husband, felt his absence, but she hadn't allowed this sense of loss to destroy her life.

"Perhaps you aren't grieving as intensely as you once were," Cole amended. "But I wonder, really wonder, if you honestly have laid your husband to rest."

"Of course I have," she answered with a gentle nod of her head, not wanting to talk about Lonny.

"I don't mean to sound unsympathetic," Cole said, his tone compassionate. "I understand, believe me I do. Emotional pain is familiar territory for us both. It seems to me that sustaining this kind of grief is like pitching a tent in the barren soil and lingering there, afraid of what lies just beyond."

"You're exaggerating, Cole."

"Maybe," he agreed. "You're a lovely woman, Robin. Witty. Intelligent. Outgoing. I'm sure one of the first questions anyone asks you is how long it's been since your husband died. And I'll bet when you tell them, they seem surprised."

That was true, and Robin wondered how Cole had guessed.

"Most young widows remarry."

"Are you suggesting that because I didn't immediately find my way back into matrimonial bliss I'm a candidate for therapy? Come on, Cole, even you must realize how ridiculous that is."

"Even me?" he asked, chuckling.

Jeff came racing toward them, his face flushed with excitement. "They're filming a movie," he cried, pointing toward a congested area farther down the pier. "There's cameras and actors and everything. Can I go watch some more?"

Robin nodded. "Just don't get in anyone's way. Understand?"

Jeff nodded. "I won't. Promise. Here, Mom, hold my snake." He entrusted her with his precious package before racing back down the pier.

"He's a fine boy, Robin."

"He loves you already. You and Blackie."

"And what about his mother?"

The knot in her throat thickened. "She loves you, too."

Cole grinned. "She just isn't sure if she can let go of her dead husband to take on a live one. Am I right?"

His words hit their mark. "I don't know," she admitted finally. "Maybe it's because I'm so afraid you want to marry me because Jeff reminds you of Bobby. Or because you've created a fantasy wife and think I'll fit the role."

Her words seemed to shock him. "No. You've got that all wrong. Jeff is a wonderful plus in this relationship, but it's *you* I fell in love with. It's you I want to grow old with. You, and you alone, not some ideal. If you want to know the truth, I think you're stirring up all this turmoil because you're afraid of ever marrying again. The little world you've made is tidy and safe. But is this what Lonny would have wanted for you?" He gripped her firmly by the shoulders. "If Lonny were standing beside you right now, and you could ask him about marrying me, what would he say?"

"I don't understand."

"If you could seek Lonny's advice, what would he tell you? Would he say, 'Robin, look at this guy. He's in love with you. He thinks the world of Jeff, and he's ready to embark on a new life. This is an opportunity too good for you to pass up. Don't be a fool. Marry him.'?"

"That sounds like something my friend Angela would say."

"I think I'm going to like this friend of yours just as long as she doesn't try to set you up with another one of her divorced cousins," Cole said, laughing. His eyes grew warm as he gazed at her, and she suspected he was longing to take her in his arms and kiss her doubts away. But he didn't. Instead, he looked over his shoulder and sighed. "I think I'll go check and see what Jeff's up to. I'll leave you to yourself for a few minutes. I don't mean to pressure you, but I do want you to think about what I said."

"You aren't pressuring me," she whispered, staring out over the water.

Cole left her then, and her hands gripped the steel railing as she raised her eyes to the sky. "Oh, Lonny," she whispered. "What should I do?"

CHAPTER TEN

"COLE WANTS ME to ask your advice." Robin continued to look up at the cloudless blue sky. "Oh, Lonny, I honestly don't know what's right for Jeff and me anymore. I love Cole. I love you. But at the same time I can't help wondering about Cole's motives...."

Robin paused, waiting. Not that she expected an answer. Lonny couldn't give her one. He never did; he never would. But unlike the other times she'd spoken to him, she needed a response, even though expecting one was totally illogical.

With every breath she drew, Robin knew that, but the futility of it all hit her, anyway. Her frustration came, so hard and unexpectedly powerful that it felt like a body blow. Robin closed her eyes, hoping the warmth of the sun would take away this bitter ache, this dreadful loneliness.

She felt so empty. Hollow all the way through.

Her fists clenched at her sides as tears filled her eyes. Embarrassed, she glanced around, grateful that the film crew had attracted most of the sightseers. No one was around to witness her distress. She brushed the tears from her cheeks.

Anger, which for so many years had lain dormant inside her, gushed forth in an avalanche of grief and pain. The tears spilled down her cheeks. Her lips quivered. Her shoulders shook. Her hands trembled. It was as if the emotion was pounding against her chest and she was powerless to do anything but stand there and bear it.

The anger consumed her now. Consumed her because she hadn't allowed it to when Lonny was first killed. It had been more important to put on a brave front. More important to hold herself together for Jeff and for Lonny's parents. More important to deal with the present than confront the past.

Lonny had died and Robin was furious with him for leaving her alone with a child to raise. Leaving her alone to deal with filing taxes and taking out the garbage and repairing leaking pipes. All these years she'd managed on her own. And she'd bottled the anger up inside, afraid of ever letting it go.

"Robin."

Cole's voice, soft and urgent, reached out from behind her. At the sound, she turned and walked into his arms, sobbing, needing his comfort and his love in equal measure. Needing him as she'd never needed anyone before.

She didn't know how long he held her. He was whispering soothing words to her. Gentle words. But she heard none of them over the sound of her own suffering.

Once she started crying, Robin couldn't seem to stop. It was as if a dam had burst inside her and the anguish, stored for too many years, came pouring out.

Cole's arms were securely wrapped around her, shielding her. She longed to control this outburst, longed to explain, but every time she tried to speak her sobbing only grew worse.

"Let it out," he whispered. "You don't have to say anything. I understand."

"He doesn't answer," she sobbed. "I asked him... Lonny never answers me...because he can't. He left me..."

"He didn't want to die," Cole assured her.

"But he did...he did."

Cole didn't argue with her. He simply held her tenderly, stroking the back of her head as though reassuring a small child.

It took several minutes for Robin to compose herself enough to go on. "Part of me realises that Lonny didn't want to leave me, didn't want to die. But he did and I'm so angry at him."

"That anger is what makes us human," Cole told her. He continued to comfort her and, gradually, bit by bit, Robin felt her composure slip back into place.

She sensed Jeff's presence even before he spoke.

"What wrong with my mom?" he asked Cole.

"She's dealing with some emotional pain," Cole explained, speaking as one adult to another.

"Is she going to be all right?"

Robin hadn't wanted her son to see her crying and made a concerted effort to break away from Cole, to reassure Jeff herself. Cole loosened his hold, but kept his arm around her shoulders.

"I'm fine, Jeff. Really."

"She doesn't look so good."

Her son had developed the irritating habit of not talking to her when she was upset. Jeff and Cole had done it that day her son had run away to the fort. He and Cole had carried on an entire conversation about her while she was in their midst then, too.

Cole led her to a bench and they all sat down.

Jeff plopped himself next to her and reached for her hand, patting it several times. Leaning toward Cole, he said earnestly, "Chocolate might help. One time Mom told me there wasn't anything in this world chocolate couldn't cure."

She'd actually said that? Robin started to smile. Wrapping her arms around her son, she hugged him close, loving him so much her heart seemed about to burst.

Jeff wasn't all that keen on being cuddled, especially in public, but although he squirmed he put up with his mother's sudden need to hold him.

When she'd finished, Jeff rolled his eyes and once more directed his comments to Cole. "She gets weird like this every once in a while. Remember what happened that day I ran away?"

"I remember," Cole said, and Robin smiled at the trace of amusement she heard in his voice.

"Will you stop excluding me from this conversation? I'm going to be all right. I just had this overpowering need to cry, but don't worry, it's passed."

"See what I mean," Jeff muttered to Cole.

"But Jeff's right," Robin said, ignoring her son's comment. "Something chocolaty would definitely help."

"You'll be OK by yourself for a couple of minutes?" Cole asked.

"I'll be fine. I...don't know exactly what came over me, but I'm going to be just fine."

"I know you are." He kissed her, his lips gentle against her cheek.

The two of them left and once more Robin was alone. She didn't really understand why the pain and anger had hit her so hard now, after all this time. Except that it had something to do with Cole. But the last place she would ever have expected to give in to her grief was on Fisherman's Wharf with half of San Francisco looking on.

Jeff returned less than a minute later, running to her side with a double-decker chocolate ice-cream cone. "Cole's bringing two more for him and me," he explained. "I told the guy it was an emergency and he gave me this one right away."

"That was thoughtful of you," Robin said, wondering what the vendor must have thought. Smiling, she ran her tongue over the ice cream, savoring the cold chocolate. As profoundly as she'd wept, she felt almost giddy with relief now, repressing the urge to throw back her head and laugh.

Cole arrived, and with Jeff on her left and Cole on her right she sat on the concrete bench and ate her ice-cream cone.

"I told you this would work," Jeff told Cole smugly.

"And to think I scoffed at your lucky baseball cap," she teased, feeling much better.

When they finished the cones, Cole gathered up their packages and led them back to where he'd parked his car.

Blackie was there to greet them the instant they returned to Orchard Street. Jeff ran into the backyard to play with the dog, and Cole walked Robin to her door. He accepted her offer of coffee.

"I'm probably going to be leaving soon for my property," he said, watching her closely. He sat down at the table, his hands cupping the mug as though to warm them. "Will you be all right?"

Robin nodded. She walked over and stood beside him and pressed a hand to his strong jaw. "I realise you delayed going up there today because of Jeff and his baseball game. We're both grateful."

Cole placed his hand over hers and harshly expelled his breath. "I feel responsible for what you went through there on the pier. I should never have said what I did. I'm sorry, Robin, it wasn't any of my business."

"You only said what I needed to hear."

He smiled. "If I did, it was because of what happened to me in

Seattle. I find it more than a little amazing that the two of us would come to grips with our pain while standing on a pier—me in Seattle, you here in San Francisco. I returned home with this incredible sense of release. For the first time since Bobby and Janice's deaths, I surrendered my grief. In a way it was as though I reached up and God reached down and together we came to an understanding."

That so completely described what Robin had been feeling that for a long moment she couldn't say anything. What Cole had told her earlier about carrying the pain with her, dragging it everywhere she went, was right on the mark, too. He understood; he'd done the same thing himself. A surge of love swelled within her.

"I know you don't want to hear this," he was saying. "I honestly don't mean to pressure you. But once I returned from Seattle and realised I was falling in love with you I started thinking about having another baby." He hesitated and took a gulp of his coffee the way a thirsty man attacks a cold beer. He stood up abruptly, nearly knocking the chair backward. "I better go before I say or do something else I shouldn't."

Robin followed him into the entryway, not wanting him to leave, but not quite ready to give him what he needed.

He paused at the screen door and his eyes immediately found hers. He couldn't seem to keep himself from touching her, brushing an auburn curl from her cheek. His knuckles grazed her skin lightly, and Robin's eyes closed of their own accord at the sensation that shot through her. Her heart was full, and she seemed to have all the answers now—except to the one question that was the most important in her life. And Jeff's.

"I'll see you next week some time," Cole said roughly, pulling his hand away. Without another word, he walked out the door, pausing at the top of the porch steps.

He called for his dog and in response both Blackie and Jeff came running.

"You're not leaving, are you?" Jeff asked breathlessly.

"I'm taking Blackie for the rest of the weekend. You think you can get along without him till Monday, sport?"

Jeff shrugged and stuck his fingers in the hip pockets of his blue jeans. "I suppose. Where are you taking him?"

"To my property." Cole didn't turn towards Robin. It was as if he had to ignore her in order to walk away from her.

"Oh, yeah!" Jeff said enthusiastically. "I remember your saying something about it once. You're building a house, aren't you?"

"Remodelling one. My grandfather lived there as a boy and he willed it to me, only it's been a lot of years since anyone's properly cared for that old house and there's plenty of work that needs to be done."

"I'll work for you," Jeff piped in eagerly. He made up a fist and flexed his arm, revealing the meager muscles. "I know it doesn't look like much, but I'm strong. Just ask anyone."

Cole tested Jeff's muscles, pretending to be impressed. "Yes, I can tell you're strong, and I'm sure I couldn't ask for a harder worker." Jeff beamed until Cole added regretfully, "I'll take you up there another time, sport."

Jeff's face fell with disappointment.

Before she even realised what she was doing, Robin moved on to the porch. "Cole."

He turned to face her, but the movement seemed reluctant.

Perhaps it was because she didn't want to be separated from him any more than he wanted to be away from her. Perhaps it was the thought of Jeff's being disappointed when he'd already had so many other disappointments in his young life. Perhaps it was this newborn sense of freedom she was just beginning to experience.

She stepped towards Cole. "Could Jeff and I go up to the property with you?"

Jeff didn't wait for Cole to answer before leaping excitedly into the air. "Hey, Mom, that's a great idea! Really great. Can we, Cole? Blackie and I can help you, and Mom can... Well, she can do things like make us some grub and bring us lemonade and other stuff women do when their men are working."

"I'll have you both know I pound a mean hammer," Robin felt obliged to inform them. If she was going to Cole's farm, she fully intended to do her share.

Cole looked perplexed for a moment, as if he wasn't sure he'd heard her correctly. "I'd love to have you come—if you're sure that's what you want."

Robin just nodded. All she knew was that she couldn't bear to be separated from him any longer.

"Just be warned the house is only half done. The plumbing isn't in yet."

"We'll manage, won't we, Jeff?"

"Sure," Jeff said eagerly. "Anyway, boys got it easy."

Cole laughed. "How long will it take you to pack?"

"We're ready now, aren't we, Blackie?" Jeff almost jitterbugged across the front lawn in his enthusiasm.

"Give me a few minutes to throw some things together," Robin said, grinning. Jeff was smiling, too, ear to ear, as he raced past her into the house and up the stairs.

Cole's eyes held Robin's in silent communication—until Jeff came bursting out of the house, dragging his sheets and quilt with him, straight from his bed.

"Jeff," she cried, aghast, "what are you doing?"

"I took everything off my bed. I'm willing to go without plumbing, but I need certain comforts." He piled the bedding at their feet. "You two can go back to looking at each other. I'll get everything else we need."

"Jeff," Robin groaned, casting Cole an apologetic glance. "I'll pack my own things, thank you."

"You want me to get your sheets, too?" he called from inside the house.

"No." She scooped up the bedding and dashed into the house, taking the stairs two at a time. She discovered Jeff sitting on the edge of her bed, his expression pensive.

"What's wrong?"

"Are you ever going to marry Cole?" her son asked.

At the unexpectedness of the question, Robin's heart flew to her throat, then slid back into place. Briefly she wondered if Cole had brought up the subject with her son, but instinctively knew that he hadn't. "W-what makes you ask that?"

He shrugged. "Lots of things. Every time I turn around you two are gazing into each other's eyes. Either that, or kissing. I try to pretend I don't notice, but it's getting as bad as some of those movies you like to rent. And when you were crying on the pier, I saw something. Cole had his arms around you and he was looking real sad. Like...like he wished he could do the crying for you. It's the same look Grandpa sometimes gives Grandma when he figures out how she feels about something, and she doesn't even have to talk. Do you know what I mean?"

"I think so," Robin said, casually walking over to her dresser drawer and taking out a couple of old sweatshirts. "And what would you think if I said I was considering marrying Cole?"

Robin expected shouts of glee and wild shrieks, but instead, her son crossed his arms over his chest and moved his mouth in odd ways, stretching it sharply to one side and then the other. "You're serious, aren't you?"

"Yes." She folded and refolded one of the sweatshirts, her heart pounding in anticipation. "It would mean a lot of changes for all of us."

"How many other people are involved in this?"

Robin hesitated, not understanding Jeff's concern. "What do you mean?"

"Will I get an extra set of grandparents in this deal?"

"Uh...probably. I haven't talked to Cole about that yet, but I assume so."

"That means extra gifts on my birthday and at Christmas. If that's the case, I say we should go for it."

"Jeffrey Leonard Masterson, you shock me!"

"A kid thinks that way. It shouldn't come as any surprise."

Robin shook her head in dismay at her son's sudden materialistic attitude towards her possible marriage. She was still frowning as she stepped outside.

Cole was in his garage, loading up the trunk of his four-wheel-drive vehicle when Robin joined him. She handed him one small suitcase and a bag of groceries she'd packed at the last moment.

Cole stowed them away, carefully avoiding her eyes. "I take it you said something to Jeff about us?'' She could hear amusement in his voice.

''Yes. How'd you know?''

''He brought down a paper bag full of clothes, and asked what kind of presents he could expect from my parents at Christmas. He also asked if there were any aunts or uncles in the deal.'' Robin's embarrassment must have showed, because Cole started chuckling.

''That boy's got a mercenary streak in him I knew nothing about,'' she muttered.

Cole was still grinning. ''You ready?''

She nodded, drawing an unsteady breath, eager for this adventure to begin. Jeff and Blackie were already in the back seat when Robin slipped in the front to wait for Cole.

''Are we going to sing camp songs?'' Jeff asked, bracing his elbows on the back of their seats and leaning forward. He didn't wait for a response, but immediately launched into the timeless ditty about bottles of beer on the wall. He sang ninety-nine verses of that, then performed a series of other songs until they came off the freeway and wound up on a narrow country road with little traffic.

Jeff had tired of singing by then. ''Knock knock,'' he called out.

''Who's there?'' Robin said, falling in with his game.

''Eisenhower.''

''Eisenhower who?''

Jeff snickered. ''Eisenhower late, how about you?'' With that, the ten-year-old broke into belly-gripping guffaws, as if he should be receiving awards for his ability to tell jokes.

Cole's mouth was twitching and Robin had to admit that she was amused, too.

''The turnoff for the ranch is about a mile up the road,'' Cole explained. ''Now remember, this is going to be a lot like camping. It's still pretty primitive.''

''You don't need to worry,'' Robin said, smiling at him.

A couple of minutes later, Cole slowed about to turn down the long driveway. It was then that Robin saw the sign. Her heart jumped to her throat and her hands started to shake.

''Stop!'' she screamed. ''Stop!''

Cole slammed on the brakes, catapulting them forward. "Robin, what is it?"

Robin threw open the front door and leapt out of the car, running to the middle of the road. She stared at the one word on the sign even as the tears filled her eyes.

Cole's farm was named *Paradise*.

CHAPTER ELEVEN

"ROBIN, I DON'T UNDERSTAND," Cole said for the third time. His dark eyes were filled with worry.

"I bet my allowance she's crying again," Jeff muttered, poking his head out the side window. "Something weird's going on with my mother. She's been acting goofy all day. What do you think it is?"

"I'm not really sure," Cole said as he continued to study Robin.

For her part, Robin couldn't take her eyes off the sign. Jeff was right about her crying; the tears streamed unrestrained down her face. But these were tears of joy. Tears of gratitude. Tears of acknowledgment. It was exactly as Cole had described. She'd reached up and God had reached down and together they'd come to an understanding. She'd finally resolved her dilemma with Cole.

Unable to stop herself, Robin hurled her arms around Cole's neck. Her hands roamed his face. His wonderful, wonderful face.

Because her eyes were blurred with emotion, she couldn't accurately read Cole's expression, but it didn't matter. Her heart spilled over with love for him.

"Robin…"

She didn't let him finish, but began spreading a long series of kisses across his face, starting with his eyelids. "I love you, I love you," she repeated between kisses, moving from his cheek to his nose and downward.

Cole put his arms around her waist and pulled her closer. Robin was half-aware of the car door slamming and Jeff marching on to the road to join them.

"Are you two going to get all mushy on me again?"

Robin barely heard her son. Her mouth had unerringly found Cole's. When the kiss ended, his teeth tugged gently at her lower lip.

The unexpected sharp sound of a hand clap brought her out of her dream world. Her eyes immediately went to Jeff, who was looking very much like a pint-size adult. His face and eyes were as stern as she'd ever seen them.

"Do the two of you realise where you're standing?" Jeff demanded as though he'd recently been hired by the state police to make sure this type of thing didn't happen. "There are proper places to kiss, but the middle of the road isn't one of them."

"He's right," Cole said, his eyes devouring Robin. He didn't want to release her and did so with a reluctance that tugged at her heart.

"Come with me," Jeff said, taking his mother firmly by the hand and leading her back to the car. He paused in front of the door and glanced at Cole. "She might have a fever. She acts a little weird sometimes, but it's never been as bad as today."

"Robin," Cole said, grasping her hand, "can you explain now?"

She nodded. "It's the sign—Paradise. Tell me about it. Tell me why your grandfather named his place Paradise."

"I'm not entirely sure," Cole said, puzzled. "He lived here his whole life and always said this land was all he'd ever needed. From what I remember, he once told me he thought of this place as the Garden of Eden. I can only assume that's why he named it Paradise."

Robin nodded, unsurprised by his explanation. "When Lonny and I were first married, we talked...we dreamed about someday buying some land and raising animals. Enough land for Jeff to have a pony and for me to have a huge garden. We decided this land would be our own piece of heaven on earth and...from that we came up with the idea of naming it Paradise."

Slowly Cole shook his head, and she could tell he didn't completely understand.

"This afternoon, when I was standing on Fisherman's Wharf, you suggested I talk over my feelings about our getting married with Lonny."

"What I suggested," Cole reminded her gently, "was that you *imagine* what he'd say to advise you. I certainly didn't expect you to really communicate with him."

"I know this won't make any sense to you, but I've talked to Lonny lots of times over the years. This afternoon, what hit me so hard was the fact that Lonny would never answer me. That realisation was what finally forced me to deal with the pain. To forgive Lonny for dying.''

Jeff was looking at her as if he was about to suggest they call a doctor.

''Here you were wanting to marry me and I didn't know what to do. I had trouble believing your proposal was prompted by anything more than the desire to replace the family you'd lost. I do love you, and I desperately wanted to believe you loved me—and Jeff. But I wasn't sure....''

''And you're sure now?''

She nodded enthusiastically. ''Yes. With all my heart, I'm confident that marrying you would be the right thing for all of us.''

''Of course we're going to marry Cole!'' Jeff cried. ''Good grief, if you had any doubts, all you had to do was ask me and I would've told you. It's obvious we belong together.''

''Yes, it is, isn't it,'' Robin whispered. ''Cole,'' she said, gripping both his hands with her own. ''I'd consider it a very great honour to become your wife.''

''Jeff?'' Cole said, tearing his eyes away from Robin. ''I want to know what you think.''

The boy's face beamed and his eyes sparkled. ''I'd consider it a very great honour to become your son.''

Cole brushed his lips across Robin's and then reached for Jeff, hauling him into his arms and squeezing him tight. Blackie started barking then, wanting out of the car. Robin quickly moved to open the passenger door, and the black Lab leapt out. She crouched down and wrapped her arms around his thick neck, hugging him. ''You're going to have a whole family now, Blackie,'' she murmured happily.

TWO HOURS LATER, just at dusk, Robin was standing in the middle of the yard. She'd loved everything about Paradise, just as she'd known she would. The house and property were nothing like the place she and Lonny had dreamed about, but she hadn't expected them to be. The four-bedroom house was much larger than anything they'd ever hoped to own. The land was filled with Ponderosa pine trees, and the rocky ground was more suitable to grazing a few sheep or cattle than planting crops.

Cole was showing Jeff the barn, and Robin had intended to join them, but the evening was filled with a sweet-smelling breeze and she'd stopped to breathe in the fresh cool air. She folded her arms and stood there, smiling into the clear sky. A multitude of twinkling stars were just beginning to reveal themselves.

Cole walked quietly up behind her, and slipped his arms around her waist, pulling her against him. "Have I told you how much I love you?"

"In the last fifteen minutes? No, you haven't."

"Then allow me to correct that situation." He nibbled the back of her neck gently. "I love you to distraction."

"I love you, too."

He sighed then, and whispered hoarsely, "It was a difficult decision to marry me, wasn't it?"

Robin agreed with a nod.

"Had I given you so many reasons to doubt me?"

"No," she said quickly, turning in his arms. She pressed her palms against his jaw. "I had to be sure in my heart you weren't trying to replace the son you'd lost with Jeff. And I had to be equally certain you loved me for myself and not because I was Jeff's mother and we came as a package deal."

He shook his head decisively. "Jeff's a great kid, don't get me wrong, but there's never been any doubt in my mind how I felt about you. The first time we met, you hit me square between the eyes. I didn't mean to fall in love again. I didn't even want it."

"I don't think I did, either," Robin confessed.

"Past experience had taught us both that loving someone only causes pain. I loved Janice, but I could never make her happy. When we divorced I accepted my part in the breakup."

"But she had a drinking problem, Cole. You can't blame yourself."

"I don't, not entirely, but I accept a portion of the blame for what went wrong. It tore me apart to see Bobby caught in the middle, and in an effort to minimise the pain I didn't fight for custody. He was an innocent victim of the divorce, and I didn't want him to suffer any further distress. I was willing to do anything I could to spare him. Later, when I realised how serious Janice's problem with alcohol had become, I tried to obtain custody, but before I could get the courts to move on it, the accident happened. Afterward, I was left to deal with the guilt of having waited too long.

"The thought of ever marrying again, having children again, terrified me. I couldn't see making myself vulnerable a second time." He paused, and a slow, gentle smile spread across his face, smoothing away the tension. "All that changed when I met you. It was as if life was offering me a second chance. And I knew I had to grab hold of it with both hands or forever live with regret."

"Oh, brother," Jeff said as he dashed into the yard. "Are you two at it again?"

"We're talking," Robin explained.

"Your mouths are too close together for talking." He strolled past them, Blackie at his side. "I don't suppose you thought about making me anything to eat, did you, Mom?"

"I made sandwiches."

"Great. Are there enough for Blackie to have one?"

"I think so. There's cans of pop and some corn chips in the kitchen, too."

"Great," Jeff repeated, hurrying into the house.

"Are you hungry?" Robin asked Cole.

"Yes," he stated emphatically, "but my appetite doesn't seem to be for food. How long will you keep me waiting to make you my wife?"

"I'll have to call my parents and my brother and make the arrangements. It's important to me that we have a church wedding. It doesn't have to be fancy, but I'd like to invite a handful of good friends and—"

"How long?"

"To make the arrangements? I'm not exactly sure. Three, possibly four months to do it properly. Maybe longer."

"One month," Cole said.

"What do you mean, one month?"

"I'm giving you exactly thirty days to arrange whatever you want, but that's as long as I'm willing to wait."

"But, Cole—"

He swept her into his arms then and his mouth claimed hers in a fury of desire. Robin found herself trembling and she clutched his shirt, her fingers bunching the material as she strove to regain her equilibrium.

"Cole..." She felt chilled and feverish at the same time. Needy, yet wealthy beyond her wildest dreams.

"One month?" he repeated.

"One month," she agreed, pressing her face against his broad warm chest. They'd both loved, profoundly, and they'd lost what they'd valued most. For years, in their own ways, they'd sealed themselves off from others, because no one else could understand their pain. Then they'd found one another, and nothing would ever be the same again. Their love was the mature love that came when one had suffered and lost and been left to rebuild a shattered life. The love they shared was stronger than either could ever have hoped for.

"Do you see what I was telling you about?" Jeff muttered to Blackie, sitting on the back porch steps. "I suppose we're going to have to put up with this for a while."

Blackie munched on a corn chip, apparently more interested in sharing Jeff's meal than listening to his comments.

"I can deal with it, if you can," Jeff continued. "I suspect I'll be getting at least one brother out of this deal, and if we're lucky maybe two. A sister would be all right, too, I guess—" he sighed deeply "—but I'll have to think about that. Girls can be a real headache, if you know what I mean."

The dog wagged his tail as Jeff slipped him another corn chip. "And you know what, Blackie? It's gonna be Father's Day soon. My very first. And I've already got a card picked out. It's got a picture of a father, a mother and a little boy with a baseball cap. And there's a dog on it that looks just like you!"

FIRST COMES MARRIAGE

FIRST COMES MARRIAGE

CHAPTER ONE

"YOU MUST BE Zachary Thomas," Janine said breathlessly as she whirled into the office. "I'm sorry I'm late, but I got hung up in traffic on Fourth Avenue. I didn't realize they'd torn up the whole street." Still a little winded, she unfastened her coat, tossed it over the back of the leather chair and plopped herself down, facing the large executive desk.

The man on the other side blinked twice as though he didn't quite know what to think.

"I'm Janine Hartman," she gasped out, flattening her hand over her chest. She drew in a deep steadying breath. "Gramps said if he wasn't back from his appointment, I should introduce myself."

"Yes," Zachary said after a moment of strained silence. "But he didn't tell me you'd be wearing—"

"Oh, the bandanna dress," Janine said, smoothing one hand over her lap. The entire dress had been constructed of red and blue bandannas; it featured a knee-length zigzag hemline and closely hugged her hips. "It was a gift. And since I'm meeting the girl who made it later, I thought the least I could do was wear it."

"I see. And the necklace?"

Janine toyed with the colored Christmas-tree lights strung between large bright beads on a bootlace that dangled from her neck. "It's a bit outrageous, isn't it? That was a gift, too. I think it's kind of cute, though. Don't you? Pamela is so clever."

"Pamela?"

"A teenager from the Friendship Club."

"I...see," Zach said, frowning.

"I do volunteer work there and the two of us hit it off the moment we met. Pam's mother doesn't live in the area and she's at that awkward age and needs a friend. For some reason she took a liking to me, which was fine because I think she's wonderful.''

"I see."

Janine doubted that he did.

"The necklace is *different* I'll grant you," Zach was saying—which wasn't admitting to much. His dark eyes narrowed as he studied the multicolored bulbs.

Now that she'd met Zachary Thomas, Janine could understand why her grandfather was so impressed with him, if appearances were anything to judge by. In his well-tailored suit, he was the very picture of a high-powered executive, crisp, formal and in control. He was younger than she'd assumed, possibly in his early thirties, but it was difficult to tell. His facial features were attractive enough, she noted, but he wasn't strikingly handsome. Still, she found herself fascinated by the strength of character she saw in the uneven planes of his face. His dark hair was cut military short. His jaw was strong, his cheekbones high and his mouth full. That was the way she'd describe him physically, but there was apparently much more to the man than met the eye. At least, her grandfather was convinced of it.

Several months earlier Anton Hartman had merged his well-established business supply firm with the up-and-rising company owned by Zachary Thomas. Together the two men had quickly dominated the market.

For weeks now, Gramps had wanted Janine to meet Zachary. His name had popped up in every conversation, no matter what they were discussing. To say her grandfather thought highly of his partner was a gross understatement.

"Gramps has spoken...highly of you," she said next.

A hint of a smile—just the merest suggestion—touched the edges of his mouth, giving her the impression that he didn't smile often. "Your grandfather has one of the keenest business minds in the country."

"He's incredible, isn't he?"

Zachary's nod betrayed no hesitation.

There was a polite knock on the door, and almost immediately afterward, a tall middle-aged woman wearing a navy-blue pin-striped suit stepped into the room. "Mr. Hartman phoned," she announced primly. "He's been delayed and suggested you two meet him at the restaurant."

"I see." Zach's lean dark face tightened briefly before he cast Janine an uneasy glance. "Did he say how long he was going to be?"

"I'm sorry, Mr. Thomas, but he didn't."

Janine glanced at her watch. She was scheduled to meet Pam at three. If they were delayed much longer, she'd be late.

She scowled at Zach's apparent reluctance to entertain her in Gramp's absence. "Maybe it would be best if we rescheduled lunch for another day," she offered brightly. She wasn't any happier about the prospect of waiting in a restaurant, just the two of them, than he was. "Gramps is held up, I'm meeting Pam later, and you're obviously a busy man."

An uncomfortable silence followed her remark. "Is it your habit not to show up when your grandfather is expecting you?" he asked sharply.

Janine bristled. "Of course not." She swallowed the words to defend herself. Her suggestion hadn't been unreasonable and he had no right to insinuate that she was inconsiderate and rude.

"Then I suggest we meet your grandfather at the restaurant as he requested," he finished stiffly.

"By all means," she said, forcing a smile. She stood and reached for her coat, watching Zach from the corner of her eye. He didn't like her. The realization had a peculiar effect on Janine. She felt disappointed and a little sad. Zach hadn't said much, and actually there hadn't been time for a real conversation, but she'd sensed his attitude almost from the first. He thought of her as spoiled and frivolous, probably because he knew she didn't hold a responsible job and loved to travel. Part of her longed to explain that there were good reasons she'd chosen the life-style she had. But from the looks he was giving her, it would be a waste of breath to justify herself.

Besides, it was more important to maintain the peace, however strained, for Gramps's sake, Janine decided. She'd have enjoyed getting to know Zach, perhaps even becoming friends, but that didn't seem likely. It was unfortunate, really.

That morning, before Gramps had left the house, he'd been as excited as a little boy about their luncheon date. He'd come down the stairs whistling when he'd joined her for breakfast, his blue eyes sparkling. When she'd refused the use of the limousine, he'd spent the next fifteen minutes giving her detailed directions, as though she'd never driven in downtown Seattle.

Almost as an afterthought, he'd mentioned that he had a morning meeting with an important client. If he hadn't returned by the time she arrived, she was to go directly to Zach's office, introduce herself and wait for him there.

Shrugging into a raincoat, Zachary moved toward the door. "Are you ready?"

She nodded, burying her hands in her pockets.

Thankfully the restaurant her grandfather had chosen was close by. By tacit agreement, they began to walk the few short blocks, although Janine had trouble matching her stride with Zach's much longer one.

Struggling to keep up with him, Janine studied Zachary Thomas, trying to determine exactly what disturbed her about the man. His height was a good example. He wasn't tall—under six feet, she guessed—and since she was almost five-eight there wasn't more than a few inches' difference between them. Why, then, did he make her feel much shorter?

He must have sensed her scrutiny because he turned and glared at her. Janine offered him a feeble smile, and felt the color rise in her cheeks. Zach's quick dismissive glance did nothing to boost her ego. She wasn't vain, but Janine knew she was attractive. Over the years, plenty of men had told her so, including Brian, the man who'd broken her heart. But she could have warts on her nose for all the notice Zachary Thomas gave her.

If he found the bandanna dress disconcerting, then he was probably put off by her hairstyle as well. She wore it short, neatly trimmed in the back with extra-long bangs slanted across her forehead. For years Janine had worn her hair shoulder-length, parted in the middle. One afternoon a few weeks earlier, for no particular reason, she'd decided to have it cut. She was in the mood for something radical and the style she now sported seemed more appropriate to the pages of a fashion magazine. Pam had been crazy about the change, insisting she looked phenomenal. Janine wasn't convinced. Her one comfort was that, given time, the thick dark length would return.

Janine suspected Zach had characterized her as flamboyant, if not downright flashy. She in turn would describe him as austere and disciplined, perhaps solitary. Her grandfather saw all that, she knew, and a good deal more.

"Mr. Hartman is waiting for you," the maître d' informed them when they arrived at the plush waterfront restaurant. He led them across the thick carpet to a high semi-circular booth upholstered in blue velvet.

"Janine, Zach." Anton Hartman smiled broadly as they approached. The years had been good to her grandfather. His bearing was still straight and confident, though his hair had grown completely white. His deep blue eyes, only a little faded, were filled with warmth, and wisdom. "I apologize for the inconvenience."

"It wasn't any problem," Zach answered for both of them before Janine could respond—as if he'd expected her to complain!

Ignoring him, Janine removed her coat and kissed her grandfather's leathery cheek with affection.

"Janine," he began, then gasped. "Where did you ever get that...dress?"

"Do you like it?" She threw out her arms and whirled around once to give him the full effect. "I know it's a bit unconventional, but I didn't think you'd mind."

Gramps's gaze flickered to Zach, then back to her. "On anyone else it would be scandalous, but on you, my dear, it's a work of art."

"Honestly, Gramps," she said, laughing softly. "You never could lie very well." She slid into the booth next to her grandfather, forcing him into the center, between her and Zach. Gramps looked a bit disgruntled, but after her turbulent first encounter with Zach, she preferred to keep her distance from the man. For that matter, he didn't seem all that eager to be close to her, either.

She glanced at him and noted, almost smugly, that he was already studying the menu. No doubt he found ordinary conversation a waste of time. Janine reached for her own menu. She was famished. At breakfast, she'd only had time for coffee and a single piece of toast, and she had every intention of making up for it now.

When the waiter came to take their order, Janine asked for the seafood entrée and soup *and* salad. She'd decide about dessert later, she said. Once he'd left, Gramps leaned toward Zach. "Janine never has to worry about her weight." He made this sound as if it was a subject of profound and personal interest to them both. "Her grand-mother was the same way. How my Anna could eat, and she never gained an ounce. Janine's just like her."

"Gramps," Janine whispered under her breath. "I'm sure Zach couldn't care one way or the other how much I weigh."

"Nonsense," Gramps said and gently patted her hand. "I hope you two had the chance to introduce yourselves."

"Oh yes." Janine returned automatically.

"Your granddaughter is everything you claimed," Zachary said, but the inflection in his voice suggested something entirely different to Janine than it did to her grandfather. She guessed that to Anton, he seemed courteous and complimentary. But he was telling Janine he'd found her to be the spoiled darling he'd long suspected. He didn't openly dislike her, but he wasn't too impressed with her, either.

Unfortunately, that was probably due to more than just the dress and the lightbulb necklace.

Janine watched for her grandfather's reaction to Zach's words and she knew she was right when his gaze warmed and he nodded, ob-viously pleased by his partner's assessment. Zachary Thomas was clever, Janine had to grant him that much.

"How did the meeting with Anderson go?" Zach asked.

For a moment her grandfather stared at him blankly. "Oh, Ander-son... Fine, fine. Everything went just as I'd hoped." Then he cleared his throat and carefully spread the linen napkin across his lap. "As you both know," he said, "I've been wanting the two of you to meet for some time now. Janine is the joy of my life. She's kept me young and brought me much happiness over the years. I fear that, without her, I would have turned into a bitter old man."

His look was so full of tenderness that Janine had to lower her eyes and swallow back a rush of tears. Gramps had been her salvation too. He'd taken her in after the deaths of her parents, raised her with a gentle hand and loved her enough to allow her to be herself. It must have been difficult for him to have a six-year-old unexpectedly thrust into his life, but he'd never complained.

"My only son died far too young," Anton admitted slowly, painfully.

"I'm sorry," Zachary murmured.

The genuine compassion Janine heard in his voice surprised her. And it definitely pleased her. Zach's respect and affection for her grandfather won her immediate approval—even if the man didn't seem likely to ever feel anything so positive toward *her*.

"For many years I mourned the loss of my only child," Anton continued, his voice gaining strength. "I've worked all my life, built an empire that stretches across these fifty states, and in the process have become a wealthy man."

Janine studied her grandfather closely. He was rarely this serious. He wasn't one to list his accomplishments, and she wondered at his strange mood.

"When Zach brought his business into the area, I saw in him a rare gift, one that comes along seldom in life. It's said that there are men in this world who make things happen, those who watch things happen, and then those who wonder what happened. Zachary is a man who makes things happen. In many ways, the two of us are alike. That's one of the primary reasons I decided to approach him with a proposal to merge our companies."

"I'm honored that you should think so, sir."

"Sir," Anton repeated softly and chuckled. He raised his hand, motioning for the waiter. "You haven't called me that in six months, and there's no reason to start again now."

The waiter returned with a bottle of expensive French champagne. Soon glasses were poured and set before them.

"Now," Anton continued, "as I said earlier, I have the two people I love most in this world together with me for the first time, and I don't mind telling you, it feels good." He raised his glass. "To happiness."

"Happiness," Janine echoed, sipping her champagne. Her eyes met Zach's above the crystal flute and she saw a glint of admiration. If she were dining on it, she'd starve—to quote a favorite expression of her grandfather's—but it was just enough for her to know he would think kindly of her because of her love for Anton.

Her grandfather chuckled and whispered something in his native tongue, a German dialect from the old country. Over the years she'd picked up a smattering of the language, but when she'd repeated a few phrases to a college German professor, he'd barely recognized the words. Gramps paused and his gaze lingered on Janine, then went to Zach. Whatever Gramps was muttering appeared to please him. His blue eyes fairly twinkled with delight.

"And now," he said, setting his glass aside. "I have an important announcement to make."

He looked to Janine and his face softened with deep affection. "I feel as though I've been an impossible burden to you, child, what with running this company," he said thoughtfully. "Never in all my dreams did I expect to accumulate so much in a single lifetime. I realize I've stayed in the business far longer than I should. It's time for me to retire and do a little traveling."

"It's past time," Janine argued. For years, she'd been urging her grandfather to lessen his heavy work schedule. He'd often spoken of revisiting his birthplace and the surrounding countries. He talked at length of cousins and friends he'd left behind in the small German settlement in what was now part of the Soviet Union.

"This is where Zachary comes into the picture," Anton explained. "I know myself all too well. Full retirement would be impossible for me. If I stopped working, I'd shrivel up and die. That's just the way I am," he said simply.

Neither Janine nor Zachary disputed his words.

"I'll never be able to keep my fingers out of the business, yet I want to enjoy my travels. I couldn't do that if I was fretting about what was happening at the home office." He paused as if he expected one of them to contradict him. "I believe I've come upon a solution.

As of this afternoon, Zachary, I'm handing over the reins to you. You will assume my position as chairman of the board. I realize this is sooner than we discussed, but the time is right and I hope you'll agree.''

"But, Anton—"

"Gramps—"

Anton held up his hand. "I've thought about this long and hard," he said confidently. "I find Zach's honesty unquestionable, his loyalty certain and his intelligence keen. He's shrewd, perceptive and insightful. I know of no better man, and there's no better time."

Janine studied Zach, and she noted that he seemed uncomfortable with the praise. "Thank you," was all he said.

"A share of this company will belong to you someday, Janine," Anton said next. "Do you have any objections to this appointment?"

She opened her mouth, but nothing came out. Of course she approved. What else could she do? "Whatever you decide is fine with me."

Anton turned his attention to the other man. "Zachary do you accept?"

Although their acquaintance had been brief, Janine knew instinctively that it took a lot to fluster this man. But her grandfather had managed to do so.

Zachary continued to stare at him as though he couldn't quite believe what he was hearing. But when he spoke, his voice was well modulated, revealing little of his emotions. "I'm honored."

"For the next few months, we'll be working closely together, much as we have in the past, but with a difference. No longer will I be teaching you the ropes. I'll be giving them to you."

The first course of their luncheon order arrived, and to Janine's delight, the conversation flowed smoothly. Her grandfather made sure of that. He was jubilant and entertaining, witty and charming. It would have been impossible not to be affected by his good humor.

When they'd finished the meal, Zachary glanced at his watch, his look regretful. "I'm sorry to leave so soon, but I have an appointment."

Janine noted the time and took a last sip of her coffee. "I should be leaving, too.'' She reached for her purse and coat, then slid out of the booth, waiting for her grandfather to join her.

"If neither of you objects, I'm going to linger over my coffee,'' Anton said, nodding toward the steaming cup.

"Of course.'' Janine leaned over to kiss him goodbye.

Zachary walked out to the street with her. Before he left, he shook her hand. "It's been a pleasure, Miss Hartman.''

"You're sure?'' she teased, unable to stop herself.

"Yes.'' His eyes held hers and he bestowed on her what she suspected was a rare smile. She walked away feeling oddly excited about their meeting. Zach wasn't an easy person to know, but she had the impression that he was everything her grandfather claimed and more.

GRAMP'S MOOD remained cheerful when he arrived home later that evening. Janine was in the library sipping herbal tea with her feet tucked under her as she watched the local news.

Sitting down in the wingback leather chair next to her, Gramps crossed his legs and reached for one of his Havana cigars. Janine watched him light it and shook her head affectionately; she loved her grandfather dearly and wished he'd stop smoking, though she no longer bothered to express that wish. He was the kind of man who did exactly as he chose, got exactly what he wanted. He was obviously pleased with the way their luncheon had gone, and she wondered briefly if Zach had said anything about her afterward. Somehow she doubted it.

"Well,'' he said after a moment, "What do you think of Zachary Thomas?'' He blew a steady stream of smoke at the ceiling while he awaited her answer.

All afternoon, Janine had prepared herself for his question. Several complicated answers had presented themselves to her, clever replies that would sidestep her true feelings, but she used none of them now. Her grandfather expected the truth, and it was her duty to give it to him.

"I'm not exactly sure. He's not an easy man to know, is he?''

Anton chuckled. "No, he isn't, but I've never known you to walk away from a challenge. The boy's a little rough around the edges, but on the inside, he's pure gold.''

Janine hadn't thought of Zach in those terms—a challenge. Frankly, she doubted there would be much reason for her to have any future contact with him. Gramps and Zach would be working closely together, but she had little if anything to do with the business.

"I've earned his trust, but it took time," Gramps was saying now.

"I'm glad you've decided to retire," she said absently, half listening to the weather report.

"Zachary will change," her grandfather added.

He had her full attention now. "Gramps," she said patiently, holding in a laugh. "Why should he? He's achieved considerable financial success. Everything's looking good for him. What possible reason could there be for him to change?"

Before Anton answered, he stood and poured himself a liberal dose of brandy, swirling it slowly in the bottom of the snifter. "You're going to change him," he said after a thoughtful moment.

"Me?" Janine laughed outright. "I'm going to change Zachary Thomas?" she repeated in wide-eyed disbelief. That would be the day!

"Before you argue with me, and I can see that's what you're dying to do, I have a story I want to tell you. A rather sad one as it happens."

Janine picked up the remote control and snapped off the television. She'd often listened to grandfather's parables. "So tell me."

"It's about a boy, born on the wrong side of the tracks to an alcoholic father and a weak mother. He never had much of a chance in life. His father was abusive enough for the state to remove the lad and his younger sister from the home. He was barely eight and subjected to a long series of foster homes, but he refused to be separated from his sister. He'd promised her he'd always be there to take care of her.

"Once there wasn't any alternative and the two were placed in separate homes. Beside himself with worry for his sister, the young boy ran away. The authorities were in a panic, but three days later, he turned up two hundred miles away at the home where they'd placed Beth Ann.''

"He probably felt responsible for her."

"Yes. Which made matters much worse when she drowned in a swimming accident when he was twelve."

"Oh, no." A pain squeezed Janine's heart at the agony the boy had suffered at the death of his sister.

"He blamed himself, of course," Anton said softly.

"The poor kid."

"This lad never seemed to belong to anyone after that," Gramps continued, staring into his brandy. "He never quite fit in, but that wasn't entirely his fault." He paused to take another puff on his cigar. "His mother died a month after his sister. They were the only ones who had ever truly loved the boy. He lost contact with his father, which was probably for the best. So his family was gone and no one seemed to want this troubled, hurting youth."

"Did he turn into a juvenile delinquent?" It made sense to Janine that he would; she'd dealt with several troubled teenagers through her volunteer work and was familiar with tragic patterns that so often evolved, in cases like this.

"No, I can't say that he did." Gramps dismissed her question with a short shake of his head, more interested in continuing his tale than getting sidetracked by her questions. "He drifted through childhood without an anchor and without ever being allowed to enjoy those early formative years."

"Gramps—"

He raised his hand to stop her. "When this lad was eighteen, he joined the military. He did well, which isn't surprising, considering his intelligence and the fact that he held little regard for his own well being. There was no one to mourn if he died. Because of his courage, he advanced quickly, volunteering for the riskiest assignments. He traveled all over the world to some of the most dangerous political hot spots. His duties were often top secret. There's no telling how far he might have gone had he chosen to remain in the armed services, but for some reason, he resigned. No one understood why. I suspect he wanted to start his life over. This was when he opened a business-supply company. Within a year, he had my attention. His methods were aggressive and creative. I couldn't help admiring the way he handled himself and the company. Within five years, he'd become one of my most serious rivals. I saw a strength in him that age had stolen from me. We met. We talked. As a result of these talks we joined forces.''

"Obviously you're telling me about Zachary's life.''

Anton grinned and slowly sipped his brandy. "You discovered his remoteness quickly. I thought knowing all this would help you. Zach's never had the security that a caring home and family provide. He's never really experienced love, except what he shared with his sister, Beth Ann. His life has been a long progression of painful experiences. By sheer force of will, he's managed to overcome every obstacle placed in his path. I realize Zachary Thomas isn't going to win any Mr. Personality contests, but by heaven, he's earned my respect.''

Janine had rarely heard such emotion in her grandfather's voice. "Zach told you all this?''

Anton's quick burst of laughter echoed through the room. "You're joking, aren't you? Zach has never spoken of his past to me. I doubt that he has to anyone.''

"You had him investigated?''

Gramps puffed on his cigar before answering. "It was necessary, although I'd guessed early on that his life hadn't been a bed of roses.''

"It's all very sad, isn't it?''

"You're going to be very good for him, my dear.''

Janine blinked. "Me?''

"Yes, you. You're going to teach him to laugh and enjoy life. But most important, you're going to teach him love.''

She hesitated, uncertain of her grandfather's meaning. "I don't think I understand. I realize Zach and I will probably be seeing each other now and again since he's assuming your responsibilities with the company, but I don't see how I could have any great impact on his life.''

Gramps smiled, a slow lazy smile that curved up the corners of his mouth. "That's where you're wrong, my dear. You're going to play a very big role in Zach's life, and he in yours."

Janine was still confused. "Perhaps I missed something this afternoon. I thought you made Zach the chairman of the board."

"I did." A lazy swirl of smoke circled his white head.

"I don't understand where I come into the picture."

"I don't suppose you do," he said softly. "You see, Janine, I've chosen Zachary to be your husband."

CHAPTER TWO

FOR A STUNNED MOMENT, Janine said and did nothing. "You're teasing, aren't you, Gramps?"

"No," he said, lighting a second cigar. He paused to stare at the glowing tip, his eyes filled with mischief—and with something else, less easily defined. "I'm dead serious."

"But..." Janine's thoughts were so jumbled she couldn't make sense of them herself, let alone convey her feelings to her grandfather.

"I've been giving the matter serious consideration for some time now. Zach's perfect for you and you're the ideal complement to him. You're going to have beautiful blond-haired children."

"But..." Janine discovered she was absolutely speechless. One minute she was listening to a touching parable, and the next her grandfather was telling her about the husband he'd arranged for her and the color of her children's hair.

"Once you think about it," Gramps continued confidently, "I'm sure you'll agree with me. Zach is a fine young man, and he'll make you an excellent husband."

"You...Zach talked...agreed?" The words stumbled over the end of her tongue like toppling building blocks.

"Do you mean have I suggested this arrangement to Zach?" Gramps asked. "Heavens, no. At least not yet." He chuckled as if he found the mere thought amusing. "Zach wouldn't appreciate my blatant interference in his personal affairs. With him, I'll need to be far more subtle. To be honest, I considered making this marriage part of my handing over the chairmanship, but after thinking matters through, I changed my mind. Zach would never have agreed to it. There are other ways, I decided, better ways. But I don't want you to worry about it. That's between Zach and me."

"I...see." At this point, Janine wasn't sure *what* she saw, other than one determined old man caught between two worlds. In certain respects, the old ways continued to dominate his thinking, but his success in America allowed him to appreciate more modern outlooks.

Gramps inhaled deeply on his cigar, his blue eyes twinkling. "Now, I realize you probably find the idea of an arranged marriage slightly unorthodox, but you'll get used to it. I've made a fine choice for you, and I know you're smart enough to recognize that."

"Gramps, I don't think you fully understand what you're suggesting," she said, trying to gather her scattered thoughts, hoping to find a way of explaining the ridiculousness of this whole scheme without offending him.

"But I do, my child."

"In this country and in this age," she continued slowly, "men and women choose their own mates. We fall in love and then marry."

Gramps frowned. "Sadly, that doesn't work," he muttered.

"What do you mean, it doesn't work?" she cried, losing her patience. "It's been that way for years and years!"

"Look at the divorce rate. I read in the newspaper recently that almost fifty percent of all marriages in this country fail. In the old country, there was no divorce. Parents decided whom a son or daughter would marry, and their decision was accepted without question. First comes marriage, and then comes love."

"Gramps," Janine said softly, wanting to reason this out with him. Her grandfather was a logical man; surely if she explained it properly, he'd understand. "Things are done differently now. First comes love, then comes marriage."

"What do you young people know about love?"

"A good deal, as it happens," she returned, lying smoothly. Her first venture into the emotion had ended in a broken heart and a shattered ego, but Gramps knew little if anything about Brian.

"Pfft!" he spat. "What could you possibly know of love?"

"I realize," she said, thinking fast, "your father arranged your marriage to Grandma, but that was years ago, and in America such customs don't exist. You and I live here now, in the land of the free. The land of opportunity."

Gramps gazed down into his brandy for a long moment, lost in thought. Janine doubted he'd even heard her.

"I'll never forget the first time I saw my Anna," he said in a faraway voice that was haunting and gentle. "She was sixteen and her hair was long and blond and fell in braids all the way to her waist. My father spoke to her father and while they were talking, Anna and I sat at opposite ends of the room from each other, too shy to look at each other. I wondered if she thought I was handsome. To me, she was the most beautiful girl in the world. Even now, after all these years, I can remember how my heart beat with excitement when I first saw her. I knew—"

"But Gramps that was nearly sixty years ago! Marriages aren't decided by families any longer. A man and a woman discover each other without a father introducing them. Maybe the old ways were better back then, but it's simply not done like that anymore." Gramps continued to stare into his glass, lost in a world long since enveloped by the passage of time.

"The next day, Anna's parents visited our farm and again our two fathers spoke. I tried to pretend I wasn't concerned, determined to accept whatever our families decided. But when I saw our fathers shake hands and slap each other on the back, I knew Anna would soon be mine."

"You loved her before you were married, didn't you?" Janine asked softly, hoping to prove her point.

"No," he returned flatly, without hesitation, "How could I love her when I'd only seen her twice before the wedding ceremony? We hadn't said more than a handful of words to each other. Love wasn't necessary for us to find happiness. Love came later, after we arrived in America."

"Wasn't it unusual for a marriage to be arranged even then?" There had to be some point for her to contend, Janine mused.

"Perhaps in other parts of the world, but not in Vibiskgrad. We were a small farming community. Our world had been ravaged by war and hate. We clung to each other, holding on to our own traditions and rituals. Soon our lives became impossible and we were forced to flee our homes."

"As I said before, I can understand how an arranged marriage—back then—might be the best for everyone involved. But I can't see it working in this day and age. I'm sorry to disappoint you, Gramps, but I'm not willing to accept Zachary Thomas as my husband, and I'm sure he would be equally unwilling to marry me."

Briefly Gramps's face tensed with a rare display of disappointment and indignation, then quickly relaxed. Janine had seldom questioned his authority and had never openly defied him.

"I suppose this idea is a shock to you, isn't it?" he said.

If it astonished her, she couldn't wait to hear what Zachary Thomas thought! They'd only met once, but he hadn't disguised his opinion of her. He wouldn't take kindly to Gramps's plan of an arranged marriage—especially to a woman he viewed as spoiled and overindulged.

"All I'm asking is that you consider this, Janine," Gramps said, breaking into her thoughts. "Promise me you'll at least do that. Don't reject marriage to Zach simply because you consider it old-fashioned."

"Oh, Gramps..." Janine hated to refuse him anything. "It isn't just me. What about Zach? What about *his* plans? What if he—"

Gramps dismissed her questions with an abrupt shrug. "How often do I ask something of you?", he persisted.

Now he was going to use guilt. "Not often," she agreed, frowning at him for using unfair tactics.

"Then consider Zach for your husband!" His eyes brightened. "The two of you will have such beautiful children. A grandfather knows these things."

"I promise I'll think about it." But it wouldn't do any good! However, discretion was a virtue Janine was nurturing, and there had never been a better time than now to employ it.

GRAMPS DIDN'T MENTION Zach Thomas or even hint at the subject of her marrying his business partner again until the following evening. They'd just sat down to dinner, prepared to sample Mrs. McCormick's delicious fare, when Gramps looked anxiously at Janine. "So?" he asked breathlessly.

From the moment he'd walked into the house that afternoon, Gramps's mood had been light and humorous. He was grinning now as he handed her the platter of thinly sliced marinated and grilled flank steak. It happened to be one of Janine's favorite meals. "So?" he repeated, smiling at her. "What did you decide?"

Janine helped herself to a crisp dinner roll, taking her time buttering it while her thoughts chased each other in frantic circles. "Nothing."

His smile collapsed into a frown. "You promised me you'd consider marrying Zach. I gave you more time than Anna's father gave her."

"You have to know now?"

"Now!"

"But, Gramps, a simple yes or no doesn't answer something as complex as this. You're asking me to decide on a lifelong commitment in less than twenty-four hours." She was stalling for time, and Gramps had probably guessed as much. Frankly, she didn't know what to tell him. She couldn't, wouldn't, marry Zach—even if he was willing to marry her—but at the same time she hated disappointing her grandfather.

"What's so difficult? Either you marry him, or not."

"I don't understand why you've decided to match me up with Zach Thomas," she cried. "What's wrong with Peter?" She'd been dating the other man casually for the last few months. Her heart was too bruised after what had happened with Brian for her to consider dating anyone seriously.

"You're in love with that whitewashed weakling, that..."

Janine signed loudly, regretting the fact she'd introduced Peter into their conversation. "He's very nice."

"So is chocolate mousse!" Gramps muttered. "Peter Donahue would make you a terrible husband. I'm shocked you'd even consider marrying him."

"I hadn't actually thought about him in those terms," she clarified. Peter was witty and fun, but Gramps was right; they weren't suited as husband and wife.

"I thank the good Lord you've been given some sense."

Janine took a deep breath and finally asked a question that had been nagging at her all afternoon. "Did—did you arrange my father's marriage?"

Gramps lowered his eyes, but not before he could disguise the pain there. "No. He fell in love with Patrice while he was in college. I knew from the first that the match wasn't a good one, but Anna reminded me this was America and young people fell in love by themselves. She convinced me they didn't need a father's guiding hand the way we did in the old country."

"Do you think he would have listened if you'd wanted to arrange a marriage?"

Her grandfather hesitated, and his hand tightened on the water glass. "I don't know, but I'd like to think he would have."

"Instead he married my mother."

Neither spoke for a long moment. Janine remembered little of her parents, only bits and pieces of memories, mostly unconnected. What she did recall were terrible fights and accusations, a house filled with strife. She could remember hiding under her bed when the shouting started, pressing her hands to her ears. It was her father who used to find her, who comforted her. Always her father. Her memory included little of her mother. Even pictures didn't jar her recollection, although Janine had spent hour upon hour looking at the photographs, hoping to remember something. But the woman who had given birth to her had remained a stranger to her in life and in death.

"You're the only consolation I have from Steven's marriage," Anton said hoarsely. "At least Steven and Patrice gave you to me before they died."

"Oh, Gramps. I love you so much and I hate with everything that's in me to disappoint you, but I can't marry Zach and, frankly, I can't see him agreeing to marry me."

Her grandfather quieted after that, seeming to mull over her words as he finished his dinner. "I suppose I seem like a feeble old man, still trying to live in the old ways."

"Gramps, no, I don't think that at all."

He planted his elbows squarely on the table and linked his fingers, gazing at her. His brow was puckered in a contemplative frown.

"Perhaps it would help me understand if you told me what you want in a husband."

She hesitated, then glanced away, avoiding eye contact. Once she'd been so certain of what she wanted. "To be perfectly honest, I'm not sure. Romance, I suppose."

"Romance." Slowly Gramps rolled the word off his tongue as though it were an expensive delicately flavored wine.

"Yes," she said with a hard nod of her head, gaining confidence.

"And exactly what is romance?"

"Well..." Now that she'd been called upon to define it, Janine wasn't sure she could put that magical feeling into words. "It's an awareness that comes from the heart."

"The heart," her grandfather repeated, smacking his palm against his chest.

"Romance is the knowledge that a man would rather die than live his life without me," she said, warming to the subject.

"You want him to die?"

"No, just be willing."

Gramps frowned. "I don't think I understand."

"Romance is forbidden trysts on lonely Scottish moors," she added, thinking of an historical romance she'd read as a teenager.

"There aren't any moors in the Seattle area."

"Don't distract me," she said, smiling, her thoughts gaining momentum. "Romance is desperate passion."

"That sounds more like hormones to me."

"Gramps, please!"

"How can I understand when all you say is ridiculous things? You want romance. First you claim it's a feeling in the heart, then you say it's some kind of passion."

"It's more than that. It's walking hand in hand along the beach at twilight and gazing into each other's eyes. It's speaking of love without ever having to say the words." She paused, feeling a little foolish at getting so carried away. "I don't know that I can adequately describe it. I don't think anyone can."

"That's because you haven't experienced it."

"Maybe not," she agreed reluctantly. "But I will someday."

"With Zach," he said with complete assurance and a wide grin.

Janine didn't bother to argue anymore. Gramps was being obstinate and arguing with him was pointless. The only recourse she had was time itself. Soon enough he'd realize that neither she nor Zach was going to willingly fall in with his scheme. Then, and only then, would he drop the subject.

A WEEK PASSED and Gramps hadn't mentioned another word about arranging a marriage between her and Zachary Thomas. It was a cold windy March evening and the rain was coming down in torrents. Janine loved nights like this and was curled up in her favorite chair with a mystery novel when the doorbell chimed. Gramps had gone out for the evening and she wasn't expecting anyone.

She turned on the porch light, and looked out the peephole to discover Zach standing there, a briefcase clenched in his hand. His shoulders were hunched against the pelting rain.

"Zach," she said in surprise, throwing open the door.

"Hello, Janine," he said politely, stepping inside the house. "Is your grandfather here?"

"No." She pressed the novel against her chest, her heart pounding hard and fast. "He went out."

Zach frowned, clearly confused. "He asked me to stop by. There were some business matters he wanted to discuss. Did he say when he'd be returning home?"

"No, but I'm sure if he asked you over, then it'll be soon. Would you care to wait for him?"

"Please."

She took his raincoat and led him into the library where she'd been reading. A gentle fire was burning, and its warmth hugged the room. The three-story house, situated in Seattle's Mt. Baker district, was a typical turn-of-the-century home with high ceilings and spacious rooms. The third floor had once housed several servants. Charles was their only live-in help now, and his quarters had always been an apartment over the carriage house. He worked exclusively for Gramps, driving the limousine. Mrs. McCormick arrived early in the mornings and was responsible for the housekeeping chores and meal preparation.

"Can I get you something to drink?" she asked, once he was comfortably seated.

"Coffee, if you have it."

"I made a fresh pot about twenty minutes ago."

Janine brought him a cup from the kitchen, then sat across from Zach, wondering what, if anything, she should say about Gramps and his idea of an arranged marriage.

She doubted that Gramps had approached him yet. Otherwise he wouldn't be sitting there so calmly sipping coffee. If Gramps had broached the subject, she was convinced Zach wouldn't appear nearly so serene. He'd be outraged and infuriated, and studying him now, she concluded that he wasn't even slightly ruffled. It was on the tip of her tongue to warn him about what was coming, but she decided against it. Better that he learn of Gramps's plans the same way she had.

Lacing her fingers together, she smiled, feeling awkward and a little gauche. "It's nice to see you again."

"You, too. I'll admit I'm a bit disappointed, though."

"You are?"

"On the drive over, I was trying to guess what you might be wearing this time. A dress made from bread sacks? A blouse constructed out of men's socks?"

She muttered under her breath, miffed by his teasing tone. He had the uncanny ability to make her feel fifteen all over again. So much for any possibility that they'd ever be compatible. And Gramps seemed to think he knew them both so well.

"I'll admit that an Irish cable-knit sweater and wool slacks are a pleasant surprise," he said.

A flicker of admiration sparked in his dark eyes, something that had been sadly missing the first time they'd met.

In that instant, Janine knew.

She went stock-still, almost dizzy with the realization. Not only had Gramps approached Zach, but they'd apparently reached some sort of agreement. Otherwise Zach would never have been this friendly, this openly appreciative of her charms. Nor would he arrive unannounced when Gramps had specifically stated that he'd be gone for the evening.

They were obviously plotting against her. Well, she had no intention of putting up with it. None. If Zach and Gramps thought they could lure her into marriage, they had a real surprise coming.

Squaring her shoulders she slid to the edge of her chair. "So you gave in to the pressure," she muttered, shooting him a scalding look. Unable to stay seated, she stormed to her feet and started pacing, rubbing her palms together as she cornered her thoughts. "Gramps got to you, didn't he?"

"I beg your pardon?" Zach stared up at her, his eyes wide and curious.

"And you agreed?" She slapped her hands against the sides of her legs and groaned, "I don't believe it, I simply don't believe it. I thought better of you than this."

"What don't you believe?"

"Of all the men I've met over the years, I would have sworn you were the type who'd refuse to be bought. I'm disappointed in you, Zach."

He remained calm and unperturbed, which infuriated her more than anything he could have said or done.

"I haven't the slightest idea what you're talking about," was all he said.

"Oh, sure, play the innocent," she snapped. She was so incensed that she continued to pace in heavy hurried steps. Standing still was impossible.

In response, Zach merely glanced at his watch and drank his coffee. "Does your grandfather know you suffer from these bouts of hysteria?"

"Funny, Zach, very funny."

He exhaled an exaggerated sigh. "All right, I'll take the bait. What makes you think I've been bought? By the way, before I forget, what exactly am I getting in exchange."

"Technically you're not getting anything, and I want that understood this very minute, because I refuse to be sold." Arms akimbo, she turned to glare down at him with the full force of her disdain. "What did he offer you? The entire company? Vast sums of money?"

Zach shrugged. "He's offered me nothing."

"Nothing," she repeated slowly, feeling unreasonably insulted. "He was just going to *give* me away." The realization was enough to deflate the billowing sails of her pride. Stunned, she sat back down in her chair. "I thought the bride's family was supposed to supply some kind of dowry. Gramps didn't even offer you money?"

"Dowry?" Zach repeated the word as if he'd never heard it before.

"Gramps's family received a cow and ten chickens for my grandmother," she said, as if that would explain everything. "But apparently I'm not even worth a single hen."

Zach set his coffee aside and sat straight in his chair. "I think we'd better begin this conversation again. I'm afraid I lost you back there when you said something about my cracking under pressure. Perhaps you should enlighten me about what I'm supposed to have done that's so terrible."

Janine just glared at him.

"Humor me."

"All right, if you insist. It's obvious that Gramps talked to you about the marriage."

"Marriage," he repeated in a shocked voice. His face went blank. "To whom?"

"Me, of course."

Zach flung himself out of the chair, bolting to his feet. "To you?"

"Don't look so horrified! My ego's taken about all it can for one evening. I'm not exactly the Wicked Witch of the West, you know. Some men would be more than happy to marry me." Not Brian, and certainly not Peter, but she felt it was important that Zach think she was sought after.

"Marriage between us is…would be impossible. It's completely out of the question. I don't ever plan to marry—I have no use for a wife or family."

"Tell that to Gramps."

"I have every intention of doing exactly that." His face tightened and Janine guessed her grandfather was due for an earful once he arrived. "What makes that crazy old man think he can order people's lives around like this?" he asked angrily.

"His marriage was arranged for him and for his father before him. Trust me, Zach, I argued until I was exhausted, but Gramps hasn't given up his old-country beliefs and he thinks the two of us—now this is really ridiculous—are perfect for each other."

"If you weren't so serious, I'd find this highly amusing."

Janine noticed that he seemed rather pale. "I appear to have jumped to conclusions earlier. I apologize for that but, well, I thought...I assumed Gramps had spoken to you already and you'd agreed."

"Was that when you started mumbling something about a cow and a few chickens?"

She nodded and her long bangs fell over her eyes. Absently she pushed them aside. "For a moment there, I thought Gramps was offering me to you gratis. I know it's silly, but I felt downright insulted by that."

For the first time since they'd entered into this conversation, Zach's face softened enough to grant her a faint smile. "Your grandfather loves you, no question."

"I know." Feeling self-conscious, she threaded her fingers through her hair. "I've used every argument I could come up with to combat this insane idea of his. I explained the importance of romance and told him how vital it was for men and women to fall in love with the person of their own choice. Apparently he doesn't accept that times have changed."

"He wouldn't listen to you?"

"He listened," she replied, feeling defeated, "but he disputed everything I said. Gramps claims the modern version of love and marriage is a complete failure. With the divorce rate what it is, I'm afraid I don't have much of an argument."

"That's true enough," Zach said, looking frustrated.

"I explained that men and women fall in love and then decide to marry, but Gramps insists it's better if marriage comes first."

"Dear Lord." Zach rubbed a hand over his face. "Now that I

think about it, your grandfather has been introducing you into every conversation, telling me how wonderful you are.''

Janine gasped softly. ''He'd done the same to me about you, too, weeks before we even met.''

Pressing his lips together, Zach nodded. ''A lot of things are beginning to make sense.''

''What are we to do?'' Janine wondered aloud. ''I mean, it's perfectly obvious we're going to have to agree on a plan of action. I hate to disappoint Gramps, but at the same time I'm not willing to be married off like...like...'' Words failed her.

''Especially to me.''

Although his low words were devoid of emotion, Janine recognized the pain behind his statement. Knowing what she did about his past, the fact that he'd experienced only brief patches of love in his life and little or no approval tugged at her heart.

''I didn't mean it to sound like that,'' she insisted. ''My grandfather wouldn't have chosen you if he didn't think you were pretty special. He prides himself on his ability to judge character, and from the first, he's been impressed with you.''

''Let's not kid ourselves, Janine,'' Zach returned, his voice hardening. ''You're an uptown girl. We're about as suited as satin and burlap.''

''I agree with you there, but not for the reasons you think. From the minute I stepped into your office, you made it clear you thought of me as some kind of snob. I'm not, but I refuse to waste my breath arguing with you.''

''Fine.''

''Instead of hurling insults at each other,'' she suggested tightly, crossing her arms in a show of indignation, ''why don't we come up with a plan that will counter Gramps's preposterous idea?''

''That isn't necessary,'' he countered. ''I'm not willing.''

''And you think I am?''

Zach said nothing.

Janine expelled her breath with as much force as she could. ''It seems to me the perfect solution is for one of us to marry someone else. That would quickly put an end to this whole thing.''

"I already told you I have no intention of marrying," he said emphatically. "You're the one who insinuated you had plenty of men hanging around just waiting for you to say 'I do.'"

"None that I'd honestly consider marrying, for heaven's sake," she grumbled. "Besides, I'm not currently in love with anyone."

Zach laughed, if the sound that came from his throat could be called a laugh. "Then find a man who's current. If you fall in and out of love that easily, surely there's got to be at least one prospect on the horizon."

"There isn't. *You're* going to have to come up with someone! If you think you're such hot stuff, go out there and sweep some sweet young thing off her feet," she muttered sarcastically.

"I'm not willing to sacrifice my life so you can get off scot-free." His words were low and furious.

"But it's perfectly all right for *me* to sabotage mine. That makes a whole lot of sense."

"Okay," he said after a tense moment. He paused, raking one hand through his hair. "That idea's obviously not going to work. We'll have to come up with something better."

Janine gestured toward him. "It's your turn, bright boy."

He glared at her, seeming to dislike her even more. In all honesty, Janine wasn't too pleased with the way she was behaving, either. She'd been sarcastic and needlessly rude, but then, Zach had driven her to it. He could be the most unpleasant man.

Still Janine was about to say something conciliatory when the sound of the front door opening distracted her. Her gaze flew to Zach and he nodded, reassuring her he would handle this situation.

They returned to their chairs and were seated by the time Gramps appeared in the library doorway.

"Zach, I'm sorry for the delay. I'm pleased to see Janine entertained you." Her grandfather turned toward her with a bright smile as if to tell her he approved and hoped she'd taken advantage of this time alone with Zach.

"We did manage to have a stimulating conversation," Zach said, his eyes briefly linking with Janine's.

"Good. Good."

Zach stood and reached for his briefcase. "There were some figures you wanted to go over with me?"

"Yes." Looking pleased with himself, Gramps led the way out of the room. Zach followed him, with a glance back at Janine that said he'd get in touch with her later.

Later turned out to be almost a week. She'd been puttering around outside, trimming back the rosebushes and deciding where to plant the geraniums this year, when Mrs. McCormick came to tell her she was wanted on the phone.

"Hello," Janine said cheerfully.

"We need to talk," Zach said without preamble.

"Why?" she demanded. If he was going to keep her hanging for six anxious days, then she wasn't going to give the impression she was thrilled to hear from him.

"Your grandfather laid his cards on the table this afternoon. I thought you might be interested in hearing what he's offering me to take you off his hands."

CHAPTER THREE

"ALL RIGHT," Janine said, bracing herself. "What's he offering you? Huge bonuses?"

"No," Zach said quickly.

"Cash? I want to know exactly how much."

"He didn't offer me money."

Janine frowned. "What then?"

"I think we should meet and talk about it."

If her grandfather had openly approached Zach with the arranged-marriage idea, Janine knew darn well that Gramps would have made it worth Zach's while. Despite his impassioned claims to the contrary, it wouldn't have surprised Janine to discover that the newly appointed chairman of the board of Hartman-Thomas Business Supply had taken the bait.

"You want us to meet?" she repeated in a faltering voice.

"There's a good Italian restaurant on University Way—Italian 642. Have you heard of it?"

"No, but I'll find it."

"Good. Meet me there at seven." Zach paused, then added, "And listen, it might not be a good idea to let your grandfather know we're meeting. He might misunderstand our getting together."

"Right," Janine agreed.

Zach hesitated once more. "We have a lot to discuss."

Janine's heartbeat accelerated, and she felt the perspiration break out on her forehead. "Zach," she began, needing to know, "you haven't changed your mind, have you? I mean, you're not actually considering this ridiculous idea of his? You can't... We agreed, remember?" She swiped at her forehead with the back of her free hand as she waited for him to answer.

"You don't have anything to worry about," he finally said.

Replacing the telephone receiver, Janine had the sudden horrible sensation of being completely at her grandfather's mercy. He was an unshakably stubborn man who almost always got what he wanted through sheer determination. Faced with a mountain, Anton Hartman either climbed it, tunneled through it or forged a path around it; failing such active alternatives, he settled down in the foothills and waited for the mountain to dissolve. He claimed he won a majority of his battles by simply displaying patience. Janine called it not knowing when to pack up and go home.

She knew her grandfather's methods, but then so did Zach. But she hoped Anton's candidate for her husband would at least have the internal fortitude to withstand a few bribes, however tempting. Apparently he did, because he'd told her she had nothing to worry about. Yet on the other hand he sounded downright eager to discuss the subject with her.

"He *says* he never wants to marry," she muttered aloud in an effort to reassure herself. Indeed, Zachary Thomas was the last man Janine could imagine humming "The Wedding March"—especially when someone else was directing the band.

Janine was waiting in the library, coat draped over her arm, when her grandfather arrived home at six-thirty. He kissed her dutifully on the cheek and reached for the evening newspaper, scanning the headlines as he settled into his comfortable leather chair.

"Zach called," she said without thinking. She hadn't intended to mention that to Gramps.

Anton nodded. "I thought he might. You meeting him for dinner?"

"Dinner? Zach and me?" she squeaked. "No, of course not! Why would you even think I'd agree to a dinner date with…him?" Darn, how could she have nearly forgotten her promise to keep their meeting a secret? She detested lying to her grandfather, but there wasn't any help for it.

"But you are dining out?"

"Yes." She couldn't very well deny that, dressed as she was and carrying her coat.

"Then you're seeing Peter Donahue again?"

"No. Not exactly," Janine said uncomfortably, "I'm meeting a...friend."

"I see." The corners of Gramps's mouth quirked into a knowing smile.

Janine could feel the telltale heat saturating her face. She was a terrible liar, and always had been. Gramps knew as surely as if she'd spelled it out that she was meeting Zach. And when she told Zach she'd let it slip, he'd be furious with her, and rightly so.

"What did Zach want?"

"What makes you think he wanted anything?" Janine asked fervently. Her heart was thundering as she edged her way toward the door. The sooner she escaped, the better.

"You just said Zach phoned."

"Oh. Yes, he did, earlier, but it wasn't important. Something about...something." Brilliant! She rushed out of the house before Gramps could question her further. What a fool she was. Like a dunce she'd blurted out the very thing she'd wanted to keep secret.

By the time Janine located the Italian restaurant in the University district and found a parking place, she was ten minutes late.

Zach was sitting in a booth in the farthest corner of the room. He frowned when he saw her and glanced at his watch just so she'd know she'd kept him waiting.

Ignoring his disgruntled look, Janine slid onto the polished wooden bench, removed her coat and casually announced, "Gramps knows."

Zach's frown deepened. "What are you talking about."

"Gramps knows I'm having dinner with you," she explained. "I don't know what came over me. The minute he walked in the door, I told him you'd phoned—I just wasn't thinking—and when he asked why, I told him it had to do with *something*. I'm sure you'll be able to make up an excuse when he asks you later."

"I thought we agreed not to say anything about our meeting."

"I know," she said, feeling guiltier than ever. "But Gramps asked if I was going out with Peter and he just looked so smug when I told him I wasn't." At Zach's sudden movement, she burst out, "Well, what was I supposed to do?"

He grunted, which wasn't an answer one way or the other.

"If I wasn't going out with Peter, I'd have to come up with another man on the spot, and although I'm clever, I don't think that fast." She was breathless with frustration by the time she'd finished.

"Who's Peter?"

"This guy I've dated off and on for the past few months."

"And you're in love with him?"

"No, I'm not." Doubtless Zach would suggest she simply marry Peter and put an end to all this annoyance. Splendid idea.

Zach reached abruptly for the menu. "Let's order, and while we're eating we can go over what we need to discuss."

"All right," Janine agreed, grateful to leave the topic of her blunder. Besides, seven was later than she normally dined, and she was famished.

The waitress appeared then, and even as she filled Janine's water glass, her appreciative gaze never strayed from Zach. Once more Janine was struck by the knowledge that although he wasn't handsome in the traditional sense, he seemed to generate a good deal of female interest.

"I'll have the clam spaghetti," Janine said loudly, eyeing the attractive waitress, who seemed to be forgetting why she was there. The woman appeared far more interested in studying Zach than in taking their order.

"I'll have the same," Zach said, smiling briefly at the waitress as he handed her his menu. "Now, what were you saying?" he asked, returning his attention to Janine.

"As I recall, you were the one who insisted we meet. Just tell me what my grandfather said and be done with it." No doubt the offer had been generous; otherwise Zach wouldn't have suggested this dinner.

Zach's hand closed around the water glass. "Anton called me into his office to ask me a series of leading questions."

"Such as?"

Zach shrugged. "What I thought of you and—"

"How'd you answer him?"

Zach inhaled a deep breath. "I said I found you attractive, energetic, witty, a bit eccentric—"

"A bandanna dress and a string of Christmas tree lights doesn't make me eccentric," Janine insisted, her voice rising despite herself.

"If the Christmas tree lights are draped around your neck it does."

They were attracting attention, and after a few curious stares, Zach leaned closer and said, "If you're going to argue with everything I say, we'll be here all night."

"I'm sure our waitress would enjoy that," Janine snapped, then immediately regretted it. She sounded downright *jealous*—which, of course, was ridiculous.

"What are you talking about?"

"Never mind."

"Shall we return to the conversation between your grandfather and me?"

"Please," she said, properly chastised.

"Anton spent quite a long time telling me about your volunteer work at the Friendship Club and your various other community activities."

"No doubt his report was so glowing, I rank right up there with Joan of Arc and Florence Nightingale."

Zach grinned. "Something like that, but then he added that although you were constantly busy, he felt your life lacked contentment, purpose."

Janine could see it coming, as clearly as if she were standing on a track and a freight train was heading directly toward her. "Let me guess. He probably said I needed something more meaningful in my life—like a husband and children."

"Exactly." Zach nodded, his grin barely restrained. "In his opinion, marriage is the only thing that will fulfill you as woman."

Janine groaned and sagged against the back of her seat. It was worse than she thought. And to her chagrin, Zach actually looked amused by all this.

"You wouldn't look so smug if he claimed marriage was the only thing that would fulfill you as a *man*," she muttered. "Honestly, Zach, do I look like I'm wasting away from lack of purpose?" She gestured dramatically with her hands. "I'm happy, I'm busy...in fact

I'm completely delighted with my life.'' It wasn't until she'd finished that she realized she was clenching her teeth.

''Don't take it so personally.''

Janine rolled her eyes, wondering what his reaction would be if he were on the receiving end of this discussion.

''In case you didn't know it, your grandfather's a terrible chauvinist,'' he remarked, still smiling.

''Of course I know it, but he's so charming that it's easy to forgive him.''

Zach reached for his wineglass and gazed at it thoughtfully. ''What I can't figure out is why he's so keen on your marrying now. Why not last year? Or next year?''

''Heavens, I don't know. I suppose he thinks it's time. My biological clock's ticking away and the noise is probably keeping him awake nights. Heavens, by age twenty-four most of the women from the old country had four or five children.''

''He certainly seems intent on the idea of marrying you off soon.''

''Tell me about it!'' Janine cried. ''I'd bet cold cash that when he brought up the subject he insisted you were the only suitable man he'd found for me.''

''Anton also said you have a generous heart, and that he feared some fast-talker would show up one day and turn your head.''

''He said that?'' she asked weakly. Her heart plowed to a dead stop, then jolted to life again. Anton's scenario sounded exactly like her disastrous romance with Brian. She sighed deeply. ''So then he told you he wants me to marry someone he respects, someone he loves like a son. A man of discretion and wisdom and honor. A man he trusted enough to merge companies with.''

Zach arched his brows. ''You know your grandfather well.''

''I can just imagine what came next,'' Janine added scathingly and her stomach clenched at her grandfather's insidious cleverness. Zach wasn't someone who could be bought, at least not with offers of money or prestige. Instead, Gramps had used a far more subtle form of inducement. He'd addressed Zach's pride, complimented his achievements, flattered him. To hear Gramps tell it, Zachary Thomas was the only man alive capable of taking on the task of becoming Janine's husband.

"What did you tell him?" she asked, her voice so low it was a wonder Zach even heard her.

"No way."

Janine blinked back the surprise that was mingled with a fair amount of indignation. "Just like that? Couldn't you at least have mulled over the decision?" Zach was staring at her as though he thought someone should rush over and take her temperature. "Forget I said that," she muttered, fussing with her napkin in order to avoid meeting his eyes.

"I didn't want to give him any encouragement."

"That was wise." Janine picked up her water glass and downed half the contents.

"To your grandfather's credit, he seemed to accept my answer."

"Don't count on it," Janine warned.

"Don't worry, I know him, too. He isn't going to give up easily. That's the reason I suggested we meet and talk this out. If we keep in touch, we can anticipate Anton's strategy."

"Good idea."

Their salads arrived and Janine frowned when the waitress tossed Zach a suggestive glance. "So," she began in a conversational tone, once the woman had left the table, "Gramps was smart enough not to offer you a large incentive if you went along with his scheme."

"I didn't say that."

She stabbed viciously at her salad. "I hadn't expected him to stoop that low. Exactly what motivational tactics did he use?"

"Not many."

"So it seems," she hissed under her breath.

"He said something about family members having use of the limousine."

Janine's fork made a clanging sound as it hit the side of her salad bowl. "He offered to give you the limousine if you married me? That's all?"

"Not even that," Zach explained, doing a poor job of disguising his amusement, "only the *use* of it."

"Why...why, that's downright insulting." She crammed some salad into her mouth and chewed the crisp lettuce as though it were leather.

"I considered it a step above the cow and ten chickens you suggested the first time we discussed this."

"Fifty-five years ago a cow and ten chickens were worth a lot more than you seem to realize," Janine exclaimed, and immediately regretted raising her voice, because half the patrons in the restaurant turned to stare. She smiled blandly at those around her, then slouched forward over her salad.

She reached for a bread stick, she broke it in half and glared at the dry center. "The use of the limo," she repeated, indignant.

"Don't look so upset. I might have accepted."

Janine knew better. "You weren't even tempted. I assumed Gramps would at least make the offer an appealing one."

Zach was deriving far too much pleasure from this to suit her. "Your attitude isn't helping matters any," she said, frowning righteously.

"I apologize."

But he didn't look the least bit apologetic. When she'd first met Zach, Janine had assumed he was a man who rarely smiled, yet in the short time they'd spent together today, he'd barely been able to keep from laughing outright.

The waitress delivered their clam spaghetti, but when Janine took her first bite, she realized that even the pretense of eating was more than she could manage. She felt too wretched. Tears misted her eyes, which embarrassed her even more, although she struggled to hide the fact that she was upset.

"What's wrong?" Zach surprised her by asking.

Eyes averted, Janine shook her head, while she attempted to swallow. "Gramps believes I'm a poor judge of character." And she was. Brian had proved it to her, but Gramps didn't know anything about Brian. "I feel like a failure."

"He didn't mean any of it," Zach argued gently.

"But couldn't he have come up with something a little more flattering?"

"He needed an excuse to marry you off, otherwise his suggestion would have sounded crazy." Zach hesitated. "Come to think of it, the more we discuss this, the more ludicrous the whole thing seems." He chuckled softly and leaned forward to set his elbows on the table. "Who would ever have believed he'd come up with the idea of the two of us marrying?"

"Thank you very much," Janine muttered. He sat there shredding her ego and apparently found the process just short of hilarious.

"Don't let it get to you. It isn't as if you're interested in me as a husband, anyway."

"You're right about that—you're the last person I'd ever consider marrying," she lashed out, then regretted her reaction when she saw the way his face tightened.

"That's what I thought." He attacked his spaghetti as though the clams were scampering around his plate.

The tension between them mounted. When the waitress arrived to remove their plates, Janine realized she'd barely touched her meal. Zach hadn't eaten much, either.

After paying for their dinner, Zach walked her to her car, offering no further comment. As far as Janine was concerned, their meeting hadn't been the least bit productive. She felt certain that Zach was everything Gramps claimed—incisive, intelligent, intuitive. But that was at the office. As a potential husband and wife, they were completely ill-suited.

"Do you want me to keep in touch?" she asked when she'd unlocked her car door. They stood awkwardly together in the street, and Janine realized they hardly knew what to say to each other.

"I suppose we should, since neither of us is interested in falling in with this plan of his," Zach finally said. "The least we can do is set aside our differences and work together, otherwise we might unknowingly play into his hands."

"I won't be swayed and you won't be, either." Janine found the thought oddly disappointing.

"You don't have anything to worry about on my part," Zach informed her stiffly. "If and when I do marry, which I sincerely doubt, I'll choose my own bride."

It went without saying that Janine was nothing like the woman he'd want to spend his life with.

"If and when I marry, I'll choose my own husband," she said, sounding equally inflexible. As Zach had said not long before, they were as different as satin and burlap.

"I DON'T KNOW if I like boys or not," thirteen-year-old Pam Hudson admitted over a cheeseburger and French fries. "They can be such fools."

It had been a week since Janine's dinner with Zach, and it amazed her that the teenager's assessment of the opposite sex should so closely match her own.

"I'm not even sure I like Charlie anymore," Pam confessed as she stirred her catsup with a French fry. Idly she smeared the red sauce around the edges of the plate in a haphazard pattern. "I used to be so crazy about him, remember?"

Janine smiled indulgently and reminded her. "Every other word was Charlie this and Charlie that."

"He can be okay, though, you know? Remember when he brought me that long-stemmed rose and left it on my porch?"

"I remember." Janine's mind flashed to the first afternoon she'd met Zach. As they left the restaurant together, he'd smiled at her. It wasn't much as smiles went, but for some reason she didn't fully understand, she couldn't seem to forget how he'd held her gaze, his dark eyes gentle, as he murmured polite nonsense. Funny how little things about this man tended to pop up in her mind at the strangest moments.

"But last week," Pam continued, "Charlie was playing basketball with the guys, and when I walked by, he pretended he didn't even know me."

"That smarted, didn't it?"

"You bet it did," Pam confessed. "And after I tie-dyed a shirt for him, too."

"Does he wear it?"

A gratified smile lit the girl's eyes. "All the time."

"By the way, I like how you're combing your hair."

Pam beamed. "I wanted it to look more like yours."

Actually, the style suited Pam far better than it did her, Janine thought. The sides were cut close to the head, but the long bangs flopped with a life of their own, at least on Janine they did. Lately she'd taken to pinning them back.

"How are things at home?" Janine asked, watching the girl carefully. Pam's father, Jerry Hudson, was divorced and had custody of his daughter. Pam's mother worked on the East Coast. With no family in the area, Jerry worried that his daughter needed a woman's influence. He'd contacted the Friendship Club about the same time Janine had applied to be a volunteer. Since Jerry worked odd hours as a short-order cook, she'd met him only once. He was a decent sort, working hard to make a good life for himself and his daughter.

Pam was a marvelous kid, Janine mused, and she possessed exceptional creative talent. Even before her father could afford a sewing machine for her, Pam had been designing and making clothes for her Barbie dolls. The bandanna dress was one of the first projects Pam had completed on her new machine, and she'd proudly presented it to Janine. Pam had made several others since; they were popular with her friends, and she was ecstatic about the success of her ideas.

"I think I might forgive Charlie," the girl went on to say, her look contemplative. "I mean, he was with the guys and everything."

"I suppose it's not cool to let his friends know he's got a girl-friend?"

"Something like that."

Janine wasn't feeling nearly as forgiving toward Zach. He'd made such an issue of their keeping in touch, then hadn't called her once since. She didn't believe for an instant that Gramps had given up on his marriage campaign, but he'd apparently decided to let the matter rest. The pressure was off, yet Janine kept expecting some word from Zach. The least he could do was phone, she grumbled to herself, though she'd made no attempt to analyze the reasons for her disappointment.

"Maybe Charlie isn't so bad, after all," Pam murmured, then added wisely, "This is an awkward age for boys, especially in their relationships with girls."

"Say," Janine teased, "who's supposed to be the adult here, anyway? That's my line."

"Oh, sorry,"

Smiling, Janine stole a French fry from Pam's plate and popped it into her mouth.

"So when are you leaving for Scotland?" Pam wanted to know.

"Next week."

"How long are you going to be gone?"

"Ten days." The trip had come as a complete surprise—a gift from her grandfather. One night shortly after she'd met Zach for dinner, Gramps had handed her an airline ticket. When she'd asked why, his reply had been vague, even cryptic—something about her needing to get away. Since Janine had always dreamed of visiting Scotland, she'd leapt at the offer.

It wasn't until she'd driven Pam home that Janine thought she should let Zach know she was going to be out of the country. It probably wasn't important, but then, he'd made a point of saying they should keep in touch...

JANINE PLANNED HER VISIT to the office carefully, making sure Gramps would be occupied elsewhere. Since she'd been shopping for her trip, she was carrying several department and clothing store bags. She was doing this for a reason. She wanted her visit to appear unplanned, as if in the course of a busy day, she'd suddenly remembered their agreement.

"Hello," she said to Zach's efficient secretary, smiling cheerfully. "Is Mr. Thomas available? I'll only need a moment of his time."

The older woman clearly disapproved of this intrusion, but although she pursed her lips, she didn't verbalize her objection. She pushed the intercom button and Janine unexpectedly felt a tingle of awareness at the sound of Zach's strong masculine voice.

"This is a pleasant surprise," he said, standing as Janine breezed into the room with a flair a Paris model might have envied.

She set her bags on the floor and with an exaggerated sigh, eased herself into the chair opposite his desk and crossed her long legs.

"I'm sorry to drop in unannounced," she said casually, "but I have some news."

"It's no problem." His gaze fell to the bags heaped on the floor. "Looks like you've had a busy afternoon."

"I was shopping."

"So I see. Any special reason?"

"It's my trousseau." Melodramatically, she pressed the back of her hand against her forehead. "I can't take the pressure anymore. I've come to tell you I've told my grandfather to go ahead and arrange the wedding. Someday, somehow, we'll learn to love each other."

"This charade isn't the least bit amusing. Now what's so important that it can't—"

"Mr. Thomas," his secretary announced crisply over the intercom, "Mr. Hartman is here to see you."

Janine's eyes rounded in panic as her startled gaze flew to Zach, who looked equally alarmed. It would be the worst possible thing for Gramps to discover Janine alone with Zach in his office. She hated to think what interpretation he'd put on that.

"I'll just be a minute," Zach said, reading the hysteria in her eyes. She marveled at how composed he sounded. He pointed toward a closed door and ushered her into a small room—or a huge closet—that was practically a home away from home. A bar, refrigerator, small stove, sink and other conveniences were neatly arranged inside the compact area. No sooner was she inside than the door was slammed shut behind her. The room was in total darkness. A second later, the door was jerked open again, letting in a shaft of light, and three large shopping bags were tossed in.

Janine felt utterly ridiculous. She kept as still as she could, almost afraid to breathe for fear of being discovered.

With her ear pressed against the door, she tried to listen to the conversation, hoping to discover just how long Gramps intended to plant himself in Zach's office.

Unfortunately, she could barely hear a thing. She risked opening the door a crack; a quick glance revealed that both men were turned away from her, presenting her with a clear view of their backs. That explained why she couldn't decipher their conversation.

It was then Janine spotted her purse. Strangling a gasp, she eased the door shut and staggered away from it. She covered her mouth as she took a deep calming breath. When she found the courage to edge open the door and peek again, she saw that all her grandfather had to do was glance downward.

Sweet heaven, if he shuffled his feet, his shoe would catch the strap and he'd drag it out of the office with him.

Zach turned away from the window, and for the first time Janine could hear and see him clearly.

"I'll take care of that right away," he said evenly. He was so calm, so composed, as though he often kept women hidden in his closet. He must have spied Janine's purse because his eyes widened briefly and his gaze flew accusingly toward her.

Well, for heaven's sake, she hadn't purposely left it out there for Gramps to trip over! He wasn't even supposed to be in the building. That very morning, he'd told her he was lunching at the Athletic Club with his longtime friend, Burt Coleman. Whenever Gramps ate the noonday meal with his cronies, he ended up spending the afternoon playing pinochle. Apparently, he'd changed his habits, just so her hair would turn prematurely gray.

Several tortured minutes passed before Zach escorted Gramps to the door. The instant it was closed, Janine stepped into the office, blinking against the brightness after her wait in the dark. "My purse," she said in a strangled voice. "Do you think he saw it?"

"It would be a miracle if he didn't. Of all the stupid things to do."

"I didn't purposely leave it out here!"

"I'm not talking about that," Zach growled. "I'm referring to your coming here in the first place. Are you crazy?"

"I...had something to tell you and I was in the neighborhood." So much for her suave, sophisticated facade. Zach was right, of course; she could have told him just as easily by phone. But for some perverse reason, she'd wanted to tell him in person about her trip.

Zach looked furious. "For the life of me I can't think of a solitary thing that's so important you'd attempt anything this foolish. If your grandfather were to see the two of us together, he'd immediately jump to the wrong conclusion. Until this afternoon, everything's been peaceful. Anton hasn't once mentioned your name and, frankly, I appreciated that.''

His words stung. ''You're right, of course. I...I won't make the mistake of coming again—ever,'' she vowed, trying to sound digni-fied and aloof. She gathered her things as quickly as possible and hurried out of the office, not caring who saw her leave, including Gramps.

''Janine, you never did say why you came.'' Zach had followed her to the elevator.

Janine stared at the light above the elevator that indicated the floor number, as though it was a message of the utmost importance. Her hold on the bags was precarious, and something was dragging against her feet, but she couldn't have cared less. ''I'm sorry to have imposed on your valuable time. Now that I think about it, it wasn't even important.''

''Janine,'' he coaxed, apparently regretting his earlier outburst. ''I shouldn't have yelled.''

''Yes, I know,'' she said smoothly. The elevator opened and with as little ceremony as possible, she slipped inside. It wasn't until she was over the threshold that she realized her purse strap was tangled around her feet.

So much for a dignified exit.

CHAPTER FOUR

"THE CASTLE OF CAWDOR was built in the fifteenth century and to this day remains the seat of the earl of Cawdor," the tour guide intoned as Janine and several other sightseers viewed the famous landmark. "William Shakespeare used the castle in his play *Macbeth* for the slaying of King Duncan I, thane of Cawdor, in 1040."

For the first few days of Janine's visit to Scotland, she'd been content to explore on her own. The tours, however, helped fill in the bits and pieces of history she might otherwise have missed.

The castle of Cawdor was in northeastern Scotland. The following day, she planned to rent a car and take a meandering route toward Edinburgh, the political heart of Scotland. From what she'd read, Edinburgh Castle was an ancient fortress, built on a huge rock, that dominated the city's skyline. Gramps had booked reservations for her at an inn on the outskirts of town.

The Bonnie Inn, with its red-tiled roof and black-trimmed gables, had all the charm she'd expected, and more. Janine's room offered more character than comfort, but she felt its welcome as if she were visiting an old friend. A vase filled with fresh flowers and dainty jars of bath salts awaited her.

Eager to explore, she strolled outside and investigated the extensive garden. There was a chill in the April air and she tucked her hands in her pockets, watching with amusement as the partridges fed on the lush green lawn.

"Janine?"

At the sound of her name, she turned, and to her astonishment discovered Zach standing not more than ten feet away. "What are you doing here?" she demanded.

"Me? I was about to ask you the same question."

"I'm on vacation. Gramps gave me the trip as a gift."

"I'm here on business," Zach explained, and his brow tightened into a suspicious frown.

Janine was doing her own share of frowning. "This is all rather convenient, don't you think?"

Zach took immediate offense. "You don't honestly believe I planned this, do you?"

"No," she agreed reluctantly.

Zach continued to stand there, stiff and wary. "I had absolutely nothing to do with this," he stated.

"If you hadn't been so rude to me the last time we met," she felt obliged to inform him, with a righteous tilt to her chin, "you'd have known well in advance that Gramps was sending me here, and we could have avoided this unpleasant surprise."

"If you hadn't been in such an all-fired hurry to leave my office, you'd have discovered I was traveling here myself."

"Oh, that's perfect! Go ahead and blame me for everything," she shrieked, glowering at him. "As I recall you were madder than a wet hen at my being anywhere near your precious office."

"All right, I'll admit I might have handled the situation poorly," Zach said, and the muscles in his jaw hardened. "But as you'll recall, I did apologize."

"Sure you did," she said, "after you'd trampled all over my ego. I've never felt more of a fool in my life."

"You?" Zach shouted. "It may surprise you to know I don't make a habit of hiding women in my office."

"Do you think I enjoyed being stuffed in that...closet like a bag of dirty laundry?"

"What was I supposed to do? Hide you under my desk?"

"It might have been better than a pitch-black closet."

"If you're so keen on casting blame, let me remind you, I wasn't the one who left my purse in full view of your grandfather," Zach said. "I did everything but perform card tricks to draw his attention away from it."

"You make the entire episode sound like I'm the one at fault," Janine snapped.

"I'm not the one who popped in unexpectedly. If you had a job like everyone else…"

"If I had a job," she echoed, outraged. "You mean all the volunteer work I do doesn't count? Apparently the thirty hours a week I put in mean nothing. Sure I've got a degree. Sure I could probably have my pick of a dozen different jobs, but why take employment away from someone who really needs it when so many worthwhile organizations are hurting for volunteers?" She was breathless by the time she finished, and so angry she could feel the heat radiating from her face.

She refused to tolerate Zach's offensive insinuations any longer. From the first time they'd met, Zach had clearly viewed her as spoiled and frivolous, without a brain in her head. And it seemed that nothing had altered his opinion.

"Listen, I didn't mean—"

"It's obvious to me," she cut in bluntly, "that you and I are never going to agree on anything." She was so furious she could barely keep her anger in check. "The best thing for us to do is completely ignore one another. It is quite apparent that you don't want anything to do with me and, frankly, I feel the same way about you. So, good day, Mr. Thomas." With that she walked away, her head high and her pride intact.

For the very first time with this man, she'd been able to make a grand exit. It should have felt good. But it didn't.

An hour later, after Janine had taken the tourist bus into Edinburgh, she found she was still brooding over her latest encounter with Zachary Thomas. If there was any humor at all in this situation, it had to be the fact that her usually sage grandfather could possibly believe she and Zach were in any way suited to each other.

Determined to put the man out of her mind, Janine wandered down Princes Street, which was packed with shoppers, troupes of actors giving impromptu performances, and strolling musicians. Her mood couldn't help but be influenced by the festive flavor, and she soon found herself smiling despite the unpleasant confrontation with her grandfather's business partner.

Several of the men who passed her in the street were dressed in kilts and traditional woolen caps called Glengarries. Janine felt as if she'd stepped into another time, another world, as the air swirled with bagpipe music. The city itself seemed gray and gloomy, a dull background for the colorful sights and sounds, the excitement, of ages past.

It was as Janine walked out of a dress shop that she bumped into Zach a second time. He stopped, his eyes registering surprise and what looked to Janine like a hint of regret—as though confronting her twice in the same day was enough to try anyone's patience.

"I know what you're thinking," he said, pinning her with his dark intense gaze.

"And I'm equally confident that you don't." She gathered her packages close and edged against the shop window to avoid hindering other pedestrians on the crowded sidewalk.

"I came here to do some shopping," Zach said gruffly. "I wasn't following you."

"You can rest assured I wasn't traipsing after *you*."

"Fine," he said.

"Fine," she repeated.

But neither of them moved for several nerve-racking seconds. Janine assumed Zach was going to say something else. Perhaps she secretly hoped he would. If it was impossible for them to be friends, Janine would have preferred that they remain allies. They should be uniting their forces instead of battling each other. Without a word, Zach gestured abruptly and wheeled around to join the stream of people hurrying down the sidewalk.

A half hour later, with more packages added to her collection, Janine strolled into a fabric store, wanting to purchase a sizable length of wool as a gift for Pam. She ran her fingertips along several thick bolts of material, marveling at the bold color combinations. The wool felt soft, but when she lifted a corner with her palm, she was amazed at how heavy it was.

"Each clan has its own tartan," the white-haired lady in the shop explained. Janine enjoyed listening to her voice, with its enthusiastic warmth and distinct Scottish burr. "Some of the best-known tartans

come in three patterns that are to be worn for different occasions—
everyday, dress and battle.''

Intrigued, Janine watched as the congenial woman walked around
the table to remove a blue-and-green plaid. Janine had already seen
that pattern several times. The shop owner continued by explaining
that tourists were often interested in this particular tartan, called
Black Watch, because it was assigned to no particular clan. In choosing Black Watch, they weren't aligning themselves with any one clan,
but showing total impartiality.

Pleased, Janine purchased several yards of the fabric. She was
shuffling her packages in her arms as she made her way down the
narrow street when she caught sight of Zach watching a troupe of
musicians. She started to move away, then for no reason she could
name, paused to study him. Her view of him really hadn't changed
since that first afternoon. She still thought Zach Thomas opinionated,
unreasonable, and...all right, she was willing to admit it, attractive.
Very attractive, in a sort of rough-hewn way. He lacked the polish,
the superficial sophistication of a man like Brian, but he had a vigor
that seemed thoroughly masculine. He also had the uncanny ability
to set her teeth on edge with a single look. No other man could irritate
her so quickly.

The musicians began a lively song and Zach laughed unself-
consciously. His rich husky tenor sounded smooth and relaxed as it
drifted across the street toward her. Janine knew she should have
pulled away then, but she couldn't. Despite everything, she was intrigued.

Zach must have felt her scrutiny because he suddenly turned and
their eyes locked before Janine could withdraw her gaze. The color
rose to her cheeks and for a long moment, neither moved. Neither
smiled.

It was in Janine's mind to cross the street, swallow her pride, and
put an end to this pointless antagonism. In the past several weeks her
pride had become familiar fare; serving it up once more shouldn't be
all that difficult.

She was entertaining that thought when a bus drove past her belch-
ing a thick cloud of black smoke, momentarily blocking her view of

Zach. When the bus had passed, Janine noticed he'd returned his attention to the musicians.

Disheartened, she headed in the opposite direction. She hadn't gone more than a block when she heard him call her name.

She stopped and waited for him to join her. With an inquiring lift of an eyebrow, he reached for some of her packages. She nodded, repressing a shiver of excitement as his hand brushed hers. Shifting his burden, he slowed his steps to match Janine's. Then he spoke for the first time. "We need to talk."

"I don't see how we can. Every time you open your mouth you say something insulting and offensive."

Only moments earlier, Janine had been hoping to put an end to this foolishness, yet here she was provoking an argument, acting just as unreasonable as she accused him of being. She stopped midstep, disgusted with herself. "I shouldn't have said that. I don't know what it is about us, but we seem to have a difficult time being civil to each other."

"It might have something to do with the shock of finding one another here."

"Which brings up another subject," Janine added fervently. "If Gramps was going to arrange for us to meet, why send us both halfway around the world to do it?"

"I used to think I knew your grandfather," Zach murmured. "But lately, I'm beginning to wonder. I haven't a clue why he chose Scotland."

"He came to me with the airline ticket, reminding me it'd been almost a year since I'd traveled anywhere," Janine said. "He told me it was high time I took a vacation, that I needed to get away for a while. And I bought it hook, line and sinker."

"You?" Zach cried, shaking his head, clearly troubled. "Your grandfather sent me here on a wild-goose chase. Yes, there were contacts to make, but this was a trip any one of our junior executives could have handled. It wasn't until I arrived at the inn and found you booked there that I realized what he was up to."

"If we hadn't been so caught up with who was to blame for that fiasco at your office, we might have been able to prevent this. At least, we'd have realized what Gramps was doing.''

"Exactly," Zach said. "Forewarned is forearmed. Obviously, we've got to put aside our differences and stay in communication. That's the key. Communication.''

"Absolutely," Janine agreed, with a firm nod of her head.

"But finding ourselves thrown together at every opportunity is only going to lead to trouble.''

"I couldn't agree with you more.''

"The less time we spend together, the better." He paused when he noticed she was standing in front of the bus stop.

"If we allow Gramps to throw us together like this, it'll only encourage him. We've got to be very firm about this, before things get completely out of hand.''

"You're right." Without asking, he took the rest of the packages from her arms, adding them to the bags and parcels he already carried. "I rented a car. I don't suppose you'd accept a ride back to the inn?''

"Please." Janine was grateful for the offer. They'd started off badly, each willing to blame the other, but fortunately their relationship was beginning to improve. That pleased her. She'd much rather have Zachary for a friend than an enemy.

They spoke very little on the twenty-mile ride back to the Bonnie Inn. After an initial exchange of what sites they'd viewed and what they'd purchased, there didn't seem to be much more to say. They remained awkward and a little uneasy with each other. Battle-weary. And Janine was all too aware of how intimate the confines of the small rented car were. Her shoulder and her thigh were within scant inches of brushing against Zach, something she was determined to ignore.

The one time Janine chanced a look in his direction, she noticed how intent his features were, as if he were driving a difficult and dangerous course instead of a well-maintained road with only light traffic. His mouth was compressed, bracketed by deep grooves, and his dark eyes had narrowed. He glanced away from the road long enough for their eyes to meet. Janine smiled and quickly looked away, embarrassed that he'd caught her studying him so closely. She wished she could sort through her feelings, analyze all her contradictory emotions in a logical manner. She was attracted to Zach, but not in the same way she'd been attracted to Brian. Although Zach infuriated her, she admired him. Respected him. But he didn't send her senses whirling mindlessly, as Brian had. Then again, she didn't think of him as a brother, either. Her only conclusion was that her feelings for Zach were more confusing than ever.

After thanking him for the ride and collecting her parcels, she left Zach in the lobby and tiredly climbed the stairs to her room. She soaked in a hot scented bath, then changed into a blue-and-gold plaid kilt she'd bought that afternoon. With it, she wore a thin white sweater under her navy-blue blazer. She tied a navy scarf at her neck, pleased with the effect. A little blush, a dab of eye shadow and she was finished, by now more than ready for something to eat.

Zach was waiting to be seated in the dining room when she came downstairs. He wore a thick hand-knit sweater over black dress slacks and made such a virile sight she found it difficult not to stare.

The hostess greeted them both with a warm smile. "Dinner for two?"

Janine reacted first, flustered and a little embarrassed. "We're not together," she said quickly. "This gentleman was here before me." Anything else would be negating the agreement they'd made earlier.

Zach frowned as he followed the hostess to a table set against the wall, close to the massive stone fireplace. The hostess returned and directed Janine to a table against the same wall, so close to Zach that she could practically read the menu over his shoulder. She was reading her own menu when Zach spoke. "Don't you think we're both being a little silly?"

"Yes," she admitted. "But we agreed this afternoon that being thrown together like this could lead to trouble."

"I honestly don't think it would hurt either of us to have dinner together, do you?"

"No...I don't think it would." They'd spend the entire meal talking across the tables to each other, anyway.

He stood up, grinning. "May I join you?"

"Please." She couldn't help responding with a smile.

He pulled out the chair across from her, his gaze appreciative. "Those colors look good on you."

"Thanks." She had to admit he looked darkly vibrant—and wonderfully masculine—himself. She was about to return his compliment when it dawned on her how senselessly they were challenging fate.

"It's happening already," she whispered heatedly, leaning toward him in order not to be overheard.

"What?" Zach glanced around him as though he expected ghostly clansmen to emerge from behind the thick drapes.

"You're telling me how good I look in blue and I was about to tell you how nice you look and we're smiling at each other and forming a mutual admiration society. Before either of us will be able to figure out what happened, we'll be married."

"That's ridiculous."

"Sure, you say that now, but I can see real trouble here."

"Does this mean you want me to go back to my table and eat alone?"

"Of course not. I just think it would be best if we limited the compliments. All right?"

"I'll never say anything nice about you again."

Satisfied, Janine nodded. "Thank you."

"You might want to watch that, as well," he warned with a roguish grin. "If we're too formal and polite with each other, that could lead us straight to the jewelers. Before we know what's happening, we'll be choosing wedding bands."

Janine's lips quivered with a barely restrained smile. "I hadn't thought about that." They glanced at each other and before either could hold it in, they were laughing, attracting the attention of everyone in the dining room. As abruptly as they'd started, they stopped, burying their faces in the menus.

After they'd ordered, Janine shared her theory with Zach, a theory that had come to her on their drive back to the inn. "I think I know why Gramps arranged for us to meet here."

"I'm dying to hear this."

"Actually, I'm afraid I'm the one responsible." She slumped

against the shield-back chair and heaved a sigh of remorse. Every part of her seemed aware of Zach, which was exactly what she didn't want. She sighed again. "When Gramps first mentioned the idea of an arranged marriage, I tried to make him understand that love wasn't something one ordered like...like dinner from a menu. He genuinely didn't seem to grasp what I was saying and wanted to know what a woman needed to fall in love."

"And you told him a trip to Scotland?" Zach's eyes sparkled with the question.

"Of course not. I told him a woman needed romance."

Zach leaned forward. "I hate to appear dense, but I seem to have missed something."

Pretending to be annoyed with him, Janine explained, "Well, Gramps asked me to define romance..."

"I'd be interested in finding that out myself." Zach wiped the edges of his mouth with his napkin. Janine suspected he did it to cover a growing need to smile.

"It isn't all that easy to explain, you know," Janine said. "And remember this was off the top of my head. I told Gramps romance was forbidden trysts on Scottish moors."

"With an enemy clan chieftain?"

"No, with the man I loved."

"What else did you tell him?"

"I don't remember exactly. As I recall, I said something about a moonlight stroll on the beach, and desperate passion."

"I wonder how he'll arrange that?"

"I don't think I want to find out," Janine murmured. In light of how seriously Gramps had taken her impromptu definition, she almost dreaded the thought of what he might do next.

When they'd finished, their plates were removed by the attentive waiter and their coffee served. To complicate her feelings, she found she was a little sad their dinner was about to end.

They left the dining room, and Zach escorted her up the stairs. "Thank you for being willing to take a risk and share dinner with me," he said, his voice deadpan. "I enjoyed it, despite the, uh, danger."

"I did, too," Janine said softly. More than she cared to admit. Against her better judgment, her mind spun with possible ways to delay their parting, but she decided against each one, not wanting to tempt fate any more than she already had.

Zach walked her to her room, pausing outside her door. Janine found herself searching for the right words. She longed to tell him that she'd enjoyed spending the evening with him, talking and laughing together, but she didn't know how to say it without sounding like a woman in love.

Zach appeared to be having the same problem. He raised one hand as though to touch her face, then apparently changed his mind, dropping his hand abruptly. She felt strangely disappointed.

"Good night," he said curtly, stepping back.

"Good night," she echoed, turning to walk into her room. She closed the door and leaned against it, feeling unsettled but at a loss to understand why.

After ten restless minutes she ventured out again. The country garden was well lit, and a paved pathway led to rocky cliffs that fell off sharply. Even from where she stood, Janine could hear the sea roaring below. She could smell its salty tang, mixed with the scent of heath, a wild purple flower that bloomed in spring. Thrusting her hands into her blazer pockets, Janine strolled along a narrow path into the garden. The night air was cool and she had no intention of walking far, not more than a few hundred feet. She'd return in the morning when there was much more to be seen. Then she planned to walk as far as the cliffs with their buffeting winds.

The moon was full and so large it seemed to take up the entire sky, sending streaks of silvery light across the horizon. With her arms cradling her middle, she gazed up at it, certain she'd never felt more peaceful or serene. She closed her eyes, savoring the luxurious silence of the moment.

Suddenly it was broken. "So we meet again," Zach said from behind her.

"This is getting ridiculous." Janine turned to him and smiled, her heart beating hard and fast. "Meeting on the moors..."

"It isn't exactly a tryst," Zach said.

"Not technically."

They stood side by side, looking into the night sky, both at a loss for words. During their meal they'd talked nonstop, but now Janine felt tongue-tied and ill at ease. If they'd been worried about having dinner together, they were placing themselves at even greater risk alone in the moonlight.

Janine knew it. Zach knew it. But neither suggested leaving.

"It's a beautiful night," Zach said at last, linking his hands behind his back.

"It is, isn't it?" Janine replied brightly, as if he'd introduced the most stimulating topic of her entire vacation.

"I don't think we should put any stock in this," he surprised her by saying next.

"In what?"

"In meeting here, as if we'd arranged a tryst. Of course you're a beautiful woman and it would only be natural if a man...any red-blooded man were to find himself charmed. I'd blame it on the moonlight, wouldn't you?"

"Oh, I agree completely. I mean, we've been thrust together and it would only be natural if the two of us...were to find ourselves momentarily...attracted to each other. That would be normal, but it doesn't mean anything."

Zach moved behind her. "You're right, of course." He hesitated, then murmured, "You should have worn a thicker jacket." Before she could assure him she was perfectly comfortable, he ran his hands slowly down the length of her arms, as though to warm her. Unable to restrain herself, Janine sighed softly and leaned against him, soaking up his warmth and his strength.

"This presents something of a problem, doesn't it?" he whispered, his voice husky and close to her ear. "Isn't moonlight supposed to do something strange to people?"

"I...think it only affects werewolves."

He chuckled and his breath shot a series of incredible light-as-air sensations along her neck. Janine felt she was about to crumple at his feet. Then his chin brushed the side of her face and she sighed once more, delighting in the baffling exciting feel of him.

His hands on her shoulders, Zach urged her around so that she faced him, but not for anything would Janine allow her gaze to meet his.

He didn't say anything.

She didn't, either.

Janine suffered a series of mixed worries, afraid to voice even one. Zach apparently felt the same way, because he didn't seem any more eager to explain things than she did. Or to stop them....

After a moment, Zach pressed his hands over her cheekbones. Leisurely, his thumbs stroked the line of her jaw, her chin. His eyes were dark, his expression unreadable. Janine's heart was churning over and over, dragging her emotions with it. She swallowed tightly, then moistened her lips.

He seemed to find her mouth mesmerizing, and focused his gaze there. From somewhere deep inside her, she found the strength to warn him that her grandfather's plan was working. She opened her mouth to speak, but before she could utter a single word, Zach's arms came around her and drew her close against his strongly muscled body. She felt his comforting warmth seep through her, smelled the faint muskiness of his skin. The sensations were unlike anything she'd ever experienced. Then he lowered his mouth to hers.

The immediate shock of pleasure the contact sent through her was almost frightening. She couldn't keep from trembling.

He drew back slightly. "You're cold. You should have said something."

"No, that's not it." Even her voice was quivering.

"Then what is?"

In response she kissed him back. She hadn't meant to, but before she could stop herself, she wove her arms around his neck and slanted her mouth over his. She was immersing herself in his strength, just as he was immersing himself in her tenderness.

Zach's shoulders were heaving when at last she pulled her mouth away and pressed her face against his chest.

"Dear Lord," he whispered. He hastily broke away from her as if he'd suddenly realized what they were doing.

Janine was too stunned to react. In an effort to hide his effect on her, she rubbed her hands over her face as though struggling to wake up from a deep sleep.

"That shouldn't have happened," Zach said stiffly.

"You're telling me," she returned raggedly. "It certainly wasn't the smartest move we could have made."

Zach jerked his fingers roughly through his hair and frowned. "I don't know what came over me. Over us. We both know better."

"It probably has something to do with the moon and the fact that we're both tired," Janine said soothingly, offering a convenient excuse. "When you stop to think about it, the whole thing's perfectly understandable. Gramps arranged this meeting, hoping something like this would happen. Clearly the power of suggestion is stronger than either of us realized."

"Clearly." But he continued to frown.

"Oh, gee," Janine said glancing at her watch, unable to read the numbers in the dark. Her voice was high and wavering. "Will you look at the time? I can't believe it's so late. I really should be getting back inside."

"Janine, listen. I think we should talk about this."

"Sure, but not now." All she wanted to do was escape and gather some perspective on what had happened. It had all started so innocently, almost a game, but quickly turned into something far more serious.

"All right, we'll discuss it in the morning." Zach didn't sound too pleased. He walked through the garden with her, muttering under his breath. "Damn it!" he roared, again shoving his fingers through his hair. "Damn it, I knew I should never have come out here."

"There's no need to be so angry. Blame this crisp clean air. It obviously disrupts the brain and interferes with the wave patterns or something."

"Right," Zach said, his voice still gruff.

"Well, good night," Janine managed cheerfully when they reached the staircase.

"Good night," Zach returned, his tone equally nonchalant.

Once Janine was in her room, she threw herself on the bed and covered her eyes with one hand. Oh, no, she lamented silently.

They'd crossed the line. Tempted fate. Spit in the eye of common sense.

They'd kissed.

Several minutes later, still shaking, Janine got up and undressed. She slid under the blankets and tried to find a relaxing position. But she didn't feel the least bit like sleeping. Tomorrow she'd have to make polite conversation with Zach and she didn't know if she could bear it. She was sure he'd feel just as uncomfortable with her. She'd noted how he could barely look at her when they entered the inn.

Tossing aside the blankets, Janine decided there was only one option left. She had to leave Scotland, and the sooner the better. Reaching for the phone, she called the airport, booked a seat on the earliest flight home and immediately set about packing her bags.

Not bothering to even try to sleep, she crept down the stairs a little before midnight and checked out of the inn.

"You're leaving sooner than you anticipated, aren't you, Miss Hartman?" the night manager asked, after calling for a cab.

"Yes," she said.

"I hope everything was satisfactory?"

"It was wonderful." She pulled a folded piece of paper from her purse and placed it on the counter. "Would you see to it that Mr. Thomas receives this in the morning?"

"Of course." The young man tucked it in a small cubbyhole behind him.

Satisfied that Zach would know she was leaving and wouldn't be concerned by her hurried return to Seattle, she turned away from the desk and sat in a chair in the small lobby to wait for the cab.

About fifteen minutes later, Janine watched silently as the cabdriver stowed her luggage in the trunk. She paused before climbing into the back seat of the car and glanced one last time at the muted moonlit landscape, disappointed that she wouldn't have an opportunity to visit the cliffs.

The ride to the airport seemed to take an eternity. She felt a burning sense of regret at leaving Scotland. She'd fallen in love with the country during her short visit and hoped someday to return. Although the memory of her evening stroll through the garden would always bring with it a certain chagrin, she couldn't completely regret that time with Zach. In fact, she would always remember the contentment she'd experienced in his arms. She wasn't foolish enough to give it any credence, however.

Janine arrived at the airport several hours before her flight was scheduled to leave. She spent the time drinking coffee and glancing through fashion magazines, several of which she tucked in her luggage to give to Pam later.

Carrying a cup of coffee in one hand, she approached the airline counter with her ticket in the other. By accident, the bag she had draped over her shoulder collided with the man standing next to her. An automatic apology formed on her lips, but before she could voice it, that same man turned to face her.

"Zach," she cried, nearly dropping her coffee in shock. "What are you doing here?"

CHAPTER FIVE

"YOU THINK this is intentional, don't you?" Zach demanded. "It's obvious you're the one traipsing after me this time. You found the note I slipped under your door and—"

"I checked out just before midnight so I couldn't possibly have read your note," she returned stiffly. She noticed that he didn't mention the message she'd left for him at the front desk. "And furthermore I left word for you."

"I didn't get it."

"Then there's been a misunderstanding."

"To say the least," Zach muttered. "A misunderstanding..." His tone was doubtful, as if he suspected she'd purposely arranged to fly home with him. A sense of righteous indignation filled her, and she launched into a heated protest.

"Excuse me, please."

The interruption was from a uniformed airline employee who was leaning over the counter and waving in an effort to gain their attention.

"May I have your ticket?" she asked Janine. "You're holding up the line."

"Of course. I'm sorry." The best thing to do, she decided, was to ignore Zach completely. Just because they were booked on the same flight home didn't mean they had to have anything to do with each other. Evidently they'd both panicked after their encounter in the garden. He was as eager to escape as she was.

Okay, so she'd ignore him and he'd ignore her. She'd return to her life, and he'd return to his. From this point forward, they need never have contact with each other again. Then they'd both be satisfied.

The clerk took the ticket from Janine and punched several numbers into her computer. "I'll give you your seat assignment now," she remarked, concentrating on the screen.

Standing on tiptoe, Janine leaned toward the woman and lowered her voice to a whisper. "Could you make sure I'm as far removed from Mr. Thomas's seat as possible?"

"Miss," the attendant said impatiently, "this flight is booked solid and has been for weeks. The only reason we were able to give you and your...friend seats was because of a last-minute cancellation. I'll do the best I can, but I can't rearrange everyone's seat assignments just before the flight."

"I understand," Janine said, feeling foolish and petty. But the way her luck had been running, Zach would end up sitting in the seat beside her, believing she'd purposely arranged that, too.

They boarded the flight separately; in fact, Zach was one of the last passengers to step onto the plane.

By that time, Janine was settled in the second row of the first-class section, flipping through the pages of the flight magazine. Zach strolled past her, intent on the ticket clenched tightly in his hand.

Pretending she hadn't seen him seemed the best tactic, and she turned to gaze out the window.

"It seems I've been assigned to sit here," Zach announced brusquely, loading his carry-on luggage in the compartment above the seats.

Janine had to bite her tongue to keep from insisting she'd had nothing to do with that. She'd even tried to prevent it, but she doubted Zach would have believed her.

"Before you claim otherwise, I want you to know I didn't arrange this," he said, sitting down stiffly beside her.

"I know that."

"You do?"

"Of course," Janine confirmed. "The fates are against us. I don't know how my grandfather arranged our meeting at the airport or the adjoining seats, any more than I know why I stumbled on you my first day at the Bonnie Inn. We might never have crossed paths. But somehow, some way, Gramps is responsible." She thought it best not to mention their stroll in the moonlight. If it was important to lay blame for that, she'd accept it.

"So you're not ready to unleash the full force of your anger on me?"

"I don't see how I can be upset with you—or the reverse. Neither of us asked for this."

"Exactly."

Janine yawned loudly and covered her mouth. "Oh, excuse me. I didn't sleep last night and now it's catching up with me."

Her yawn was contagous and soon Zach's hand was warding off his own admission of drowsiness. The flight attendant came by with coffee, which both Zach and Janine declined.

"Frankly, I'd be more interested in a pillow," Janine said yawning again. The attendant handed her one, a thick blanket and a couple of small pillows, then offered the same to Zach. He refused both, intending to work on some papers he'd withdrawn from his briefcase. The minute the plane was safely in the air, Janine laid her head back and closed her eyes. Almost immediately she felt herself drifting into a peaceful slumber.

She stirred twice in the long hours that followed, but both times a gentle voice soothed her back to sleep. Sighing, she snuggled into the warmth, feeling more comfortable than she had in weeks.

She began to dream and could see herself walking across the moors, wearing traditional Scottish dress, while bagpipes wailed in the background.

Then, on the crest of a hill, Zach appeared, lavishly dressed in a Black Watch kilt and tam-o'-shanter; a set of bagpipes was draped over his shoulder. Their eyes met and the music ceased. Then out of nowhere her grandfather appeared, standing halfway between the two of them, looking pleased and excited. He cupped his hands over his mouth and shouted to Janine.

"Is this romance?"

"Yes," she shouted back.

"What else do you need?"

"Love."

"Love," Gramps repeated, frowning. He turned to Zach, apparently seeking some kind of assistance.

Zach started fiddling with the bagpipes, avoiding the question. He scowled as he concentrated on his task.

"Look at the pair of you," Gramps called. "You're perfect together. Zach, when are you going to wake up and realize what a beauty my Janine is?"

"If I do marry, you can be sure I'll choose my own bride." Zach hollered.

"You!" Janine shouted back. "I'd prefer to pick out my own husband!"

"You're falling in love with Zach!" Gramps declared, elated.

"I—I—" Janine was so flustered she couldn't complete her thought, which only served to please her grandfather more.

"Look at her, boy," Gramps directed his attention back to Zach. "See how lovely she is. And think of what beautiful children you'll have."

"Gramps! Enough about our beautiful babies! I'm not marrying Zach!"

"Janine." Zach's voice echoed in her ear.

"Keep out of this," she cried. He was the last person she wanted to hear from.

"You're having a dream."

Her eyes fluttered open to discover Zach's face unbelievably close to her own and her head nestled against his chest. "Oh..." she mumbled, bolting upright. "Oh, dear...I am sorry. I didn't realize I was leaning on you."

"I hated to wake you, but you seemed to be having a nightmare."

She blinked against the lights and tried to focus her attention on him, but it was difficult, and to complicate matters her eyes started to water. She wiped her face with one sleeve, then straightening, she removed the pillows from behind her back and folded the blanket, doing her best to disguise how badly her hands were trembling.

"You're worried about what happened after dinner last night, aren't you?"

Janine released a pent-up breath, and smiled at him brightly as she lied. "Nothing really happened."

"In the garden, when we kissed. Listen," Zach said in a low voice, glancing quickly around to ensure that no one could overhear their conversation, "I think it's time we talked this out."

"I... You're right, of course." She didn't feel up to this, but she supposed it was best dealt with before she had to face her grandfather.

"Egos aside."

"By all means," Janine agreed. She braced herself, not knowing what to expect. Zach had made his views on the idea of an arranged marriage plain from the first; for that matter so had she. Brian had taught her a valuable lesson, a painful lesson, one that wouldn't easily be forgotten. She'd given him her heart and her trust, and he'd betrayed both. Falling in love had been the most shattering experience of her life, and she had no intention of repeating it any time soon.

"I'd be a liar if I didn't admit how pleasant kissing you was," Zach said, "but I wish it had never happened. It created more problems than it solved."

Janine wasn't exactly flattered by his admission. Keeping egos out of this was harder than it sounded, she thought ruefully. Her face must have spelled out her thoughts because Zach elaborated. "Before I arrived in Scotland, we barely knew each other. We met that first afternoon over lunch—with Anton—and talked a couple of times, but basically we remained strangers."

"We had dinner one night," Janine reminded him, irked he could so casually dismiss that evening.

"Right," he acknowledged. "Then we met at the Bonnie Inn and, bingo, we were having dinner together and strolling in the moonlight, and before either of us quite knew how it happened, we were kissing."

Janine nodded, listening quietly.

"There are several factors we can take into account, but if we were going to place blame for that kiss, I'm afraid I'm the one at fault."

"You?"

"Me," he confirmed with a grimace. "Actually, I'm prepared to accept full responsibility. I doubt you were aware of what was happening. It didn't take me long to realize you're completely innocent—''

"Now just a minute," Janine snapped. Once more he was taking potshots at her dignity. "What do you mean by that?"

"It's obvious you haven't had a lot of sexual experience and—"

"In other words I'm so incredibly naive that I couldn't possibly be held accountable for a few kisses in the moonlight?"

"Something like that."

"Oh, brother," she muttered.

"There's no need to feel offended."

"I wasn't exactly raised in a convent school, you know. And for your information, I've been kissed by more than one man."

"I'm sure you have. We're getting sidetracked here—"

"I'm sorry you found me so inept. A man of your vast worldly experience must have been sorely disappointed by someone as unsophisticated and artless as me, and—"

"Janine," he said firmly, stopping her. "You're putting words in my mouth. All I was saying is that we—*I*—let matters get out of hand and we can't blame your grandfather for what happened."

"I'm willing to accept my part in this. I can also see where this conversation is leading."

"Good," Zach said. It was clear his composure was slipping. "You tell me."

"You think that because I enjoyed spending time with you and we shared this mildly romantic evening and—"

"Mildly romantic?"

"Yes, you did say egos aside, didn't you? I'm just being honest."

"Fine," he said, tight-lipped.

"Now you seem to think that because you have so much more experience than I do, there's a real danger I'd swoon at your feet if we repeated the experience." She rested her hand over her heart in melodramatic fashion and batted her eyelashes furiously.

"Janine, you're behaving like a child," he informed her coldly.

"Of course I am. That's exactly what you seem to expect of me."

Zach's fingers tightened on the armrest. "You're purposely misconstruing everything I said."

"Frankly, whatever you're trying to say isn't necessary. You're thinking that we had a borderline interest in each other and now we've crossed that border. Right? Well, I'm telling you that you needn't concern yourself." She sucked in a deep breath and glared at him. "I'm right, aren't I? That's what you think, isn't it?"

"Something like that, yes."

Janine nodded grimly. "And now you think because you've held me in your arms and you lost your control long enough to kiss me, I'm suddenly going to start entertaining thoughts of the M word."

"The M word?"

"Marriage."

"That's ridiculous," Zach said, forcefully returning the flight magazine to the seat pocket in front of him.

"Well?" she demanded.

"I think the temptation might be there and we should both beware of that type of thought."

"Oh, honestly, Zach," she said sarcastically, "you overestimate yourself."

"Listen, I wasn't the one mumbling something about our having beautiful babies. We kiss, and the next thing I know you're studying diaper-folding techniques."

"I was having a dream! That has absolutely nothing to do with what we're talking about now."

"You could've fooled me." He reached for the same magazine he'd recently rejected and turned the pages hard enough to rip them in two. "I don't think this discussion is getting us anywhere."

Janine sighed. "You were right, though. We did need to clear the air."

Zach made a gruff indistinguishable reply.

"I promise to do my best to keep out of your magnetic force field, but if I occasionally succumb to your overwhelming charm and forget myself, I can only beg your forgiveness."

"Enough, Janine."

He looked so annoyed with her that she couldn't help smiling. Zach

Thomas was a man of such colossal ego it would serve him right if she pretended to faint every time he glanced in her direction. The image filled her mind with laughter.

Zach leaned his head back and closed his eyes, effectively concluding their conversation. Janine gazed out the window at the first signs of sunrise, thinking about all kinds of things—except her chaotic feelings for the man beside her.

After what seemed a lifetime, the pilot announced that the plane would soon be approaching Seattle-Tacoma International Airport. Home sounded good to Janine, although she fully intended to have a heart-to-heart talk with her grandfather about his matchmaking efforts.

Once they'd landed, she cleared customs quickly. She struggled with her two large pieces of luggage, pulling one by the handle and looping the long strap of the second over her shoulder. Zach was still dealing with the customs agent when she maneuvered her way outside into the bright morning sunlight, intending to flag down a cab.

"Here," Zach said, joining her, "I'll carry one of those for you." He'd managed to travel with only his briefcase and one garment bag, which was neatly folded and easily handled.

"Thank you," she said breathlessly.

"I thought we'd agreed to limit our expressions of gratitude toward each other," he grumbled, frowning as he lifted the suitcase.

"I apologize. It slipped my mind."

Zach continued to grumble. "What'd you pack in here, anyway? Bricks?"

"If you're going to complain, I'll carry it myself."

He muttered something she couldn't hear and shook his head. "I'll get us a cab."

"Us?"

"We're going to confront your grandfather."

"Together? Now?" She was exhausted, mentally and physically. They both were.

"The sooner the better, don't you think?"

The problem was, Janine hadn't given much thought to what she was going to say. She fully intended to challenge Gramps but she'd planned to wait for the most opportune time. And she'd hoped to speak to him privately. "He might not even be home," she argued, "and if he is, I don't know if now would really be best."

"I want this matter settled once and for all."

"So do I," she said vehemently. "But I think we should choose when and how we do this a little more carefully, don't you?"

"Perhaps..." His agreement seemed hesitant, even grudging. "All right, we'll do it your way."

"It isn't my way. It just makes sense to organize our thoughts first. Trust me, Zach, I want this thing cleared up as badly as you do."

His reply was little more than a grunt, but whether it was a comment on the weight of her suitcase or her tactics in dealing with Anton, she didn't know.

"And furthermore," she said, making a sweeping motion with her arm, "we've got to stop doubting each other. Nobody's following anyone and neither of us is in any danger of falling in love because we were foolish enough to kiss."

"Fine," Zach muttered as he set her suitcase down. He raised his hand to hail a taxi. To Janine's mingled relief and annoyance, a cab immediately squealed to a halt by the curb.

"How is it we always seem to agree with each other and yet we constantly find ourselves at odds?"

"I wish I knew," he said, looking weary in body and spirit. The cabdriver jumped out and opened the trunk, storing her suitcases neatly inside. Zach threw his garment bag in on top.

"We might as well still share this taxi," he said, holding the door for her.

"But isn't the Mt. Baker district out of your way?"

"I do need to talk to your grandfather. There're some estimates I need to give him."

"But can't it wait until tomorrow? Honestly, Zach, you're exhausted. One day isn't going to make any difference. For that matter Gramps might not even be at the house."

Zach rubbed his eyes with the heels of his hands, then glanced irritably in her direction. "Honestly, Janine," he mocked, "you're beginning to sound like a wife already."

Biting her tongue to keep back her angry retort, Janine crossed her arms and glared out the side window. Indignation seeped through her with every breath she drew. Of its own accord, her foot started an impatient tapping. She could hardly wait to part company with this rude unreasonable man.

Apparently Zach didn't know when to quit, because he added, "Now you even look like one."

With a saccharine smile, she slowly turned to him and in an even more saccharine voice inquired, "And what's that supposed to mean?"

"Look at you, for heaven's sake. First you start nagging me and then—"

"Nagging you!" she exploded. "Let's get one thing straight, right now, Zachary Thomas. I do not nag."

Zach rolled his eyes, then turned his head to glare out the window on his side.

"Sir, sir," Janine said, sliding forward in the seat. She politely tapped the driver on the shoulder.

The middle-aged man with a deep receding hairline glanced at her. "What is it, lady?"

"Sir," she said, offering him her warmest, most sincere smile. "Tell me, do I look like the kind of woman who would nag?"

"Ah... Look, lady, all I do is drive a cab. You can ask me where a street is and I can tell you. If you want to go uptown, I can take you uptown. But when it comes to answering personal-type questions, I prefer to mind my own business."

"Are you satisfied?" Zach murmured.

"No, I'm not." She crossed her arms once more and stared straight ahead.

The cabdriver's eyes met hers in the rearview mirror, and Janine tried to smile, but when she caught a glimpse of herself, she realized her effort looked more like a grimace.

"Me and the Mrs. been married for near twenty years now," the driver said suddenly, stopping at a red light just off the James Street exit. "Me and the Mrs. managed to stay married through the good times and the bad. Can't say that about a lot of folks."

"I don't suppose your wife is the type who nags, though, is she?" Zach made the question sound more like a statement, sending Janine a look that rankled.

"Betsy does her fair share. If you ask me, nagging's just part of a woman's nature."

"That's ridiculous," Janine countered stiffly. She should have known better than to draw a complete stranger into the discussion, especially another male who was sure to take Zach's side.

"I'll tell you the real reason me and the missus managed to stay together all these years," the cabbie continued in a confiding tone. "We never go to bed angry at each other. I know I look like an easygoing kind of guy, but I've got a temper on me. Over the years, me and Betsy have had our share of fights, but we always kiss and make up."

Janine smiled and nodded, sorry she'd ever gotten involved in this conversation.

"Go on," the cabbie urged.

Janine's puzzled gaze briefly met Zach's.

"Go on and do what?" Zach wanted to know.

"Kiss and make up." The cabbie turned to smile at them and wink at Janine. "If my wife was as pretty as yours, mister, I wouldn't be hesitating."

He turned his attention back to his driving.

Janine nearly swallowed her tongue. "We are not married."

"And have no intention whatsoever of marrying," Zach added quickly.

The driver chuckled. "That's what they all say. The harder they deny it, the more in love they are."

He turned off Broadway and a few minutes later pulled into the circular driveway that led to Janine's house. As the talkative cabbie leapt out of the car and dashed for the trunk, Janine opened her door and climbed out.

Apparently, Zach had no intention of taking her advice, because he, too, got out of the cab. It was while they were tussling with the luggage that the front door opened and Mrs. McCormick hurried outside. Her white hair was tucked into a tight bun at the back of her head and she wore the ever present bib apron.

"Janine," she cried, her blue eyes lighting up with surprise. "What are you doing back so soon? We weren't expecting you for another two days."

"I missed your cooking so much, I couldn't bear to stay away any longer," Janine said, throwing her arms around the plump older woman in a warm hug. "Has Gramps been giving you any trouble?"

"Not a bit."

Zach paid the cabbie, who got back into the cab, but not before he'd winked at Janine again. "Remember what I told you," he yelled, backing out of the driveway and speeding off.

"How much was the fare?" Janine asked, automatically opening her purse.

"I took care of it," Zach said, reaching for his garment bag and the heavier of Janine's two suitcases. He said it as though he expected an argument from her, but if that was the case, Janine didn't plan to give him one.

"Is Gramps home?" Janine curved her arm affectionately around the housekeeper's thick waist as she spoke.

"He went out real early this morning, but I'm expecting him back soon."

"Good," Zach mumbled, following them into the house.

"I imagine you're both starved," Mrs. McCormick said, heading toward the kitchen. "Give me a few minutes and I'll whip you up something that'll make you both glad you're home."

Left alone with Zach once more, Janine wasn't sure what to say to him. They'd spent almost twenty-four hours in each other's company. They'd argued. They'd talked. They'd laughed. They'd kissed.

"Janine—"

"Zach—"

They spoke simultaneously, then exchanged nervous smiles.

"You first," Zach said, gesturing toward her.

"I...I just wanted to say thanks for everything. I'll be in touch," she said. "By phone," she quickly assured him. "So you don't need to worry about me dropping into the office unannounced."

He grinned sheepishly. "Remember, communication is the key."

"I agree one hundred percent."

They stood facing each other in the foyer. "You wanted to say something?" she prompted after a moment.

"Yes." Zach exhaled sharply, then drew a hand along the side of his jaw. "What that cabbie said is true—even for us. I don't want us to part with any bad feelings. I shouldn't have said what I did back there—about nagging. You don't nag, and I had no right to say you did."

"I overreacted." The last thing she'd expected from Zach was an apology. His eyes, dark and tender, held hers, and without even re-alizing what she was doing, Janine took a step forward. Zach met her and she was about to slip into his arms when the sound of the front door opening drove them apart.

"Janine," Anton cried, delighted. "Zach. My, my, this is a pleas-ant surprise." He chuckled softly as he removed his coat. "Tell me, was your tryst on the moors as romantic as I hoped?"

CHAPTER SIX

"OUR BEST BET is to present a united front," Janine said to Zach four days later. They'd met at her house early in the afternoon to outline their strategy. Gramps was gone for the day, but by the time he returned, Zach and Janine planned to be ready to talk him out of this marriage idea. The sooner Anton realized his ploy wasn't working, the better. Then they could both get on with their lives and forget this unfortunate episode.

"It's important that we stand up to him together," Janine explained when Zach didn't comment. From the moment he'd arrived, he'd given her the impression that he'd rather not be doing this. Well, she wasn't overjoyed about plotting against her grandfather, either, but in this instance it was necessary. "If we don't, I'm afraid Gramps will continue to play us against each other."

"I'm here, aren't I?" Zach grumbled, looking none too pleased. He certainly wasn't in one of his better moods.

"Listen, if you're going to act like this—"

"Like what?" he demanded, standing up slowly. He walked over to the silver tea service and poured himself a cup of coffee. When he'd finished, he ambled to the fireplace and leaned against the mantel.

"Like you're doing me a big favor," Janine elaborated.

"You're the one who's left *me* dangling for three days. Do you realize what I've been forced to endure? Anton kept giving me these smug smiles, looking so pleased with himself and the way things had worked out in Scotland. Yesterday he went so far as to mention the name of a good jeweler."

Before Janine could stop herself, she was on her feet, arms akimbo, glaring at Zach. "I thought you were going to call me! Weren't you the one who claimed communication is the key? Then it's as if you'd dropped off the face of the earth! And for your information, it hasn't exactly been a Sunday school picnic around here, either."

"It may surprise you to learn that I have other things on my mind besides dealing with you and your grandfather."

"Implying I don't have anything to do with *my* time?" she snapped.

"No," he said slowly, after a moment. "Damn it, Janine, we're arguing again."

She sighed regretfully. "I know. We've got to stop this infernal squabbling. It's counterproductive."

Zach's nod was curt and she saw that he was frowning. "What troubles me most is the way your grandfather found us the other day. We were standing so close and you were staring up at me with those baby blues of yours, silently begging me to kiss you."

"I most certainly was not," she denied, knowing Zach was right. Her cheeks grew pink. She *had* wanted him to kiss her, but she hated having to admit that she would have walked into his arms without a second's hesitation. It was best, she decided, to blame that unexpected longing on the exhausting flight home.

Zach shook his head and set his coffee cup carefully on the mantel. He thrust both hands into his pockets, still slouching against the fireplace wall. "The problem is, I was ready to do it. If your grandfather hadn't walked in when he did, I would have kissed you."

"You would?" she asked softly, feeling almost light-headed at his words.

Zach straightened, and a nerve in his jaw jerked, calling her attention to the strong chiseled lines of his face. "I'm only human," he said dryly. "I'll admit I'm as susceptible to a beautiful woman as the next man, especially when she all but asks me to take her in my arms."

That was too much. Janine pinched her lips together to keep from crying out in anger. Taking a moment to compose herself, she closed her eyes and drew in a deep calming breath. "Instead of blaming each other for something that *didn't happen*, could we please return to the subject at hand, which happens to be my grandfather?"

"All right," Zach agreed readily. "I apologize. I shouldn't have said anything." He walked to the wing-back leather chair and sat down. Leaning forward, he rested his elbows on his knees. "What do you think you should say to him?"

"Me? I thought...I'd hoped...you'd want to do the talking."

Zach shook his head. "Tact doesn't seem to be my strong point lately."

"Okay, okay, I'll do the talking, if that's what you really want." She gazed silently down at the richly patterned carpet, collecting her thoughts. "I think we should say something about how much we both love and respect him and that we realize his actions have been motivated by his concern for us both and his desire for our happiness. We might even go so far as to thank him—" She stopped abruptly when Zach gave a snort of laughter. "All right, if you think you could do any better, you do the talking."

"If it was up to me I'd just tell that meddling old fool to stay out of our lives."

"Your sensitivity is really heartwarming," she muttered. "First this whole thing was one big joke to you, and you really enjoyed tormenting me."

"You're exaggerating."

"As I recall you played that cow-and-ten-chickens business for all it was worth, but I notice you're singing a different tune now and frankly—"

The library door opened, interrupting her tirade. Her grandfather and his longtime friend, veterinarian Dr. Burt Coleman, walked into the room, unaware that Janine and Zach were inside.

"Zach. Janine," Gramps said, grinning broadly.

"Gramps," Janine burst out, rushing to her feet. They weren't prepared for this, and Zach was being impossible, so she said the first thing that came to mind. Pointing at Zach, she cried, "I don't know how you could possibly expect me to marry that man. He's stubborn and rude and we're completely wrong for each other." She was trembling by the time she finished, and collapsed gracelessly into the nearest chair.

"In case you haven't figured it out yet, you're no angel yourself," Zach growled, glaring at Janine.

"Children, please," Gramps implored, advancing into the library, hands held out in supplication. "What seems to be the problem?"

"I want the subject settled once and for all," Zach said forcefully. "I'm not about to be saddled with Janine for a wife."

"And I want to be *your* wife? In your dreams, Zachary Thomas!"

"We realize you mean well," Zach added, his face looking pinched. He completely ignored Janine. "But neither of us appreciates your matchmaking efforts."

Gramps walked over to the leather chair recently occupied by Zach and sat down. He smiled weakly at each of them, his shoulders sagging. "I thought...I'd hoped you two would grow fond of each other."

"You mean if we don't murder each other first," Zach grumbled.

"I'm sorry to disappoint you, Gramps, I really am," Janine said, feeling wretched. "But Zach and I don't even like each other. We can barely carry on a civil conversation. He's argumentative and unreasonable—"

"And she's illogical and stubborn."

"I don't think we need to trade insults to get our message across," Janine said stiffly. Her face was so hot, she felt as if her cheeks were on fire.

"There's no hope?" Anton's expression altered, as if he were in pain.

"None whatsoever," Zach said, his voice surprisingly even. "I'm sure Janine will make some man a wonderful wife one day, but unfortunately, he won't be me."

Her grandfather slumped against the back of his chair. "You're sure?"

"Positive," Zach said, loud enough to convince Mrs. McCormick who was working in the kitchen.

"I love you, Gramps," said Janine, "and I'd do most anything you wanted, but I can't and won't marry Zach. We realize you have our best interests at heart, but neither of us is romantically interested in the other."

Burt Coleman remained just inside the library, looking as if he'd rather be anyplace else. His discomfort at witnessing this family scene was obvious. "I think it'd be best if I came back another time," he murmured as he turned to leave.

"No," Anton argued, gesturing his friend back. "Come in. You know Zachary Thomas, don't you?"

The two men nodded toward each other, but Janine noticed how rigidly Zach held himself. This meeting with Gramps hadn't gone the way she'd hoped or planned. She'd wanted everything to be calm and rational, a discussion uncluttered by messy emotions. Instead they'd ended up practically attacking each other, and worse, Janine had been the one to throw the first punch.

Without asking, she walked over to the tea service and poured Gramps and his friend a cup of hot coffee. Burt sat across from her grandfather, clearly ill at ease at being thrust into this awkward situation.

"I should be going," Zach announced starkly. "Good to see you again, Dr. Coleman."

"You, too," Gramps's friend said, glancing briefly toward Zach. His puzzled gaze quickly returned to Anton.

"I'll walk you to the front door," Janine said, eager to make her own escape. She closed the library door behind her.

Both she and Zach paused in the entryway. Janine tried to smile, but Zach was staring at her steadily, and her heart clenched like a fist inside her chest. They'd done what they had to do; she should be experiencing relief that the confrontation she'd dreaded for days was finally over. Instead she felt a strange sadness, one she couldn't fully understand or explain.

"Do you think we convinced him?"

"I don't know," Zach answered, keeping his tone low. "Your grandfather's a difficult man to read. It could be he'll never bring up the subject of our marrying again and we're home free. I'd like to think that's the case. Just as likely, though, he'll give us a few days' peace while he regroups. I don't expect him to give up quite so easily."

"No, I don't suppose he will."

Zach looked at his watch. "I should be going," he said again.

Janine was reluctant to see him leave, but there wasn't any reason to detain him. Her hand was on the doorknob when she suddenly hesitated and turned around. "I didn't mean what I said in there," she blurted in a frenzy of regret.

"You mean you do want us to marry?"

"No," she cried, aghast. "I'm talking about when I said you were stubborn and rude. That isn't entirely true, but I had to come up with some reason for finding you so objectionable. But I don't really believe it."

"It was the same with me. I don't find you so intolerable, either. I was trusting that you knew it was all an act for your grandfather's sake."

"I did," she assured him, but her pride *had* been dented, though that wasn't anything new.

"The last four days have been difficult at best," Zach went on. "Not only was Anton gloating about Scotland, but like I told you, he's been giving me these amused looks and odd little smiles. A couple of times I heard him murmuring something in his native tongue—I'm afraid to guess what."

"Well, I know what he was saying, because he's been doing the same thing to me. He's talking about babies."

"Babies?" Zach echoed, his eyes round and startled.

"Ours in particular."

"Good Lord." One corner of Zach's mouth lifted, as if he found the thought of them as parents amusing. Or unlikely.

"That was my reaction, too. Every time I've seen Gramps in the last few days, he's started talking about...well, you know."

Zach nodded. "I do know. Things haven't been pleasant for either of us."

"Our setting Gramps straight was for the best." But if that was the case, why did she feel this terrible letdown? "If he accepts us at our word, and he just might, then I guess this is goodbye."

"Yes, I suppose it is," Zach responded, but he made no effort to leave.

Janine was glad, because these few moments gave her the opportunity to memorize his proud sharp features. She stored them for the future, when there would be no reason for her to have anything but the most infrequent contact with Zach.

"Unless, of course, your grandfather continues to find ways to throw us together."

"Of course," Janine added quickly, hating the way her heart soared at the prospect. "Naturally, we'd be forced to confront him again. We can't allow ourselves to be his pawns."

Zach was about to say something more, when the library door flew open and Burt Coleman hurried out, the urgency on his face unmistakable. "Janine, I think we should call a doctor for your grandfather."

"What's wrong?"

"I'm not sure. He's gone terribly pale and he seems to be having trouble breathing. I think it might be his heart."

With Zach following, Janine ran into the library, her own heart in jeopardy. Dr. Coleman was right—she'd never seen her grandfather look worse. His breath came noisily and his eyes were closed as he rested his head against the back of the chair. He looked old, far older than she could ever remember seeing him. A sense of panic filled her as she raced across the room to the desk where there was a phone.

"I'm fine," Gramps said hoarsely, opening his eyes and slowly straightening. He raised his hand in an effort to stop Janine. "There's no need for everyone to go into a tizzy just because an old man wants to rest his eyes for a few minutes." His smile was weak, his complexion still pale. "Now don't go calling any doctor. I was in last week for a checkup and I'm fit as a fiddle."

"You don't look so fit," Zach countered and Janine noted that his face seemed almost as ashen as her grandfather's. Kneeling beside the older man, Zach grasped his wrist and began to check his pulse.

"I'm fine," Gramps insisted.

"Are you in any pain?"

Gramps's gaze moved from his partner to Janine. "None," he answered, dismissing their concern with a short hard shake of his head.

"Dr. Coleman?" Janine looked to her grandfather's longtime friend. "Should I phone his doctor?"

"What does Burt know about an old man and his heart?" Gramps objected. "Burt's expertise is with horses."

"Call the doctor. Having him checked over isn't going to hurt," Burt said after a moment.

"Fiddlesticks," Gramps roared. "I'm in perfect health."

"Good," Janine said brightly. "But I'll just let Dr. Madison reassure me." She punched out the phone number and had to speak loudly in order to be heard over her grandfather's protests. A couple of minutes later, she replaced the receiver and told Zach, "Dr. Madison says we can bring him in now."

"I'm not going to waste valuable time traipsing downtown. Burt and I were going to play a few hands of cribbage."

"We can play tomorrow," Dr. Coleman said gruffly. "You keep forgetting, Anton, we're retiring."

"I've got things to do at the office."

"No, you don't," Zach said firmly. "You've got a doctor's appointment. Janine and I are going to escort you there and we aren't going to listen to a single argument. Do you understand?"

Gramps's gaze narrowed as if he were preparing a loud rebuttal. But he apparently changed his mind, because he relaxed and nodded sluggishly, reluctantly. "All right, if it'll make you feel better. But I'm telling you right now, you're going to look like a fine pair of fools."

The next two hours felt like two years to Janine. While Dr. Madison examined Gramps, she and Zach paced the waiting room. Several patients came and went.

"What could be taking so long?" Janine asked, wringing her hands nervously. "Do you think we did the right thing bringing him here? I mean, should we have gone directly to the hospital emergency room instead?"

"I doubt he would have agreed to that," Zach said.

"Do you honestly believe I would have listened to him?" She sat on the edge of a chair and gripped her hands together so tightly her knuckles whitened. "It's ridiculous, but I've never thought of Gramps as old. He's always been so healthy, so alive. I've never once considered what would happen if he were to become ill."

"He's going to be fine, Janine."

"You saw him," she cried, struggling against the dread and horror that churned inside her.

Zach's hand clasped hers and the fears that had torn at her composure only seconds earlier seemed to abate with his touch. He lent her confidence and strength, and she was badly in need of both.

When the door leading to the doctor's office opened, they both leapt to their feet. Zach's hand tightened around hers before he released it.

"Dr. Madison can talk to you now," the nurse told them briskly. She led the way to a compact office and explained that the doctor would be with them in a few minutes. Janine sat in one of the thickly cushioned chairs and ran her gaze over the framed degrees on the walls.

Dr. Madison came into the room moments later. He paused to shake hands with Zach and nod politely toward Janine. "My tests don't show anything we need to be too concerned about," he said, shuffling through the papers on his desk.

"What happened? Why was he so pale? Why was he gasping like that?" Janine demanded.

Dr. Madison frowned and folded his hands. "I really couldn't say. He claims he hadn't been doing any strenuous exercise."

"No, he was drinking coffee and talking to a friend when it happened."

Dr. Madison nodded. "Did he recently receive any negative news regarding his business?"

"No," Janine replied, glancing at Zach. "If anything, the business is doing better than ever. Gramps is getting ready to retire. I hate the thought of anything happening to him now."

"I don't know what to tell you," Dr. Madison said with a thoughtful frown. "He should take it easy for the next couple of days, but there's nothing to worry about that I can find."

Janine sighed and closed her eyes. "Thank God."

"Your grandfather's getting dressed now," Dr. Madison said. He stood, signaling the end of their interview. "He'll join you in a few minutes."

"Thank you, Doctor," Zach said fervently.

Relief washed through Janine like a tidal wave. She got up and smiled at Zach. It was a smile full of gratitude. A smile one might share with a good friend when something has gone unexpectedly right. The kind of smile a woman would share with her husband. The thought hit her full force and she quickly lowered her gaze to cover her reaction.

When Gramps joined them in the waiting room, he looked immeasurably better. His blue eyes were filled with indignation and his skin tone was a healthy pink. "I hope the pair of you are satisfied," he said huskily, buttoning his coat. "The better part of the afternoon was wasted with this nonsense."

"You were a hundred percent right, Gramps," Janine said brightly. "You're as fit as a fiddle and we wasted valuable cribbage time dragging you down here."

"I should have been back at the office hours ago," Zach put in, sharing a smile with Janine.

"And whose fault is that?" Anton demanded. He brushed off his sleeves as though he'd been forced to pick himself up off the floor, no thanks to them.

Once more Janine and Zach shared an intimate look. They both seemed to realize at the same moment what they were doing and abruptly glanced away.

Zach drove Gramps and Janine back to the house, Gramps protesting loudly all the while that they'd overreacted and ruined his afternoon. His first concern seemed to be rescheduling his cribbage game.

Janine walked Zach back to his car. "Thanks for everything," she said, folding her arms around her middle to repress the sudden urge to hug him.

"If you're worried about anything, give me a call," Zach said as he opened the car door. He hesitated fractionally, then lifted his head and gazed directly into her eyes. "Goodbye, Janine."

She raised her hand in farewell and a sadness settled over her. "Goodbye, Zach," she said forcing a lightness into her voice. "Thanks again."

For the longest moment, he said nothing, although his eyes still held hers. Finally he repeated, "Call me if you need anything, all right?"

"I will."

But they both knew she wouldn't. It was best to end this now. Make a clean cut.

Janine stood in the driveway until Zach's car was well out of sight. Only then did she return to the house.

"THIS IS REALLY GOOD of you," Patty St. John whispered, handing the sleeping infant to Janine. "I don't know what I would've done if I'd had to drag Michael to the interview. I need this job so badly."

"I'm happy to help." Janine peered down at the sweet face of the sleeping six-month-old baby. "I apologize if it was inconvenient for you to bring Michael here, but I've been sticking close to the house for the past few days. My grandfather hasn't been feeling well."

"It isn't any problem," Patty whispered, setting the diaper bag on the floor. She glanced around the house. "This place is really something. I didn't have any idea that you...well, you know, that you were so well off."

"This house belongs to my grandfather," Janine explained, gently rocking Michael in her arms. The warmth and tenderness she felt toward the baby was a revelation. It was understandable, though, when she thought about it. Gramps had spent last week constantly telling her what remarkable babies she and Zach would have, and here she was with one in her arms. All the maternal instincts she didn't know she had came bubbling to the surface.

"I'll be back in about an hour," Patty said. She leaned over and kissed Michael's soft forehead. He didn't so much as stir.

Still carrying the baby, Janine walked to the door with her friend. "Good luck."

Patty gave a strained smile and crossed her fingers. "Thanks. I'm going to need it."

No sooner had the door closed when Anton walked into the living room. He paused when he saw Janine gently rocking in the old chair that had once belonged to his wife. His face relaxed into a broad grin.

"Is that a baby you've got there?"

Janine smiled. "Nothing gets past you, does it, Gramps?"

He chuckled. "Who's he belong to?"

"Patty St. John. You might remember my mentioning her. She's another volunteer at the Friendship Club. She quit her job when Michael was born, but now she'd like to find some part-time work."

"Are you volunteering to baby-sit for her?"

"Just for today," Janine explained. "Her regular sitter has the flu."

"I thought you were going out?" Gramps muttered, with a slight frown. "You haven't left the house all week. Fact is, you're becoming a recluse."

"I've had other things to do," she returned, not raising her voice for fear of disturbing the baby.

"Right. The other things you had to do were keep an eye on your grandfather," he protested. "You think I didn't notice? How long do you plan on being my shadow? You should be gadding about, doing the things you normally do, instead of worrying yourself sick over me. I'm fine, I tell you. When are you going to listen to me?"

"Dr. Madison said to keep an eye on you for a few days."

"It's been a week."

Janine didn't need her grandfather to tell her that. She was beginning to suffer from cabin fever. She'd spoken to hardly anyone all week. She hadn't heard from Zach, either. Not that she'd expected to. Perhaps Gramps had taken them at their word. Or else he was doing what Zach had suspected and simply regrouping for the next skirmish.

Michael stirred in her arms and she gently placed him against her shoulder, rocking him back to sleep.

"I'm going to the office tomorrow," Gramps announced, eyeing her defiantly as though he anticipated a challenge.

"We'll see," she said, delaying the showdown.

Yawning, baby Michael raised his head and looked around. Gramps's weathered face broke into a tender smile. "All right," he agreed easily. "We'll see." He offered the little boy his finger and Michael gripped it firmly in his hand, then started to chew on it.

Janine laughed, watching her grandfather react to the baby. After a couple of minutes, Michael grew tired of the game with Anton's finger and yawned again, arching his back. Janine decided it was time to check his diaper. She got up, reaching for the bag Patty had left.

"I'll be back in a minute," she told her grandfather.

She was halfway across the living room when Anton stopped her. "You look real good with a baby in your arms. Natural."

Janine smiled. She didn't dare let him know how right it felt to hold one.

While she was changing the baby, she heard the doorbell ring. Normally she would have answered it herself, but since she was busy, either Gramps or Mrs. McCormick would see to it.

Michael was happily investigating his toes and making cooing sounds as Janine pulled up his rubber pants. "You're going to have to be patient with me, kiddo," she told him, carefully untwisting the legs of his corduroy overalls and snapping them back in place. When she'd finished, she lifted him high above her head and laughed when Michael squealed delightedly. They were both smiling when she returned to the living room.

Gramps was sitting in the chair closest to the grand piano, and across from him sat Zach.

Janine's heart lurched as her eyes instantly flew to Zach's. The laughter drained out of her. "Hello, Zach," she said, striving to sound as nonchalant as possible, tucking Michael against her hip. She cast a suspicious glare at her grandfather, who smiled back, the picture of innocence.

"Zach brought some papers for me to sign," Gramps explained.

"I didn't mean to interrupt you," she apologized. Her gaze refused to leave Zach's. He smiled that slanted half-smile of his that wasn't really a smile at all. The one she'd always found so appealing. Something seemed to pass between them—a tenderness, a hunger.

"Janine's not interrupting anything, is she?" Gramps asked.

"No," Zach responded gruffly. He seemed to be taking in everything about her, from the acid-washed jeans and oversize pink shirt to the gurgling baby riding so casually on her hip.

Gramps cleared his throat. "If you'll excuse me a moment, I'll go get a pen," he said, leaving them alone together.

"How have you been?" Zach asked, his eyes riveted to her.

"Fine. Just fine."

"I see you haven't had any problems finding another admirer," he murmured, nodding at Michael.

Zach kept his tone light and teasing, and Janine followed his lead. "Michael St. John," she said, turning slightly to give Zach a better view of the baby, "meet Mr. Thomas."

"Hello," Zach said, holding up his palm. He looked questionably awkward around children. "I take it you're watching him for a friend."

"Yes, another volunteer. She's looking for a part-time job, but there's a problem finding one with the right hours. She's at an interview."

"I see."

Janine sank down on the ottoman in front of Zach's chair and set Michael on her knee. She focused her attention on gently bouncing the baby. "Now that your life is back in order," she said playfully, glancing up at Zach, "have you discovered how much you miss me?"

He chuckled softly. "It's been how long since we last talked? Seven days? I'm telling you, Janine, I haven't had a single disagreement with anyone in all that time."

"That should make you happy."

"You're right. It should." He shook his head. "Unfortunately it doesn't. Damn it all, Janine, I was bored to death. So the answer is yes, I missed you."

CHAPTER SEVEN

BEFORE JANINE HAD A CHANCE to respond, Gramps wandered back into the living room, pen in hand.

"You said you had some papers you wanted me to sign," Anton reminded Zach.

With obvious reluctance, Zach tore his gaze from Janine's. He opened his briefcase and brought out several papers. "Go ahead and read these over."

"Do you need me to sign them or not?" her grandfather grumbled.

Once more Zach dragged his gaze away from Janine. "Sure, go ahead."

Muttering under his breath, Gramps took the documents to the small table, scanned them and quickly scrawled his name.

Janine knew she should leave; the two men probably wanted to discuss business. But she couldn't make herself stand up and walk away. Not when Zach had actually admitted that he'd missed her.

Gramps broke into her thoughts. "Janine, I—"

"I was just going," she said quickly. She clambered to her feet, securing her hold on Michael.

But Gramps surprised her.

"I want you to stay," he declared. "I wanted to talk to you and Zach. Fact is, I owe you both an apology. Burt and I had a good long talk the other day and I told him how I'd tried to arrange a marriage between the two of you. He laughed and called me an old fool, claimed it was time I stepped out of the Dark Ages."

"Gramps," Janine said anxiously, unwilling to discuss the subject that had brought such contention, "Zach and I have already settled that issue. We realize why you did it and...and we've laid it to rest, so there's no need to apologize."

"I'm afraid there is," Gramps insisted. "Don't worry, Burt

pointed out the error of my ways. Haven't got any new tricks up my sleeve.'' He rose to bring Zach the signed papers, then sat wearily in the chair across from them. He'd never looked so fragile, so old and beaten.

''Janine's a wonderful woman,'' Zach said unexpectedly. ''I want you to know I realize that.''

''She's got her faults,'' Gramps responded, reaching for a cigar, ''but she's pretty enough to compensate.''

''Thank you very much,'' Janine whispered sarcastically and was rewarded with an off-center grin from Zach. Gramps didn't seem to hear her; if he had, he was ignoring her comment.

''I only want the best for her, but when I approached her about marrying you, she put up a big fuss. Fact is, it would have been easier to pluck a live chicken. When it came right down to it, she said she needed *romance*.'' Gramps pronounced the word as if it were one that evoked instant amusement.

''There isn't a woman alive who doesn't need romance,'' she wailed, defending herself.

''I'm from the old country,'' Gramps continued. ''Romance wasn't something I knew about from personal experience, and when I asked Janine to explain, she had some trouble defining it herself. Said it was a tryst on the moors and a bunch of other hogwash. That's the reason I sent you both to Scotland.''

''We figured that out soon enough,'' Zach said dryly.

''As you'll recall,'' Janine found herself rejoining, ''that definition was off the top of my head. I'll have you know romance isn't easy to explain, especially to a man who scoffs at the entire idea.''

Anton chuckled, moving the cigar to the side of his mouth. ''It's unfortunate the two of you caught on to me so soon. I was looking forward to arranging the desperate passion part.''

''Desperate passion?'' Zach echoed.

''Yes. Janine said that was all part of romance, too. I may be over seventy, but I know about passion. Oh, yes, Anna and I learned about that together.'' His blue eyes took on a faraway look and his lips curved in the gentlest of smiles. He glanced at Janine and his smile widened.

"I'm pleased you find this so amusing," Janine snapped.

Gramps dismissed her anger with a flick of his hand and looked at Zach. "I suppose you've discovered she's got something of a temper?"

"From the start!" Zach declared.

"It may come as a surprise to you, Zachary Thomas," said Janine, "but you're not exactly Mr. Perfect."

"No," Zach countered smoothly. "I think your grandfather was thinking more along the lines of Mr. Right."

"Oh, brother!"

"Now, children, I don't see that arguing will do any good. I've willingly accepted defeat. Trying to interest you in each other was an old man's way of setting his world right before he passes on."

The doorbell chimed and, grateful for an excuse to leave the room, Janine hurried to answer it. Patty St. John stood there, her face cheerless, her posture forlorn.

"I wasn't expecting you back nearly so soon."

"They'd already hired someone," Patty explained, walking into the foyer and automatically taking her son from Janine. She held the infant close, as if his small warm body might absorb her disappointment. "I spent the entire day psyching myself up for this interview and it was all for nothing. Ah, well, who wants to be a receptionist at a dental clinic, anyway?"

"I'm so sorry," Janine murmured.

"Was Michael any problem?"

"None at all," Janine assured her, wishing she could think of something encouraging to say. "I'll get his things for you."

It took Janine only a minute to collect Michael's diaper bag, but when she returned to the entryway, she discovered Zach talking to Patty. Janine saw him hand her friend his business card and overheard him suggesting she report to the personnel office early the following week.

"Thanks again," Patty said enthusiastically to both of them. She lifted Michael's hand. "Say bye-bye," she coaxed the baby, then raised his arm and moved it for him.

Janine let her out, with Zach standing next to her. Gramps had gone into the library, and Zach glanced anxiously in that direction before lowering his voice to a whisper. "Can you meet me later?"

"When?"

"In an hour." He checked his watch, then mentioned the number of a pier along the waterfront. Janine had just managed to clarify the location when Gramps returned.

Zach left the house soon afterward and Janine was able to come up with an excuse half an hour later. Gramps was reading and didn't bother to look up from his mystery novel, although Janine suspected she saw the hint of a smile, as if he knew full well what she was up to. She didn't linger to investigate. The last time she'd agreed to a clandestine meeting with Zach had been the night they'd met at the Italian restaurant, when she'd all but blurted out the arrangements to her grandfather.

Zach was waiting for her, grim-faced. He stood against the pier railing, the wind whipping his raincoat against his legs.

"I hope there's a good reason for this, because I don't think Gramps is a fool," Janine announced when she joined him. "He'll more than likely figure out that I'm meeting you if I'm not back soon." She buried her hands in her jacket pockets, turning away from the wind. The afternoon sky was gray, threatening rain.

"Am I interrupting something important?"

"Not really." Janine wouldn't have minded listing several pressing engagements, but she'd canceled everything for the next two weeks, wanting to stay close to home in case her grandfather needed her.

Zach clasped his hands behind his back and started strolling down the pier the wind ruffling his neatly trimmed hair. Janine followed. "I'm worried about Anton," he said suddenly, stopping and facing Janine.

"Why?" Perhaps there was something she didn't know about his health, something Dr. Madison hadn't told her.

"He doesn't look good."

"How do you mean?" Although she asked, she already knew the answer. She'd felt the same thing the past few days. Gramps was aging right before her eyes.

"I think you know."

"I do," she admitted reluctantly.

"Furthermore I'm worried about you."

"Me?" she asked, her voice rising. "Whatever for?"

"If, God forbid, anything should happen to Anton," Zach said, drawing in a ragged breath, "what will happen to you? You don't have any other family, do you?"

"No," she told him, her chest tightening at the thought. "But I'm not worried about it. There are several friends who are very close to the family, Burt Coleman for one, so I wouldn't be cast into the streets like an orphan. There's no need for you to be concerned. I'm not."

"I see." Zach frowned as he walked to the farthest end of the pier, seeming to fix his gaze on the snow-capped peaks of the Olympic mountains far in the distance.

Janine hurried to catch up with him. "Why do you ask?" she demanded.

"He's always said he was concerned about your not having any other family. But it wasn't until recently that I really understood some of his motivations in trying to arrange a marriage between us."

"Good, then you can explain it to me, because frankly, I'm at a loss. He admitted he was wrong, but I don't think he's given up on the idea. He'd do just about anything to see the two of us together."

"I *know* he hasn't given up on us."

"What did he do? Up the ante?"

Zach chuckled and his features relaxed into a smile as he met her eyes. "Nothing so explicit. He simply told me that he's getting on in years and hates the thought of you being left so alone when he dies."

"I'll adjust. I'm not a child," she insisted, although her heart filled with dread at the thought of life without her cantankerous, generous-hearted grandfather.

"I don't doubt you would." Zach hesitated, then resumed strolling, apparently taking it for granted that she'd continue to follow him.

"I have plenty of friends."

Zach nodded, although Janine was certain he hadn't heard her. He stopped abruptly and turned to look at her. "What I'm about to say is going to shock you."

Janine stared up at him, not knowing what to expect.

"When you think about it, our getting married makes an odd kind of sense."

"What?" Janine couldn't believe what she was hearing.

"From a practical point of view," he rushed to explain. "With the business in both our names, plus the fact that we're both alone. I realize I'm not exactly Prince Charming..." Zach paused as if he expected her to contradict him. When she didn't, he frowned but eventually continued, "The problem has more to do with whether we can get along. I don't even know if we're capable of going an entire day without arguing."

"What are you suggesting?" Janine asked, wondering if she was reading more into this conversation than he intended.

"Nothing yet. Frankly, I'm trying to be as open and as honest as I can and it's damn difficult." He gripped the railing with both hands and braced himself, as though expecting a fierce wind to uproot him.

"Are you thinking that our getting married wouldn't be such a bad idea after all?" Janine ventured. Initially he'd made a joke of the whole thing, infuriating her. Then he'd seen it as an annoyance. Now he seemed to have changed his mind again.

"I...don't know yet. I'm mulling over my thoughts, which I'm willing to confess are hopelessly tangled at the moment."

"Mine aren't much better."

"Does this mean you'd consider the possibility?"

"I don't know." Janine had thought she was in love once. She remembered how Brian had gently wooed her, how he'd done everything a romantic hero should do. He'd sent her flowers, said all the things a woman longs to hear and then, without a pause, he'd casually broken her heart. When she thought about it now, she couldn't really imagine herself married to Brian. But Zach, who'd never made any romantic gestures, seemed somehow to fit into her life almost naturally. And yet...

As she pondered these contradictions, Zach started walking again. "I realize I'm not the kind of husband you want," he was saying, "and not near as good as you deserve. I'd like to be the man of your dreams, but I'm not. Nor am I likely to change at this stage of my life." He paused, chancing a look in her direction. "What are you thinking?"

Janine sighed and concentrated as hard as she could, but her mind was filled with so many questions, so many doubts. "Would you mind very much kissing me?"

Shock widened his dark eyes. He glanced around, then scowled. "Now? Right here?"

"Yes."

"There are people everywhere. Is this really necessary?"

"Would I ask you to do it if it weren't?"

As he searched her face, she moistened her lips and looked up at him, tilting her head slightly. Slowly, reluctantly, Zach slipped one arm around her waist and drew her close. Her heart reacted immediately, leaping into a hard fast rhythm that made her feel slightly breathless. He lifted her chin with his free hand and slowly lowered his mouth to hers.

The instant his lips grazed hers, Janine was flooded with a sensual languor. It was as if they'd returned to the moors of Scotland with the full moon overhead pouring magic onto their small corner of the earth. Everything around them faded. No longer did Janine hear the sound of water slapping against the wooden columns of the pier. The blustery day went calm.

She supported her hands on his chest, breathing erratically, when he stopped kissing her. Neither spoke. Janine wanted to, but none of her faculties seemed to be working at the moment. She parted her lips and Zach lowered his mouth to hers once more. Only this time it was a full-fledged kiss, deep and probing. His hands slid up her back as his mouth abandoned hers to explore the sweep of her neck.

Several glorious moments passed before he shuddered, raised his head and drew back slightly, although he continued to hold her. "Does that answer your question?"

"No," she answered, hating the way her voice trembled. "I'm afraid it only raised more."

"I know what you mean," Zach admitted, briefly closing his eyes.

"This last week apart was something of an eye-opener for me. I thought I'd be glad to put this matter between your grandfather and us to rest. If you want the truth, I thought I'd be glad to be rid of you. I was convinced you felt the same way." He paused, waiting for some kind of response from her.

"The days seemed so empty," she whispered.

His eyes burned into hers, and he nodded his head. "You were constantly on my mind, and I found myself wishing you were there to talk to." He groaned. "Heaven knows you deserve a different kind of husband than I could possibly be."

"What about you? I've heard you say a hundred times that when it comes to finding a wife, you'll choose your own."

He blinked, as though he didn't recognize his own words for a moment. Then he shrugged. "Once I got to know you, I realized you're not so bad."

"Thanks." So much for wine and roses and sweet nothings whispered in her ear. But then again, she'd had those things and they hadn't brought her happiness.

"I hate to admit it, but our getting married makes sense. We seem to like each other well enough, and there's a certain...attraction." Zach was frowning a little as he spoke. "It would be a good move for both of us from a financial viewpoint, as well." He gripped her by the shoulders and gazed into her eyes. "The question is, Janine, can I make you happy?"

Her heart melted at the way he said it, at the simplicity, the sincerity of his words. "What about you? Will you be content being married to me?"

The apprehension in his face eased. "I think so. We'll be good for each other. This isn't any grand passion. But I'm fond of you and you're fond of me."

"Fond?" Janine repeated, breaking away.

"What's wrong with that?"

"I hate that word," Janine said through gritted teeth. "Fond sounds so watered down...so weak. I'm not looking for a grand passion, as you put it, but I want a whole lot more than *fond*." She gestured dramatically with her hands. "A man is fond of his dog or a favorite place to eat, not his wife." She spoke so vehemently that she was starting to attract attention from other strollers. "Would it be too much for you to come up with another word?"

"Stop looking at me as if it were a matter of life and death," he said.

"It's important," she insisted.

Zach looked distinctly uncomfortable. "I run a business. There are more than a hundred outlets in fifty states. I know the office-supply business inside out, but I'm not good with words. If you don't like the word *fond*, you choose another one."

"All right," she said thoughtfully, biting the corner of one lip. Her eyes brightened. "How about cherish?"

"Cherish." Zach repeated it as if he'd never heard the word before. "Okay, it's a deal. I'll cherish you."

"And I'll cherish you," she said emphatically, nodding with satisfaction.

They walked along the pier until they came to a seafood stand, where Zach bought them each a cup of steaming clam chowder. They found an unoccupied picnic table and sat down, side by side.

Occasionally they stopped eating to smile at each other. An oddly exciting sensation attacked Janine's stomach every time that happened. Finally, finishing her soup, she licked the back of the white plastic spoon. She kept her eyes carefully lowered as she said, "I want to make sure I understand. Did we or did we not just agree to get married?"

Zach hesitated, his spoon halfway between his cup and his mouth as an odd, still look crossed his face. He swallowed once. "We decided to go through with it, both realizing this isn't the traditional love match, but one based on practical and financial advantages."

Janine dropped her spoon into the plastic cup. "If that's the case, the wedding's off."

Zach threw back his head and stared into the sky. "Now, what did I say that was so terrible?"

"Financial and practical advantages! You make the whole thing sound as appealing as a dentist appointment. There's got to be more reason than that for us to marry."

Shrugging, Zach gestured helplessly with his hands. "I already told you I wasn't any good at this. Perhaps we'd do better if you explained why you're willing to marry me."

She hesitated and before she could prevent it, a smile tugged at the corners of her mouth. "You won't like my reason any better than I like yours." She looked all around to be sure no one could overhear, then leaned toward him. "When we kissed a few minutes ago, the earth moved. I know it's a dreadful cliché, but that's exactly what I felt."

"The earth moved," Zach repeated deadpan.

"It happened when we were in Scotland, too. I don't know what's going on between us or even if we're doing the right thing, but there's definitely...something, something special."

She wasn't surprised when Zach scowled. "You mean to say you're willing to marry me because I'm a good kisser?"

"It makes a whole lot more sense to me than that stuff about financial advantages."

"You were absolutely correct," he said evenly. "I don't like your reason. Is there anything else that makes the prospect appealing?"

Janine giggled. "You know," she reflected, "Gramps was right. We're going to be very good for each other."

A flash of light warmed his eyes and his hand reached for hers. He entwined their fingers as their eyes met. "Yes, we are."

THE WEDDING WAS ARRANGED so fast that Janine barely had time to reconsider their decision. They applied for a license that same afternoon. When they returned to the house, Gramps shouted for joy, slapped Zach across the back several times and repeatedly hugged Janine, claiming she'd made an old man happy.

Janine was so busy, the days and nights soon mingled together and she lost all track of time. There were so many things to do—fittings and organizing caterers and inviting guests—that for the following five days she didn't so much as talk to Zach even once.

The day before the ceremony, the garden was buzzing with activity. Mrs. McCormick was busy supervising the men who were assembling the wedding canopy and setting up the tables and chairs.

Exhausted, Janine wandered outside and glanced toward the bold blue sky, praying the sunshine would hold for at least another day. The lawn was lush and green, and freshly mowed. The roses were in bloom, perfuming the air with their rich fragrance.

"Janine."

She recognized his voice immediately. She turned around to discover Zach striding purposely toward her, and her heart reacted of its own accord. She felt as though they'd been apart for a year instead of just a few days. She wore jeans and a sweatshirt and wished now that she'd chosen something less casual. In contrast, Zach was strikingly formal, dressed in a handsome pin-striped suit and dark tie. She was willing to admit she didn't know him as well as she should—as well as a woman who was about to become his wife. His habits, his likes and dislikes, were a mystery to her, yet those details seemed minor. It was the inner Zach she was coming to understand. The little she'd learned was enough to assure her that she'd made the right decision.

"Hello," she called, walking toward him. She noted that he looked as tired as she felt. Apparently he'd been just as busy, though the wedding preparations had been left to her.

They met halfway and stopped abruptly, gazing at each other. Zach didn't hug her or make any effort to touch her.

"How are you holding up?" he asked.

"Fine," she answered. "How about you?"

"I'll live." He glanced over at the activity near the rose garden and sighed. "Is there someplace we can talk privately?"

"Sure." Janine's heart leapt to her throat at the sober manner in which he was studying her. "Is everything all right?"

He reassured her with a quick nod. "Of course."

"I don't think anyone's in the kitchen."

"Good." Hand at her elbow, he guided her toward the house. Her fingers were trembling as she pulled out a chair and sat down at the oak table. As he lowered himself into a chair opposite her, she gripped the edge of the table. His eyes had never seemed darker. "Tomorrow's the day."

He said this as if he expected it to come as a shock to Janine. It didn't—but she understood what he was telling her. Time was closing in on them, and if they wanted to back out, it would have to be now.

"Believe me, I know," she said, and her fingers tightened on the table. "Have you had a change of heart?"

"Have you?"

"No, but then again, I haven't had much time to think."

"I've done nothing *but* think about this wedding," Zach said, raking his hands through his hair.

"And?" she prompted, needing reassurance.

He shrugged. "We may both have been fools to agree to this."

"It all happened so fast," Janine said in a weak voice. "One minute we agreed on the word *cherish*, and the next thing I remember, we were deciding we'd be good for each other."

"Don't forget the kissing part," he added. "As I recall, that had quite a bit to do with this decision."

"If you're having second thoughts, I'd rather you said so now than after the ceremony."

His eyes narrowed fleetingly before he slowly shook his head. "No."

"You're sure?"

He answered her by leaning forward, slipping his hand behind her neck, and kissing her soundly. Tenderly. When they broke apart, they were silent. Not talking, not wanting to.

Janine gazed into his dark warm eyes and suddenly she could hardly breathe.

"This is going to be a real marriage," he said forcefully, as if he were expecting an argument.

She nodded. "I most certainly hope so, Mr. Thomas." And her voice was strong and clear.

LESS THAN TWENTY-FOUR HOURS later, Janine stood at Zach's side, prepared to pledge her life to his. She'd never felt more uncertain— or, at the same time, more confident—of anything she'd ever done.

Zach seemed to understand what she was feeling. His eyes held hers as she repeated the words that would bind them.

When she'd finished, Zach slipped his arm around her waist and drew her close to his side. The pastor smiled down on them, then looked to the fifty or so family friends who had gathered on Anton's lawn and said, "I present to you Mr. and Mrs. Zachary Thomas."

A burst of spontaneous applause followed his words.

Before Janine fully realized what was happening, they were mingling with their guests. One minute she was standing in front of the pastor, trembling but unafraid, and the next she was a wife.

"Janine, Janine." Pam rushed to her side before anyone else. "You look so beautiful," she said softly, and bright tears shone in her eyes.

Janine hugged her young friend. "Thank you, sweetheart."

Pam gazed up at Zach and slowly shook her head. "He sure is handsome."

"I think so, too."

Zach arched his brows, cocked his head toward her and murmured, "You never told me that."

"There's no need for you to get a swelled head."

"My children," Gramps said, rejoining them. He hugged Janine close, and she saw that his eyes were as bright as Pam's. "You've never been more beautiful. I swear you look more like my Anna every year."

It was the highest compliment Gramps could have paid her. From the pictures Gramps kept of his wife, Janine knew her grandmother had been exceptionally beautiful.

"Thank you," she said, and lovingly kissed his cheek.

"I have something for you," Pam insisted, thrusting a neatly wrapped box into Janine's hands. "I made them myself," she announced proudly. "I think Zach will like them, too."

"Oh, Pam, you shouldn't have," Janine murmured. Sitting down on the cushioned folding chair, she peeled away the paper and lifted the lid. The moment she did, her breath jammed in her throat. Inside were the sheerest white baby-doll pajamas Janine had ever seen. Her smile faltered as she glanced up to find several people staring at her.

Zach's hand, resting at the nape of Janine's neck, tightened as he spoke, though his voice was warm and amused. "You're right, Pam. I like them very much."

CHAPTER EIGHT

JANINE SAT NEXT to Zach in the front seat of his car. Dressed in a pink suit and matching broad-brimmed hat, she clutched her small floral bouquet. Although the entire wedding had been arranged in seven short days, it had been a lovely affair.

Zach had taken care of planning the short honeymoon trip. All he could spare was three days, so instead of scheduling anything elaborate, he'd suggested they go to his summer place in Ocean Shores, a coastal town two and a half hours by car from Seattle. Janine had willingly agreed.

"So you think I'm handsome," Zach said, keeping his eyes on the road. Neither of them had said much since they'd set off.

"I knew if I said anything it'd go straight to your head, and obviously I was right," she answered. Then, unable to hold back a wide yawn, she pressed the back of her hand to her mouth.

"You're exhausted."

"Are you always this astute?"

"Testy, too."

"I don't mean to be," she apologized. She'd been up before five that morning and in fact, hadn't slept well the entire week. This wasn't exactly the ideal way to start a marriage, and definitely not a honeymoon. There was an added stress, too, that had to do with the honeymoon. Zach had made it understood that he intended their marriage to be a real one, but surely he didn't expect them to share a bed so soon. Or did he?

Every now and again as they drove, she glanced in his direction, wondering what she should say, if anything. Even if she did decide to broach this delicate subject, she wasn't sure how.

"Go ahead and rest," Zach suggested. "I'll wake you when we arrive."

"It shouldn't be too much longer now, should it?"

"Another fifteen minutes or so."

"Then I'll stay awake." Nervously, she twisted the small floral bouquet. Unwrapping Pam's gift had made her all the more apprehensive, but delaying the subject any longer was impossible.

"Zach...are we going to...you know..." she stammered feeling like a complete fool.

"If you're referring to what I think you're referring to, the answer is no. So relax."

"No?" He didn't need to sound so casually certain about it, as if the idea was neither here nor there.

"Why do you ask? Are you having second thoughts about...that?"

"No. Just some reservations."

"Don't worry. When it happens, it happens. The last thing we need to do is pressure one another."

"You're right," she answered, relieved.

"All we need is some time to become comfortable. There's no reason to rush into the physical aspect of our marriage, is there?"

"None whatsoever," she agreed quickly, perhaps too quickly, because when she glanced at him again, Zach was frowning. Yet he seemed so willing to wait, as though their lovemaking was of minor importance. As he'd said, this marriage wasn't one of grand passion. Well, that much was certainly true.

Before another five minutes had passed, Zach left the highway and drove into the resort town of Ocean Shores. He didn't stop in the business district, but headed directly down a side street toward the ocean front. The sun was setting as he pulled into a driveway and turned off the engine.

Janine was too enthralled with the house to say a word.

The wind whipped at them ferociously when they climbed out of the car. Janine held onto her hat with one hand, still clutching the flowers, and to Zach with the other. The sun cast a pink and gold reflection over the rolling hills of sand.

"Home, sweet home," Zach said, nudging her toward the house.

The front door opened before they reached it and a trim middle-aged man stepped onto the porch to greet them. He was grinning broadly. "Hello, Zach. I trust you had a safe trip."

"We did."

"Everything's ready. The cupboards are stocked. The firewood's stacked against the side of the house, and dinner's all prepared."

"Wonderful, Harry, thanks." Zach placed his hand on Janine's shoulder. "This is my wife, Janine," he said, and hesitated. "We were married this afternoon."

"Your wife?" Harry repeated, looking more than a little surprised. "Why that's fantastic. Congratulations to you both."

"Thank you," Janine answered politely.

"Harry Gleason looks after the place for me when I'm not around."

"I'm pleased to meet you, Harry."

"So Zach got himself a wife," Harry said, rubbing the side of his jaw in apparent disbelief. "I couldn't be more—"

"Pleased," a frowning Zach supplied for him, ushering Janine toward the front door.

"Right," Harry said. "I couldn't be more pleased."

Still holding on to her hat, Janine tilted back her head to look over the modern and sprawling single-story house.

"Go on inside," Zach instructed. "I'll get the luggage."

Janine started to protest, suddenly wanting him to follow the traditional wedding custom of carrying her over the threshold. She paused, and Zach gave her a puzzled frown. "Is something wrong?"

"No." She had no real grounds for complaint. She wasn't even sure why it mattered. Swallowing her disappointment, she made her way into the house. She stopped just inside the front door and gazed with wide-eyed wonder at the immense living room with its three long sofas and several upholstered chairs. A brick fireplace took up an entire wall; another was dominated by a floor-to-ceiling window that looked out over the ocean. Drawn to it, Janine watched the waves crash against the shore with a mighty force, as though to punish the sand for some imagined wrong.

Zach followed her inside, carrying their luggage, barely taking time to appreciate the scene before him. "Harry's putting the car away," he said.

"This place is incredible," Janine breathed, gesturing around her. She removed her hat and placed it next to the flowers on the coffee table. She trailed after Zach, and discovered a hallway off which were four bedrooms with an equal number of baths. At the back of the house, she found an exercise room, an office, and an ultramodern kitchen where a pot of coq au vin was simmering on the burner.

In the formal dining room, the long polished mahogany table was set for two. On the deck, designed to take advantage of the ocean view, she found a steaming hot tub along with a bottle of French champagne on ice.

Zach returned as she wandered back into the kitchen and a strained silence fell between them. He was the first to speak. "I put your suitcases in the master bedroom," he said brusquely, shoving his hands into his pockets. "I'm in the one across the hall."

She nodded, not taking time to question her growing sense of disappointment. They'd agreed to delay their wedding night, hadn't they?

"Are you hungry?" he asked, walking to the stove, and lifting the pot's lid, as she had done earlier.

"Only a little. I was thinking about slipping into the hot tub, unless you want to eat first."

"Sure. The hot tub's fine. Whatever you want."

Janine unpacked and located her swimsuit, then changed into it quickly. The warm water sounded appealing. And maybe it would help her relax. Draping a thick beach towel over her arm, she returned to the kitchen, but Zach was nowhere to be seen. Not waiting for him, she walked out to the deck and gingerly stepped into the hot tub. The water felt like a soothing liquid blanket and she slid down, letting it lap just under her breasts.

Zach sauntered onto the deck a minute later, still dressed in his suit. He stopped short when he saw her. "I...didn't realize you'd be out so soon," he said, staring at her with undisguised appreciation. He inhaled sharply and occupied himself by uncorking the bottle of champagne, then pouring himself a liberal glass. He gulped it down, then reached for a second one and filled it for Janine. "You're coming in, aren't you?" she asked, when he handed her the crystal flute.

"Actually, no," he said abruptly. "I won't join you, after all. There were several things I wasn't able to finish at the office this week, and I thought I'd look over some papers. You go ahead and enjoy yourself."

He was going to *work* on their wedding night! But she didn't feel she had any right to comment or complain. She was determined to conceal her bitter disappointment.

"The water's wonderful," she said, as cheerfully as she could manage, hoping her words would convince him to join her.

Zach nodded, but his eyes now avoided Janine. "It looks...great." He strode to the end of the deck, raked his fingers through his hair, then twisted around to face her. He seemed about to say something, but apparently changed his mind.

Baffled by his odd behavior, Janine set aside the glass of champagne and stood up so abruptly that water sloshed over the edges of the tub. "You don't need to say it," she muttered, climbing out and grabbing her towel.

"Say what?"

"You warned me before the wedding, so I walked into this with my eyes wide open. Well, you needn't worry. I got the message the minute we arrived at the house."

Zach again downed his champagne as though it were water. "What the hell are you talking about?"

"Never mind." Vigorously, she rubbed her arms with the towel.

"No," he barked impatiently, "I want you to tell me."

Against her better judgment, she pointed a quaking finger toward the front door. "You went out of your way to tell me how *fond* of me you were and how there wasn't going to be any grand passion. Great. Fine. Perfect. I agreed to those terms. That's all dandy with me, but—"

"But what?" he demanded.

She squared her shoulders, anticipating an argument. "But every bride should at least be carried over the threshold."

"The threshold?" he cried, looking at her as if she were a prime candidate for intensive counseling. He took two steps away from her and then abruptly turned around. "You're joking, aren't you?"

She cocked her chin defiantly, refusing to meet his dark eyes. With a lump the size of a watermelon blocking her throat, she dared not try to answer him.

"You're serious. You're actually serious about this!" He sounded utterly astonished. "If it's so important to you, then I'll be more than happy to oblige."

Tears were burning for release, but by sheer force of will, Janine managed to hold them at bay. "You're the last man on this earth I'd ever allow to carry me anywhere. I'd rather throw myself over this deck than let you touch me."

"Oh, great, we're fighting. I suppose you're going to ask for a divorce and make this the shortest marriage in Washington history."

Janine paled. Divorce was such an ugly word, and it struck her as hard and viciously as a slap across the face. Despite her efforts, scalding tears brimmed and spilled down her cheeks. With as much dignity as she could muster, which admittedly wasn't much, Janine turned and walked back into the house, leaving a wet trail in her wake.

"Janine," Zach shouted, following her into the kitchen. He hurried ahead of her and planted himself in the doorway, blocking her exit. "Damn it, Janine, arguing with you was the last thing I intended."

With her head held high, she stared past him to a painting of yellow flowers on the dining-room wall. When the tears in her eyes blurred the flowers beyond recognition, she defiantly rubbed the moisture away.

"I'm sorry," he whispered, reaching for her as if he needed to hold her, to touch her. But then his arms fell abruptly to his sides. "I should have realized the wedding traditions would be important to you. To be honest, I completely forgot about the threshold business."

"It's not just that, it's everything. The determined effort to bury yourself in your work. How many other men bring a briefcase with them on their honeymoon? I feel like excess baggage in your life— and we haven't even been married twenty-four hours." She didn't want Zach to swoon at her feet, overcome with passion, but she hadn't expected him to make her feel about as desirable as a load of dirty laundry, either.

Zach looked perplexed. "What does my catching up on reading have to do with any of this?"

His question only irritated her more. "You don't have the foggiest notion of how impossible you are, do you?"

He didn't answer her right away, but seemed to be studying her, weighing his answer before he spoke. "I just thought I might have time to read over some papers," he said slowly. "Apparently that bothers you."

Janine placed her hands on her hips. "Yes, it bothers me."

Zach frowned. "Since we've already agreed to delay the honeymoon part, what would you suggest we do for the next few days?"

"Do you think maybe we could spend the time having fun? Becoming better acquainted?"

"I guess I do seem like a stranger to you," he allowed. "No wonder you're so nervous."

"I am *not* nervous. Just tired and trying hard not to say or do anything that will make you think of me as a...a nag."

"A nag?" Zach repeated incredulously. "I don't think of you as anything but lovely. The truth is, I'm having one heck of a time keeping my eyes off you."

"You are?" The towel she was holding slipped unnoticed to the floor. "I thought you said you didn't know how to say anything romantic."

"That was romantic?"

"And very sweet. I was beginning to think you didn't find me...attractive."

Astonished, Zach stared at her. "You've got to be kidding!"

"I'm not."

"I can see that the next few days are going to be difficult," he said. "You'll just need to be patient with me, all right?"

"All right," she agreed, already feeling worlds better.

"How about if I dish up dinner while you're changing?"

"Great."

By the time she arrived back in the kitchen, wearing warm charcoal slacks and a sweater that was the color of fresh cream, Zach had prepared their meal and poured the wine. He stood behind her chair, politely waiting for her.

"Before we sit down there's something I need to do."

The last thing Janine expected was to be lifted in his strong arms. A gasp of surprise lodged in her throat as her startled gaze flew to his.

"What are you doing?"

"I thought you said you wanted to be carried over the threshold."

"Yes, but you're doing it all wrong. You're supposed to carry me from the outside in—not the other way around."

Zach shrugged, unconcerned. "There's nothing traditional about this marriage. Why start now?" He made a show of pretending his knees were buckling under her weight as he staggered through the living room.

"This is supposed to be serious," she chastised him, but no matter how hard she tried, she couldn't keep the laughter out of her voice.

With a good deal of feigned effort, he managed to open the front door and then ceremoniously step onto the porch. Slowly he released her, letting her feet drop first, holding her upper body close against his chest for a long moment. The humor left his eyes. "There," he said tenderly. "Am I forgetting anything?"

It wouldn't hurt to kiss me, Janine told him in her heart, but the words didn't make it to her lips. When Zach kissed her again, she wanted it to be *his* idea.

"Janine?"

"Everything's perfect. Thank you."

"Not quite," he muttered. He turned her to face him, then covered her mouth with his own. Janine trembled, slipping her arms around his neck and giving herself completely to the kiss. She quivered at the heat that began to warm her from the inside out. This kiss was better than any they'd ever shared, and she hadn't thought that possible. And what that meant, she had no idea.

Zach lifted his mouth abruptly from hers, but his eyes remained closed. Almost visibly he pulled himself together, and when he broke away he seemed completely in control of himself again. Janine sighed inwardly, unsure of what she'd expected.

THE NEXT TWO DAYS flew past. They took long walks on the shore, collecting shells. They rented mopeds and raced along the beach. They launched kites into the sky and delighted in their colorful dipping and soaring. The day before they were scheduled to return to Seattle, Zach declared that he intended to cook dinner. Following that announcement, he informed her he had to go into town to buy the necessary groceries. After the first night, he'd given Harry a week off, and Janine had been fixing simple meals for them.

"What are you serving?" she wanted to know when he pulled into the parking lot of the town's only grocery store. "At least tell me that so I can buy an appropriate wine."

"Wine," he muttered under his breath. "I don't normally serve wine with this dish."

She followed him in, but when he discovered her traipsing down the aisle after him, he gripped her by the shoulders and directed her back outside. "I am an artist, and I insist upon working alone."

Janine had a difficult time not laughing outright.

"In order to make this dinner as perfect as possible, I must concentrate completely on the selection of ingredients. You, my dear sweet wife," he said, pressing his index finger to the tip of her nose, "are too much of a distraction. A lovely one, but nevertheless a distraction."

Janine smiled, her heart singing. Zach was not free with his compliments, and she found herself prizing each one.

While Zach was busy in the grocery store, Janine wandered around town. She bought a lifelike ceramic sea gull, which she promptly named Chester, and a bag of saltwater taffy. Then on impulse, she purchased a bottle of lotion in case they decided to lie out in the sun, tempting a tan.

By the time she returned to the car, Zach was waiting for her. She was licking a double-decker chocolate ice-cream cone and feeling incredibly happy.

"Did the master chef find everything he needed?" she asked. Two brown paper bags were sitting on the floor and she restrained herself from peeking inside.

"Our meal tonight will be one you'll long remember, I promise you."

"I'm glad to hear it." Holding out her ice-cream cone, she asked. "Do you want a taste?"

"Please." He rejected the offer of the cone itself and instead bent forward and lowered his mouth to hers. As she gazed into his dark heavy-lidded eyes her heart accelerated and she was filled with a sudden intense longing. Janine wasn't sure what was happening between them, but it felt, quite simply, right.

Although the kiss was fleeting, a shiver of awareness twisted its way down her back. Neither of them spoke or moved. He'd meant the kiss to be gentle and teasing, but it had quickly found another purpose. For a breathless second, the smile faded from his eyes. He continued to hold her, and his breathing was rapid and hard.

After nearly two full days alone together, Janine found it amusing that when he finally chose to kiss her, he'd do it in a crowded parking lot.

"I don't remember chocolate being quite that rich," he murmured. He strove for a casual tone, but Janine wasn't fooled. He was as affected by the kiss as she, and struggling just as hard to disguise it.

They were both uncharacteristically quiet on the short drive back to the house. Until the kiss, they'd spent companionable days together, enjoying one another's company. Then, in the space of no more than a couple of seconds, all that had changed.

"Am I banished from the kitchen?" Janine asked once they were inside the house, forcing an airy note into her voice.

"Not entirely," Zach surprised her by saying. "I'll need you later to wash the dishes."

Janine laughed and pulled her suntan lotion out of her bag. While Zach puttered around inside, she changed into her swimsuit, then dragged the lounge chair into the sun to soak up the last of the afternoon's rays.

Zach soon joined her, carrying a tall glass of iced tea. "You look like you could use this."

"Thanks. If I'd known how handy you were in the kitchen, I'd have let you assume the duties long before now."

He set the glass down beside her and headed back to the kitchen. "You'd be amazed at the list of my talents," he threw over his shoulder.

Kissing was certainly one of them, she thought. The sample he'd given her earlier had created a sharp unexpected need for more. If she was a sophisticated experienced kind of woman, she wouldn't have any problem working her way back into his arms. It would all appear so effortless and casual. He'd kiss her, and she'd kiss him back, and before either of them realized what was happening, they'd truly be husband and wife.

Lying on her back with her eyes closed, Janine imagined how wonderful it would be if Zach were to take her in his arms and make love to her....

She awoke from her doze with a start. She hurried inside to change, and by the time she was finished, Zach announced that dinner was ready to be served. He'd set the patio table so they could eat on the deck.

"Do you need any help?" she asked, trying to peek inside the kitchen.

"None. Sit down before everything cools." He pointed to the chair and waited until she was comfortable.

"I only have a spoon," she said, after unfolding the napkin on her lap. He must have made a mistake.

"A spoon is all you'll need," he shouted to her from inside the kitchen.

Playfully she asked, "You went to all this trouble for soup?"

"Wait and see. I'll be there in a minute."

He sounded so serious, Janine couldn't keep from smiling. She was running through a list of words to praise his efforts—"deliciously unique," "refreshingly different"—when Zach walked onto the deck, carrying a tin can with a pair of tongs.

"Good grief, what's that?" she asked in dismay.

"Dinner," he said. "The only real cooking I ever did was while I belonged to the Boy Scouts."

As though he was presenting lobster bisque, he set the steaming can in front of her. Janine leaned forward, almost afraid to view its contents.

"Barbecue beans. With sliced hot dogs," he announced proudly.

"And to think I doubted you."

Her reservations vanished, however, the moment she tasted his specialty. The beans were actually very good. He surprised her, too, by bringing out dessert, a concoction consisting of graham crackers covered with melted chocolate and marshmallows. He'd warmed them in the oven and served them on a cookie sheet.

Janine ate four of what Zach called "some-mores." He explained that once they'd been tasted, everyone asked for "some more."

"I don't know how you've managed to stay single all these years," she teased, forgetting for the moment that they were married. "If the news about your talent in the kitchen got out, women would be knocking down your door."

Zach chuckled, looking extraordinarily pleased with himself.

An unexpected thought entered Janine's mind, filling her with curiosity. It astonished her now that she'd never asked Zach about other women in his life. It would be naive to assume he'd never had involvements. She'd had her relationship with Brian; surely there were women in Zach's past.

She waited until later that night when they were sipping wine and listening to classical music in front of the fireplace. Zach seemed relaxed, sitting with one knee raised and the other leg stretched in front of him. Janine lay on her stomach, staring into the fire.

"Have you ever been in love?" She was striving for a casual tone.

Zach didn't answer her right away. "Would you be jealous if I said I had?"

"No." She sounded more confident than she felt.

"I thought not. What about you?"

She took her time answering, too. She'd thought she was in love with Brian. It wasn't until later, after the pain of Brian's rejection had eased, that she realized she'd been in love with the *idea* of being in love.

"No," she said, feeling completely honest in her response. What she felt for Zach, whom she was only beginning to know, was already a thousand times stronger than anything she'd ever felt for a man. She didn't know how to explain it, so she avoided the issue by reminding him, "I asked you first."

"I'm a married man. Naturally I'm in love."

"You're fond of me, remember?"

"I thought you detested that word."

"I do. Now stop tiptoeing around the subject. Have you ever really been in love—I mean head over heels in love? You don't need to go into any detail—a simple yes or no will suffice."

"A desperate-passion kind of being in love?"

"Yes," she told him, growing impatient. "Don't make fun of me and please don't give me a list of all the women you've been *fond* of."

He grew so quiet and so intense that her smile began to fade. She pulled herself into a sitting position and looped her arms around her bent knees.

Zach stared at her for a long moment. As she watched the harsh pain move into his eyes, Janine felt her chest tighten.

"Yes," he answered in a hoarse whisper. "I've been in love."

CHAPTER NINE

"HER NAME was Marie."

"Marie," Janine repeated the name as though she'd never heard it before.

"We met in Europe when I was on assignment with the armed services. She spoke five languages fluently and helped me learn my way around two of them in the time we worked together."

"She was in the service with you?"

"I was army, she worked for the secret service. We were thrown together for a top-secret project that was only supposed to last a few days and instead dragged on for weeks."

"This was when you fell in love with her?" The ache inside her chest wouldn't go away. Her heart felt weighted down with the pain.

"We both were aware the assignment was a dangerous one, and our working closely together was essential." He paused, sighing deeply. "To make a long story short, I fell in love with her. But she didn't love me."

"And then what?"

"I wanted her to leave the service and marry me. She wasn't interested. If you insist on knowing the details, I'll give them to you."

"No."

Zach took a sip of his wine. "I left the army shortly after that. I didn't have the heart for it anymore. Unlike Marie—her work, with all its risks, was her whole life. She was the most dedicated and bravest woman I've ever known. Although it was painful at the time, she was right to reject my proposal. Marriage and a family would have bored her within a year. It was painful, don't misunderstand me. I loved her more than I thought it possible to care for another human being."

They both were silent for a moment, then Janine asked, "What did you do once you left the army?"

"Over the years, I'd managed to put aside some money, make a few investments. Once I was on my own, I decided to go into business for myself. I read everything I could get my hands on about the business-supply field and modeled the way I dealt with my clients and accounts after your grandfather's enterprise. Within five years, I was his major competitor. We met at a conference last year, and decided that instead of competing against each other, we'd join forces. And as they say, the rest is history."

"Was she pretty?" Even as she asked the question, Janine knew it was ridiculous. What possible difference would it make if his Marie was a former Miss America or had a face like a gorilla? None. Zach had loved Marie. Loved her as he would probably never love again. Loved her more than he'd thought it was possible to love another human being. By comparison, what he felt for her, Janine, was indeed only fondness.

"She was blond and, yes, she was beautiful."

Janine made a feeble attempt at a smile. "Somehow I knew that."

Zach shook himself lightly as if dragging himself back to the present and away from the powerful lure of the past. "You don't need to worry. It was a long time ago."

"I wasn't worried," Janine muttered. She got to her feet and collected their wineglasses. "I'm a little tired. If you don't mind I think I'll go to bed now."

Zach was still staring into the fire and Janine doubted that he'd even heard her. She didn't need a crystal ball to realize he was thinking of the beautiful Marie.

No more than ten minutes after she'd turned out her bedroom light, Janine heard Zach move down the hallway to his room. It sounded for a moment as if he'd hesitated in front of her door, but Janine convinced herself that was just wishful thinking.

From the moment Zach had told her about the one great love of his life, Janine had felt as if a lump were building inside her. A huge lump of disillusionment that seemed to be located somewhere between her heart and her stomach. With every breath she took, it grew larger. Good grief, why should she care about Marie? Zach had never confessed to any deep feeling for her. He hadn't cheated her out of anything that was her right.

An hour later, she lay on her side, still wide awake, her hands pressed to her stomach. She didn't mind that Zach had loved another woman so deeply, but what did hurt was that he could never love her with the same intensity. Marrying her, he'd claimed, made practical and financial sense. He was *fond* of her.

Like a romantic idiot, Janine had been frolicking through their short marriage, confident they would soon be in love with each other and live happily ever after with their two-point-five children in their happy little home with the white picket fence.

Zach had loved Marie, who'd dedicated herself to serving her country.

The most patriotic thing Janine had ever done was cast her vote at election time. She didn't think she should include the two occasions she'd made coffee at Red Cross meetings.

Marie was a linguist. After two years of high-school French, Janine was a master at conjugating verbs, but hopelessly lost in real conversation.

"I had to ask," she groaned to herself. She was fairly confident that Zach would never have mentioned Marie if she hadn't forced the subject. How blissful her ignorance had been. How comfortable.

She could never be the great love of his life and would always remain in the background. Far in the background...

When Janine heard Zach moving around the house a few hours later, she rolled over and glanced at the clock, sure it was still the middle of the night. Then she noticed it was midmorning; they'd planned to be on the road before now. Tossing aside the blankets, she stumbled out of bed and reached blindly for her robe. But she wasn't paying attention, because she collided with the wall and gave a loud shout of pain. She cupped her hand over her nose and closed her eyes. Tears rolled slowly down her cheeks.

"Janine." Zach pounded on the door. "Are you all right?"

"No," she cried, still holding her nose. She glanced in the mirror and lowered her hand. Just as she'd suspected, her nose was bleeding.

"Can I come in?" Zach asked next.

"No...go away." She headed for the adjoining bathroom, tilting back her head as far as she could and pressing both hands over her nose.

"You sound funny. I'm coming in."

"No," she hollered again, "Go away." She groped for a washcloth. The tears rained down now, more from humiliation than pain.

"I'm coming in," Zach shouted, sounding distinctly irritated.

Before Janine could protest, the bedroom door flew open and Zach stalked inside. He stopped abruptly in the bathroom doorway. "What happened?"

Pressing the cold cloth over the lower half of her face with one hand, Janine gestured violently with the other, demanding that he leave.

"Let me look at that," he said, obviously determined to deal with her bloody nose, as well as her anger. He pushed gently against her shoulders, lowering her onto the edge of the bathtub, and carefully removed the cloth.

"What did you do? Meet up with a prize fighter?"

"Don't you dare make fun of me!" The tears ran down her cheeks again and plummeted like raindrops against her silk collar.

It took only a minute or so to control the bleeding. Zach seemed to know exactly what to do. Janine no longer had any desire to fight, and she allowed him to do what he wanted.

Gently, Zach brushed the tears from her cheeks. "Do you want me to kiss it and make it better?"

Without waiting for an answer, Zach's mouth captured hers. Janine felt herself go completely and utterly still. Her heart started to explode and before she realized what she was doing, she'd linked her arms around his neck and was clinging to him helplessly. Zach kissed her forehead and her eyes. His thumbs brushed the remaining moisture from her cheeks. Then he nuzzled her neck. Trembling, she immersed herself in his tenderness. No matter what had happened in the past, Zach was hers for this minute, for this day.

Zach lifted Janine to her feet and seemed to be leading her toward the bed. She might have been tempted to let him, if she hadn't learned about his love for Marie. Knowing she would always place a distant second in his affections was a crippling blow to her pride—and to her heart. It would take time and effort to accept that she could never be the woman who evoked an all-consuming passion in him.

With that thought in mind, she gently pushed him away, needing to put some distance between them before it was too late.

Accepting Janine's decision, Zach dropped his arms and moved to lean against the doorjamb, as if he needed its support to remain upright.

Janine couldn't look at him, couldn't speak. She turned away and began fumbling with her clothes.

"I'll give you a few minutes to dress while I start loading up the car," Zach said a moment later, sounding oddly unlike himself.

Janine nodded miserably. There was nothing she could say. Nothing she could do. He'd wanted to make love to her, and she'd turned him away.

While he packed the car, Janine dressed. She met him fifteen minutes later, her suitcase in hand. She was determined to be cool. But not too cool. Friendly, she decided, but not excessively friendly.

"I'm ready," she announced, with her most cheerful smile.

Zach locked up the house, and in a few moments they were on their way. Deciding to pretend there was nothing out of the ordinary, Janine chatted amicably during the drive home. If Zach noticed anything was wrong, he didn't comment. For his part, he seemed as hesitant as she to talk about what had happened. They seemed to be of one mind about the morning's incident. The whole thing was best forgotten.

Only once did Zach refer to it. He asked her if her nose was causing her any pain, but she quickly assured him she was fine. She flashed a smile bright enough to blind him and immediately changed the subject.

The Seattle sky was gray and drizzling rain when they pulled into the parking garage at the downtown condominium owned by Zach. Silently, she helped him unload the car. They were both unusually quiet as they rode the elevator to the tenth floor.

Zach paused outside his door and eyed her skeptically. "Am I obligated to haul you over the threshold again, or is once enough?"

"Once is enough."

"Good." He grinned and unlocked the door, then pushed it open for her to precede him. Curious, she quickened her pace as she walked inside. The living room was a warm mixture of leather and wood, and its wide window offered a breathtaking view of the Seattle skyline.

"It's lovely."

He nodded, seeming pleased at her reaction. "If you don't like it, we can move. I suppose now that we're married, we should think about purchasing a house soon."

"Why?" she inquired innocently.

"I'm hoping we'll have children someday. Whenever you're ready, that is. There's no pressure, Janine."

"I...know that." She looked past him at the panoramic view, and wrapped her arms around her middle, her heart reacting immediately to his words.

Walking to his desk, Zach pushed the "play" button on his answering machine. A long stream of apparently business-related messages followed.

Janine was much too interested in exploring the condominium to stand and listen to three days' worth of communications. She wandered from room to room, eager to see her new home. In the hallway, she noted Zach had diplomatically left her luggage on the carpet outside the two bedrooms. His was in the master. In his own way, he was telling her that where she slept would be her own decision. If she wished to become his wife in the fullest sense, all she had to do was place her suitcase in the master bedroom. Nothing more needed to be said.

It didn't take Janine longer than a second to decide. She lifted her suitcase and headed toward the guest bedroom. When she looked up, Zach was standing in the hall, studying her, his expression pained.

"Unless you need me for anything, I'm going to the office," he said gruffly.

"That'll be fine."

His gaze moved past her and rested meaningfully on the mattress in the guest bedroom. He cocked one eyebrow questioningly as though to offer her the opportunity to reconsider. "Are you sure you'd rather sleep in here?" he asked.

"I'm sure."

Zach dragged his fingers through his hair. "I was afraid of that." A minute later, he was gone.

ZACH DIDN'T COME HOME for dinner that night. Janine had been in the bathroom when the phone rang, and Zach had left her a message on the machine that he'd be late. So she ate by herself in front of the television, feeling abandoned and unloved. She was just putting the dishes into the dishwasher when he arrived home.

"Sorry I'm late."

"No problem," she lied, never having felt more alone.

Zach glanced through the mail on his desk, although Janine was sure he'd looked at it earlier. "You got the message I wouldn't be home for dinner?"

"Yes. Did you want anything to eat? I could fix you something."

"I ate earlier. Thanks anyway."

They watched an hour's worth of television and then decided to go to bed.

Janine changed into her pajamas—the same no-nonsense type she'd been wearing all week, for she couldn't bring herself to wear the dainty baby-dolls that Pam had given her—and had just finished washing her face. She was coming out of the bathroom, her tooth-brush clenched between her teeth, when she nearly collided with Zach in the hallway. She'd forgotten her slippers and was going to her bedroom to retrieve them. They'd already said their good-nights, and Janine hadn't expected to see him again until morning. She wasn't prepared for this encounter, and the air between them was thick with tension.

She had to force herself not to carelessly toss her toothbrush aside. Not to tell him how she longed for him to love her with the same intensity he had with Marie.

His hands reached out to steady her, and when she didn't immediately move away, he ran the tips of his fingers down her thick brown hair, edging her long bangs to the side of her face so he could gaze into her blue eyes.

Janine lowered her head and closed her eyes. "Esh-bloo me," she managed, but it was difficult to speak with a toothbrush poking out of her mouth.

"Pardon?"

Janine hurried back to the bathroom and rinsed out her mouth. Turning, she braced her hands against the edge of the sink. "I said excuse me for bumping into you."

"Will you be comfortable in the guest room?"

"Yes, fine."

He held a thick blanket in his arms. "I thought you might need this."

"Thanks," she said as smoothly as possible, coming out of the bathroom to take the blanket from him. She longed to be swept off her feet. She wanted love. She wanted passion.

He was offering a warm blanket.

"I...phoned Gramps," she said, looking for a way to delay their parting, and cursing herself for her weakness.

"I intended to get hold of him myself, but got sidetracked."

"He sounded chipper. Dr. Coleman and a couple of his other friends were at the house and the four of them were playing pinochle."

"I'm pleased to hear he's enjoying his retirement."

"I am, too."

A short silence followed.

"Good night, Janine," Zach said after a moment. He glanced, frowning, into the guest room.

"Good night," she said awkwardly.

Janine was certain neither of them slept a wink that night. They were across the hall from each other, but they might as well have been on opposite sides of the state, so great was the emotional distance between them.

In the morning, when Zach's alarm rang, Janine was already wide awake. She threw back her covers, dressed and had coffee waiting when he entered the kitchen.

Zach seemed surprised to see her. "Thanks," he murmured, when she handed him a cup. "That's a very...wifely thing to do."

"What? Make coffee?"

"Get up to see your husband off to work."

"I happened to be awake and figured I might as well get out of bed."

He opened the refrigerator, reached for the orange juice and poured himself a glass. "I see." He replaced the carton and leaned against the counter. "You did agree that our marriage would be a real one."

"Yes, I did," she said somewhat defensively. But that agreement had been before she'd learned about the one great love of his life. Zach had warned her their marriage would be advantageous for a variety of reasons, the least of which was love. At the time, Janine had willingly agreed, convinced their relationship would find a storybook ending. One day they'd gaze at each other and realize they were madly in love. Now she understood that would never happen. And she didn't know if she could stand it.

"Janine," Zach said, distracting her, "is something wrong?"

"What could possibly be wrong?"

"Obviously something's bothering you. You look like you've lost your best friend."

"You should have told me," she burst out, running from the kitchen.

"Told you what?" Zach shouted, following her down the hall.

Furious, she hurried into her bedroom and sat on the end of the mattress, her hands clenched into tight fists at her sides.

"What are you talking about?" he demanded, blocking the doorway.

"About...this other woman you loved."

"Marie? What about her? What's she got to do with you and me?"

"You said you lost your heart when she rejected you. You loved her... She was brave and wonderful, and I'm not any of those things. I don't take pain very well and...I'd like to be patriotic but all I do is vote and all I know in French are verbs."

"What's any of that got to do with you and me?" Zach repeated hoarsely, then tossed his hands into the air. "What the hell has that got to do with anything?"

Knowing she'd never be able to explain, Janine shook her head, sending her bangs fanning out in several directions. "All you are is *fond* of me."

"Correction," Zach said as he stepped into the bedroom. "I *cherish* you."

"It isn't enough," she said, feeling miserable and wretched and unworthy.

"What do you mean it isn't enough? According to you the only reason you married me was that I was a good kisser, so you can't fault me for *my* reasons."

"I don't, it's just that you...you never told me about loving someone else, and if loving her wasn't bad enough, she was a hero, too. All you feel for me is fondness. Well, I don't want your fondness, Zachary Thomas," she cried, leaping to her feet. She tried to collect her scattered thoughts. "If you cared for me, then you would have told me about Marie before. Not mentioning her was a form of dishonesty. You were completely...unfair."

Zach's expression darkened and he buried his hands in his pockets. "You, my dear, didn't say one word to me about Brian."

Janine was so shocked she sank back into the bed. Zach still glared at her, challenging her to contradict him. Slowly gathering her composure, she stood, her eyes narrowing as she studied her husband. "Who told you about Brian?"

"Your grandfather."

"How did he know? I never said a word to him about Brian. Not one solitary word."

"Obviously he knew."

"Obviously." Janine had never felt more like weeping. "I suppose he told you that Brian lied to me and claimed to love me when all the while he was seeing another girl on the side." Another, more troubling thought entered her mind. "I...bet Gramps used the story to make you feel sorry for me, sorry enough to agree to marry me."

"Janine, no."

She covered her face with both hands, humiliation burning her cheeks. It was all so much worse than she'd ever imagined. "You felt sorry for me, didn't you?"

Zach paced the length of the bedroom. "I'm not going to lie to you, although I have a notion it would be better if I did. Your grandfather didn't mention that you'd fallen in love with Brian until after the day we took him to the doctor."

"He waited until we got to know each other a little better," Janine whispered, still dealing with the realization that her grandfather had known about Brian all along.

"By then I'd discovered I liked you."

"The word *like* is possibly even worse than *fond*," she muttered.

"Just hear me out, would you?"

"All right," she sighed, fearing that nothing he said now mattered, anyway. Her pride had just suffered another major blow. The one love of his life had been this marvelous patriot, while Janine had fallen for a weak-willed womanizer.

"It isn't as bad as it seems," Zach tried to assure her.

"I can just imagine what Gramps told you."

"All he said was that he was afraid you'd never learn to trust your own judgment again. For quite a while now, he's watched you avoid any hint of a relationship. It was as though you'd retreated from men and were content to just lick your wounds."

"That's not true. I was seeing Peter Donahue on a regular basis."

"Safe dates with safe men. There was never any likelihood of your falling in love with Peter and you knew it. It was the only reason you went out with him."

"Is...is what happened with Brian why Gramps decided to play matchmaker?"

"I suspect that was part of it. Also his concern for your future. But I don't fully understand his intentions even now. I don't think it matters. He wanted you to be happy and secure. Anton knew I'd never purposely hurt you. And in his eyes, the two of us were perfect for each other." Zach sat down next to her and reached for her hand, lacing her fingers with his own. "Does it matter so much? We're married now."

She looked away from him, and swallowed tightly. "I...may not be blond and gorgeous or even brave, but I deserve a husband who'll love me. Both Gramps and you failed to take that into account. I don't want your pity, Zach Thomas."

"Good, because I don't pity you. You're my wife, and frankly, I'm happy about it. We can have a good life, if you'll put this nonsense behind you."

"You'd never have chosen me on your own. I knew what you thought of me from the first moment we met. You thought, you assumed I was a rich spoiled woman who'd never had anything real to worry about. I bet you thought I'd consider a broken nail a major disaster."

"All right, I'll admit I had the wrong impression, but that was before," Zach insisted.

"Before what?"

"Before I got to know you."

Janine's shoulders heaved with barely suppressed emotion. "As I recall you suggested the reason you'd be willing to marry me was because I wasn't so bad. I guess I should have swooned with the sheer thrill of such compliments."

Zach's sigh was filled with frustration. "I told you before I wasn't ever going to say the stuff you women like to hear. I don't know a damn thing about romance. But I care about you, Janine, I honestly care. Isn't that enough?"

"I need more than that," she said miserably. It was the promise of their future, the promise of learning about love together, that had intrigued her.

Zach frowned. "You told me even before we were married that you didn't need romantic words. You were content before I ever mentioned Marie. How has my telling you changed anything?"

She saw that Zach was losing his patience with her. She lowered her gaze to the thick carpet and swallowed hard. "I really wish I could explain, but it does make a difference. I'm sorry, Zach, I really am."

A lifetime seemed to pass before he spoke again. "So am I," he whispered before turning away. A moment later the front door opened and almost immediately closed again. Zach had left her.

"What did you expect?" she wailed, covering her face with both hands. "Did you think he was going to fall at your knees and declare his undying love?" The picture of the proud and mighty Zach Thomas playing the role of besotted husband was almost comical. If he'd done that for any woman it would have been the brave and beautiful Marie. Not Janine.

AFTER THAT DISASTROUS morning, their relationship grew more strained than ever. Zach left for work early and returned late, usually past dinnertime. Janine never questioned where he was or who he was with, although she nearly had to bite off her tongue to keep from asking.

Zach proved to be a model housemate, if not a husband—cordial, courteous and remote. For her part, she threw herself into her volunteer work at the Friendship Club, spending several hours each week with the youngsters. She did her best to hide her unhappiness from her grandfather, although that was difficult.

"You look pale," he told her when she joined him for lunch one afternoon, several days after her return from Ocean Shores. "Are you losing weight?"

"I wish," she said, attempting to make a joke of it. They sat in the dining room, with Mrs. McCormick wandering in and out, casting Janine concerned glances. Janine resisted the urge to leap up and do aerobic exercises to demonstrate that she was in perfect health.

"You can't afford to get much thinner," Gramps said, eyeing her solemnly. He placed a dinner roll on the side of her plate and plunked the butter dish down in front of her.

"I'm not losing weight," she chided, spreading a thick layer of butter on the roll in order to please him.

"I took that sea gull you gave me into the office," Gramps said as he continued to study her. "Zach saw it and asked me where I got it. When I told him, he didn't say anything, but I could tell he wasn't pleased. Do you want it back?"

"No, of course not." Janine dropped her gaze. She'd never intended for Gramps to take Chester into the office. On impulse, she'd given him the ceramic bird, reluctant to have it around the condominium to remind her of those first glorious days with Zach.

"I wish I knew what was wrong with you two," Gramps burst out in an uncharacteristic display of frustration. He tossed his napkin onto his dinner plate. "You should be happy! Instead, the pair of you look like you're recovering from a bad bout of flu. Zach's working so many hours it's a wonder he doesn't fall over from sheer exhaustion."

Janine carefully tore the roll into quarters. She toyed with the idea of bringing up the subject of Brian, but in the end, she didn't.

"So you say you're fine, and there's nothing wrong between you and Zach," Gramps muttered sarcastically. "Funny, that's exactly what he said when I asked him. Only he told me to mind my own business—not quite in those words, but I got the message. The thing is, the boy looks as pathetic as you do. I can't understand it—you're perfect for each other!"

Gramps reached into his pocket for a cigar. "I'll be seeing Zach this afternoon and I fully intend to give that boy a piece of my mind. By all rights, you should be a happy bride." He tapped one end of the cigar against the table.

"We'll be fine, Gramps. Please stay out of it."

For a long moment, he said nothing; he only stared at the cigar between his fingers. "You're sure you don't want me to talk some sense into that boy?" he finally asked.

The mental picture of him trying to do so was enough to bring a quivering smile to her lips. "I'm sure," she said, then glanced at her watch. Pam would be waiting for her. "But since you're seeing Zach, would you mind letting him know I'll probably be late for dinner? He...should go ahead and eat without me."

"Do you do this often?" His question was an accusation.

"No," she replied, shaking her head. "This is the first time. Pam needs my help with a school project and I don't know when we'll be finished."

Gramps glowered as he lit his cigar, puffing mightily before he spoke. "I'll tell him."

AS IT TURNED OUT, Janine spent longer with Pam than she'd expected. The homework assignment wasn't difficult, but Pam begged Janine to stay with her. Pam's father was working late and the girl seemed to need Janine more than ever. They cooked dinner together, then ate in front of the television while Pam chatted away about her friends and life in general.

It was almost nine by the time Janine pulled into the parking garage. The first thing she noticed was Zach's car. The atmosphere had been so terribly falsely courteous between them that she dreaded each encounter, however brief. Since that first morning, Zach hadn't made any effort to talk to her about her role in his life. Janine wasn't looking for a long flowery declaration of love. Just a word or two more profound than *fond* or *like* to let her know she was important to him.

Drawing a deep calming breath, she headed for the condominium. She'd just unlocked the door when Zach stormed into the room like a Minnesota blizzard. "Just where the hell have you been?" he demanded.

Janine was so shocked by his fierce anger that she said nothing.

"I demand as your husband to know exactly where you were." Zach jammed his fingers viciously through his hair.

She removed her sweater, hanging it carefully in the entryway closet along with her purse. Zach scowled at her silence, fists clenched at his sides. "Do you have any idea of the time? Did it so much as cross your mind that I might have been concerned about you?"

Janine turned to face him. "You knew where I was," she said calmly.

"All Anton said was that you'd be late. Not where you were going or who you were with. So naturally I was worried."

"I'm sorry. Next time I'll leave you Pam's phone number in case you need to contact me." Janine yawned and covered her mouth with both hands. The day had been exhausting. "If you don't mind, I think I'll go to bed now. Unless there's anything else you'd like to know?"

He glared at her, then shook his head, before wheeling around abruptly and walking away.

Hours later, Janine was awakened from a light sleep by a gruff sobbing sound coming from the other room. It didn't take her more than a moment to realize it was Zach. Was he having a nightmare?

Tossing aside the blankets, she hurried out of bed and into his room. The cries of anguish grew louder and more intense. In the light from the hallway, she could see him thrashing about, the bedding in disarray.

"Zach," she cried, rushing to his side. She sat on the edge of the bed and placed her hands gently on his shoulders. "Wake up. You're having a dream. Just a dream. It's okay...."

Zach's eyes slowly opened. "Janine." He ground out her name as though in torment, and reached for her, hauling her into his arms with such force that he left her breathless. "Dear Lord," he said, his voice so husky she could barely understand him. "I thought I'd lost you."

Her vision cleared as she slowly reached to brush aside an errant sobbing sound, coming from somewhere in the room. She was more content to listen closely. *Zach*. It was the sound of a man. Of course, with the shadows, she carried him off bed and into his room. It was if salt to any sensation of bitterness in the wind into no reality, she could lie for minutes about the rocking in silence.

CHAPTER TEN

"ZACH, I'M FINE," Janine whispered. Emotion clogged her throat at the hungry way his eyes roamed her face. He seemed to have difficulty believing, even now, that she was unhurt.

"It was so real," he continued, his chest heaving. He covered his face as if to block out the vivid images the dream had induced. Making room in the large bed, he brought her down beside him. His hands repeatedly stroked her hair from her face as he released several jagged breaths. "We were at the ocean," he told her, "and although I'd warned you against it, you decided to swim. A huge wave knocked you off your feet and you were drowning. Heaven help me, I tried, but I couldn't get to you fast enough." He closed his eyes briefly. "You kept calling out to me and I couldn't find you. I just couldn't get to you fast enough."

"Zach," she whispered, her mouth so close to his that their breath mingled, "I'm right here. It was only a dream. It wasn't real."

He nodded, but his eyes still seemed troubled, refusing to leave her face. Then ever so slowly, as though he expected her to object, he moved his mouth even closer to hers. "I couldn't bear to lose you. I'd rather die myself."

Helpless to deny him anything, Janine turned her face to receive his kiss.

His hands tangled her thick dark hair, effectively holding her captive, while his mouth seized hers in a devouring kiss that sent her senses swirling into a place where nothing mattered except his touch. Overcome for a moment by the fierce tenderness she felt in him, Janine eagerly fed his need.

"Janine, oh, my dear sweet Janine. I couldn't bear to lose you."

"I'm here...I'm here." Melting against him, she molded her body to the unyielding contours of his, offering her lips and her heart to his loving possessiveness. Again and again, he kissed her. Janine slid her hands up his chest and twined them around his neck. This was what she'd longed for from the first, the knowledge that he needed her, and she gloried in the warm sensations.

With a groan, he reluctantly dragged his mouth from hers. He held her clasped firmly to his chest and his breathing was both harsh and rapid. Complete and utter peace combined with a delirious sense of happiness, and she released a deep sigh. Pressing her ear to his muscled chest, she listened, content, to the heavy pounding of his heart.

"Did I frighten you?" he asked after a moment.

"No," she whispered.

He resumed stroking her hair as she nestled more securely in his arms. Zach had made her feel wondrous, exciting things every time he'd kissed her, but the way he held and touched her now went far beyond those kisses. She'd experienced a bonding with Zach, a true joining of spirits that had been missing until now. He had told her he would cherish her, but she hadn't believed it until this moment. Tears clouded her eyes and she struggled to restrain them.

For a long time neither of them spoke. But Janine didn't need words. Her eyes were closed as she savored these precious moments.

When Zach did speak, his voice was little more than a hoarse whisper. "I had a sister who drowned. Her name was Beth Ann, and I promised I'd always be there for her—but I failed her. I couldn't bear to lose you, too."

Janine tightened her hold, knowing how difficult it must be for him to speak of his sister.

"I never forgave myself." His body tensed and his fingers dug roughly into her shoulder. "Losing Beth Ann still haunts me. She wouldn't have drowned if I'd been with her. She—"

Lifting her head slightly, Janine's misty gaze met his. "It wasn't your fault. How could it have been?"

"But I was responsible for her," he returned harshly.

Janine suspected that Zach had rarely, if ever, shared his sorrow or his guilt over his sister's death with anyone. A low groan worked its way through him and he squeezed his eyes tightly shut. "For years, I've drummed out the memories of Beth Ann's death. The nightmare was so real, only this time it wasn't her—it was you.''

"But I'm safe and sound. See?" She pressed her hands to both sides of his face, smiling down on him.

He sighed and smiled back, a little uncertainly. "I'm all right now. I shouldn't have burdened you with this."

"It wasn't a burden."

His arms tightened around her, and he inhaled deeply as if soaking in her scent, absorbing her softness. "Stay with me?"

She nodded, satisfied that he needed her.

Within minutes, Janine felt herself drifting into drowsiness. From Zach's relaxed, even breathing, she knew he was already asleep.

When Janine next stirred, she was lying on her side, and Zach was cuddling her spoon fashion, his arm looped about her waist. At some point during the night, she'd slipped under the covers, but she had no recollection of doing so. A small satisfied smile touched the edges of her mouth. She rolled carefully onto her back so as not to disturb Zach, and wondered what she should do. When Zach woke and found her in bed with him, she feared he might regret what had happened, regret asking her to stay. In the harsh light of day, he might feel embarrassed that he'd told her about his sister's death and the guilt he bore.

Closing her eyes, Janine debated with herself. If she slipped from his bed and returned to her own room, he might think she was rejecting him, shocked by his heart-wrenching account of Beth Ann's death.

"Janine?" He whispered her name, his voice still husky with sleep.

Her eyes flew open. "I...we fell asleep. What time is it?"

"Early. The alarm won't go off for another couple of hours."

She nodded, hoping to disguise any hint of disappointment in her voice. He didn't want her with him, she was sure of it. He was embarrassed to find her still in his bed. "I'll leave now if you want."

"No."

The single word was filled with such longing that Janine thought she'd misunderstood him. She managed to tip her head back far enough to meet his gaze. The light from the hall allowed her to see the passion smoldering in his rich dark eyes. Turning onto her side so she faced him, Janine lovingly traced the lines of his face.

"I'm sorry about the way I behaved over...Marie," she whispered. "I was jealous and I knew I was being ridiculous, but I couldn't help myself."

The corners of his eyes crinkled with his smile. "I'll forgive you, if you're willing to overlook the way I behaved when you arrived home last night."

She answered him with a light kiss, and he hugged her to him. Janine surrendered to the sheer pleasure of being in Zach's arms, savoring the rush of warm sensations that sprang to life inside her.

"I don't know how to say all the words you deserve to hear, but I know one thing, Janine. I love you. It happened without my even being aware of it. One day I woke up and realized how important you'd become to me. It wasn't the grand passion you wanted, and I'm sorry for that. The love I feel for you is the quiet steady kind. It's buried deep in my heart, but trust me, it's there. You're the most important person in my life."

"Oh, Zach, I love you so much."

"You love me?"

"I have for weeks, even before we were married, I think. That's what bothered me so much when I learned about Marie. I wanted you to love me with the same intensity that you felt for her...that I feel for you."

"It isn't like that. It never was. Marie was as brave as she was beautiful, but what we shared was never meant to last. And she was smart enough to realize it. I fell in love with her, but she was too much of a professional ever to involve her heart. She was the kind of person who thrives on excitement and danger. It wasn't until you and I met that I realized if I were ever to marry, it would be to someone like you."

"Someone like me?"

He kissed her briefly. "A woman who's warm and gentle and caring. Someone unselfish and—" he hesitated "—and desirable."

Her throat tightened with emotion. It was all she could do to meet his gaze. Zach found her desirable. He wanted to make love to her.

He didn't need to say the words; the message was there for her to read in his eyes. It wasn't the desperate passion she'd once assumed she wanted, but the love she felt coming from him, his need to have her a part of his life, was far more potent than any action he could have taken, any words he could have said.

Feeling weak with her love, Janine whispered, simply, "Love me, Zach."

Zach's mouth found hers with a sweet desperate ardor. If she was suffering any lingering doubts they vanished like mist in the sun as his lips devoured hers, twisting her into tight knots of desire.

His arms locked around her and he rolled onto his back, pulling her with him so that her softness pressed against the full length of his hard muscular frame. His hands outlined her face as though he half expected her to stop him.

"Make me your wife," she whispered, bending forward to brush her moist mouth over his.

Zach groaned, and then he did the strangest, most wonderful thing. He laughed. The robust sound echoed across the room and was so infectious that it made Janine grin.

"My sweet Janine," he said. "You've lit up my life." And then he kissed her again, leaving her with no doubts at all.

For a long time afterward, their happiness could be heard in their sighs and gasps and whispered words of love....

THE BUZZING SOUND refused to go away. Janine moaned softly and flung out her hand, hoping to find the source of the distraction. But before she could locate it, the noise ceased abruptly.

"Good morning, wife," Zach whispered close to her ear.

Her eyes remained closed as she smiled leisurely. "Good morning, husband." Rolling onto her back, she held her arms open wide to him. "I had the most marvelous dream last night."

Zach chuckled softly. "That wasn't any dream."

"But it must have been," she said, slipping her arms around his neck and smiling lazily. "Nothing could be that incredible in real life."

"I didn't think so, either, but you proved me wrong." He kissed her tenderly, and then so thoroughly that by the time he lifted his head, Janine was breathless.

Slowly, almost against her will, her eyes drifted open. His gaze was dark with desire. "You'll be late for work," she warned him.

His smile filled with sensual laziness. "Who cares?"

"Not me," she murmured. And with a small cry of pleasure, she willingly gave herself to her husband.

Zach was already an hour late for the office when he dragged himself out of bed and headed for the shower. Wearing her husband's pajama top, Janine wandered into the kitchen and prepared a pot of coffee, going through the motions by rote. She leaned her hip against the counter and smiled softly into space, hardly aware of the passage of time.

A few minutes later, or perhaps it was longer, Zach stepped behind her and slid his arms around her waist, nuzzling her neck.

"Zach," she protested, but not too strenuously. She closed her eyes and cradled her arms over his, leaning back against his solid strength. "You're already late."

"I know," he murmured. "If I didn't have an important meeting this morning, I'd skip work altogether."

Twisting around in his arms, Janine tilted back her head to gaze into his eyes. "You'll be home for dinner?"

"Keep looking at me like that and I'll be home for lunch."

Janine smiled. "It's almost that time now."

"I know," he growled, reluctantly pulling away from her. "We'll go out to dinner tonight to celebrate," he said, kissing her again. His mouth was hot on her own, feverish with demand and need and passion. He lifted his head, but his eyes remained shut. "Then we'll come home and celebrate."

Janine sighed. Married life was beginning to agree with her.

At precisely five, Zach was back. He stood just inside the door, loosening his tie, when Janine appeared. A smile traveled to his mouth as their eyes met and held. Neither moved. They stared at each other as if they'd spent years apart instead of a few short hours.

Janine was feeling distinctly light-headed. "Hi," she managed to say, shocked that her voice sounded more like a hoarse whisper than the cheery greeting she'd intended. "How'd the meeting go?"

"Bad."

"Bad?"

He nodded slowly and stepped forward, placing his briefcase on the edge of his desk. "I was supposed to be listening to an important financial report, but unfortunately all I could think about was how much longer the thing would take so I could get back home to my wife."

"Oh." That wasn't the most intelligent bit of conversation she'd ever delivered, but just looking at Zach was enough to wipe out all her normal thought processes.

"It got to be almost embarrassing." His look was intimate and loving as he advanced two more steps toward her. "In the middle of it, I started smiling, and then I embarrassed myself further by laughing outright."

"Laughing? Something was funny?"

"I was thinking about your definition of romance. The tryst on the moors was supplied by your grandfather, the walk along the beach, hand in hand, was supplied by me after the wedding. But the desperate passion, my dear sweet wife, was something we found together."

Her eyes glazed over with moisture.

"Dear sweet heaven, Janine, I love you."

They started toward each other then, but stopped abruptly when the doorbell chimed. Zach's questioning eyes met hers. Janine shrugged, not knowing who it could possibly be.

The second Zach answered the door, Anton flew into the room, looking more determined than Janine had ever seen him.

"All right, you two, sit down," he ordered, waving them in the direction of the sofa.

"Gramps?"

"Anton?"

Janine glanced at Zach, but he looked as mystified as she did. So she just shrugged and complied with her grandfather's demand. Zach sat down next to her.

Gramps paced the carpet directly in front of them, looking thoroughly disgruntled.

"Janine and I had lunch the other day," Anton said, directing his words to Zach. "Two things were made clear to me then. First and foremost she's crazy in love with you, but I doubt she's told you that."

"Gramps—" Janine started, but her grandfather silenced her with a single look.

"The next thing I realized is that she's unhappy. Terribly unhappy. Being in love is difficult enough but—"

"Anton," Zach broke in, "if you'd—"

Gramps cut him off with the same laser-eyed look he'd sent Janine. "Don't interrupt me, boy. I'm on a roll and I'm not about to stop now. If I noticed Janine was a little melancholy at lunch, it was nothing compared to what I've been noticing about you." Suddenly he ceased his pacing and planted himself squarely in front of Zach. "All week I've been hearing complaints and rumors about you. Folks in the office claim you're there all hours of the day and night, working until you're ready to drop. The fact is, I know you, Zach, probably better than anyone else does. You're in love with my granddaughter, and it's got you all tangled up inside."

"Gramps—"

"Shh." He dismissed Janine with a hard shake of his head. "Now I may be an old man, but I'm not dense. Maybe the way I went about bringing the two of you together wasn't the smartest way, or the conventional way, but by golly it worked." He hesitated long enough to smile proudly. "In the beginning I had my doubts. Janine put up a bit of fuss."

"I believe you said something about how it's easier to pluck a live chicken," Zach inserted, slanting a secret smile at Janine.

"True enough. I never knew that girl had so much spunk. But the fact is, Zachary, as you'll recall, you weren't all that keen on the idea yourself. You both think because I'm retirement age I don't notice things. But I do. You were two lonely people, filling up your lives with unimportant relationships, avoiding love, avoiding life. I care about you. Too damn much to sit back and do nothing."

"It worked out," Janine said, wanting to reassure him.

"At first I thought it had. I arranged the trip to Scotland and it looked like everything was falling neatly into place, like one of those old movie scripts. I couldn't have been more pleased when you announced that you were going to marry. It was sooner than I'd anticipated, but I assumed that meant matters between the two of you were progressing nicely. Apparently I was wrong. Now I'm worried."

"You don't need to be."

"That's not the way I see it," Gramps said with a fierce glare. "Tell him you love him, Janine. Look Zach in the eye and put aside that silly pride of yours. He needs to know it. He needs to hear it. I told you from the first that he wasn't going to be an easy man to know, and that you'd need to be patient with him. What I didn't count on was that damnable pride of yours."

"You want me to tell Zach I love him? Here? Now?"

"Yes!"

Janine turned to her husband and, feeling a little self-conscious, lowered her eyes.

"Tell him," Gramps barked.

"I love you, Zach," she said softly. "I really do."

Gramps gave a loud satisfied sigh. "Good, good. Okay, Zach, it's your turn."

"My turn?"

"Tell Janine what you feel and don't go all arrogant on me."

Zach's hand reached for Janine's. He lifted her palm to his mouth and brushed his lips against the tender skin there. "I love you," he whispered.

"Add something else," Gramps instructed, gesturing toward him. "Something along the lines that you'd be a lost and lonely soul without her. Women like to hear that sort of thing. Damn foolishness, I know, but necessary."

"I'd be a lost and lonely soul without you," Zach repeated, then looked back to Janine's grandfather. "How'd I do?"

"Better than most. Is there anything else you'd like him to say, Janine?"

She released an expressive sigh. "I don't think so."

"Good. Now I want the two of you to kiss."

"Here? In front of you?"

"Yes," Gramps insisted.

Janine slipped into Zach's arms. The smile he shared with her was so devastating that she felt her heart race with anticipation. Her eyes fluttered closed as his mouth settled on hers, thrilling her with promises for all the years to come.

Gently, provocatively, Zach moved his mouth over hers, ending his kiss all too soon to suit Janine. From the shudder that coursed through him, Janine knew it was all too soon to suit him, too. Reluctantly they pulled apart. Zach looked deeply into her eyes, and Janine responded with a soft smile.

"Excellent, excellent."

Janine had all but forgotten her grandfather's presence. When she tore her gaze away from Zach, she discovered Gramps sitting across from them, his hands braced against the arms of the leather chair. He looked exceedingly proud of himself. "Are you two going to be all right now?"

"Yes, sir," Zach answered for them both, his eyes hazy with desire as he smiled at Janine. She could feel herself blushing, and realized her eyes were foggy with the same longing.

"Good!" Gramps declared, nodding once for emphasis. A slow grin overtook his mouth. "I knew all the two of you needed was a little assistance from me." He paused and inhaled deeply. "Since you're both getting along so well, maybe now would be the time to bring up the subject of children."

"Anton," Zach said, slowly rising to his feet. He moved across the room and opened the door. "If you don't mind, I'll take care of that myself."

"Soon?" Gramps wanted to know.

Zach's eyes met Janine's. "Soon," he promised.

HERE COMES TROUBLE

CHAPTER ONE

"MARYANNE SIMPSON of the New York Simpsons, I presume?"

Maryanne glared at the man standing across the room from her in the reception area of the radio station. She pointedly ignored his sarcasm, keeping her baby-blue eyes as emotionless as possible.

Kramer Adams—Seattle's most popular journalist—looked nothing like the polished professional man in the black-and-white photo that headed his daily column. Instead he resembled a well-known dishevelled television detective. He even wore a wrinkled raincoat, one that looked as if he'd slept in it for an entire week.

"Or should I call you Deb?" he taunted.

"Ms Simpson will suffice," she said in her best finishing-school voice. The rival newspaperman was cocky and arrogant and the best damn journalist Maryanne had ever read. Maryanne was a good columnist herself, or at least she was desperately striving to become one. Her father, who owned the *Seattle Review* and twelve other daily newspapers nationwide, had seen to it that she was given this once-in-a-lifetime opportunity with the Seattle paper. She was working hard to prove herself. Perhaps too hard. That was when the trouble had begun.

"So how's the heart?" Kramer asked, reaching for a magazine and idly flipping through the dog-eared pages. "Is it still bleeding with all those liberal views of yours?"

Maryanne ignored the question, removed her navy blue wool coat and neatly folded it over the back of a chair. "My heart is just fine, thank you."

With a sound she could only describe as a snicker, he threw himself down on the padded chair and indolently brought an ankle up to rest on his knee.

Maryanne sat across from him, stiff and straight in the high-backed chair, and boldly met his eyes. Everything she needed to know about Kramer Adams could be seen in his face. The strong well-defined lines of his jaw told her how stubborn he could be. His eyes were dark, intelligent and intense. And his mouth, well, that was another story altogether. It seemed to wrestle with itself before ever breaking into a smile, as if a gesture of amusement went against his very nature. Kramer wasn't smiling now. And Maryanne wasn't about to let him know how much he intimidated her. Some emotion must have shone in her eyes, because he said abruptly, "You're the one who started this, you know?"

Maryanne was well aware of that. But this rivalry between them had begun unintentionally, at least on her part. The very day that the morning edition of the competition, the *Seattle Sun*, published Kramer's column on solutions to the city's housing problem, the *Review* had run Maryanne's piece on the same subject. Kramer's article was meant to be satirical while Maryanne's was deadly serious. Her mistake was in stating that there were those in the city who apparently found the situation amusing, and she blasted anyone who behaved so irresponsibly. This was not a joking matter, she'd pointed out.

It was as if she'd read Kramer's column and set out to reprimand him personally for his cavalier attitude before the entire western half of Washington state.

Two days later, Kramer's column poked fun at her, asking what Ms High Society could possibly know about affordable housing. Clearly a debutante had never had to worry about the roof over her head, he'd snarled. But more than that, he'd made her suggestions to alleviate the growing problem sound both frivolous and impractical.

Her next column came out the same evening and referred to tough pessimistic reporters who took themselves much too seriously. She went so far as to make fun of a fictional Seattle newsman who resembled Kramer Adams to a T.

Kramer retaliated once more, and Maryanne seethed. Obviously she'd have to be the one to put an end to this silliness. She hoped that not responding to Kramer's latest attack would terminate their rivalry, but she should have known better. An hour after her column on community spirit had hit the newsstands, KJBR, a local radio station, called, requesting Maryanne to give a guest editorial. She'd immediately agreed, excited and honored at the invitation. It wasn't until later that she learned Kramer Adams would also be speaking. The format was actually a celebrity debate, a fact of which she'd been blithely unaware.

The door opened and a tall dark-haired woman walked into the station's reception area. "I'm Liz Walters," she said, two steps into the room. "I produce the news show. I take it you two know each other?"

"Like family," Kramer muttered with that cocky grin of his.

"We introduced ourselves no more than five minutes ago," Maryanne rebutted stiffly.

"Good," Liz said without glancing up from her clipboard. "If you'll both come this way, we'll get you set up in the control booth."

From her brief conversation with the show's host, Brian Campbell, Maryanne learned that the show taped on Thursday night wouldn't air until Sunday evening.

When they were both seated inside the control booth, Maryanne withdrew two typed pages from her bag. Not to be outdone, Kramer made a show of pulling a small notepad from the huge pocket of his crumpled raincoat.

Brian Campbell began the show with a brief introduction, presenting the evening's subject: the growing popularity of the Seattle area. He then turned the microphone over to Maryanne, who was to speak first.

Forcing herself to relax, she took a deep calming breath, tucked her long auburn hair behind her ears and started speaking. She managed to keep her voice low and as well modulated as her nerves would allow.

"The word's out," she said, glancing quickly at her notes. "Seattle has been rated one of the top cities in the country for several years running. Is it any wonder Californians are moving up in droves, attracted by the increasing economic growth, the lure of pure fresh air and beautiful clean waters? Seattle has appeal, personality and class."

As she warmed to her subject, her voice gained confidence and conviction. She'd fallen in love with Seattle when she'd visited for a two-day stopover before flying to Hawaii. The trip had been a college graduation gift from her parents. She'd returned to New York one week later full of enthusiasm, not for the tourist-cluttered islands, but for the brief glimpse she'd had of the Emerald City.

From the first, she'd intended to return to the Pacific Northwest. Instead she'd taken a job as a non-fiction editor in one of her father's New York publishing houses; she'd been so busy that travelling time was limited. That editorial job lasted almost eighteen months, and although Maryanne thoroughly enjoyed it she longed to write herself, and put her journalism skills to work.

Samuel Simpson must have sensed her restlessness because he mentioned an opening at the *Seattle Review,* a long-established paper, when they met in Nantucket over Labour Day weekend. Maryanne had plied him with questions, mentioning more than once how she'd fallen in love with Seattle. Her father had grinned, chewing vigorously on the end of his cigar, and looked towards his wife of twenty-seven years before he'd casually reached for the telephone. After a single call that lasted less than three minutes, Samuel announced the job was hers. Within two weeks, Maryanne was packed and on her way west.

"In conclusion I'd like to remind our audience that there's no turning back now," Maryanne said. "Seattle sits as a polished jewel in the beautiful Pacific Northwest. Seattle, the Emerald City, awaits even greater prosperity, even more progress."

She set her papers aside and smiled in the direction of the host, relieved to be finished. She watched in dismay as Kramer scowled at her, then slipped his notepad back inside his pocket. He apparently planned to wing it.

Kramer—who needed, Brian declared, no introduction—leaned towards the microphone. He glanced at Maryanne, frowned once more, and slowly shook his head.

"Give me a break, Ms Simpson!" he cried. "Doesn't anyone realise it rains here? Did you know that until recently, if Seattle went an entire week without rain, we sacrificed a virgin? Unfortunately we were running low on those until you moved into town."

Maryanne barely managed to restrain a gasp.

"Why do you think Seattle has remained so beautiful?" Kramer continued. "Why do you think we aren't suffering from the pollution problems so prevalent in Southern California and elsewhere? You seem to believe Seattle should throw open her arms and invite the world to park on our unspoiled doorstep. My advice to you, and others like you, is to go back where you came from. We don't want you turning Seattle into another LA—or New York."

The hair on the back of Maryanne's neck bristled. Although he spoke in general terms, his words seemed to be directed solely at her. He was telling her, in effect, to pack up her suitcase and head home to Mommy and Daddy where she belonged.

When Kramer finished, they were each given two minutes for a rebuttal.

"Some of what you have to say is true," Maryanne admitted through clenched teeth. "But you can't turn back progress. Only a fool," she said pointedly, "would try to keep families from settling in Washington state. You can argue until you've lost your voice, but it isn't going to help. The population in this area is going to explode in the next few years whether you approve or not."

"That's probably true, but it doesn't mean I have to sit still and let it happen. In fact, I intend to do everything I can to put a stop to it. We in Seattle have a way of life to protect and a duty to future generations. If growth continues in this vein, our schools will soon be overcrowded, our homes so overpriced that no one except those from out of state will be able to afford housing—and that's only if they can find it. If that's what you want, then fine, bask in your ignorance."

"What do you suggest?" Maryanne burst out. "Setting up road blocks?"

"That's a start," Kramer returned sarcastically. "Something's got to be done before this area becomes another urban disaster."

Maryanne rolled her eyes. "Do you honestly think you're going to single-handedly turn back the tide of progress?"

"I'm sure as hell going to try."

"That's ridiculous."

"And that's our Celebrity Debate for this evening," Brian Campbell said quickly, cutting off any further argument. "Join us next week when our guests will be City Council candidates Nick Fraser and Robert Hall."

The microphone was abruptly switched off. "That was excellent," the host said, flashing them a wide enthusiastic smile. "Thank you both."

"You've got your head buried in the sand," Maryanne felt obliged to inform Kramer, although she knew it wouldn't do any good. She dropped her notes back in her bag and snapped it firmly shut, as if to say the subject was now closed.

"You may be right," Kramer said with a grin. "But at least the sand is on a pollution-free beach. If you have your way, it'll soon be cluttered with—"

"I have my way?" she cried. "You make it sound as though I'm solely responsible for the Puget Sound growth rate."

"You are responsible, and those like you."

"Well, excuse me," she muttered sarcastically. She nodded politely to Brian Campbell, then headed back to the reception room where she'd left her coat. To her annoyance Kramer followed her, grumbling every step of the way.

"I don't excuse you, Deb."

"I asked you to use my name," she said furiously, "and it isn't Deb."

Crossing his arms over his chest, Kramer leaned lazily against the doorjamb while she retrieved her wool coat.

Maryanne crammed her arms into the sleeves and nearly tore off the buttons in her rush to leave. The way he stood there studying her did little to cool her temper.

"And another thing..." she muttered.

"You mean there's more?"

"You're darn right there is. That crack about virgins was intolerably rude! I...I expected better of you."

"Hell, it's true."

"How would you know?"

He grinned that insufferable grin of his, infuriating her even more.

"Don't you have anything better to do than follow me around?" she demanded, stalking out of the room.

"Not particularly. Fact is, I've been looking forward to meeting you."

Once she'd recovered from the shock of learning that he'd be her opponent in this radio debate, Maryanne had eagerly anticipated this evening, too. Long before she'd arrived at the radio station, she'd planned to tell Kramer how much she admired his work. This silly rivalry between them was exactly that: silly. She hadn't meant to step on his toes and would have willingly called and cleared the air if he hadn't attacked her in print at the earliest opportunity.

"Sure you wanted to meet me. Hurling insults to my face must be far more fun."

He laughed at that and Maryanne was amazed at how rich and friendly his amusement sounded.

"Come on, Simpson, don't take everything so personally. Admit it. We've been having a good time poking fun at each other."

Maryanne didn't say anything for several moments. Actually he was partially right. She *had* enjoyed their exchanges, although she wouldn't have admitted that earlier. She wasn't entirely sure she wanted to now.

"Admit it," he coaxed, again with a grin.

That uneven smile of his was her undoing. "It hasn't exactly been *fun*," she answered reluctantly, "but it has been...interesting."

"That's what I thought." He thrust his hands into his pockets, looking pleased with himself.

She glanced at him appraisingly. The man's appeal was definitely of the rugged variety: his outrageous charm—Maryanne wasn't sure charm was really the right word—his craggy face and solid compact build. She'd been surprised to discover he wasn't as tall as she'd imagined. In fact, he was probably less than six feet.

"Word has it Daddy was the one responsible for landing you this cushy job," he commented, disrupting her assessment.

"Cushy?" she cried, infuriated. "You've got to be kidding!" She often put in twelve-hour days slaving over her computer, trying to come up with a column that was both relevant and entertaining. In the four weeks since she'd joined the *Seattle Review* staff, she'd worked damn hard. She had something to prove to herself, not only to herself but to her peers.

"So being a journalist isn't everything it's cracked up to be?"

"I didn't say that," she returned heatedly. To be perfectly honest, Maryanne had never tried harder at anything. Her pride and a whole lot more was riding on the outcome of the next few months. Samuel Simpson's daughter or not, she was on probation, after which her performance would be reviewed by the managing editor.

"I wonder if you've ever done anything without Daddy's approval."

"I wonder if you've always been this rude."

He chuckled at that. "Almost always. As I said, don't take it personally."

With her leather bag securely tucked under her arm, she headed for the exit, which Kramer was effectively blocking. "Excuse me, please."

"Always so polite," he murmured before he straightened, allowing her to pass.

Kramer followed her to the lift, annoying her even more. Maryanne felt his scrutiny, and it flustered her. She knew she was reasonably attractive, but she also knew that no one was going to rush forward with a banner and a tiara. Her mouth was just a little too full, her eyes a little too round. Her hair had been fire-engine red the entire time she was growing up, but it had darkened to a deep auburn in her early twenties, a fact for which she remained truly grateful. Maryanne had always hated her red hair and the wealth of freckles that accompanied it. No one else in her family had been cursed with red hair, not to mention freckles. Her mother's hair was a beautiful blonde and her father's a rich chestnut. Even her younger brothers had escaped her fate. If it weren't for the distinctive high Simpson forehead and deep blue eyes, Maryanne might have suspected she'd been adopted. But that wasn't the case. Instead she'd been forced to discover early in life how unfair heredity could be.

The lift arrived, and both Maryanne and Kramer stepped inside. Kramer leaned against the side—he always seemed to be leaning, Maryanne noticed. Leaning and staring. He was studying her again; she could feel his eyes as profoundly as a caress.

"Would you kindly stop?" she snapped.

"What?"

"Staring at me!"

"I'm curious."

"About what?" She was curious about him, too, but far too civilised to make an issue of it the way he was doing.

"I just wanted to see if all that blue blood showed."

"Oh, honestly!"

"I am being honest," he answered. "You know, you intrigue me, Simpson. Have you eaten?"

Maryanne's heart immediately raced with excitement at the off-hand question. He seemed to be leading up to suggesting they dine together. Unfortunately she'd been around Kramer long enough to realise she couldn't trust the man. Anything she said or did would more than likely show up in that column of his.

"I've got an Irish stew simmering in a pot at home," she murmured, dismissing the invitation before he could offer it.

"Great! I love stew."

Maryanne opened her mouth to tell him she had no intention of asking him into her home. Not after the things he'd said about her in his column. But when she turned to tell him so, their eyes met.

Brown eyes clashed with blue ones. His were deep and dark and almost...she couldn't be sure, but she thought she saw a faint glimmer of admiration. The edge of his mouth quirked upward with an unmistakable hint of challenge. He looked as if he expected her to reject him.

Against her better judgement, and knowing she'd live to regret this, Maryanne found herself smiling.

"My apartment's on Spring Street," she murmured.

"Good. I'll follow you."

She lowered her gaze, feeling chagrined and already a little regretful about the whole thing. "I didn't drive."

"Is your chauffeur waiting?" he asked, his voice and eyes mocking her in a manner that was practically friendly.

"I took a cab," she said, glancing away from him. "It's a way of life in Manhattan and I'm not accustomed to dealing with a car. So I don't have one." She half expected him to make some derogatory comment and was thankful when he didn't.

"I'll give you a lift, then."

He'd parked his car, a surprisingly stylish sedan, in a lot close to the waterfront. The late-September air was brisk, and Maryanne braced herself against it as Kramer cleared the litter off the passenger seat for her.

She slipped inside, grateful to be out of the chill. It didn't take her more than a couple of seconds to realise that Kramer treated his car the same way he treated his raincoat. The front and the back seat of the sedan were both cluttered with empty paper cups, old newspapers and several paperback novels. Mysteries, she noted. The great Kramer Adams read mysteries. A container filled with loose change was propped inside his ashtray.

While Maryanne searched for the seatbelt, Kramer raced around the front of the car, slid inside and quickly started the engine. "I hope there's a place to park off Spring."

"Oh, don't worry," Maryanne quickly assured him, "I've got valet service."

Kramer murmured something under his breath. Had she made an effort, she might have been able to hear, but she figured she was probably better off not knowing.

He turned up the heater and Maryanne was warmed by a blast of air. "Let me know if that gets too hot for you."

"Thanks, I'm fine."

"Hot" seemed to describe their relationship. From the first, Maryanne had inadvertently got herself into scalding water with Kramer, water that came closer to boiling point each time a new column appeared. "Hot" also described the way they seemed to ignite sparks off each other. The radio show had proved that much.

Nevertheless, Maryanne was grateful for the opportunity to bridge their differences, because, despite everything, she genuinely admired Kramer's writing.

They chatted amicably enough until Kramer pulled into the crescent-shaped driveway of the Seattle, the luxury apartment complex where she lived.

Max, the doorman, opened her car door, his stoic face breaking into a smile as he recognised her. When Kramer climbed out of the driver's side, Maryanne watched as Max's smile slowly turned into a frown, as though he wasn't certain Kramer was appropriate company for a respectable young lady.

"Max, this is Mr Adams from the *Seattle Sun*."

"Kramer Adams?" Max's expression altered immediately. "I read your work faithfully, Mr Adams. You gave ol' Larson hell last month. From what I heard, your column was what forced him to resign from City Council."

Kramer had given Maryanne hell, too, but she refrained from mentioning it. She doubted Max had ever read her work or was even aware that Kramer had been referring to her in his column earlier in the month.

"Would you see to Mr Adams's car?" Maryanne asked.

"Right away, Ms Simpson."

Burying his hands in his pockets, Kramer followed Maryanne into the extravagantly decorated foyer with its huge crystal chandelier and bubbling fountain. "My apartment's on the eleventh floor," she said, pushing the elevator button.

"Not the penthouse suite?" he teased.

Maryanne smiled weakly in response. While they rode upward, she concentrated on taking her keys from her bag to hide her sudden nervousness. Her heart was banging against her ribs. Now that Kramer was practically at her door, she wondered how she'd let this happen. After the things he'd called her, the least of which were Ms

High Society, Miss Debutante and Daddy's Darling, she felt more than a little vulnerable sharing his company.

"Are you ready to change your mind?" he asked, as though he'd read her thoughts.

"No, of course not." she lied.

She noticed—but sincerely hoped Kramer didn't—that her hand was shaking when she inserted the key.

She turned on the light as she walked into the spacious apartment. Kramer followed her, his brows raised at the sight of the modern white leather and chrome furniture. There was even a fireplace.

"Nice place you've got here," he said, glancing around.

She thought she detected sarcasm in his voice, then decided it was what she could expect from him all evening; she might as well get used to it.

"I'll take your raincoat," she said. Considering the fondness with which he wore the thing, he might well choose to eat in it, too.

To Maryanne's surprise, he handed it to her, then walked over to the fireplace and lifted a family photo from the mantel. The picture had been taken several summers earlier, when they'd all been sailing off Martha's Vineyard. Maryanne was looking into the wind and laughing at the antics of her younger brothers. It certainly wasn't her most flattering photo. In fact she looked as if she was gasping for air after being too long underwater. The wind had caught her red hair, its colour even more pronounced against the backdrop of white sails.

"The two young men with me are my brothers. My mom and dad are at the helm."

Kramer stared at the picture for several seconds and then back at her. "So you're the only redhead."

"How kind of you to mention it."

"Hey, you're in luck. I happen to like redheads." He said this with such a lazy smile that Maryanne couldn't possibly be offended.

"I'll check the stew," she said, after hanging up their coats. She hurried into the kitchen and lifted the lid of the pot. The pungent aroma of stewing lamb, vegetables and basil filled the apartment.

"You weren't kidding, were you?" Kramer asked, sounding mildly surprised.

"Kidding? About what?"

"The Irish stew."

"No. I put it on this morning, before I left for work. I've got one of those all-day cookers.'' After living on her own for the past couple of years, Maryanne had become a competent cook. When she'd rented her first apartment in New York, she used to stop off at a deli on her way home, but that had soon become monotonous. Over the course of several months, she'd discovered some excellent recipes for simple nutritious meals. Her father wasn't going to publish a cookbook by her, perhaps, but she did manage to eat well.

"I thought the stew was an excuse not to have dinner with me," Kramer remarked conversationally. "I didn't know what to expect. You're my first deb.''

"Some white wine?" she asked, ignoring his comment.

"Please.''

Maryanne got a bottle from the refrigerator and expertly removed the cork. She filled them each a glass, then handed Kramer his and carried the bottle into the living-room, where she set it on the polished glass-topped coffee table. Sitting down on one end of the white leather sofa, she slipped off her shoes and tucked her feet beneath her.

Kramer sat at the other end, resting his ankle on his knee, making himself at home. "Dare I propose a toast?" he asked.

"Please.''

"To Seattle," he said, his mischievous gaze meeting hers. "May she forever remain unspoiled.'' He reached over and touched the rim of her glass with his.

"To Seattle," Maryanne returned. "The most enchanting city on the West Coast.''

"But, please, don't let anyone know," Kramer coaxed in a stage whisper.

"I'm not making any promises," she whispered back.

They tasted the wine, which had come highly recommended by a friend at the paper. Maryanne had only recently learned that wines from Washington state were quickly gaining a world reputation for excellence. Apparently the soil, a rich sandy loam over a volcanic base, was the key.

They talked about the wine for a few moments, and the conversation flowed naturally after that, as they compared experiences and shared impressions. Maryanne was surprised by how much she was enjoying the company of this man she'd considered a foe. Actually, they did have several things in common. Perhaps she was enjoying his company simply because she was lonely, but she didn't think that was entirely true. She'd been too busy with work to do any socialising; she occasionally saw a few people from the paper, but other than that she hadn't had time to establish any friendships.

After a second glass of wine, feeling warm and relaxed, Maryanne was willing to admit exactly how isolated she'd felt since moving to Seattle.

"It's been so long since I went out on a real date."

"There does seem to be a shortage of Ivy League guys in Seattle."

She giggled and nodded. "At least Dad's not sending along a troupe of eligible men for me to meet. I enjoyed living in New York, don't get me wrong, but every time I turned around a man was introducing himself and telling me my father had given him my phone number. You're the first man I've had dinner with that Dad didn't handpick for me since I moved out on my own."

"I hate to tell you this, sugar, but I have the distinct impression your daddy would take one look at me and have me arrested."

"That's not the least bit true," Maryanne argued. "My dad isn't a snob, only…only if you do meet him take off the raincoat, OK?"

"The raincoat?"

"It looks like you sleep in it. All you need is a hat and a scrap of paper with 'Press' scrawled on it sticking out of the band—you'd look like you worked for the *Planet* in Metropolis."

"I hate to disillusion you, sugar, but I'm not Ivy League and I'm not Superman."

"Oh, darn," she said, snapping her fingers. "And we had such an interesting thing going." She was feeling too mellow to remind him not to call her sugar.

"So how old are you?" Kramer wanted to know. "Twenty-one?"

"Three," she amended. "And you?"

"A hundred and three in comparison."

Maryanne wasn't entirely sure what he meant, but she let that pass, too. It felt good to have someone to talk to, someone who was her contemporary, or at least close to being her contemporary.

"If you don't want to tell me how old you are, then at least fill in some of the details of your life."

"Trust me, my life isn't nearly as interesting as yours."

"Bore me, then."

"All right," he said, drawing a deep breath. "My family was dirt-poor. Dad disappeared about the time I was ten and Mom took on two jobs to make ends meet. Get the picture?''

"Yes." She hesitated. "What about women?''

"I've had a long and glorious history.''

"I'm not kidding, Kramer.''

"You think I was?''

"You're not married.''

"Not to my knowledge.''

"Why not?''

He shrugged as if it was of little consequence. "No time for it. I came close once, but her family didn't consider my writing career noble enough. Her father tried to fix me up with a job.''

"What happened?''

"Nothing much. I told her I was going to work for the newspaper, and she claimed if I really loved her I'd accept her father's generous offer. It didn't take me long to decide. I guess she was right—I didn't love her.''

He sounded nonchalant, as if the episode hadn't cost him a moment's regret, but just looking at him told Maryanne otherwise. Kramer had been deeply hurt. Every sarcastic irreverent word he wrote suggested it.

In retrospect, Maryanne mused one afternoon several days later, she'd thoroughly enjoyed her evening with Kramer. They'd eaten, and Kramer had raved about her Irish stew until she flushed at his praise. She'd made them cups of café au lait while Kramer built a fire. They'd sat in front of the fireplace and talked for hours. He'd told her more about his own large family, his seven brothers and sisters. How he'd worked his way through two years of college, but was forced to give up his education when he couldn't afford to continue. As it turned out, he'd been grateful because that decision had led to his first newspaper job. And, as they said, the rest was history.

"You certainly seem to be in a good mood," her coworker, Carol Riverside, said as she strolled past Maryanne's desk later that same afternoon. Carol was short, with a pixielike face and friendly manner. Maryanne had liked her from the moment they'd met.

"I'm in a fabulous mood," Maryanne said, smiling. Kramer had promised to pay her back by taking her out to dinner. He hadn't set a definite date, but she half expected to hear from him that evening.

"In that case, I hate to be the bearer of bad tidings, but someone has to tell you, and I was appointed."

"Tell me? What?" Maryanne glanced around the huge open office and noted that several faces were staring in her direction, all wearing sympathetic looks. "What's going on?" she demanded.

Carol moved her arm out from behind her and Maryanne noticed that she was holding a copy of the rival newspaper's morning edition. "It's Kramer Adams's column," Carol said softly, her eyes wide and compassionate.

"W-what did he say this time?"

"Well, let's put it this way. He titled it, 'My Evening with the Debutante.'"

CHAPTER TWO

MARYANNE WAS much too furious to stand still. She stalked her living-room like a caged panther, her mind spitting and churning. A slow painful death was too good for Kramer Adams.

Her phone rang and she went into the kitchen to answer it. She reached for it so fast and hard that she nearly ripped it off the wall. Rarely did she allow herself to become this angry, but complicating her fury was a deep and aching sense of betrayal. "Yes," she said forcefully.

"This is Max," her doorman announced. "Mr Adams is here. Shall I send him up?"

For an instant Maryanne was too stunned to speak. The man had nerve, she'd say that much for him. Raw courage, too, if he knew the state of mind she was in.

"Ms Simpson?"

It took Maryanne only about a second to decide. "Send him up," she said with deceptive calm.

Arms hugging her waist, Maryanne continued pacing. She was going to tell this man in no uncertain terms what she thought of his duplicity, his trickery. He might have assumed from their evening together that she was a gentle, forgiving soul who would quietly overlook this treachery. Well, if that was his belief, Maryanne was looking forward to enlightening him.

Her doorbell chimed and she turned to glare at it with narrowed eyes. Wishing her heart would stop pounding, she gulped in a deep breath, then walked calmly across the living-room and opened the door.

"Hello, Maryanne," Kramer said, his eyes immediately meeting hers.

She stood exactly where she was, imitating his tactic of leaning against the frame and blocking the threshold.

"May I come in?" he asked mildly.

"I haven't decided yet." He was wearing the raincoat again, which looked even more disreputable than before.

"I take it you read the article?" he murmured, one eyebrow raised.

"Read it?" she nearly shouted. "Of course I read it, and so, it seems, did everyone else in Seattle. Did you honestly think I'd be able to hold my head up after that? Or was that your intention—humiliating me and…and making me a laughingstock?" She stabbed her index finger repeatedly against his solid chest. "And if you think no one'll figure out it was me just because you didn't use my name, think again."

"I take it you're angry?" He raised his eyebrows again, as if to suggest she was overreacting.

"Angry! Angry? That isn't the half of it, buster!" The problem with being raised in a God-fearing, flag-loving family was that the worst thing she could think of to call him out loud was *buster*. Plenty of other names flashed through her mind, but none she dared to verbalise. No doubt Kramer would delight in revealing this in his column, too.

Furious, she grabbed his tie and jerked him into the apartment. "You can come inside," she said.

"Thanks. I think I will," Kramer said wryly. He smoothed his tie, which drew her attention to the hard defined muscles of his chest. The last thing Maryanne wanted to do was notice how virile he looked, and she forced her gaze away from him.

Because it was impossible to stand still, she resumed her pacing. With the first rush of anger spent, she had no idea what to say to him, how to make him realise the enormity of what he'd done. Abruptly, she paused at the edge of her living-room and pointed an accusing finger at him. "You have your nerve."

"What I said was true," Kramer stated, boldly meeting her glare. "If you'd bothered to read the article all the way through, objectively, you'd have noticed there were several complimentary statements."

"'An idealist, an optimist…'" she said, quoting what she remembered, the parts that had offended her the most. "You made me sound like Mary Poppins!"

"Surprisingly unspoiled and gentle," Kramer returned, "and very much a lady."

"You told the entire city I was lonely," she cried, mortified even to repeat the words.

"I didn't say you were lonely," Kramer insisted, sounding all too reasonable and controlled. That infuriated her even more. "I said you were away from your family for the first time."

She poked his chest again as she punctuated her speech. "But you made it sound like I should be in a day-care centre!"

"I didn't imply anything of the kind," he contended. "And I did mention what a good cook you are."

"I'm supposed to be grateful for that? As I recall you said, I was 'surprisingly adept in the kitchen'—as if you were amazed I knew the difference between a goldfish bowl and an oven."

"You're blowing the whole thing out of proportion."

Maryanne barely heard him. "The comment about my being insecure was the worst. You want security, buster, you're looking at security. My feet could be molded in cement, I'm that secure." Defiant angry eyes flashed to him as she pointed at her shoes.

Kramer didn't so much as blink. "You work twice as hard as anyone else at the *Review,* and twice as many hours. You push yourself because you've got something to prove."

A strained silence followed his words. Everything he said was true. She *did* work hard, she *was* trying to prove herself, and Kramer knew it. Except in high school and college, she'd had no experience working for a newspaper.

"Did you wake up one morning and decide to play Sigmund Freud with my life?" she cried. "Who, may I ask, gave you that right?"

"What I said is true, Maryanne. I don't expect you to admit it to me, but if you're honest you'll at least admit it to yourself. Your family is your greatest asset and your weakest link. From everything I've read about the Simpsons, they're good people, but they've cheated you out of something important."

"Exactly what do you mean by that?" she snapped, ready to defend her father to the death, if need be. How dared this pompous, arrogant, argumentative man insult her family?

"You'll never know if you're a good enough journalist to get a job like this without your father's help. He handed you this plum position and at the same time cheated you out of a just reward."

Maryanne opened her mouth, an argument hot on the tip of her tongue. Instead, she lowered her gaze, realising there was nothing she could say to defend herself. From the moment she arrived at the *Seattle Review,* she'd known that Carol Riverside was the one who'd earned the right to be the local-affairs columnist, not her. And yet Carol had been wonderfully supportive and kind.

"It wasn't my intention to insult you or your family," Kramer continued.

"Then why did you write that column?" she demanded, her voice heaving. "Did you honestly think I was going to be flattered by it?"

He'd been so quick with the answers that his silence caught her attention more effectively than anything he could have said. She watched as he started pacing. He drew his fingers roughly through his hair and his shoulders rose in a distinct sigh.

"I'm not entirely sure. In retrospect, I believe I wanted to set the record straight. At least that was my original intent. I realise I wrote more than I should have, but the piece was never meant to ridicule you. Whether you know it or not, you impressed the hell out of me the other night."

"Am I supposed to be grateful you chose to thank me publicly?"

"No," he answered sharply. Once more he jerked his fingers fiercely through his hair. He didn't wince, but Maryanne did—which was interesting, since only a few minutes earlier she'd been day-dreaming about the joy she'd experience watching this man suffer.

"Inviting myself to dinner the other night was an impulse," he admitted grudgingly. "The words slipped out before I realised what I was saying. I don't know who was more surprised, you or me. I tried to act like I knew what I was doing, play it cool, that sort of thing. The fact is, I discovered I like you. Trust me, I wasn't in any frame of mind to talk civilly to you when you arrived at the radio station. All along I'd assumed you were a spoiled rich kid, but I was wrong. Since I'd published several pieces that suggested as much, I felt it was only fair to set the record straight. Besides, for a deb you aren't half-bad."

"Why is it every time you compliment me I feel a knife between my shoulder blades?"

"We certainly don't have a whole lot in common," Kramer continued thoughtfully. "I learned most everything I know on the streets, not in an expensive private school. I doubt there's a single political issue we can agree on. You're standing on one side of the fence and I'm way over on the other. We're about as far apart as any two people could ever be. Socially. Economically. And every other way I could mention. We have no business even speaking to one another, and yet we sat down and shared a meal and talked for hours.''

''I felt betrayed by that column.''

''I know. I apologise, although the damage is already done. I guess I didn't realise it would offend you. That wasn't what I intended at all.'' He released a giant sigh and paused, as though collecting his thoughts. ''After I left your place, I felt good. I can't remember a time I've enjoyed myself more. You're a charming, interesting—''

''You might have said that in your column!''

''I did, only you were obviously too upset to notice it. When I got home that night, I couldn't sleep. Every time I'd start to drift off, I'd think of something you'd said, and before I knew it I'd be grinning. Finally I got up and sat at my desk and started writing. The words poured out of me as fast as I could type them. The quality that impressed me the most about you is your honesty. There isn't a pretence in you, and the more I thought about that the more I realised how you've been cheated.''

''And you decided it was your duty to point all this out—for everyone in town to read?''

''No, it wasn't. That's why I'm here. I admit I went further than I should have and came over to apologise.''

''If you're telling me this to make me feel better, it isn't working.'' Her ego was rebounding somewhat, but he still had a lot of apologising to do.

''To be honest, I didn't give the column a second thought until this afternoon, when someone in the office said I'd really done it now. If I was hoping to make peace with you, I'd failed. This friend said I was likely to get hit by the wrath of a woman scorned and suggested I run for cover.''

''Rightly so!''

''Forgive me, Maryanne. It was arrogant in the extreme of me to publish that piece. If it'll help you feel any better, you can blast me to kingdom come in your next column. I solemnly promise I'll never write another word about you.''

''Don't be so humble—it doesn't suit you,'' she muttered, gnawing on her lower lip. ''Besides, I won't be able to print a rebuttal.''

''Why not?''

''I don't plan on working for the *Review* any longer, or at least not after tomorrow.'' The idea seemed to emerge fully formed; until that moment she hadn't known exactly what she was going to say.

The silence following her words was fraught with tension. ''What do you mean?''

''Don't act so surprised. I'm quitting the paper.''

''What? Why?'' Kramer had been standing during their whole conversation, but he suddenly seemed to find it necessary to sit. He slowly lowered himself on the sofa, his face pale and tight. ''You're over-reacting! There's no need to do anything so drastic.''

''There's every need. You said so yourself. You told me I've been cheated, that if I'm even half as good a reporter as I think I am I would have got this 'plum position' on my own. I'm just agreeing with you.''

He nodded stiffly.

''As painful as this is to admit, especially to you,'' she went on, ''you're right. My family is wonderful, but they've never allowed me to fall flat on my face. Carol Riverside is the one who deserved the chance to write that column. She's been with the paper for five years—I'd only been there five minutes. But because my name is Simpson, and because my father made a simple phone call, I was given the job. Carol was cheated. She should have been furious. Instead, she was kind and helpful.'' Maryanne sat down next to Kramer and propped her feet on the coffee table. ''And maybe worse than what happened to Carol is what happened to me as a result of being handed this job. What you wrote about my wondering if I had what it takes to make it as a journalist hit too close to home. All my life my father's been there to tell me I can be anything I want to be and then he promptly arranges it for me.''

''Quitting the *Review* isn't going to change that,'' Kramer argued. ''Come on, Maryanne, you're taking this all too seriously.''

''Nothing you say is going to change my mind,'' Maryanne informed him primly. ''The time has come for me to cut myself loose and sink or swim on my own.''

Her mind was galloping ahead, adjusting to the coming changes. For the first time since she'd read Kramer's column that afternoon, she experienced the beginnings of excitement. She glanced around the apartment as another thought struck her. ''Naturally I'll have to move out of this place.''

''Are you going back to New York?''

"Heavens, no!" she declared, unaccountably thrilled at the reluctance she heard in his voice. "I love Seattle."

"Listen to me, would you? You're leaping into the deep end, you don't know how to swim and the lifeguard's off duty."

Maryanne barely heard Kramer, mainly because she didn't like what he was saying. How like a man to ignite a bonfire and then rush to put out the flames. "The first thing I need to worry about is finding another job," she announced. "A temporary one, of course. I'm going to continue writing, but I don't think I'll be able to support myself on that, not at first, anyway."

"If you insist on this folly, you could always free-lance for the *Sun.*"

Maryanne discounted that suggestion with a shake of her head. "I'd come off looking like a traitor."

"I suppose you're right." His eyebrows drew together as he frowned.

"You know what else I'm going to do?" She shifted her position, tucking her legs beneath her. "I've got this trust fund that provides a big interest payment every month. That's what I've been using to pay my bills. You and I both know I couldn't afford this place on what I make at the paper. I'm not going to touch those interest payments and I'll live solely on what I earn."

"I...wouldn't do that right away, if I were you."

"Why not?"

"You just said you were quitting your job." Kramer sounded uneasy. "I can see that I've started something of an avalanche here, and I'm beginning to feel mildly concerned."

"Where do you live?"

"Capitol Hill. Listen, if you're serious about moving, you need to give some thought to what kind of neighbourhood you're getting into. Seattle's a great town, don't get me wrong, but like any other place we have our problem areas." He hesitated. "Annie, I don't feel good about this."

"No one's ever called me Annie before." Her eyes smiled into his. "What do you pay for rent?"

With his hands buried deep in his pants pockets, he mumbled something under his breath, then mentioned a figure that was one-third of what she was currently dishing out every month.

"That's more than reasonable."

Surprise flashed in his eyes, and Maryanne smiled again. "If you're so concerned about my finding the right neighbourhood, then you pick one for me. Anyplace, I don't care. Just remember, you're the one who got me into this."

"Don't remind me." Kramer's frown darkened.

"I may not have appreciated what you said about me in your column," Maryanne said slowly, "but I'm beginning to think good things might come of it."

"I'm beginning to think I should be dragged to the nearest tree and hanged," Kramer grumbled.

"Hi." Maryanne slipped into the booth opposite Kramer at the greasy spoon called Mom's Place. She smiled, feeling like a child on a grand adventure. Perhaps she *was* going off the deep end, as Kramer had so adamantly claimed the day before. Perhaps, but she doubted it. Everything felt incredibly right.

Once the idea of living on her own—on income she earned herself, from a job she'd been hired for on her own merits—had taken hold in her mind, it had fast gained momentum. She could work days and write nights. The arrangement was perfect.

"Did you do it?"

"I handed in my notice first thing this morning," she said, reaching for the menu. Kramer had insisted on meeting her for a late lunch and suggested this greasy spoon with its faded neon sign that flashed Home Cooking. She had the impression he ate there regularly.

"I talked to the managing editor first thing this morning and told him I was leaving."

"I don't imagine he took kindly to that," Kramer muttered, lifting a white ceramic mug half-full of coffee. He'd been wearing a frown from the moment she'd entered the diner. She had the feeling it was the same one he'd left her apartment with the night before, but it had deepened slightly since she'd last seen him.

"Larry wasn't too upset, but I don't think he appreciated my suggestion that Carol Riverside take over the column, because he said something I'd rather not repeat about how he was the one who'd do the promoting and demoting, not me, no matter what my name was."

Kramer took a sip of coffee and grinned. "I'd bet he'd like my head if it could be arranged, and frankly I don't blame him."

"Don't worry, I didn't mention your name or the fact that your column was what led to my decision."

Maryanne doubted Kramer even heard her. "I'm regretting that column more with each passing minute. Are you sure I can't talk you out of this?"

"I'm sure."

He sighed and he shook his head. "How'd the job hunting go?"

The waitress came by, automatically placing a filled mug of coffee in front of Maryanne. She fished a pad from the pocket of her pink apron. "Are you ready to order?"

"I'll have a turkey sandwich on rye, no sprouts, a diet soda and a side of potato salad," Maryanne said with a smile, handing her the menu.

"You don't need to worry, we don't serve sprouts here," she said, scribbling down the order.

"I'll have the chilli, Barbara," Kramer said. The waitress nodded and strolled away from the booth. "I was asking how your job hunting went," Kramer reminded Maryanne.

"I found one!"

"Where? And what will you be doing? And for how much?"

"You're beginning to sound like my father."

"I'm beginning to *feel* like your father. Annie, you're a babe in the woods. You don't have a clue what you're getting involved in. Heaven knows I've tried to talk some sense into you, but you refused to listen. And, as you so delight in reminding me, I'm the one responsible for all this."

"Stop blaming yourself." Maryanne reached across the table for her water glass. "I'm grateful, I honestly am—though, trust me, I never thought I'd be saying that. But what you wrote was true. By insulting me, you've given me the initiative to make a name for myself without Dad's help and—"

He closed his eyes. "Just answer the question."

"Oh, about the job. It's for a…service company. It looks like it'll work out great. Actually, I didn't think I'd have any chance of getting hired, since I don't have much experience, but they took that into consideration. You see, it's a new company and they can't afford to pay much. Everyone seems friendly and helpful. The only drawback is my salary and the fact that I won't be working a lot of hours at first. In fact, the money is a lot less than I was earning at the paper.

But I expect to be able to sell a couple of articles soon. I'll get along all right once I learn to budget.''

"How much less than the paper?"

"If I tell you, you'll only get angry." His scowl said he'd be even angrier if she didn't tell him. From the way he was glaring at her, Maryanne knew she'd reached the limits of his patience. She muttered the amount and promptly lowered her gaze.

"You aren't taking the job," Kramer said flatly.

"Yes, I am. It's the best I could do for now. Besides, it's only temporary. It isn't all that easy to find work, you know. I must have talked to fifteen companies today. No one seemed too impressed with my double degree in Early American History and English. I wanted to find employment where I can use my writing skills, but that didn't happen, so I took this job.''

"Annie, you won't be able to live on so little."

"I realise that. I've got a list of the community newspapers and I'm going to contact them about doing free-lance work. I figure between the writing and my job, I'll do all right.''

"Exactly *what* will you be doing?" he demanded.

"Cleaning," she mumbled under her breath.

"What did you say?"

"I'm working for Rent-A-Maid."

"Dear Lord," Kramer groaned. "I hope you're kidding."

"Get your mind out of the gutter, Adams. I'm going to work six hours a day cleaning offices and spend the rest of the time doing research for my articles. Oh, and before I forget, I gave your name as a reference.''

"You're going to go back and tell whoever hired you that you're terribly sorry, but you won't be able to work there, after all," Kramer announced, and the hard set of his mouth brooked no argument.

Maryanne was saved from having to tell him she had no intention of quitting, because the waitress, bless her heart, appeared with their orders at precisely that moment.

"Now what about an apartment?" Maryanne asked. After his comment about living in a safe neighbourhood, she was more than willing to let him locate one for her. "Have you had a chance to check into that for me?"

"I hope you didn't give your notice at the Seattle."

Swallowing a bite of her sandwich, Maryanne nodded eagerly.

"First thing this morning. I told them I'd be out by the fifteenth, which, in case you were unaware of it, happens to be early next week."

"You shouldn't have done that."

"I can't afford the place! And I won't be able to eat in restaurants everyday or take cabs or buy things whenever I want them." She smiled proudly as she said it. Money had never been a problem in her life—it had sometimes been an issue, but never a problem. She felt invigorated just thinking about her new status.

"Will you stop grinning at me like that?" Kramer burst out.

"Sorry, it's sort of a novelty to say I can't afford something, that's all," she explained. "It actually feels kind of good."

"In a couple of weeks it's going to feel like hell." Kramer's face spelled out apprehension and gloom.

"Then I'll learn that for myself." She noticed he hadn't touched his meal. "Go ahead and eat your chilli before it gets cold."

"I've lost my appetite." He immediately contradicted himself by reaching for a small bottle of hot sauce and dousing the chilli with several hard shakes.

"Now did you or did you not find me a furnished studio apartment to look at this afternoon?" Maryanne pressed.

"I found one. It's nothing like you're used to, so be prepared. I'll take you there once we're finished lunch."

"Tell me about it," Maryanne said eagerly.

"There's one main room, small kitchen, smaller bathroom, tiny closet, no dishwasher." He paused as if he expected her to jump to her feet and tell him the whole thing was off.

"Go on," she said, reaching for her soda.

"The floors are pretty worn but they're hardwood."

"That'll be nice." She didn't know if she'd ever lived in a place that didn't have carpeting, but she'd adjust.

"The furniture's solid enough. It's old and weighs about a ton, but I don't know how comfortable it is."

"I'm sure it'll be fine. I'll be working just about everyday, so I can't see that there'll be a problem," Maryanne returned absently. As soon as she'd spoken, she realised her mistake.

Kramer stabbed his spoon into the chilli. "You seem to have forgotten you're resuming your job hunt. You won't be working for Rent-A-Maid, and that's final."

"You sound like a parent again. I'm old enough to know what I can and can't do, and I'm going to take that job whether you like it or not, and *that's final.*"

His eyes narrowed. "We'll see."

"Yes, we will," she retorted. Kramer might be an astute journalist, but there were several things he had yet to learn about her, and one of them was her stubborn streak. The thought produced a small smile as she realised she was thinking of him in a way that suggested a long-term friendship. He was right when he said they stood on opposite sides of the fence on most issues. He was also right when he claimed they had no business being friends. Nevertheless, Kramer Adams was the most intriguing man she'd ever known.

Once they'd finished their meal, Kramer reached for the bill, but Maryanne insisted on splitting it. He clearly wasn't pleased about that but let it pass. Apparently he wasn't going to argue with her, which suited Maryanne just fine. He escorted her to his car, parked outside the diner, and Maryanne slid inside, absurdly pleased that he'd cleaned up the front seat for her.

Kramer hesitated when he joined her, his hands on the steering wheel. "Are you sure you want to go through with this?"

"Positive."

"I was afraid you were going to say that." His mouth twisted. "I can't believe I'm aiding and abetting this nonsense."

"You're my friend, and I'm grateful."

Without another word, he started the engine.

"Where's the apartment?" Maryanne asked as the car progressed up the steep Seattle hills. "I mean, what neighbourhood?"

"Capitol Hill."

"Oh, how nice. Isn't that the same part of town you live in?" It wasn't all that far from the Seattle, either, which meant she'd still have the same telephone exchange. Maybe she could even keep her current number.

"Yes," he muttered. He didn't seem to be in the mood for conversation and kept his attention centred on his driving, instead. He pulled into a parking lot behind an eight-storey post-World War II brick building. "The apartment's on the fourth floor."

"That'll be fine." She climbed out of the car and stared at the old structure. The garbage dumpster was backed against the wall and full to overflowing. Maryanne had to step around it before entering by a side door. Apparently there was no lift, and by the time they reached the fourth floor she was so winded she couldn't have found the breath to complain, anyway.

"The manager gave me the key," Kramer explained as he paused in the hallway and unlocked the second door on the right. Kramer wasn't even breathing deeply, while Maryanne was leaning against the wall, dragging deep breaths into her oxygen-starved lungs.

Kramer opened the door and waved her in. "As I said, it's not much."

Maryanne walked inside and was immediately struck by the sparseness of the furnishings. One overstuffed sofa and one end table with a lamp on a dull stained wood floor. She blinked, squared her shoulders and forced a smile to her lips. "It's perfect."

"You honestly think you can live here after the Seattle?" He sounded incredulous.

"Yes, I do," she said with a determination that would have made generations of Simpsons proud. "How far away is your place?"

Kramer walked over to the window, his back to her. He exhaled sharply before he announced, "I live in the apartment next door."

CHAPTER THREE

"I DON'T NEED a baby-sitter," Maryanne protested. She had some trouble maintaining the conviction in her voice. In truth, she was pleased to learn that Kramer's apartment was next door, and her heart did a little jig all its own.

Kramer turned away from the window. His mouth was set in a thin straight line, as if he was going against his better judgement in arranging this. "That night at the radio station," he mumbled softly. "I knew it then."

"Knew what?"

Slowly, he shook his head, apparently lost in his musings. "I took one look at you and deep down inside I heard a small voice cry out, 'Here comes trouble.'"

Despite his fierce look, Maryanne laughed.

"Like a fool I ignored it, although Lord only knows how I could have."

"You're not blaming me for all this, are you?" Maryanne asked, placing her hands on her hips, prepared to do battle. "In case you've forgotten, you're the one who invited yourself to dinner that night. Then you got me all mellow with wine—"

"You were the one who brought out the bottle. You can't blame me for that." He was muttering again, and he buried his hands deep in the pockets of his raincoat.

"I was only being a good hostess."

"All right, all right, I get the picture," he said through clenched teeth, shaking his head again. "I was the one stupid enough to write that column afterward. I'd give a week's pay to take it all back now. No, make that a month's pay. This is the last time," he vowed, "that I'm ever going to set the record straight. Any record." He jerked his hand from his pocket and stared at it for several moments.

Maryanne crossed to the large stuffed sofa covered with fading chintz fabric and ran her hand along the armrest. It was nearly threadbare in places and nothing like the supple white leather of her sofa at the Seattle. "I wish you'd stop worrying about me. I'm not as fragile as I look."

Kramer snickered softly. "A dust ball could bowl you over."

A ready argument sprang to her lips, but she quickly swallowed it. "I'll take the apartment, but I want it understood, right now, that you have no responsibilities towards me. I'm a big girl and I'll manage perfectly well on my own. I have in the past and I'll continue to do so in the future."

Kramer didn't respond immediately. Instead he grumbled something she couldn't hear. He seemed to be doing a lot of that since he'd met her. Maybe it was a long established habit, but somehow she doubted it.

Kramer drove her back to the Seattle, and the whole way there Maryanne could hardly contain a feeling of delight. For the first time, she was taking control of her own life. Kramer, however, was all too obviously experiencing no such enthusiasm.

"Do I need to sign anything for the apartment? What about a deposit?"

"You can do that later. You realise this studio apartment is the smallest one in the entire building. My own apartment is three times that size."

"Would you stop worrying?" Maryanne told him. A growing sense of purpose filled her, and a keen exhilaration unlike anything she'd ever felt.

Kramer pulled into the circular driveway at her building. "Do you want to come up for a few minutes?" she asked.

His dark eyes widened as if she'd casually suggested they play a round of Russian roulette. "You've got to be kidding."

She wasn't.

He held up both hands. "No way. Before long, you'll be serving wine and we'll be talking like old friends. Then I'll go home thinking about you, and before I know how it happened—" He stopped abruptly, as if he'd already said too much. "No, thanks."

"Goodbye, then," she said, disappointed. "I'll see you later."

"Right. Later." But the way he said it suggested that if he didn't stumble upon her for a decade or two it would be fine with him.

Maryanne climbed out of his car and was about to close the door when she hesitated. "Kramer?"

"Now what?" he barked.

"Thank you," she said softly.

Predictably, he started mumbling and drove off the instant she closed the door. In spite of his sour mood, Maryanne found herself smiling.

Once inside her apartment, she was immediately struck by the contrast between this apartment at the Seattle and the place Kramer had shown her. One was grey, cramped and dingy, the other polished and spacious and elegant. Her mind's eye went over the dreary apartment on Capitol Hill, and she felt a growing sense of excitement as she thought of different inexpensive ways to bring it colour and character. She'd certainly faced challenges before, but never one quite like this. Instinctively she knew there would be real satisfaction in decorating that place with her newly limited resources.

Turning her new apartment into a home was the least of her worries, however. She had yet to tell her parents that she'd quit her job. Their reaction was as predictable as Kramer's.

The phone seemed to draw her. Slowly she walked across the room toward it, sighing deeply. Her fingers closed tightly around the receiver. Before she could change her mind, she closed her eyes, punched out the number and waited.

Her mother answered almost immediately.

"I was sitting at my desk," Muriel Simpson explained. She sounded delighted to hear from Maryanne. "How's Seattle? Are you still as fascinated with the Northwest as you were before?"

"More than ever," Maryanne answered without a pause; what she didn't say was that part of her fascination was now because of Kramer.

"I'm pleased you like it so well, but I don't mind telling you, sweetie, I miss you something dreadful."

"I haven't lived at home for years," Maryanne reminded her mother.

"I know, but you were so much closer to home in Manhattan than you are now. I can't join you for lunch the way I did last year."

"Seattle's lovely. I hope you'll visit me soon." But not too soon, she prayed.

"Sometime this spring, I promise," Muriel replied. "I was afraid once you'd settled there all that rain would get you down."

"Mother, honestly, New York City has more annual rainfall than Seattle."

"I know, dear, but in New York the rain all comes in a few days. In Seattle it drizzles for weeks on end, or so I've heard."

"It's not so bad." Maryanne had been far too busy to pay much attention to the weather. Gathering her courage, she forged ahead. "The reason I called is that I've got a bit of exciting news for you."

"You're madly in love and want to get married."

Muriel Simpson was looking forward to grandchildren and had been ever since Maryanne's graduation from college. Both her brothers, Mark and Sean, were several years younger, so Maryanne knew the responsibility had fallen on her. For the past couple of years they'd been introducing her to suitable young men.

"It's nothing that dramatic," Maryanne said, then, losing her courage, she crossed her fingers behind her back and blurted out, "I've got a special assignment...for the—er—paper." The lie nearly stuck in her throat.

"A special assignment?"

All right, she was stretching the truth about as far as it would go, and she hated doing it. But she had no choice. Kramer's reaction would look tame compared to her parents' if they ever found out she was working as a janitor. Rent-A-Maid gave it a fancy name, but basically she'd been hired to clean. It wasn't a glamorous job, nor was it profitable, but it was honest work and she needed something to tide her over until she made a name for herself in her chosen field.

"What kind of special assignment?"

"It has to do with work." Maryanne decided it was best to let her family assume the "assignment" was with the newspaper. She wasn't happy about this, in fact she felt downright depressed to be misleading her mother this way, but she dared not hint at what she'd actually be doing. The only comfort she derived was from the prospect of showing them her published work in a month or two.

"It's not anything dangerous, is it?"

"Oh, heavens, no," Maryanne said, forcing a light laugh. "But I'm going to be involved in it for several weeks, so I won't be mailing you any of my columns, at least not for a while. I didn't want you to wonder when you didn't hear from me."

"Will you be travelling?"

"A little." Only a few city blocks, as a matter of fact, but she couldn't very well say so. "Once everything's completed, I'll get in touch with you."

"You won't even be able to phone?" Her mother's voice carried a hint of concern.

Not often, at least not on her budget, Maryanne realised regretfully.

"Of course I'll phone," she hurried to assure her mother. She didn't often partake in subterfuge, and being new to the game she was making everything up as she went along. She hoped her mother would be trusting enough to accept her at her word.

"Speaking of your columns, dear, tell me what happened with that dreadful reporter who was harassing you earlier in the month."

"Dreadful reporter?" Maryanne repeated uncertainly. "Oh," she said with a flash of insight. "You mean Kramer."

"That's his name?" Her mother's voice rose indignantly. "I hope he's at least stopped using that column of his to irritate you."

"It was all in good fun, Mother." All right, he *had* irritated her, but Maryanne was willing to forget their earlier pettiness. "We're friends now. In fact, I like him quite a lot."

"Friends," her mother echoed softly. Slowly. "I don't suppose your newfound friend is married, is he? You know your father and I started our own relationship at odds with each other, don't you?"

"Mother, honestly. Stop matchmaking."

"Just answer me one thing. Is he married or not?"

"Not. He's in his early thirties and he's handsome." A noticeable pause followed the description. "Mother?"

"You're attracted to him, aren't you?"

Maryanne wasn't sure if she should admit it, but on the other hand she'd already given herself away. "Yes," she said stiffly, "I am...a little. There's a lot to like about him, even though we don't always agree. He's very talented. I've never read a column of his that didn't make me smile—and think. He's got this—er—interesting sense of humour."

"So it seems. Has he asked you out?"

"Not yet." *But he will,* her heart told her.

"Give him time." Muriel Simpson's voice had lowered a notch or two, and again Maryanne could almost hear the wheels turning in her mother's head. "Now, sweetie, before we hang up, I want you to tell me some more about this special assignment of yours."

They talked for a few minutes longer, and Maryanne surprised herself at the way she managed to avoid answering her mother's direct questions. She hated this subterfuge, and she hated the guilt she felt afterward. She tried to reason it away by reminding herself that her motives were good. If her parents knew what she was planning, they'd be sick with worry. But she couldn't remain their little girl forever. She had something to prove, and for the first time she was going to compete like a real contender—without her father standing on the sidelines, bribing the judges.

MARYANNE DIDN'T HEAR from Kramer for the next three days, and she was getting anxious. At the end of the week, she'd be finished at the *Review*; the following Monday she'd be starting at Rent-A-Maid. To her delight, Carol Riverside was appointed as her replacement. The look the managing editor tossed Maryanne's way suggested he'd given Carol the job not because of her recommendation, but despite it.

"I'm still not convinced you're doing the right thing," Carol told her over lunch on Maryanne's last day at the paper.

"But *I'm* convinced, and that's what's important," Maryanne returned. "Why is it everyone's so afraid I'm going to fall flat on my face?"

"It's not that, exactly."

"Then what is it?" she pressed. "I don't think Kramer stopped grumbling from the moment I announced I was quitting the paper, finding a job and moving out on my own."

"And well he should grumble!" Carol declared righteously. "He's the one who started this whole thing. You're such a nice girl. I can't see you getting mixed up with the likes of him."

Maryanne had a sneaking suspicion her friend wasn't saying this out of loyalty to the newspaper. "Mixed up with the likes of him? Is there something I don't know about Seattle's favourite journalist?"

"Kramer Adams may be the most popular newspaper writer in town, but he's got a biting edge to him. Oh, he's witty and talented, I'll give him that, but he has this scornful attitude that makes me want to shake him till he rattles."

"I realise he's a bit cynical."

"He's a good deal more than cynical. The problem is he's so darn entertaining that his attitude is easy to overlook. I'd like two minutes alone with that man just so I could set him straight. He had no business saying what he did about you in that 'My Evening with the Debutante' piece. Look where it's led!''

For that matter, Maryanne wouldn't mind spending two minutes alone with Kramer, either, but for an entirely different reason. The speed with which the thought entered her mind surprised her enough to produce a soft smile.

"Only this time his words came back to hit him in the face," Carol continued.

"Everything he wrote was true," Maryanne felt obliged to remind her friend. She hadn't been all that thrilled when he'd decided to share those truths with the entire western half of Washington state, but she couldn't fault his perceptions.

"Needless to say, I'm not as concerned with Kramer as I am with you," Carol said, gazing down at her sandwich. "I've seen that little spark in your eye when you talk about him, and frankly it worries me."

Maryanne immediately lowered her betraying eyes. "I'm sure you're mistaken. Kramer and I are friends, but that's the extent of it." She wasn't entirely sure Kramer would even want to claim her as a friend; she rather suspected he thought of her as a nuisance.

"Perhaps it's friendship on his part, but it's a lot more on yours. I'm afraid you're going to fall in love with that scoundrel."

"That's crazy," Maryanne countered swiftly. "I've only just met him." Carol's gaze narrowed on her like a diamond drill bit and Maryanne sighed. "He intrigues me," she admitted, "but that's a long way from becoming emotionally involved with him."

"I can't help worrying about you. And, Maryanne, your falling in love with Kramer worries me more than the fact that you're cleaning offices or found yourself an apartment on Capitol Hill."

Maryanne swallowed tightly. "Kramer's a talented respected journalist. If I was going to fall in love with him, which I don't plan to do in the near future, but if I *did* fall for him, why would it be so tragic?"

"Because you're sweet and caring and he's so..." Carol paused and stared into space. "Because he's so scornful."

"True, but underneath that gruff exterior is a heart of gold. At least I think it's there," Maryanne joked.

"Maybe, but I doubt it," Carol went on. "Don't get me wrong—

I respect Kramer's talent. It's his devil-may-care attitude that troubles me.''

But it didn't trouble Maryanne. Not in the least. Perhaps that was what she found most appealing about him. Yet everything Carol said about Kramer was true. He did tend to be cynical and a bit sardonic, but he was also intuitive, reflective and, despite Carol's impression to the contrary, considerate.

Since it was her last day at the paper, Maryanne spent a few extra minutes saying goodbye to her co-workers. Most were sorry to see her go. There had been a fair amount of resentment directed at her when she'd first arrived, but her hard work seemed to have won over all but the most sceptical doubters.

On impulse, Maryanne stopped off at the diner where Kramer had met her earlier in the week, hoping he'd be there. Her heart flew to her throat when she saw him sitting in a booth by the window, a book propped open in front of him. He didn't look up when she walked in.

Nor did he notice her when she approached his booth. Without waiting for an invitation, she slid in across from him.

"Hi," she murmured, keeping her voice low and secretive. "Here comes trouble to plague you once more."

Slowly, with obvious reluctance, Kramer dragged his gaze from the novel. Another mystery, Maryanne noted. "What are you doing here, Trouble?"

"Looking for you."

"Why? Have you thought up any other ways to test my patience? How about walking a tightrope between two skyscrapers? That sounds right up your alley."

"I hadn't heard from you in the past couple of days." She paused, hoping he'd pick up the conversation. "I thought there was something I should do about the apartment. Sign a lease, give the manager a deposit, that sort of thing."

"Annie—"

"I hope you realise I don't even know the address. I only saw it that one time."

"I told you not to worry about it."

"But I don't want anyone else to rent it."

"They won't." He laid the book aside just as the waitress appeared carrying a glass of water and a menu. Maryanne recognised her from the other day. "Hello, Barbara," she said, reading the woman's plastic name tag. "What's the special for the day? Mr Adams owes me a meal and I think I'll collect it while I've got the chance." She waited for him to ask her what she was talking about, but he apparently remembered his promise of dinner to pay her back for the Irish stew he'd eaten at her house the first evening they'd met.

"Cabbage rolls, with soup or salad," Barbara said, reaching for her pad and pencil while Maryanne quickly scanned the menu.

"I'll have a cheeseburger and a chocolate shake," Maryanne decided.

Barbara grinned. "I'll make sure it comes up with Mr Adams's order."

"Thanks," she said, handing her back the menu. Barbara sauntered off toward the kitchen, scribbling on her order pad as she walked.

"It was my last day at the paper," Maryanne announced.

"I'll ask you one more time—are you sure you want to go through with this?" Kramer demanded. "Hell, I never thought for a moment you'd want that apartment. Damn it all, but you're a stubborn woman."

"Of course I'm taking the apartment."

"That's what I thought." He closed his eyes briefly. "What did the Rent-A-Maid agency say when you told them you wouldn't be taking the job?"

Purposely Maryanne stared out the window. "Nothing."

He cocked an eyebrow. "Nothing?"

"What could they say?" she asked, trying to ignore the doubt reflected in his eyes. Maybe she was getting good at this lie-telling business, which wasn't a comforting thought. The way she'd misled her mother still bothered her.

Kramer drew one hand across his face. "You didn't tell them, did you? Apparently you intend to play the Cinderella role to the hilt."

"And you intend to play the role of my wicked stepmother to perfection."

He didn't say anything for a long moment. "Is there a part in that fairy tale where Cinderella gets locked in a closet for her own good?"

"Why?" she couldn't resist asking. "Is that what you're going to do to me?"

"Don't tempt me."

"I wish you had more faith in me."

"I do have faith in you. I have faith that you're going to make my life hell for the next several months while you go about proving yourself. Heaven knows what possessed me to write that stupid column, but, trust me, there hasn't been a minute since it hit the streets that I haven't regretted it. Not a single minute."

"But—"

"Now you insist on moving into the apartment next to mine. That's just great. Wonderful. Whatever peace I have in my life will be completely and utterly destroyed."

"That's not true!" Maryanne cried. "Besides, I'd like to remind you, you're the one who found that apartment, not me. I have no intention of pestering you."

"Like I said, I figured just seeing the apartment would be enough to put you off. Now I won't have a moment to myself again. I know it, and you know it." His eyes were darker and more brooding than she'd ever seen them. "I wasn't kidding when I said you were trouble."

"All right," Maryanne said, doing her best to disguise her crushing sense of defeat. "It's obvious you never expected me to take the place. I suppose you arranged it to look as bleak as you could. Don't worry, I'll find somewhere else to live. Another apartment as far away from you as I can possibly get." She was out of the booth so fast, so intent on escaping, that she nearly collided with Barbara.

"What about your cheeseburger?" the waitress asked.

Maryanne glanced at Kramer. "Wrap it up and give it to Mr Adams. I've lost my appetite."

The tears that blurred her eyes only angered her more. Furious with herself for allowing Kramer's words to wound her, she hurried down the street, headed in the direction of the Seattle waterfront. It was growing dark, but she didn't care; she needed to vent some of her anger, and a brisk hike would serve that purpose nicely.

She wasn't concerned when she heard hard quick footsteps behind her. As the wind whipped at her, she shivered and drew her coat closer, tucking her hands in her pockets and hunching her shoulders forward.

First Carol had issued a warning, and now Kramer. Everyone seemed to believe she needed a keeper! They apparently considered her incompetent, and their doubts cut deeply into her pride.

Her head bowed against the force of the wind, she noticed a pair of male legs match steps with her own. She glanced up and discovered Kramer had joined her.

For the longest time, he said nothing. They were halfway down a deserted pier before he spoke. "I don't want you to find another apartment."

"I think it would be best if I did." He'd already told her she was nothing but trouble, and, as if that wasn't bad enough, he implied she was going to be a constant nuisance in his life. She had no intention of pestering him. As far as she was concerned, he could live on the other side of town. That was what he wanted and that was what he was going to get.

"It isn't for the best," he argued.

"It is. We obviously rub each other the wrong way."

Kramer turned and gripped her by the shoulders. "The apartment's been cleaned. It's ready for you to move into anytime you want. The rent is reasonable and the neighbourhood's a good one. As I recall, this whole ridiculous business between us started over an article about the lack of affordable housing. You're not going to find anyplace else, not with what you intend to live on."

"But you live next door!"

"I'm well aware of that."

Maryanne bristled. "I won't live beside a man who considers me a pest. And furthermore you still owe me dinner."

"I said you were trouble," he pointed out, ignoring her claim. "I didn't say you were a pest."

"You did so."

"I said you were going to destroy my peace—"

"Exactly."

"—of mind," he went on. He closed his eyes briefly and expelled a sharp frustrated sigh, then repeated, "You're going to destroy my peace of mind."

Maryanne wasn't sure she understood. She stared up at him, intrigued by the emotion she saw in his intense brown eyes.

"Why the hell should it matter if you live next door to me or in the Seattle?" he exclaimed. "My serenity was shot the minute I laid eyes on you."

"I don't understand," she said, surprised when her voice came out a raspy whisper. She continued to look up at him, trying to read his expression.

"You don't have a clue, do you?" he whispered. His fingers found their way into her hair as he lowered his mouth with heart-stopping slowness towards hers. "Heaven keep me from redheaded innocents."

But heaven apparently didn't receive the message, because even as he whispered the words Kramer's arms were pulling her towards him. With a sigh of regret—or was it pleasure?—his mouth settled over hers. His kiss was light and undemanding, and despite the anger, despite his words, Maryanne felt herself melting.

With a soft sigh, she flattened her hands on his chest and slid them up to link behind his neck. She leaned against him, letting his strength support her, letting his warmth comfort her.

He pulled her even closer, wrapped his arms around her waist and half lifted her from the pier. Maryanne heard a low hungry moan; she wasn't sure if it came from Kramer or from her.

It didn't matter, she decided. Nothing mattered except this wonderful feeling of being cherished and loved and protected.

Over the years, Maryanne had been kissed by her share of men. She'd found the experience pleasant, but no one had ever set her on fire the way Kramer did now.

"See what I mean," he whispered unsteadily. "We're in trouble here. Big trouble."

CHAPTER FOUR

MARYANNE STOOD in the doorway of her new apartment, the key clenched tightly in her hand. She was embarking on her grand adventure, but now that she'd actually moved out of the Seattle she found her confidence a bit shaky.

Carol joined her, huffing and puffing as she staggered the last few steps down the narrow hallway. She sagged against the wall, panting to catch her breath.

"This place doesn't have an elevator?" she demanded, when she could speak.

"It's being repaired."

"That's what they always say."

Maryanne nodded, barely hearing her friend. Her heart in her throat, she inserted the key and turned the lock. The door stuck, so she used the force of one hip to dislodge it. The apartment was just as she remembered it: worn hardwood floors, the bulky faded furniture, the kitchen appliances that would soon be valuable antiques. But Maryanne saw none of that.

This was her new life.

She walked directly to the window and gazed out. "I've got a great view of Volunteer Park," she announced to her friend. She hadn't noticed it the day Kramer had shown her the apartment. "I had no idea the park was so close." She turned towards Carol, who was still standing in the threshold, her expression one of shock and dismay. "What's wrong?"

"Good heavens," Carol whispered. "You don't really intend on living here, do you?"

"It isn't so bad," Maryanne said with a smile, glancing around to be sure she hadn't missed anything. "I've got lots of ideas on how to decorate the place." She leaned back against the windowsill, where much of the dingy beige paint was chipped away to reveal an even dingier grey-green. "What it needs is a fresh coat of paint, something light and cheerful."

"It's not even half the size of your other place."

"There was a lot of wasted space at my apartment there." That might be true, Maryanne thought privately, but she wouldn't have minded bringing some of it with her.

"What about your neighbour?" Carol asked in a grudging voice. "He's the one who started this. The least he could do is offer a little help."

Straightening, Maryanne brushed the dust from her palms and looked away. "I didn't ask him to. In fact, I don't think he even knows when I was planning to move in."

Kramer was a subject Maryanne wanted to avoid. She hadn't talked to him since the night he'd followed her to the waterfront...the night he'd kissed her. He'd stopped off at the Seattle to leave the apartment key and a rental agreement with the doorman. Max had promptly delivered both. The implication was obvious; Kramer didn't want to see her and was, in fact, doing his best to avoid her.

Clearly he disapproved of the way things had developed on the pier that night. She supposed he didn't like kissing her. Then again, perhaps he did. Perhaps he liked it too much for his oft-lamented "peace of mind."

Maryanne knew how *she* felt about it. She couldn't sleep for two nights afterward. Every time she closed her eyes, the image of Kramer holding her in his arms danced through her mind like a waltzing couple from a 1940s movie. She remembered the way he scowled down at her when he'd broken off the kiss and how he'd struggled to make light of the incident. And she remembered his eyes, so warm and gentle, telling her another story.

"Hey, lady, is this the place where I'm supposed to bring the boxes?" A lanky youth of about fourteen stood in the doorway, holding a large cardboard box in his arms.

"Y-yes," Maryanne said, recognising the container as one of her own. "How'd you know to carry it up here?"

"Mr Adams. He promised a bunch of us guys he'd play basketball with us if we'd help unload the truck."

"Oh. How nice. I'm Maryanne Simpson," she said, her heart warming at Kramer's unexpected thoughtfulness.

"Nice to meet you, lady. Now where do you want me to put this?"

Maryanne pointed toward the kitchen. "Just stack it in the corner over there." Before she finished, a second and third youth appeared, each hauling boxes.

Maryanne slipped past them and ran down the stairs to the parking area behind the building. Kramer was standing in the back of Carol's husband's pickup, noisily distributing cardboard boxes and dire warnings. He didn't seem to notice her until she moved closer. When he did, he fell silent, a frown on his face.

"Hi," she said, feeling a little shy. "I came to thank you."

"You shouldn't have gone up and left the truck unattended," he barked, still frowning. "Anyone could have walked off with this."

"We just arrived."

"We?"

"Carol Riverside and me. She's upstairs trying to regain her breath. How long will it be before the elevator's fixed?"

"Not soon."

She nodded. Well, if he'd hoped to discourage her, she wasn't going to let him. So what if she had to walk up four flights of stairs everyday! It was wonderful aerobic exercise. In the past she'd paid good money to attend a health club for the same purpose.

Kramer returned to his task, lifting boxes and handing them to a long line of teenage boys. "I'm surprised you didn't have a moving company manage this for you."

"Are you kidding?" she joked. "Only rich people use moving companies."

"Is this all of it, or do you need to make a second trip?"

"This is it. Carol and I put everything else in storage earlier this morning. It's only costing me a few dollars a month. I have to be careful about money now, you know."

He scowled again. "When do you start with the cleaning company?"

"Monday morning."

Kramer placed his hands on his hips and glared down at her. "If you're really intending to accept that job—"

"Of course I am!"

"Then the first thing you'll need to do is ask for a raise."

"Oh, honestly, Kramer," she protested, walking backward. "I can't do that!"

"What you can't do is live on that amount of money, no matter how well you budget," he muttered. He leapt off the back of the truck as agilely as a cat. "Will you listen to me for once?"

"I am listening," she said. "It just so happens I don't agree. Quit worrying about me, would you? I'm going to be perfectly all right, especially once I start selling articles."

"I'm not a knight in shining armour, understand?" he shouted after her. "If you think I'll be racing to your rescue every time you're in trouble, then you need to think again."

"You're insulting me by even suggesting I'd accept your help." She tried to be angry with him but found it impossible. He might insist she was entirely on her own, but all the while he was lecturing her he was doling out her boxes so that she wouldn't have to haul them up the stairs herself. Kramer might claim not to be a knight riding to her rescue, but he was behaving suspiciously like one.

Two hours later, Maryanne was alone in her new apartment for the first time. Hands on her hips, she stood in the middle of her living-room and surveyed her kingdom. As she'd told Carol, it wasn't so bad. Boxes filled every bit of available space, but it wouldn't take her long to unpack and set everything in order.

She was grateful for the help Carol, Kramer and the neighbourhood teenagers had given her, but now it was up to her. And she had lots of plans—she'd paint the walls and put up her pictures and buy some plants—to make this place cheerful and attractive. To turn it into a home.

It was dark before she was finished unpacking, and by that time she was both exhausted and hungry. Actually *famished* more adequately described her condition. Her hunger and exhaustion warred with each other: she was too tired to go out and buy herself something to eat, but too hungry to go to bed without eating. Making the decision about which she should do created a dilemma of startling proportions.

She'd just decided to make do with a bowl of cornflakes, sans the milk, when there was a loud knock at her door. She jerked it open to find Kramer standing there, wearing grey sweatpants and a sweat-soaked T-shirt. He held a basketball under one arm and clutched a large white paper sack in the other.

"Never open the door without knowing who's on the other side," he warned, walking directly into the apartment. He dropped the basketball on the sofa and placed his sack—obviously from a fast-food restaurant—on the coffee table. "That chain's there for a reason. Use it."

Maryanne was still standing at the door, inhaling the aroma of french fries and hamburgers. "Yes, your majesty."

"Don't get testy with me, either. I've just lost two years of my life on a basketball court. I'm too old for this, but luckily what I lack in youth I make up for in smarts."

"I see," she said, closing the door. For good measure she clipped the chain into place and turned the lock.

"A little show of appreciation would go a long way towards soothing my injuries," he told her, sinking on to the sofa. He rested his head against the cushion, eyes drifting shut.

"You can't be that smart, otherwise you'd have managed to get out of playing with boys twenty years younger than you," she said lightly. She had trouble keeping her eyes off the white sack on the scratched mahogany coffee table.

Kramer straightened, wincing as he did so. "I thought you might be hungry." He reached for the bag and removed a napkin-wrapped hamburger, which he tossed to her before taking a second for himself. Next he set out two cardboard cartons full of hot french fries and two cans of soda.

Maryanne sat down beside him, her hand pressed against her stomach to keep it from growling. "You'd better be careful," she said. "You're beginning to look suspiciously like that knight in shining armour."

"Don't kid yourself."

Maryanne was too hungry to waste time arguing. She devoured the hamburger and fries within minutes. Then she relaxed against the back of the sofa and sighed, content.

"I came to set some ground rules," Kramer explained. "The way I figure it, you and I need to get a few things straight. Clear the air, that sort of thing."

"Sure," she agreed. It sounded like a good idea, although she was fairly certain she knew what he wanted to talk about. "I've already promised not to pester you."

"Good. I intend to stay out of your way, too."

"Perfect." It didn't really sound all that wonderful, but it seemed to be what he wanted, so she didn't have much choice. "Anything else?"

Kramer hesitated. Then he leaned forward, resting his forearms on his knees. "Yes, one other thing." He glanced in her direction with a frown. "I don't think we should...you know, kiss again."

A short silence followed his words. At first Maryanne wasn't sure she'd heard him correctly.

"I realise talking about this may be embarrassing," Kramer continued, sounding as detached as if he'd introduced the subject of football scores. "I want you to know I'm suggesting this for your own good."

"I'm pleased to hear that." It demanded some effort not to mock him by rolling her eyes.

He nodded and cleared his throat, and Maryanne could see he wasn't nearly as indifferent as he wanted her to believe.

"There appears to be a certain amount of physical chemistry between us," he continued, avoiding even a glance in her direction. "I feel that the sooner we settle this, the less likelihood there'll be for misunderstandings later on. The last thing I need is for you to fall in love with me."

"That's it!" she cried, throwing up her arms. The ridiculousness of his comment revived her enough to allow her to indulge in some teasing. "The whole thing's off. If I can't have your heart and soul, then I'm leaving right now!"

"Damn it, Annie, this is nothing to joke about."

"Who's joking?" she asked. She made her voice sound absurdly melodramatic. "I knew the minute I walked into the radio station for the Celebrity Debate that if I couldn't taste your lips there was nothing left to live for."

"If you're going to make a joke out of this, then you can forget the whole discussion." He vaulted to his feet and stuffed the wrappers from their burgers and fries into the empty sack with enough force to tear out the bottom. "I was hoping we could have a mature talk, one adult to another, but that's obviously beyond you."

"Don't get so bent out of shape," she said, trying not to smile. "Sit down before you do something silly, like leave in a huff. We both know you'll regret it." She didn't know anything of the sort, but it sounded good.

He complied grudgingly, but he stared past her, training his eyes on the darkened window.

Maryanne got stiffly to her feet, every muscle and joint protesting.

"It seems to me that you're presuming a good deal with this hands-off decree," she said with all the dignity she could muster. "What makes you think I'd even *want* you to kiss me again?"

A slow cocky grin teased the corners of his mouth. "A man can tell. My biggest fear is that you're going to start thinking things I never meant you to think. Eventually you'd end up getting hurt. I intend to make damn sure nothing romantic develops between us. Understand?"

"You think my head's in the clouds when it comes to you?"

"That's right. You're a sweet kid, stubborn and idealistic, but nonetheless naive. One kiss told me you've got a romantic soul, and frankly I don't want you fluttering those pretty blue eyes at me and dreaming of babies and a white picket fence. You and I are about as different as two people can get."

"Different?" To Maryanne's way of thinking, she had more in common with Kramer Adams than with any other man she'd ever dated.

"That's right. You come from this rich upstanding family—"

"Stop!" she cried. "Don't say another word about our economic differences. They're irrelevant. If you're looking for excuses, find something else."

"I don't need excuses. It'd never work between us and I want to make certain neither of us is ever tempted to try. If you want someone to teach you about being a woman, look elsewhere."

His words were like a slap across the face. "Naturally a man of your vast romantic experience gets plenty of requests." She turned away, so angry she couldn't keep still. "As for being afraid I might fall in love with you, let me assure you right now there's absolutely no chance of it. In fact, I think you should be more concerned about falling for me!" Her voice was gaining strength and conviction with every word. The man had such colossal nerve. At one time she might have found herself attracted to him, but that passed the minute he walked in her door and opened his mouth.

"Don't kid yourself," he argued. "You're halfway in love with me already. I can see it in your eyes."

Damn those expressive eyes of hers. Carol had said something about her eyes revealing what she felt for Kramer, too.

Maryanne whirled around, intent on composing a suitably sarcastic retort, away from his searching gaze. But before any mocking words could pass her lips, a sharp pain shot through her neck, an ache so intense it brought immediate tears to her eyes. She must have moved too quickly, too carelessly.

Her hands flew to the back of her neck.

Kramer was instantly on his feet. "What's wrong?"

"Nothing," she mumbled, easing her way back to the sofa. She sat down, hand still pressed to her neck, waiting a moment before slowly rotating her head, wanting to test the extent of her injury. Quickly, she realised her mistake.

"Annie," Kramer demanded, kneeling in front of her, "what is it?"

"I...don't know. I moved wrong, I guess."

His hands replaced hers. "You've got a crick in your neck?"

"If I do, it's all your fault. You say the most ridiculous things."

"I know." His voice was as gentle as his hands. He began to knead softly, his fingers tenderly massaging the tightened muscles.

"I'm all right."

"Of course you are," he whispered. "Just close your eyes and relax."

"I can't." How could he possibly expect her to do that when he was so close, so warm and sensual? He was fast making a lie of all her protestations.

"Yes, you can," he said, his voice low and seductive. He leaned over her, his face, his lips, scant inches from hers. His hands were working the tightness from her neck and shoulders and at the same time creating a dizzying heated sensation that extended to the tips of her fingers and the soles of her feet.

She sighed and clasped his wrist with both hands, wanting to stop him before she made a fool of herself by swaying towards him or doing something equally suggestive. "I think you should stop. Let me rephrase that. I *know* you should stop."

"I know I should, too," he admitted quietly. "Remember what I said earlier?"

"You mean the hands-off policy?"

"Yes." She could hardly hear him. "Let's delay it for a day—what do you think?"

At that moment, clear organised thought was something of a problem. "W-whatever you think is best."

"Oh, I know what's best," he whispered. "Unfortunately that doesn't seem to make a damn bit of difference right now."

She couldn't recall when it happened, but her hands seemed to have left his wrists and were splayed across the front of his T-shirt. His chest felt rigid and muscular; his heart beneath her palms pounded hard and fast. She wondered if her own pulse was keeping time with his.

With infinite slowness, Kramer lowered his mouth to hers. Maryanne's eyes drifted closed of their own accord and she moaned, holding back a small cry of welcome. His touch was even more compelling than she remembered. Kramer must have felt something similar, because his groan followed, an echo of hers.

He kissed her again and again. Maryanne wanted more, but he resisted giving in to her desires—or his own. It was as if he'd decided a few kisses were of little consequence and wouldn't seriously affect either one of them.

Wrong. Maryanne wanted to shout it at him, but couldn't.

His mouth left hers and blazed a fiery trail of kisses across her sensitised skin. His lips brushed her throat, under her chin to the vulnerable hollow. Only minutes earlier, moving her neck without pain had been impossible; now she did so freely, turning it, arching, asking—no, demanding—that he kiss her again the way he had that night at the waterfront.

Kramer complied, and he seemed to do it willingly, surrendering the battle. He groaned anew and the sound came from deep in his throat. His fingers tangled in the thick strands of her hair as his mouth rushed back to hers.

Maryanne was experiencing a renewal of her own. She felt as if she had lain dormant and was bursting to life, like a flower struggling out of winter snows into the light and warmth of spring.

All too soon, Kramer pulled away from her. His eyes met and held hers. She knew her eyes were filled with questions, but his gave her no answers.

He pulled away and abruptly stood.

"Kramer," she said, shocked that he would leave her so brusquely.

He looked back at her and she saw it then. The regret. A regret tinged with compassion. "You're so exhausted you can barely sit up. Go to bed and we'll both forget this ever happened. Understand?"

Too stunned to reply, she nodded. Maybe Kramer could forget it, but she knew she wouldn't.

"Lock the door after me. And next time don't be so eager to find out who's knocking. There isn't any doorman here."

Once more she nodded. She got up and followed him to the door, holding it open.

"Damn it, Annie, don't look at me like that."

"Like what?"

"Like that," he accused, then slowly shook his head as if to clear his thoughts. He rubbed his face and sighed, then pressed his knuckle under her chin. "The two of us are starting over first thing tomorrow. There won't be any more of this." But even as he was speaking, he was leaning forward to gently brush her mouth with his.

IT WAS THE SOUND of Kramer furiously pounding away on his electric typewriter—a heavy, outdated office model—that woke Maryanne the following morning. She yawned loudly, stretching her arms high above her head, arching her back. Her first night in her new apartment and she'd slept like a rock. The sofa, which opened into a queen-size sleeper, was lumpy and soft, nearly swallowing her up, but she'd been too exhausted to care.

Kramer's fierce typing continued most of the day. Maryanne hadn't expected to see him, so she wasn't disappointed when she didn't. He seemed determined to avoid her and managed it successfully for most of the week.

Since she'd promised not to make a nuisance of herself, Maryanne stayed out of his way, too. She started work at the cleaning company and wrote three articles in five days, often staying up late into the night.

The work for Rent-A-Maid was backbreaking and arduous. She spent three afternoons a week picking up after professional men who were nothing less than slobs. Maryanne had to resist the urge to write them each a note demanding that they put their dirty dishes in the sink and their soiled clothes in the laundry basket.

Rent-A-Maid had made housekeeping sound glamorous. It wasn't. In fact, it was the hardest, most physically exhausting job she'd ever undertaken.

By the end of the week, her nails were broken and chipped and her hands were red and chapped.

It was by chance rather than design that Maryanne bumped into Kramer late Friday afternoon. She was carrying a bag of groceries up the stairs when he bounded past her, taking the steps two at a time.

"Annie." He paused on the landing, waiting for her to catch up. "So how's it going?"

Maryanne didn't know what to say. She couldn't very well inform him that the highlight of her week was scraping a crusty patch off the bottom of an oven at one of the apartments she cleaned. She'd had such lofty expectations, such dreams. Nor could she casually announce that the stockbroker she cleaned for had spilled wine on his carpet and she'd spent an hour trying to get the stain out and broken two nails in the process.

"Fine," she lied. "Everything's just wonderful."

"Here, let me take that for you."

"Thanks." She handed him the single bag, her week's allotment of groceries. Unfortunately it was all she could afford. Everything had sounded so exciting when she started out; her plans had seemed so promising. The reality was proving to be something else again.

"Well, how do you like cleaning?"

"It's great, really great." It was amazing how easily the lie came. "I'm finding it...a challenge."

Kramer smiled absently. "I'm glad to hear it. Have you got your first paycheck yet?"

"I cashed it this afternoon." She'd spent more each week at the dry cleaners than she received in her first paycheck with Rent-A-Maid. The entire amount had gone for petrol and food and there were only a few dollars left over. Her budget was tight, but she'd make it. She'd have to.

Kramer paused in front of her door and waited while she scrabbled through her bag, searching for the key. "I hear you typing at night," she said. "Are you working on something special?"

"No."

She eyed him curiously. "How fast do you type? Eighty words a minute? A hundred? And for heaven's sake, why don't you use a computer like everyone else?"

"Sixty words a minute on a good day. And for your information, I happen to like my electric. It may be old, but it does the job."

She finally retrieved her key, conscious of his gaze on her hands.

Suddenly he grasped her fingers. "All right," he demanded. "What happened to you?"

CHAPTER FIVE

"NOTHING'S HAPPENED TO ME," Maryanne insisted hotly, pulling her hand free of Kramer's.

"Look at your nails," he said. "There isn't one that's not broken."

"You make it sound like I should be dragged before a firing squad at dawn. So I chipped a few nails this week. I'll survive." Although she was making light of it, each broken fingernail was like a small loss. She took pride in her perfect nails, or at least she had once.

His eyes narrowed as he scrutinised her. "There's something you're not telling me."

"I didn't realise you'd appointed yourself my father confessor."

Anger flashed in his dark eyes as he took the key from her unresisting fingers. He opened the door and, with one hand at her shoulder, urged her inside. "We need to talk."

"No, we don't." Maryanne marched into the apartment, plunked her bag of groceries on the kitchen counter and spun around to confront her neighbour. "Listen here, buster, you've made it perfectly clear that you don't want to have anything to do with me. That's your choice, and I'm certainly not going to bore you with the sorry details of my life."

He ignored her words and started pacing the small living area, pausing in front of the window. His presence filled the apartment, making it seem smaller than usual. He pivoted sharply, pointing an accusatory finger in her direction. "These broken nails came from swinging a dust mop around, did they? What the hell are you doing?"

Maryanne didn't answer him right away. She was angry, and his sudden concern for her welfare made her even angrier. "I told you before, I don't need a guardian."

"Against my advice, you took that stupid job. Anyone with half a brain would know it wasn't going to—"

"Will you stop acting like you're responsible for me?" Maryanne snapped.

"I can't help it. I *am* responsible for you. You wouldn't be here if I hadn't written that damn column. I don't want to intrude on your life any more than you want me to, but let's face it, there's no one else to look out for you. Sooner or later someone's going to take advantage of you."

That did it, Maryanne thought. She stalked over to him and jabbed her index finger into his chest with enough force to bend what remained of her nail. "In case you need reminding, I'm my own woman. I make my own decisions. I'll work any place I damn well please. Furthermore, I can take care of myself." She whirled around and opened her front door. "Now kindly leave!"

"No."

"No?" she repeated.

"No," he said again, returning to the window. He crossed his arms over his chest and sighed impatiently. "You haven't eaten, have you? I can tell, because you get testy when your stomach's empty."

"If you'd leave my apartment the way I asked that wouldn't be a problem."

"How about having dinner with me?"

The invitation took Maryanne by surprise. Her first impulse was to throw it back in his face. After an entire week of pretending she didn't exist, he had a lot of nerve even asking.

"Well?" he prompted.

"Where?" As if that made a difference. Maryanne was famished, and the thought of sharing her meal with Kramer was more tempting than she wanted to admit, even to herself.

"The diner."

"Are you going to order chilli?"

"Are you going to ask them to remove the bean sprouts from your sandwich?"

Maryanne hesitated. She felt confused by all her contradictory emotions. She was strongly attracted to Kramer and she admired his talent. Every time they were together she caught herself hoping they could become friends—more than friends. But, equally often, he infuriated her or left her feeling depressed. He made the most outland-ish remarks to her. He seemed to have appointed himself her legal guardian. When he wasn't issuing decrees, he neglected her as if she were nothing more than a nuisance. And to provide a finishing touch, she was lying to her parents because of him! Well, maybe that wasn't quite fair, but...

"I'll throw in dessert," he coaxed with a smile.

The smile was her Waterloo, yet she still struggled. "A la mode?"

His grin widened. "You drive a hard bargain."

Maryanne's eyes met his and although Kramer could make her angrier than anyone she'd ever known, a smile trembled on her own lips.

They agreed to meet a half-hour later. That gave Maryanne time to unpack her groceries, change clothes and freshen her make-up. She found herself humming as she applied lip gloss, wondering if she was reading too much significance into this impromptu dinner date.

When Kramer came to her door to pick her up, Maryanne noted that he'd changed out of his suit and into jeans and a fisherman's sweater. It was the first time she'd seen him without the raincoat, other than the day he'd played basketball with the neighbourhood boys. He looked good. All right, she admitted grudgingly, he looked fantastic.

"You dressed up," she said before she could stop herself, grateful at least that she'd understated her attraction to him.

"So did you. You look nice."

"Thanks."

"Before I forget to tell you, word has it the elevator's going to be fixed Monday morning."

"Really? That's the best news I've heard all week." Goodness, could she take all these glad tidings at once? First Kramer had ac-tually invited her out on a date, and now she wouldn't have to hike four flights of stairs every afternoon. Life was indeed treating her well.

They were several blocks from the apartment building before

Maryanne realised Kramer was driving in the opposite direction of the diner. She said as much.

"Do you like Chinese food?" he asked.

"I love it."

"The diner's short-staffed—one of the waitresses quit. I thought Chinese food might be interesting, and I promise we won't have to wait for a table."

It sounded heavenly to Maryanne. She didn't know how significant Kramer's decision to take her to a different restaurant might be. Perhaps it was foolish, but Maryanne hoped it meant she was becoming special to him. As if guessing her thoughts, Kramer was unusually quiet on the drive into Seattle's International District.

So much for romance. Maryanne could almost hear his thoughts. If she were a betting woman, she'd place odds on the way their dinner conversation would go. First Kramer would try to find out exactly what tasks had been assigned to her by Rent-A-Maid. Then he'd try to convince her to quit.

Only she wasn't going to let him. She was her own woman, and she'd said it often enough to convince herself. If this newsman thought he could sway her with a fancy dinner and a few well-spoken words, then he was about to learn a valuable lesson.

The restaurant proved to be a Chinese version of the greasy spoon where Kramer ate regularly. The minute they walked into the compact room, Maryanne's senses were greeted with a wide variety of tantalising scents. Pungent spices and oils wafted through the air, and the smells were so appealing it was all Maryanne could do not to follow them into the kitchen. She knew before sampling a single bite that the food would be some of the best Oriental cuisine she'd ever tasted.

An elderly Chinese gentleman greeted Kramer as if he were a long-lost relative. The two shared a brief exchange in Chinese before the man escorted them to a table. He shouted into the kitchen, and a brightly painted ceramic pot of tea was quickly delivered to their table.

Kramer and Maryanne were never given menus. Almost from the moment they were seated, food began appearing on their table. An appetiser plate came first, with several items Maryanne couldn't readily identify. But she was too hungry to care. Everything was delicious and she happily devoured one after another.

"You seem well acquainted with the waiter," Maryanne commented, once the appetiser plate was empty. She barely had time to catch her breath before a bowl of thick spicy soup was brought to them by the same elderly gentleman. He paused and smiled proudly at Kramer, then glanced at Maryanne, before nodding in a profound way.

"Wong Su's the owner. I went to school with his son."

"Is that where you picked up Chinese?"

"Yes. I only know a few words, just enough to get the gist of what he's saying," he answered brusquely, reaching for his spoon.

"What was it he said when we first came in? I noticed you seemed quick to disagree with him."

Kramer dipped his spoon into the soup, ignoring her question.

"Kramer?"

"He said you're too thin."

Maryanne shook her head, knowing immediately that he was lying. "If he really thought that, you'd have agreed with him."

"All right, all right," Kramer muttered, looking severely displeased. "I should have known better than to bring a woman to Wong Su's place. He immediately assumed there was something romantic between us. He said you'd give me many fine sons."

"How sweet."

Her words instantly captured Kramer's attention. He dropped his spoon beside the bowl with a clatter, planted his elbows on the table and glared at her heatedly. "Now don't go all sentimental on me. There's nothing between us and there never will be."

Maryanne promptly saluted. "Aye, aye, Captain," she mocked.

"Good. Well, now that's settled, tell me about your week."

"Tell me about yours," she countered, unwilling to change the subject to herself quite so easily. "You seemed a whole lot busier than I was."

"I went to work, came home…"

"…worked some more," she finished for him. Another plate,

heaped high with sizzling hot chicken and crisp vegetables was brought by Wong Su, who offered Maryanne a toothy grin.

Kramer frowned at his friend and said something in Chinese that caused the older man to laugh outright. When Kramer returned his attention to Maryanne, he was scowling again. "For heaven's sake, don't encourage him."

"What did I do?" To the best of her knowledge she was innocent of any wrongdoing.

Kramer thought it over for a moment. "Never mind, it won't do any good to tell you."

Other steaming dishes arrived—prawns with cashew nuts, then ginger beef and barbecued pork, each accompanied by small bowls of rice until virtually every inch of the small table was covered.

"You were telling me about your week," Maryanne reminded him, reaching for the dish in the centre of the crowded table.

"No, I wasn't," Kramer retorted.

With a scornful sigh, Maryanne passed Kramer the chicken. "All right, have it your way."

"You're going to needle me to death until you find out what I'm working on in my spare time, aren't you?"

"Of course not." If he didn't want her to know, then fine, she had no intention of asking again. Acting as nonchalant as possible, she helped herself to a thick slice of the pork. She dipped it into a small dish of hot mustard, which proved to be a bit more potent than she'd expected; her eyes rapidly started to water.

Mumbling under his breath, Kramer handed her his napkin. "Here."

"I'm all right." She wiped the moisture from her eyes and blinked a couple of times before reaching for her water glass. Once she'd composed herself, she returned to the subject at hand. "On the contrary, Mr Adams, whatever project so intensely occupies your time is your own concern."

"Spoken like a true aristocrat."

"Obviously you don't care to share it with me."

He gave an exaggerated sigh. "It's a novel," he said. "There now, are you satisfied?"

"A novel," she repeated coolly. "Really. And all along, I thought you were taking in typing jobs on the side."

He glared at her, but the edges of his mouth turned up in a reluctant grin. "I don't want to talk about the plot, all right? I'm afraid that would water it down."

"I understand perfectly."

"Damn it all, Annie, would you stop looking at me with those big blue eyes of yours? I already feel guilty as hell without you smiling serenely at me and trying to act so blasé."

"Guilty about what?"

He expelled his breath sharply. "Listen," he said in a low voice, leaning towards her. "As much as I hate to admit this, you're right. It's none of my business where you work or how many nails you break or how much you're paid. But damn it all, I'm worried about you."

She raised her chopsticks in an effort to stop him. "It seems to me I've heard this argument before. Actually, it's downright boring hearing it over and over again."

Kramer dropped his voice even lower. "You've been sheltered all your life. I know you don't want me to feel responsible for what you're doing—or for you. And I wish I didn't. Unfortunately I can't help it. Believe me, I've tried. It doesn't work. Every night I lie awake wondering what trouble you're going to get into next. I don't know what's going to happen first—you working yourself to death, or me getting an ulcer."

Maryanne's gaze fell to her hands, and the uneven length of her once perfectly uniform fingernails. "They are rather pitiful, aren't they?"

Kramer glanced at them and grimaced. "As a personal favour to me would you consider giving up the job at Rent-A-Maid?" He ran his fingers through his hair, sighing heavily. "It doesn't come easy to ask you this, Annie. If for no other reason, do it because you owe me a favour for finding you the apartment. But for heaven's sake, quit that job."

She didn't answer him right away. She wanted to do as he asked, because she was falling in love with him. Because she craved his approval. Yet she wanted to reject his entreaties, flout his demands. Because he made her feel confused and contrary and full of unpredictable emotions.

"If it'll do any good, I'll promise not to interfere again," he said, his voice so quiet it was almost a whisper.

"As a personal favour to you," she repeated, nodding slowly. So much for refusing to be swayed by dinner and a few well-chosen words.

Their eyes met and held for a long moment. Deliberately, as though going against every dictate of his will, Kramer reached out and brushed an auburn curl from her cheek. His touch was light yet strangely intimate, as intimate as a kiss. His fingers lingered on her cheek and it was all Maryanne could do not to cover his hand with her own and close her eyes to savour the wealth of sensations that settled around her.

Kramer's dark eyes narrowed, and she could tell he was struggling. She could read it in every line, every feature of his handsome face, but against what, she could only speculate. He didn't want to be attracted to her; that much was obvious.

As if needing to break contact with her eyes, he lowered his gaze to her mouth. Whether it was intentional or not, Maryanne didn't know, his thumb inched closer to her lips, easing towards the corner. Then, with an abrupt movement, he pulled his hand away and returned to his meal, eating quickly and methodically.

Maryanne tried to eat, but her own appetite was gone. Wong Su refused payment although Kramer tried to insist. Instead the elderly man said something in Chinese that sent every eye in the place straight to Maryanne. She smiled benignly, wondering what he could possibly have said that would make the great Kramer Adams blush.

The drive back to the apartment was as silent as the one to the restaurant had been. Maryanne considered asking Kramer exactly what Wong Su had said just before they'd left, but she thought better of it.

By unspoken agreement, they took their time walking up the four flights of stairs. "Will you come in for coffee?" Maryanne asked when they arrived at her door.

"I can't tonight," Kramer said after several all-too-quiet moments.

"I don't bite, you know." His eyes didn't waver from hers. The attraction was there—she could feel it as surely as she had his touch at dinner.

"I'd like to finish my chapter."

So he was going to close her out once again, erect that wall higher. "Don't work too hard," she said, opening the apartment door. Her disappointment was keen, but she managed to disguise it behind a shrug. "Thank you for dinner. It was delicious."

Kramer thrust his hands into his pockets. It might have been her imagination, but she thought he did it to keep from reaching for her. The idea comforted her ego and she smiled up at him warmly.

She was about to close the door when he stopped her. "Yes?" she asked.

His eyes were as piercing and dark as she'd ever seen them. "My typing. Does it keep you awake nights?"

"No," she told him and shook her head for emphasis. "The book must be going well."

He nodded, then sighed. "Listen, would it be possible..." He paused and started again. "Are you busy tomorrow night? I've got two tickets to the Seattle Repertory Theatre and I was wondering..."

"I'd love to go," she said eagerly, before he'd even finished the question.

Judging by the expression on his face, the invitation seemed to be as much a surprise to him as it was to her. "I'll see you tomorrow, then."

"Right," she answered brightly. "Tomorrow."

THE AFTERNOON was glorious, with just the right mixture of wind and sunshine. Hands clasped behind her back, Maryanne strolled across the grass of Volunteer Park, kicking up leaves as she went. She'd spent the morning researching an article she hoped to sell to a local magazine and she was taking a break.

The basketball court was occupied by several teenage boys, a couple of whom she recognised from the day she'd moved. With time on her hands and an afternoon to enjoy, Maryanne paused to watch the hotly contested game. Sitting on a picnic table, she swung her legs, content to laze away the sunny afternoon. Everything was going so well. With hardly any difficulty she'd found another job. Kramer probably wasn't going to approve of this one, either, but that was just too bad.

"Hi." A girl of about thirteen, wearing a jean jacket and tight black stretch leggings, strolled up to the picnic table. "You're Mr Adams's girlfriend, aren't you?"

Maryanne would have liked to think so, but she knew better. "What makes you ask that?"

"You moved in with him, didn't you?"

"Not exactly. I live in the apartment next door."

"I didn't believe Eddie when he said Mr Adams had a woman. He's never had anyone live with him before. He's just not the type, if you know what I mean."

Maryanne did know. She was learning not to take his attitude towards her personally. The better acquainted she became with Kramer, the more clearly she realised that he considered all women a nuisance. The first night they met, he'd mentioned that he'd been in love once, but his tone had been so casual it implied this romance was merely a long-ago mistake. He'd talked about the experience as if it meant little or nothing to him. Maryanne wasn't sure she believed that.

"Mr Adams is a really neat guy. All the kids like him a lot." The girl smiled, suggesting she was one of his legion of admirers. "I'm Gloria Masterson."

Maryanne held out her hand. "Maryanne Simpson."

Gloria smiled shyly. "If you're not his woman, are you...you know, his sweetheart?"

"Not really. We're just friends."

"That's what he said when I asked him about you."

"Oh." It wasn't as though she could expect him to admit anything more.

"Mr Adams comes around every now and again and talks to us kids in the park. I think he's checking up on us and making sure no one's into drugs or gangs."

Maryanne smiled. That sounded exactly like something Kramer would do.

"Only a few kids around here are that stupid, but you know, I think a couple of the boys might have been tempted to try something if it weren't for Mr Adams."

"Hey, Gloria." A lanky youth from the basketball court called out. "Come here, woman."

Gloria sighed loudly, then shouted. "Just a minute." She turned back to Maryanne. "I'm really not Eddie's woman. He just likes to think so."

Maryanne smiled. She wished she could say the same thing about her and Kramer. "It was nice to meet you, Gloria. Maybe I'll see you around."

"That'd be great."

"Gloria," Eddie shouted, "are you coming or not?"

The teenage girl shook her head. "I don't know why I put up with him."

Maryanne left the park soon afterward. The first thing she noticed when she got home was an envelope taped to her door.

She waited until she was inside the apartment to open it, and as she did a single ticket and a note slipped out. "I got stuck at the office," the note read. "The curtain goes up at eight—don't be late. K."

Maryanne was mildly disappointed that Kramer wouldn't be driving her to the play, but she decided to splurge and take a taxi. By seven-thirty, when the cab arrived, she was dressed and ready. She wore her best evening attire, a long black velvet skirt and matching blazer with a cream-coloured silk blouse. She'd even put on her pearl earrings and cameo necklace.

The theatre was one of the nicest in town, and Maryanne's heart sang with excitement as the usher escorted her to her seat. Kramer hadn't arrived yet and she looked around expectantly.

The curtain was about to go up when a man she mentally categorised as wealthy and a bit of a charmer settled in the vacant seat next to hers.

"Excuse me," he said, leaning towards her, smiling warmly. "I'm Griff Bradly. Kramer Adams sent me."

It didn't take Maryanne two seconds to figure out what Kramer had done. The low-down rat had matched her up with someone he considered more appropriate. Someone he assumed she had more in common with. Someone wealthy and slick. Someone her father would approve of.

"Where's Kramer?" Maryanne demanded. She bolted to her feet and grabbed her bag, jerking it so hard the tiny gold chain strap threatened to break.

Griff looked taken aback by her sharp question. "You mean he didn't discuss this evening with you?"

"He invited me to this play. I assumed... I believed the two of us would be attending it together. He didn't say a word about you. I'm sorry, but I can't agree to this arrangement." She started to edge her way out of the row just as the curtain rose.

To her dismay, Griff followed her into the aisle. "I'm sure there's been some misunderstanding."

"You bet there has," Maryanne said, loudly enough to attract the angry glares of several patrons sitting in the aisle seats. She rushed toward the exit with Griff in hot pursuit.

"If you'll give me a moment to explain—"

"It won't be necessary."

"You are Maryanne Simpson of the New York Simpsons?"

"Yes," she said, walking directly outside. Standing on the kerb, she raised her hand and shouted, "Taxi!"

Griff raced around to stand in front of her. "Surely there isn't any need to rush off like this. Kramer was doing me a good turn."

"And me a rotten one. Listen, Mr Bradly, you look like a very nice gentleman, and under any other circumstances I would have been more than happy to make your acquaintance, but there's been a terrible misunderstanding."

"But—"

"I'm sorry, I really am." A cab raced towards her and squealed to a halt.

Griff opened the back door for her, looking more charming and debonair than ever. "I don't know that my heart will recover. You're really quite lovely, you know."

Maryanne sighed. The man was overdoing it, but he certainly didn't deserve the treatment she was giving him. She smiled and apologised again, then swiftly turned her attention to the driver and recited her address.

Maryanne fumed during the entire ride back to her apartment. Rarely had she been more furious. If Kramer Adams thought he could play matchmaker with her, he was about to learn that everything he'd ever heard about redheads was true.

"Hey, lady, are you all right?" the cabbie asked.

"I'm fine," she said stiffly.

"That guy you were with back at the theatre didn't try anything, did he?"

"No, some other man did, only he's not going to get away with it." The driver pulled into her street. "That's the building there," Maryanne told him. She reached into her bag for her wallet and pulled out some of her precious cash, including a generous tip. Then she ran into the apartment building, heedless of her clothes or her high-heeled shoes.

For the first time since moving in, Maryanne didn't pause to rest on the third-floor landing. Her anger carried her all the way to Kramer's apartment door. She could hear him typing inside, and the sound added to her temper. Dragging breath through her lungs, she slammed her fist against the door.

"Hold on a minute," she heard him grumble.

His shocked look as he threw open the door would have been comical in different circumstances. "Maryanne, what are you doing here?"

"That was a rotten underhanded thing to do, you deceiving, conniving, low-down...rat!"

Kramer did an admirable job of composing himself. He buried his hands in his pockets and smiled nonchalantly. "I take it you and Griff Bradly didn't hit it off?"

CHAPTER SIX

MARYANNE WAS SO FURIOUS she couldn't find the words to express her outrage. She opened and closed her mouth twice before she collected herself enough to proceed.

"I told you before that I didn't want you interfering in my life, and I meant it."

"I was doing you a favour," Kramer countered, clearly unmoved by her angry display. In fact, he yawned loudly, covering his mouth with the back of his hand. "Griff's a stockbroker friend of mine and one hell of a nice guy. If you'd given him half a chance, you might have found that out yourself. I could see the two of you becoming good friends. Why don't you give it a try? You two might hit it off."

"The only thing I'd consider hitting is *you*." To her horror, tears of rage flooded her eyes. "Don't ever try that again. Do you understand?" Not waiting for his reply, she turned abruptly, stalked down the hall to her apartment and unlocked the door. She flung it shut with sufficient force to rattle the windows on three floors.

She paced back and forth several times, blew her nose once and decided she hadn't told him nearly enough. Throwing open her door, she rushed down the hall to Kramer's apartment again. She banged twice as hard as she had originally.

Kramer opened the door, wearing a martyr's expression. He cocked one eyebrow expressively. "What is it this time?"

"And furthermore you're the biggest coward I've ever met. If I still worked for the newspaper, I'd write a column so all Seattle would know exactly what kind of man you really are." Her voice wobbled just a little, but that didn't diminish the strength of her indignation.

She stomped back to her own apartment and she hadn't been there two seconds before there was a pounding on her door. It didn't surprise her to find Kramer Adams on the other side. He might have appeared calm, but his eyes sparked with an angry fire. They narrowed slightly as he glowered at her.

"What did you just say?" he asked.

"You heard me. You're nothing but a coward. Coward, coward, coward!" With that she slammed her door so hard that a framed family photo hanging on the wall crashed to the floor. Luckily the glass didn't break.

Her chest heaving, Maryanne picked up the photo, wiped it off and carefully replaced it. But for all her outward composure, her hands were trembling. No sooner had she completed the task when Kramer beat on her door a second time.

"Now what?" she demanded, whipping open the door. "I would have thought you got my message."

"I got it all right. I just don't happen to like it."

"Tough." She would have slammed the door again, but before she could act, a loud banging came from the direction of the floor. Not knowing what it was, Maryanne instinctively jumped back.

Kramer drew a deep breath, and Maryanne could tell he was making an effort to compose himself. "All right, Mrs McBride," Kramer shouted at the floor, "we'll hold it down."

"Who's Mrs McBride?"

"The lady who lives in the apartment below you."

"Oh." Maryanne had been too infuriated to realise she was shouting loudly enough for half the apartment building to hear. She felt ashamed at her loss of control and guilty for disturbing her neighbours—but she was still furious with Kramer.

The man in question glared at her. "Do you think it's possible to discuss this situation without involving any more doors?" he asked sharply. "Or would you rather wait until someone phones the police and we're both arrested for disturbing the peace?"

She glared back at him defiantly. "Very funny," she said, turning around and walking into her apartment. As she knew he would, Kramer followed her inside.

Maryanne moved into the kitchen. Preparing a pot of coffee gave her a few extra minutes to gather her dignity, which had been as abused as her apartment door. Mixed with the anger was a chilling pain that cut straight through her heart. Kramer's thinking so little of her that he could casually pass her on to another man was mortifying enough. But knowing he considered it a favour only heaped on the humiliation.

"Annie, please listen—"

"Did it ever occur to you that arranging this date with Griff might offend me?" she cried.

Kramer seemed reluctant to answer. "Yes," he finally said, "it did. I tried to catch you earlier this afternoon, but you weren't in. This wasn't the kind of situation I felt comfortable explaining in a note, so I took the easy way out and left Griff to introduce himself. I didn't realise you'd take it so personally."

"How else was I supposed to take it?"

Kramer glanced away uncomfortably. "Let's just say I was hoping you'd meet him and the two of you would spend the evening getting to know each other. Griff comes from a well-established family and—"

"That's supposed to impress me?"

"He's the type of man your father would arrange for you to meet," Kramer said, his voice sandpaper-gruff.

"How many times do I have to tell you I don't need a second father?" His mention of her family reminded her of the way she was deceiving them, which brought a powerful sense of remorse.

He muttered tersely under his breath, then shook his head. "Obviously I blew it. Would it help if I apologised?"

An apology, even a sincere one, wouldn't soon dissolve the hurt that had become wrapped around her heart. She looked up, about to tell him exactly that, when her eyes forcefully locked with his.

He stood a safe distance from her, his expression so tender that her battered heart rolled defencelessly to her feet. She knew she ought to throw him out of her home and refuse to ever speak to him again. No one would blame her. She tried to rally her anger, but something she couldn't explain or understand stopped her.

All the emotion must have sharpened her perceptions. Never had she been more aware of Kramer as a man. The moment felt full; the space separating them seemed to close, drawing them towards each other. She could smell the clean scent of the soap he used and hear the music of the rain as it danced against her window. She hadn't even realised, until this moment, that it was raining.

"I am sorry," he said quietly.

Maryanne nodded and wiped the moisture from her eyes. She wasn't a woman who cried easily, and the tears were a surprise.

"What you said about my being a coward is true," Kramer admitted. He sighed heavily. "You frighten me, Annie."

"You mean my temper?"

"No, I deserved that." He grinned that lazy insolent grin of his.

"What is it about me you find so unappealing?" She had to know what it was that was driving him away, no matter how much the truth damaged her pride.

"Unappealing?" His abrupt laugh was filled with irony. "I wish I could find something, *anything*, unappealing about you, but I can't." Dropping his gaze, he stepped back and cleared his throat. When he spoke again, his words were brusque, impatient. "I was a lot more comfortable with you before we met."

"You thought of me as a debutante."

"I assumed you were a pampered immature...girl. Not a woman. I expected to find you ambitious and selfish, so eager to impress your father with what you could do that it didn't matter how many people you walked over. Then we did the Celebrity Debate, and I realised none of the things I wanted to believe about you were true."

"Then why—"

"The thing you've got to understand," Kramer added forcefully, "is that I don't want to become involved with you."

"That message has come through loud and clear." She moistened her lips and cast her gaze towards the floor, afraid he'd see how vulnerable he made her feel.

Suddenly he was standing directly in front of her, so close his breath warmed her face. With one gentle finger, he lifted her chin, raising her eyes to his.

"All evening I was telling myself how noble I was," he said. "Griff Bradly is far better suited to you than I'll ever be."

"Stop saying that!"

He wrapped his arms around her waist and pulled her close. "There can't ever be anything between us," he said, his voice rough. "I learned my lesson years ago, and I'm not going to repeat that mistake." But contrary to everything he was saying, his mouth lowered to hers until their lips touched. The kiss was slow and familiar. Their bottom lips clung as Kramer eased away from her.

"That wasn't supposed to happen," he murmured.

"I won't tell anyone if you won't," she whispered.

"Just remember what I said," he whispered back. "I don't do well with rich girls. I already found that out. The hard way."

"I'll remember," she said softly, looking up at him.

"Good." And then he kissed her again.

IT WAS THREE DAYS before Maryanne saw Kramer. She didn't need anyone to tell her he was avoiding her. Again. Maybe he thought falling in love would wreak havoc with his comfortable well-ordered life. If he'd given her a chance, Maryanne would have told Kramer she didn't expect him to fill her days. She had her new job, and she was fixing up her apartment. Most important, she had her writing, which kept her busy the rest of the time. She'd recently queried a magazine about doing a humorous article on her experiences working for Rent-A-Maid.

"Here's Kramer now," Barbara whispered as she hurried past Maryanne, balancing three plates.

Automatically Maryanne reached for a water glass and a menu and followed Kramer to the booth. He was halfway into his seat when he saw her. He froze and his narrowed accusing gaze flew across the room to the middle-aged waitress.

Barbara didn't appear in the least intimidated. "Hey, what did you expect?" she called out. "We were one girl short, and when Maryanne applied for the job she gave you as a reference. Besides, she's a good worker."

Kramer didn't bother to look at the menu. Standing beside the table, Maryanne reached for her green order pad.

"I'll have the chilli," he ordered gruffly.

"With or without cheese?"

"Without," he bellowed, then quickly lowered his voice. "How long have you been working here?"

"Since Monday morning. Don't look so angry. You were the one who told me about the job. Remember?"

"I don't want you working here!"

"Why not? It's a respectable establishment. Honestly, Kramer, what did you expect me to do? I had to find another job, and fast. I can't expect to sell any articles for at least a month, if then. I've got to find some way of paying the bills."

"You could have done a hell of a lot better than Mom's Place if you wanted to be a waitress."

"Are we going to argue? Again?" she asked with an impatient sigh.

"No," he answered, grabbing his napkin just in time to catch a violent sneeze.

Now that she had a chance to study him, she saw his nose was red and his eyes rheumy. In fact he looked downright miserable. "You've got a cold."

"Are you always this brilliant?"

"I try to be. And I'll try to ignore your rudeness. Would you like a glass of orange juice or a couple of aspirin?"

"No, Florence Nightingale, all I want is my usual bowl of chilli, *without* the cheese. Have you got that?"

"Yes, of course," she said, writing it down. Kramer certainly seemed to be in a rotten mood, but that was nothing new. Maryanne seemed to bring out the worst in him.

Barbara met her at the counter. "From the looks your boyfriend's been sending me, he'd gladly cut off my head. What's with him, anyway?"

"I don't think he's feeling well," Maryanne answered in a low worried voice.

"Men, especially sick ones, are the biggest babies that ever walked the earth," Barbara said wryly. "They get a little virus and think someone should rush in to tape a documentary on their life-threatening condition. My advice to you is let him wallow in his misery all by himself.''

"But he looks like he might have a fever," Maryanne whispered.

"And he isn't old enough to take an aspirin all on his own?" The older woman glanced behind her. "His order's up. You want me to take it to him?"

"No..."

"Don't worry, if he gets smart with me I'll just whack him alongside the head. Someone needs to put that man in his place."

Maryanne reached for the large bowl of chilli. "I'll do it."

"Yes," Barbara said, grinning broadly. "I have a feeling you will."

MARYANNE ARRIVED HOME several hours later. Her feet hurt and her back ached, but she felt a pleasant glow of satisfaction. After three days of waitressing, she was beginning to get the knack of keeping orders straight and remembering everything she needed to do. It wasn't the job of her dreams, but she was making a living wage, certainly better money than she'd been getting from Rent-A-Maid. Not only that, the tips were good. Maryanne didn't dare imagine what her family would say if they found out, though. She suffered a stab of remorse every time she thought about the way she was deceiving them. In fact, it was simpler not to think about it at all.

After his initial reaction, Kramer hadn't so much as mentioned her working at Mom's Place. He clearly wasn't thrilled, but that didn't surprise her. Little, if anything, she'd done from the moment she'd met him had gained his approval.

Maryanne had grown accustomed to falling asleep most nights to the sound of Kramer's typing. She found herself listening for it when she climbed into bed. But she didn't hear it that night or the two nights that followed.

"How's Kramer?" Barbara asked her on Friday afternoon.

"I don't know." Maryanne hadn't seen him in days, but then, she rarely did.

"He must have got a really bad bug."

Maryanne hated the way her heart reacted. She'd tried not to think about him. Not that she'd been successful...

"His column hasn't been in the paper all week. The *Sun*'s been running some of his old ones—Kramer's Classics. Did you read the one last night?" Barbara asked, laughing. "He said it was a good thing the United States wasn't around when Moses was negotiating with the Egyptians. Can't you picture it? We'd get all involved in the meditations, wanting to do whatever we could to keep everything nice and friendly."

As a matter of fact, Maryanne had read the piece and been highly amused. As always she'd been impressed with Kramer's dry wit. They often disagreed—Kramer was too much of a pessimist to suit her—but she couldn't help admiring his skill with words.

Since the afternoon he'd found her at Mom's, Kramer hadn't eaten there again. Maryanne didn't consider that so strange. He went to great lengths to ensure they didn't run into each other. She did feel mildly guilty that he'd decided to stay away from his favourite diner, but it *was* his choice, after all.

During the rest of her shift, Maryanne had to struggle to keep Kramer out of her mind. His apartment had been unusually quiet for the past few days, but she hadn't been concerned about it. Now she was.

"Do you think he's all right?" she asked Barbara some time later.

"He's a big boy," the older woman was quick to remind her. "He can take care of himself."

Maryanne wasn't so sure. After work, she hurried home, convinced she'd find Kramer hovering near death, too ill to call for help. She didn't even stop at her own apartment, but went directly to his.

She knocked politely, anticipating all kinds of disasters when there was no response.

"Kramer?" She pounded on his door and yelled his name, battling down a rising sense of panic. She envisioned him lying on his bed, suffering—or worse. "Kramer, please answer the door," she pleaded, wondering if there was someone in the building with a passkey.

She'd waited hours, it seemed, before he yanked open the door.

"Are you all right?" she demanded, so relieved to see him she could hardly keep from hurling herself into his arms. Relieved, that was, until she got a good look at him.

"I was feeling just great," he told her gruffly, "until I had to get out of bed to answer the stupid door. Which, incidentally, woke me up."

Maryanne pressed her fingers over her mouth to hide her hysterical laughter. If Kramer felt anywhere near as bad as he looked, then she should seriously consider phoning for an ambulance. He wore grey sweatpants and a faded plaid robe, one she would guess had been moth fodder for years. His choice of clothes was the least of her concerns, however. He resembled someone who'd just surfaced from a four-day drunk. His eyes were red and his face ashen. He scowled at her and it was clear the moment he spoke that his disposition was as cheery as his appearance.

"I take it there's a reason for this uninvited visit?" he growled, then sneezed fiercely.

"Yes..." Maryanne hedged, not knowing exactly what to do now. "I just wanted to make sure you're all right."

"OK, you've seen me. I'm going to live, so you can leave in good conscience." He would have closed the door, but Maryanne stepped forward and boldly edged her way into his apartment.

In the weeks they'd lived next door to each other, she'd never once seen his home. The muted earth colours, the rich leather furniture and polished wood floors appealed to her immediately. Despite her worry about his condition, she smiled; this room reminded her of Kramer, with papers and books littering every available space. His apartment seemed at least twice the size of hers. He'd once mentioned that it was larger, but after becoming accustomed to her own small rooms this spaciousness of his was a pleasant shock.

"In case you haven't noticed, I'm in no mood for company," he informed her in a surly voice.

"Have you been to a doctor?"

"No."

"Do you need anything?"

"Peace and quiet," he muttered.

"You could have bronchitis or pneumonia or something."

"I'm perfectly fine. At least, I was until you arrived." He walked across the carpet—a dark green-and-gold Persian, Maryanne noted automatically—and slumped on to an overstuffed sofa piled with blankets and pillows. The television was on, its volume turned very low.

"Then why haven't you been to work?"

"I'm on vacation."

"Personally, I would have chosen a tropical island over a sofa in my own apartment." She advanced purposefully into his kitchen and stopped short when she caught sight of the dirty dishes stacked a foot high in the stainless-steel sink. She was amazed he could cram so much into such a tight space.

"This place is a mess!" she declared, hands on her hips.

"Go ahead and call the health department if you're so concerned."

"I probably should." Instead, she walked straight to the sink, rolled up her sleeves and started stacking the dishes on the counter.

"What are you doing now?" Kramer shouted from the living-room.

"Cleaning up."

He muttered something she couldn't hear, which was probably for the best.

"Go lie down, Kramer," she instructed. "When I'm done here, I'll heat you some soup. You've got to get your strength back in order to suffer properly."

At first he let that comment pass. Then, as if she was taxing him to the limit of his endurance, he called out, "The way you care is truly touching."

"I was hoping you'd notice." For someone who'd been outraged at the sight of her dishpan hands a week earlier, he seemed oddly unconcerned that she was washing his dirty dishes. Not that Maryanne minded. It made her feel good to be doing something for him.

She soon found herself humming as she rinsed off the dishes and set them in his dishwasher.

Fifteen minutes passed without their exchanging a word. When Maryanne had finished, she looked in the living-room and wasn't surprised to find him sound asleep on the sofa. A curious feeling tugged at her heart as she gazed down at him. He lay on his back with his left hand flung across his forehead. His features were relaxed, but there was nothing remotely angelic about him. Not about the way his thick dark lashes brushed the arch of his cheek—or about the slow hoarse breaths that whispered through his half-open mouth.

Maryanne felt a strong urge to brush the hair from his forehead, to touch him, but she resisted. She was afraid he'd wake up. And she was even more afraid she wouldn't want to stop touching him.

Moving about the living-room, she turned off the television, picked up things here and there and straightened a few piles of magazines. She should leave now; she knew that. Kramer wouldn't welcome her staying. She eyed the door regretfully, looking for an excuse to linger. She closed her eyes and listened to the sound of Kramer's raspy breathing.

More by chance than design, Maryanne found herself standing next to his typewriter. Feeling brave, and more than a little foolish, she dropped her gaze to the stack of paper resting beside it. Glancing over her shoulder to make sure he was still asleep, Maryanne carefully turned over the top page and quickly read the last couple of paragraphs on page 212. The story wasn't finished, but she could tell he'd stopped during a cliff-hanger scene.

Kramer had been so secretive about his project that she dared not invade his privacy any more than she already had. She neatly turned the single sheet back over, taking care to place it exactly as she'd found it.

Once again, she reminded herself that she should go back to her own apartment, but she felt strangely reluctant to end these moments with Kramer. Even a sleeping Kramer who would certainly be cranky when he woke up.

Seeking some way to occupy herself, she moved down the hall and into the bathroom, picking up several soiled towels on the way. His bed was unmade. She would have been surprised to find it in any other condition. The sheets and blankets were sagging against the floor, and two or three sets of clothing were scattered in all directions.

Without questioning the wisdom of her actions, she bundled up the dirty laundry to take to the coin-operated machine in the basement. She loaded it into a large garbage bag, then set about vigorously cleaning the apartment. Scrubbing, scouring and sweeping were skills she'd perfected in her Rent-A-Maid days. If nothing else, she'd had lots of practice cleaning up after messy bachelors.

Studying the contents of his refrigerator, more than an hour later, proved to be a humorous adventure. She found an unopened bottle of wine, a carton of broken egg shells and one limp strand of celery. Concocting anything edible from that would be impossible, so she searched the apartment until she found his keys. Then, with his garbage bag full of laundry in her arms, she let herself out the door, closing it softly.

She returned a half-hour later, clutching two bags of groceries bought with her tip money. To her delight, Kramer was still asleep. She smiled down at him indulgently before she began preparing his dinner.

She was in the kitchen peeling potatoes when she heard Kramer get up. She continued her task, knowing he'd discover she was there soon enough. He stopped cold when he did.

"What are you doing here?"

"Cooking your dinner."

"I'm not hungry," he snapped with no evidence of appreciation for her efforts.

His eyes widened as he glanced around. "Good Lord, you've cleaned the place."

"I didn't think you'd notice," she answered sweetly, popping a small piece of raw potato in her mouth. "I'll get soup to the boiling stage before I leave you to your...peace of mind. It should only take another ten or fifteen minutes. Can you endure me that much longer?"

He made another of his typical grumbling replies before disappearing. No more than two seconds had passed before he let out a bellow loud enough to shake the roof tiles.

"What did you do to my bed?" he demanded as he stormed into the kitchen.

"I made it."

"What else have you been up to? Damn it, a man isn't safe in his own home with you around."

"Don't look so put out, Kramer. All I did was straighten up the place a bit. It was a mess."

"I happen to like messes. I thrive in messes. The last thing I want or need is some neat-freak invading my home, organising my life."

"Don't exaggerate," Maryanne said serenely, as she added a pile of diced carrots to the simmering broth. "All I did was pick up a few things here and there and run a load of laundry."

"You did my laundry, too?" he exploded, running both hands through his hair. Heaven only knew, she thought, what would happen if he learned she'd read a single word of his precious manuscript.

"Everything's been folded and put away, so you needn't worry."

Kramer abruptly left the kitchen, only to return a couple of moments later. He circled the table slowly and precisely, then took several deep breaths.

"Listen, Annie," he began carefully, "it isn't that I don't appreciate what you've done, but I don't need a nurse. Or a housekeeper."

She looked up, meeting his eyes, her own large and guileless. "I quite agree," she answered.

"You do?" Some of the stiffness left his shoulders. "Then you aren't going to take offence?"

"No, why should I?"

"No reason," he answered, eyeing her suspiciously.

"I was thinking that what you really need," she said, smiling at him gently, "is a wife."

CHAPTER SEVEN

"A WIFE," KRAMER ECHOED. His dark eyes widened in undisguised horror. It was as if Maryanne had suggested he climb to the top of the apartment building and leap off.

"Don't get so excited. I wasn't volunteering for the position."

With his index finger pointing at her like the barrel of a shotgun, Kramer paced around the kitchen table again, his journey made in shuffling impatient steps. He circled the table twice before he spoke.

"You cleaned my home, washed my clothes and now you're cooking my dinner." Each word came at her like an accusation.

"Yes?"

"You can't possibly look at me with those big baby-blues of yours and expect me to believe that."

"Believe what?"

"That you're not applying for the job. From the moment we met, you've been doing all these...these sweet *girlie* things to entice me."

"Sweet girlie things?" Maryanne repeated, struggling to contain her amusement. "I don't think I understand."

"I don't expect you to admit it."

"I haven't the foggiest idea what you're talking about."

"You know," he accused once more with an angry shrug.

"Obviously I don't. What could I possibly have done to make you think that?"

"Sweet girlie things," he said again, but without the same conviction. He chewed on his bottom lip for a moment while he mulled the matter over. "All right, I'll give you an example—that perfume you're always wearing."

"Windchime? It's a light fragrance."

"I don't know the name of it. But it hangs around for an hour or so after you've left the room. You know that, and yet you wear it every time we're together.''

"I've worn Windchime for years.''

"That's not all,'' he continued quickly. "It's the way I catch you looking at me sometimes.''

"Looking at you?'' She folded her arms around her waist and rolled her eyes towards the ceiling.

"Yes,'' he returned, sounding even more peevish. He pressed his hand to his hip, cocked his chin at a regal angle and softly fluttered his thick eyelashes like fans.

Despite her efforts to hold in her amusement, Maryanne laughed outright. "I sincerely hope you're joking.''

Kramer dropped his hand from his hip. "I'm not. You get this innocent look and your lips pout just so... Why, a man—any man—couldn't keep from wanting to kiss you.''

"That's preposterous.'' But Maryanne instinctively pinched her lips together and closed her eyes.

Kramer's arm shot out. "That's another thing.''

"What now?''

"The way you get this helpless flustered look and it's all a simpleminded male can do not to rush in and offer to take care of whatever's bothering you.''

"By this time you should know I'm perfectly capable of taking care of myself,'' Maryanne felt obliged to remind him.

"You're a lamb among wolves,'' Kramer returned swiftly. "I don't know how long you intend to play out this silly charade, but personally I think you've overdone it now. This isn't your world, and the sooner you go back where you belong, the better it'll be.''

"Better for whom?''

"Me!'' he cried vehemently. "And for you,'' he added with less fervour, as though it was an afterthought. He coughed a couple of times and reached for a package of cough drops in the pocket of his plaid robe. Shaking one out, he popped it in his mouth with barely a pause.

"I don't think it's doing you any good to get so excited,''

Maryanne said with unruffled patience. "I was merely making an observation and it still stands. I believe you need a wife."

"Go observe someone else's life," he suggested, sucking madly on the cough drop.

"Aha!" she cried, waving her index finger at him. "How does it feel to have someone interfering in *your* life?"

Kramer frowned and Maryanne turned back to the stove. She lifted the lid from the soup to stir it briskly. Then she lowered the burner to simmer. When she was through, she saw with a glimmer of fun that Kramer was standing as far away from her as humanly possible, while still remaining in the same room.

"That's something else!" he cried. "You give the impression that you're in total agreement with whatever I'm saying and then go about doing exactly as you damn well please. I swear I've never met a more frustrating woman in my entire life."

"That's not true," Maryanne argued. "I quit my job at Rent-A-Maid because you insisted." It had worked out for the best, since she had more time for her writing now, but this wasn't the moment to mention it.

"Oh, right, bring that up. It's the only thing you've ever done that I wanted. I practically had to get down on my knees and beg you to leave that crazy job before you injured yourself."

"You didn't!"

"Trust me, it was a humbling experience and not one I intend to repeat. I've known you how long? A month? Lord, lord—" he paused to gaze at the ceiling "—it seems like an eternity."

"You're trying to make me feel guilty. It isn't going to work."

"Why should you feel anything of the sort? Just because living next to you is enough to drive a man to drink."

"You're the one who found me this place. If you don't like living next door to me, then I'm not the one to blame!"

"Don't remind me," he muttered.

The comment about Kramer finding himself a wife had been made in jest, a joke, but he'd certainly taken it seriously. In fact, he seemed to have strong feelings about the entire issue. Realising her welcome had worn extremely thin, Maryanne headed for his apartment door. "Everything's under control here."

"Does that mean you're leaving?"

She hated the enthusiastic lift in his voice, as if he couldn't wait to be rid of her. Although he wasn't admitting it, she'd done him a good turn. Fair exchange, she supposed; Kramer had been generous enough to her over the past month.

"Yes, I'm leaving."

"Good." He didn't bother to disguise his delight.

"But I still think you'd do well to consider what I said." Maryanne had the irresistible urge to heap coals on the fires of his indignation. "A wife could be a great help to you."

Kramer frowned heavily, drawing his eyebrows into a deep V. "I think the modern woman would find your suggestion downright insulting."

"What? That you marry?"

"Exactly. Haven't you heard? A woman's place isn't in the home any longer. It's out there in the world, forging a career for herself. Living a fuller life, and all that. It's not doing the mundane tasks you're talking about."

"I wasn't suggesting you marry for the convenience of gaining a live-in housekeeper."

His brown eyes narrowed. "Then exactly what were you saying?"

"That you're a capable talented man," she explained. She glanced surreptitiously at his manuscript, still tidily stacked by the typewriter. "But unfortunately, that doesn't mean a whole lot if you don't have someone close—a friend, a companion, a...wife—to share it with."

"Don't you worry about me, Little Miss Muffet. I've lived my own life from the time I was thirteen. You may think I need someone, but let me assure you, I don't."

"You're probably right," she admitted reluctantly. She opened his door, then hesitated. "You'll call if you want anything?"

"No."

She released a short sigh of frustration. "That's what I thought. The soup should be done in about thirty minutes."

He nodded, then, looking a bit chagrined, added, "I suppose I should thank you."

"I suppose you should, too, but it isn't necessary."

"What about the money you spent on groceries? You can't afford acts of charity, you know. Wait a minute and I'll—"

"Forget it," she snapped. "I can spend my money on whatever I damn well please. I'm my own person, remember? You can just owe me. Buy me dinner sometime." She left before he could say anything else.

Maryanne's own apartment felt bleak and lonely after Kramer's. The first thing she did was walk around turning on all the lights. No sooner had she finished when there was a loud knock at her door. She opened it to find Kramer standing there in his disreputable moth-eaten robe, glaring ferociously.

"Yes?" she inquired sweetly.

"You read my manuscript," he boomed in a voice that echoed like thunder off the apartment walls.

"I most certainly did not," she denied vehemently. She straightened her back as if to suggest she found the very question insulting.

Without waiting for an invitation, Kramer stalked into her living-room, then whirled around to face her. "Admit it!"

Making each word as clear and distinct as possible, Maryanne said, "I did not read your precious manuscript. How could I possibly have cleaned up, done the laundry, prepared a big kettle of homemade soup, and still had time to read 212 pages of manuscript?"

"How did you know it was 212 pages?" Sparks of reproach shot from his eyes.

"Ah—" she swallowed uncomfortably "—it was a guess, and from the looks of it, a good one."

"It wasn't any guess."

He marched towards her and for every step he took, she retreated two. "All right," she admitted guiltily, "I did look at it, but I swear I didn't read more than a few lines. I was straightening up the living-room and...it was there, so I turned over the last page and read a couple of paragraphs."

"Aha! Finally, the truth!" Kramer pointed directly at her "You did read it!"

"Just a few lines," she repeated in a tiny voice, feeling completely wretched.

"And?" His eyes softened.

"And what?"

"What did you think?" He looked towards her expectantly, then frowned. "Never mind, I shouldn't have asked."

Rubbing her palms together, Maryanne took one step forward. "Kramer, it was wonderful. Witty and terribly suspenseful and... I would have given anything to read more. But I knew I didn't dare because, well, because I was invading your privacy...which I didn't want to do, but I did and I really didn't want...that."

"It is good, isn't it?" he asked almost smugly, then his expression sobered as quickly as it had before.

She grinned, nodding enthusiastically. "Tell me about it."

He seemed undecided, then launched excitedly into his idea. "It's about a Seattle newspaperman, Leo, who stumbles on a murder case. Actually, I'm developing a series with him as the main character. This one's not quite finished yet—as I'm sure you know."

"Is there a woman in Leo's life?"

"You're kidding, aren't you?"

Maryanne wasn't. The few lines she'd read had mentioned a Maddie who was apparently in danger. Leo had been frantic to save her.

"You had no business going anywhere near that manuscript," Kramer reminded her.

"I know, but the temptation was so strong. I shouldn't have peeked, I realise that, but I couldn't help myself. Kramer, I'm not lying when I say how good those few lines were. Do you have a publisher in mind? Because if you don't, I have several New York editor friends I could recommend and I know—"

"I'm not using you or any influence you may have in New York. I don't want anything to do with your father's publishing company. Understand?"

"Of course, but you're over-reacting." He seemed to be doing a lot of that lately. "My father wouldn't stay in business long if he ordered the editors to purchase my friends' manuscripts, would he? Believe me, it would all be on the up and up, and if you've an idea for a series using Leo—''

''I said no.''

''But—''

''I mean it, Annie. This is my book and I'll submit it myself without any help from you.''

''If that's what you want,'' she concurred meekly.

''That's the way it's going to be.'' The stern unyielding look slipped back into place. ''Now if you don't mind, I'll quietly go back to my messy little world, sans wife and countless interruptions from a certain neighbour.''

''I'll try not to bother you again,'' Maryanne said sarcastically, since he was the one who'd invaded *her* home this time.

''It would be appreciated,'' he said, apparently ignoring her tone.

''Your apartment is yours and mine is mine, and I'll uphold your privacy with the utmost respect,'' she continued, her voice still faintly mocking. She buried her hands in her pockets and her fingers closed around something cold and metallic.

''Good.'' Kramer was nodding. ''Privacy, that's what we need.''

''Um, Kramer...'' She paused. ''This is somewhat embarrassing, but it seems I have...'' She hesitated a second time then resolutely squared her shoulders. ''I suppose you'd appreciate it if I returned your keys, right?''

''My keys?'' Kramer exploded.

''I just found them. They were in my pocket. You see, all you had in your refrigerator was one limp strand of celery and I couldn't very well make soup out of that so I had to go to the store and I didn't dare leave your door unlocked and—''

''You have my keys?''

''Yes.''

He held out his palm, casting his eyes toward the ceiling. Feeling like a pickpocket caught in the act, Maryanne dropped the keys into his hand and stepped quickly back, almost afraid he was going to grab her shoulders and shake her. Which, of course, was ludicrous.

Kramer left immediately and Maryanne followed him to the door, staring out into the hallway as he walked back to his own apartment.

THE FOLLOWING THURSDAY, Maryanne was hurrying to get ready for work when the telephone rang. She frowned and stared at it, wondering if she dared take the time to answer. It might be Kramer, but every instinct she possessed told her otherwise. They hadn't spoken all week. Every afternoon, like clockwork, he'd arrived at Mom's Diner. More often than not, he ordered chilli. Maryanne waited on him most of the time, but she might have been a robot for all the attention he paid her. His complete lack of interest dented her pride; still, his attitude shouldn't have come as any surprise.

"Hello," she said hesitantly, picking up the receiver.

"Maryanne," her mother responded, her voice rising with pleasure. "I can't believe I finally got hold of you. I've been trying for the past three days."

Maryanne immediately felt swamped by guilt. "You didn't leave a massage on my machine?"

"You know how I hate those things."

Maryanne did know that. She also knew she should have phoned her parents herself, but she wasn't sure how long she could continue with this farce. "Is everything all right?"

"Yes, of course. Your father's working too hard, but that's nothing new. The boys are busy with soccer and growing like weeds." Her mother's voice dipped slightly. "How's the job?"

"The job?"

"Your special assignment."

"Oh, that." Maryanne had rarely been able to fool her mother, and she could only wonder how well she was succeeding now. "It's going...well. I'm learning so much."

"I think you'll make a terrific investigative reporter, sweetie, and the secrecy behind this assignment makes it all the more intriguing. When are your father and I going to learn exactly what you've been doing? How I wish we'd never promised not to check up on your progress at the paper. We're both so curious."

"I'll be finished with it soon." Maryanne glanced at her watch and was about to close the conversation when her mother asked,

"How's Kramer?"

"Kramer?" Maryanne's heart zoomed straight into her throat. She hadn't remembered mentioning him, and just hearing his name sent a feverish heat through her body.

"You seemed quite enthralled with him the last time we spoke, remember?"

"I was?"

"Yes, sweetie, you were. You claimed he was very talented, and although you were tight-lipped about it I got the impression you were strongly attracted to this young man."

"Kramer's a good friend. But we argue more than anything."

Her mother chuckled. "Good."

"How could that possibly be good?"

"It means you're comfortable enough with each other to be yourselves, and that's a positive sign. Why, your father and I bickered like old fishwives when we first met. I swear there wasn't a single issue we could agree on." She sighed softly. "Then one day we looked at each other, and I knew then and there I was going to love this man for the rest of my life. And I have."

"Mom, it isn't like that with Kramer and me. I...I don't even think he likes me."

"Kramer doesn't like you?" her mother repeated. "Why, sweetie, that would be impossible."

Maryanne started to laugh then, because her mother was so obviously biased, yet sounded completely objective and matter-of-fact. It felt good to laugh again, good to find something amusing. She hadn't realised how melancholy she'd become since her last encounter with Kramer. He was still making such an effort to keep her at arm's length for fear... She didn't know exactly *what* he feared. Perhaps he was falling in love with her, but she'd noticed precious little evidence pointing to that conclusion. If anything, Kramer considered her an irritant in his life.

Maryanne spoke to her mother for a few more minutes, then rushed out the door, hoping she wouldn't be late for her shift at Mom's Place. Some investigative reporter she was!

At the diner, she slipped the apron around her waist and hurried out to help with the luncheon crowd. Waiting tables, she was learning quite a lot about character types. This could be helpful for a writer, she figured. Some of her customers were downright eccentric. She observed them carefully, wondering if Kramer did the same thing. But she wasn't going to think about Kramer....

Halfway through her shift, she began to feel light-headed and sick to her stomach.

"Are you feeling all right?" Barbara asked as she slipped past, carrying an order.

"I—I don't know."

"When was the last time you ate?"

"This morning. No," she corrected, "last night. I didn't have much of an appetite this morning."

"That's what I thought." Barbara set the hamburger and fries on the counter in front of her customer and walked back to Maryanne. "Now that I've got a good look at you, you do seem a bit peaked."

"I'm all right."

Hands on her hips, Barbara continued to study Maryanne as if memorising every feature. "Are you sure?"

"I'm fine." She had the beginnings of a headache, but nothing she could really complain about. It probably hadn't been a good idea to skip breakfast and lunch, but she'd make up for it when she took her dinner break.

"I'm not sure I believe you," Barbara muttered, dragging out a well-used phone book. She flipped through the pages until she apparently found the number she wanted, then reached for the phone.

"Who are you calling?"

She held the receiver against her shoulder. "Kramer Adams, who else? Seems to me it's his turn to play nursemaid."

"Barbara, no!" She might not be feeling a hundred per cent, but she wasn't all that sick, either. And the last person she wanted running to her rescue was Kramer. He'd only use it against her, as proof that she should go back to the cosy comfortable world of her parents.

She'd almost proved she could live entirely on her own, without relying on interest from her trust fund.

"Kramer's not at the office," Barbara said a moment later, replacing the receiver. "I'll talk to him when he comes in later."

"No, you won't! Barbara, I swear to you I'll personally give your phone number to every trucker who comes into this place if you so much as say a single word to Kramer."

"Honey," the other waitress said, raising her eyebrows, "you'd be doing me a favour!"

Grumbling, Maryanne returned to her customers.

By closing time, however, she was feeling slightly worse. Not exactly sick, but not exactly herself, either. Barbara was watching Maryanne closely, regularly feeling her cheeks and forehead and muttering about her temperature. If there was one thing to be grateful for, it was the fact that Kramer hadn't shown up. Barbara insisted Maryanne leave a few minutes early and shooed her out the door. Had she been feeling better, Maryanne would have argued.

By the time she arrived back at her apartment, she knew beyond a doubt she was coming down with some kind of virus. Part of her would have liked to blame Kramer, but she was the one who'd let herself into his apartment. She was the one who'd lingered there, straightening up the place and staying far longer than necessary.

After a long hot shower, she put on her flannel pyjamas and unfolded her bed, climbing quickly beneath the covers. She'd turned the television on for company and prepared herself a mug of soup. As she took her first sip, she heard someone knock at her door.

"Who is it?" she called out.

"Kramer."

"I'm in bed," she shouted.

"You've seen me in my robe. It's only fair I see you in yours," he yelled back.

Maryanne tossed aside her covers and sat up. "Go away."

A sharp pounding noise came from the floor, followed by an equally loud roar that proclaimed it time for "Jeopardy". Apparently, Maryanne's shouting match with Kramer was disrupting Mrs McBride's favourite television show.

"Sorry." Maryanne cupped her hands over her mouth and yelled at the hardwood floor.

"Are you going to let me in, or do I have to get the passkey?" Kramer demanded.

Groaning, Maryanne shuffled across the floor in her giant fuzzy slippers and turned the lock. "Yes?" she asked with exaggerated patience.

For the longest moment, Kramer said nothing. He shoved his hands deep into the pockets of his beige raincoat. "How are you?"

Maryanne glared at him with all the indignation she could muster, which at the moment was considerable. "Do you mean to say you practically pounded down my door to ask me that?"

He didn't bother to answer, but walked into her apartment as though he had every right to do so. "Barbara phoned me."

"Oh, brother! And what exactly did she say?" She continued to hold open the door, hoping he'd get the hint and leave.

"That you caught my bug." His voice was rough with ill-disguised worry.

"Wrong. I felt a bit under the weather earlier, but I'm fine now." The last thing she wanted Kramer motivated by was guilt. He'd succeeded in keeping his distance up to now; if he decided to see her, she wanted to be sure his visit wasn't prompted by an overactive sense of responsibility.

"You look..."

"Yes?" she prompted.

His gaze skimmed her, from slightly damp hair to large fuzzy feet. "Fine," he answered softly.

"As you can see I'm really not sick, so you needn't concern yourself."

Her words were followed by a lengthy silence. Kramer turned as though to leave. Maryanne should have felt relieved to see him go, but instead she experienced the strangest sensation of loss. She longed to reach out a hand, ask him to stay, but she didn't have the courage.

She brushed the hair from her face and smiled, even though it was difficult to put on a carefree façade.

"I'll stop by in the morning and see how you're doing," Kramer said, hovering by the threshold.

"That won't be necessary."

He frowned. "When did you get so prickly?"

"When did you get so caring?" The words nearly caught in her throat and escaped on a whisper.

"I *do* care about you," he countered.

"Oh, sure, the same way you'd care about an annoying younger sister. Believe me, Kramer, your message came through loud and clear. I'm not your type. Fine, I can accept that, because you're not my type, either." She didn't really think she had a type, but it sounded philosophical and went a long way towards salving her badly bruised ego. Kramer couldn't have made his views toward her any plainer had he rented a billboard. He'd even said he'd taken one look at her and immediately thought, "Here comes trouble."

She'd never been more attracted to a man in her life, and here she was, standing in front of him lying through her teeth, willing to walk across hot coals before she'd admit how she truly felt.

"So I'm not your type, either?" he asked, almost in a whisper.

Maryanne's heartbeat quickened. He studied her as intently as she studied him. He gazed at her mouth, then slipped his hand behind her neck and slowly, so very slowly, lowered his lips to hers.

He paused, their mouths a scant inch apart. He seemed to be waiting for her to pull away, withdraw from him. Everything inside her told her to do exactly that. He was only trying to humiliate her, wasn't he? Trying to prove how powerful her attraction to him was, how easily he could bend her will to his own.

And she was letting him.

Her heart was beating so furiously her body seemed to rock with the sheer force of it. Every throb seemed to drive her directly into his arms, right where she longed to be. She placed her palms against his chest and sighed as his mouth met hers. The touch of his lips felt warm and soft. And right.

His hand cradled her neck while his lips continued to move over hers in the gentlest explorations, as though he feared she was too delicate to kiss the way he wanted.

Gradually his hands slipped to her shoulders. He drew a ragged breath, then put his head back as he stared up at the ceiling. He exhaled slowly, deliberately.

It took all the restraint Maryanne possessed not to ask him why he was stopping. She wanted these incredible sensations to continue. She longed to explore the feelings his kiss produced and the complex responses she experienced deep within her body. Her pulse hammered erratically as she tried to control her breathing.

"OK, now we've got that settled, I'll leave." He backed away from her.

"Got what settled?" she asked swiftly, then realised she was only making a bigger fool of herself. Naturally he was talking about the reason for this impromptu visit, which had been her health. Hadn't it? "Oh, I see."

"I don't think you do," Kramer said enigmatically. He turned and walked away.

CHAPTER EIGHT

"Whose turn next?" Maryanne asked. She and her two friends were sitting in the middle of her living-room floor, having a "pity party."

"I will," Carol Riverside volunteered eagerly. She ceremonially plucked a tissue from the box that rested in the centre of their small circle, next to the lit candle. Their second large bottle of cheap wine was nearly empty, and the three of them were feeling no pain.

"For years I've wanted to write a newspaper column of my own," Carol said, squaring her shoulders and hauling in a huge breath. "But it's not at all what I thought it'd be like. I ran out of ideas for things to write about after the first week."

"Ah," Maryanne sighed sympathetically.

"Ah," Barbara echoed.

"That's not all," Carol said sadly. "I never realised the world was so full of critics. No one seems to agree with me. I—I didn't know Seattle had so many cantankerous readers. I try, but it's impossible to make everyone happy. What happens is that some of the people like me some of the time and all the rest hate everything I write." She glanced up. "Except the two of you, of course."

Maryanne nodded her head so hard she nearly toppled over. She spread her hands out at either side in an effort to maintain her balance. The wine made her yawn, loudly.

Apparently in real distress, Carol dabbed at her eyes. "Being a columnist is hard work and nothing like I'd always dreamed." The edges of her mouth turned downward. "I don't even like writing anymore," she sobbed.

"Isn't that a pity!" Maryanne cried, ritually tossing her tissue into the centre of the circle. Barbara followed suit, and then they both patted Carol gently on the back.

Carol brightened once she'd finished. "I don't know what I'd do without the two of you. You and Betty are my very best friends in the whole world," she announced.

"Barbara," Maryanne corrected. "Your very best friend's name is Barbara."

The three of them looked at each other and burst into gales of laughter. Maryanne hushed them by waving her hands. "Stop! We can't allow ourselves to become giddy. A pity party doesn't work if all we do is laugh. We've got to remember this is sad and serious business."

"Sad and serious," Barbara agreed, sobering. She reached for a fresh tissue and clenched it in her hand, waiting for the others to share their sorrows and give her a reason to cry.

"Whose idea was the wine?" Maryanne wanted to know, taking a quick sip.

Carol blushed. "I thought it would be less fattening than the chocolate ice-cream bars you planned to serve."

"Hey," Barbara said, narrowing her eyes at Maryanne. "You haven't said anything about your problem."

Maryanne suddenly found it necessary to pick lint from her jeans. Sharing what disturbed her most was a little more complicated than being disappointed in her job or complaining about fingernails that cracked all too easily, as Barbara had done. She hadn't sold a single article since she quit the paper, or even received a positive response to one of her queries. But worst of all she was falling in love with Kramer. He felt something for her, too—she knew that—but he was fighting her every step of the way. Fighting her and fighting himself.

He was attracted to her, he couldn't deny it, although he'd tried to, more than once. When they were alone together, the tension seemed to throb between them.

He was battling the attraction so hard he'd gone as far as arranging a date for her with another man. Since the evening they'd met, Kramer had insulted her, harangued her and lectured her. He'd made it plain that he didn't want her around. And yet there were times when he sought out her company. He argued with her at every opportunity, took it upon himself to be her guardian, and yet...

"Maryanne?" Carol said, studying her with concern. "What's wrong?"

"Kramer Adams," she whispered. Lifting her wineglass, she took a small swallow, hoping that would give her the courage to continue.

"I should have guessed," Carol muttered, frowning. "From the moment you moved in here, next door to that madman, I just knew he'd cause you nothing but problems."

Her friend's opinion of Kramer had never been high and Maryanne had to bite back the urge to defend him.

"Tell us everything," Barbara said, drawing up her knees and leaning back against the sofa.

"There isn't much to tell."

"He's the one who got you into this craziness in the first place, remember?" Carol pointed out righteously—as if Maryanne needed reminding. Carol then turned to Barbara and began to explain to the older woman how it had all started. "Kramer wrote a derogatory piece about Maryanne in his column a while back, implying she was a spoiled debutante, and she took it to heart and decided to prove him wrong."

"He didn't mean it. In fact, he's regretted every word of that article." This time Maryanne felt obliged to defend him. As far as she was concerned, this was old business, already resolved. It was the unfinished business, the things happening between them now, that bothered her most.

The denial. The refusal on both their parts to accept the feelings they shared. Only a few days earlier, Maryanne had tried to convince Kramer he wasn't her type and nothing about them was compatible. He'd been only too eager to agree.

But they'd been drawn together, virtually against their wills, by an attraction so overwhelming, so inevitable, they were powerless against it. This sensual and emotional awareness of one another seemed more intense every time they met. This feeling couldn't be anything except love.

"You're among friends, so tell us everything," Barbara pressed, handing Maryanne the entire box of tissues. "Remember, I've known Kramer for years, so nothing you say is going to shock me."

"For one thing, he's impossible," Maryanne whispered, having difficulty expressing her thoughts.

"He deserves to be hanged from the closest tree," Carol said scornfully.

"And at the same time he's wonderful," Maryanne concluded, ignoring Carol's comment.

"You're not..." Carol paused, her face tightening as if she was having trouble forming the words. "You don't mean to suggest you're falling in—" she swallowed "—*love* with him, are you?"

"I don't know." Maryanne clenched the soggy tissue in her hands. "But I think I might be."

"Oh, no," Carol cried, covering her mouth with both hands, "you've got to do something quick. A man like Kramer Adams eats little girls like you for breakfast. He's cynical and sarcastic and—"

"Talented and generous," Maryanne finished for her.

"You're not thinking clearly. It probably has something to do with that fever you had. You've got to remember the facts. Kramer insulted you in print, seriously insulted you, and then tried to make up for it. You're mistaking this small attack of conscience as something more, and that could be dangerous." Awkwardly, Carol rose to her feet and started pacing.

"He's probably one of the most talented writers I've ever read," Maryanne continued, undaunted by her friend's concerns. "Every time I read his work, I can't help being awed."

"All right," Carol said, "I'll concede he does possess a certain amount of creative talent, but that doesn't change who or what he is. Kramer Adams is a bad-tempered egotistical self-centred...grouch."

"I hate to say this," Barbara said softly, shaking her head, "but Carol's right. Kramer's been eating at Mom's Place for as long as I've worked there, and that's three years. I feel like I know him better than you do, and he's everything Carol says. But you know, underneath it all, there's more to him. Oh, he'd like everyone to believe he's this macho guy. He plays that role to the hilt, but after you've been around him awhile, anyone with a lick of sense would know it's all a game to him."

"I told you he's wonderful!" Maryanne exclaimed.

"The man's a constant," Carol insisted. "Constantly in a bad mood, constantly making trouble, constantly getting involved in matters that are none of his business. Maryanne here is the perfect example. He should never have written that column about her." Carol plopped back down and jerked half a dozen tissues from the box in quick succession. She handed them to Maryanne. "You've got blinders on where he's concerned. Take it from me, a woman can't allow herself to become emotionally involved with a man she plans to change."

"I don't want to change Kramer."

"You don't?" Carol echoed, her voice low and disbelieving. "You mean to say you like him as he is?"

"You just don't know him the way I do," Maryanne said. "Kramer's truly generous. Did either of you know he's become sort of a father figure for the teenagers in this neighbourhood? He's their friend in the very best sense. He keeps tabs on them and makes sure no one gets involved in drugs or is lured into gang activities. The kids around here idolise him."

"Kramer Adams does that?" Carol sounded sceptical. She arched her brows as though she couldn't completely trust Maryanne's observations.

"When Barbara told him I was coming down with a virus, he came over to check on me and—"

"As well he should!" Barbara declared. "He was the one who gave you that germ in the first place."

"I'm not entirely sure I caught it from him."

Carol and Barbara exchanged a look. Slowly each shook her head, and then all three shared a warm smile.

"I think we might be too late," Barbara said theatrically to Carol, speaking from the side of her mouth.

"She's showing all the signs," Carol agreed solemnly.

"You're right, I fear," Barbara responded in kind. "She's already in love with him."

"Good grief, no," Carol wailed, pressing her hands to her mouth. "Say it isn't so. She's too young and vulnerable."

"It's a pity, such a pity."

"I can't help but agree. Maryanne is much too sweet for Kramer Adams. I just hope he appreciates her."

"He won't," Carol muttered, reverting to her normal voice, "but then no man ever fully appreciates a woman."

"What about Alan Alda?" Maryanne demanded.

"Maybe him."

"Oh, sure, Alan," Carol agreed.

"It's such a pity men act the way they do."

"Some men," Maryanne added.

Carol and Barbara dabbed their eyes and solemnly tossed the used tissues into the growing heap in the middle of their circle.

The plan had been to gather all the used tissues and ceremonially dump them in the toilet, flush their "pity pot", and then celebrate all the good things in their lives.

The idea for this little party had been an impromptu one of Maryanne's on a lonely Friday night. She'd been feeling blue and friendless and decided to look for a little innocent fun. She'd phoned Carol and learned she was a weekend widow; her husband had gone fishing with some cronies. Barbara had thought the idea was a good one herself, since she'd just broken her longest fingernail and was in the mood for a shoulder to cry on.

A pity party seemed just the thing to help three lonely women make it through a bleak Friday night.

MARYANNE AWOKE Saturday morning with a humdinger of a headache. Wine and the ice cream they'd had at the end of the evening definitely didn't mix.

If her head hadn't been throbbing so painfully, she might have recognised sooner that her apartment had no heat. Her cantankerous radiator was acting up again. It did that some mornings, but she'd always managed to coax it back to life with a few well-placed whacks. The past few days had been unusually cold for early November—well below freezing at night.

She reached for her robe and slippers, bundling herself up like a December baby out in her first snowstorm. Cupping her hands over her mouth, she blew until a frosty mist formed.

A quickly produced cup of coffee with two extra-strength aspirin took the edge off her headache. Maryanne shivered while she slipped into jeans, sweatshirt and a thick winter coat. She suspected she resembled someone who was preparing to join an Arctic expedition.

She fiddled with the radiator, twisting the knobs and slamming her hand against the side, but the only results were a couple of rattles and a hollow clanking sound.

Not knowing what else to try, she got out her heavy cast-iron skillet and banged it against the top of the rad in hopes of reviving the ageing pipes.

The sound was deafening, vibrating through the room like a jet aircraft crashing through the sound barrier. If that wasn't enough, Maryanne's entire body began to quiver, starting at her arm and spreading outward in a rippling effect that caused her arms and legs to tremble.

"What the hell's going on over there?" Kramer shouted from the other side of the wall. He didn't wait for her to answer and a couple of seconds later came barreling through her front door, wild-eyed and dishevelled.

"What... Where?" He was carrying a baseball bat, and stalked to the middle of her apartment, scanning the interior for what Maryanne could only assume were foreign invaders.

"I don't have any heat," she announced, tucking the thin scarf more tightly around her ears.

Kramer blinked. She'd apparently woken him from a sound sleep. He was barefooted and dressed in pyjama bottoms, and although he wore a shirt, it was unbuttoned, revealing a broad muscular chest dusted with curly black hair.

"What's with you? Are you going to a costume party?"

"Believe me, this is no party. I'm simply trying to keep warm."

His gaze lowered to the heavy skillet in her hand. "Do you plan to cook on that radiator?"

"I might, but I can't seem to get it to work. In case you hadn't noticed there isn't any heat in this place."

Kramer set the baseball bat aside and moved to the far wall to look over the radiator. "What's wrong with it?"

How like a man to ask stupid questions! If Maryanne had *known* what was wrong with it, she wouldn't be standing there shivering, with a scarf swaddling her face like an old-time remedy for toothache.

"How in heaven's name am I supposed to know?" she answered testily.

"What went on here last night, anyway? A wake?"

She glanced at the mound of tissues and shrugged. He was scanning the area as if it were a crime scene and he should take caution not to stumble over a dead body.

Walking across the living-room, he picked up the two empty wine bottles and held them aloft for her inspection, pretending to be shocked.

"Very funny." She put the skillet down and removed the bottles from his hands, to be deposited promptly in the garbage.

"So you had a party and I wasn't invited." He made it sound as though he'd missed the social event of the year.

Maryanne sighed loudly. "If you must know, Carol, Barbara and I had a pity party."

"A what? You're kidding, right?" He didn't bother to hide his mocking grin.

"Never mind." She should have realised he'd only poke fun at her. "Can you figure out how to get this thing working before the next ice age?"

"Here, give me a shot at it." He gently patted the top of the radiator as he knelt in front of it. "OK, ol' Betsy, we're trusting you to be good." He began fiddling with knobs, still murmuring ridiculous endearments—like a cowboy talking to his horse.

"It doesn't do any good to talk to an inanimate object," she advised primly, standing behind him.

"You want to do this?"

"No," she muttered. Having Kramer in her home, dressed in his night clothes, did something odd to her, sent her pulse skittering erratically. She deliberately allowed her attention to wander to the scene outside her window. The still-green lawns of Volunteer Park showed in the distance and she pretended to be absorbed in their beauty.

"I thought I told you to keep that door chain in place," he mentioned casually as he worked. "This isn't the Seattle."

"Do you honestly think you need to remind me of that now?" She rubbed her hands together, hoping to generate some warmth before her fingers went numb.

"There," he said, sounding satisfied. "All she needed was a little bit of loving care."

"Thanks," Maryanne said with relief.

"No problem, only the next time something like this happens don't try to fix it yourself."

"Translated, that means I shouldn't try to fix the radiator again while *you're* trying to sleep."

"Right."

She smiled up at him, her eyes alive with appreciation. He really had been good to her from the day she'd moved in—before then, too. Discounting what he'd written about her in his column, of course. And even that had ended up having a positive effect.

It had been a week since she'd last seen him. A long week. A lonely week. Until now, she'd hardly been able to admit, even to herself, how much she'd missed him. Standing there as he was, Maryanne was struck by just how really attractive she found him. If only he'd taken time to button his shirt! She reveled in his lean strength and his aura of unquestionable authority—and that chest of his was driving her to distraction.

She wasn't the only one enthralled. Kramer was staring at her, too. The silence lingered between them, lengthening moment by moment as they gazed into each other's eyes.

"I have to go," he finally said, breaking eye contact by glancing past her, out the window.

"Right. I—I understand," she stammered, stepping back. Her hands swung at her sides as she followed him to the door. "I really do appreciate this." Already she could feel the warmth spilling into her apartment. And none too soon, either.

"Just remember to keep the door locked."

She grinned and mockingly saluted him. "Aye, aye, sir."

He left then. Maryanne hated to see him go, hated to see him walk away from her, and yet it seemed he was continually doing exactly that.

LATER THAT SAME AFTERNOON, after she'd finished her errands, Maryanne was strolling through the park when a soft feminine voice spoke from behind her.

Maryanne turned around and waved when she discovered Gloria, the teenager she'd met here earlier. But this time Gloria wasn't alone.

"This is my little sister, Katie, the pest," Gloria explained. "She's three."

"Hello, Katie," Maryanne said, smiling.

"Why am I a pest?" Katie asked, gazing at Gloria, but apparently not offended that her older sister referred to her that way.

"Because." Looking annoyed, the teenager shrugged in the same vague manner Maryanne had so often seen in her younger brothers. "Katie's three and every other word is 'why'. Why this? Why that? It's enough to drive a person straight to the loony bin."

"I have brothers, so I know exactly what you mean."

"You do?"

"They're several years younger than I am. Trust me, I know exactly what you're talking about."

"Did your brothers want to go every place you did? And did your mother make you take them even if it was a terrible inconvenience?"

Maryanne tried to disguise a smile. "Sometimes."

"Eddie wanted me to come and watch him play basketball this afternoon with Mr Adams, and I had to drag Katie along because she wanted to come to the park, too. My mom pressured me into bringing her. I didn't even get a chance to say no." Gloria made it sound as if she were being forced to swim across Puget Sound with the three-year-old clinging to her back.

"I'm not a pest," Katie insisted now, flipping her braid over one shoulder in a show of defiance. Looking up at Maryanne, the little girl carefully manipulated her fingers and proudly exclaimed, "I'm three."

"Three?" Maryanne repeated, raising her eyebrows, feigning surprise. "Really? I would have thought you were four or five."

Katie grinned delightedly. "I'm nearly four, you know."

"Mr Adams is already here," Gloria said, brightening. She frowned as she glanced down at her little sister and jerked the small arm in an effort to hurry her along. "Come on, Katie, we have to hurry. Eddie wanted me to watch him play ball."

"Why?"

Gloria groaned. "See what I mean?"

"You go on," Maryanne said, offering Katie her hand. The youngster obediently slipped her small hand into Maryanne's much larger one, willingly abandoning her cranky older sister. "Katie and I will follow behind."

Gloria looked surprised by the offer. "You mean you don't mind? I mean, Katie is my responsibility and it wouldn't be fair to palm her off on you. You're not going to kidnap her or anything, are you? I mean, I know you're not—you're Mr Adams's friend. I wouldn't let her go with just anyone, you know. But if anything happened to her, my mother would have my neck."

"I promise to take the very best care of her."

Gloria grinned, looking sheepish for having suggested anything else. "You're sure you don't mind?"

"I don't mind in the least. I don't think Katie does, either. Is that right, Katie?"

"Why?"

"Are you really sure? OK, then..." Once she'd offered a token protest Gloria raced off to join her friends.

Katie was content to skip and hop at Maryanne's side until they reached a huge pile of leaves under a chestnut tree. Almost before Maryanne realised it, Katie had slipped away from her. The child raced towards the leaves, bunching as many as she could in her small arms and carrying them back to Maryanne as though presenting her with the rarest of jewels.

"Look," she cried happily. "Leafs."

"Leaves," Maryanne corrected, bending over and grabbing an armful herself. She tossed them into the air and grinned as Katie leapt up to catch as many as she could and in the process dropped the armload she was holding.

Laughing, Maryanne clasped the child by the waist and swung her around, while Katie shrieked with delight. Dizzy, Maryanne leaned against the tree in an effort to regain her equilibrium and her breath.

It was then she noticed that Kramer had stopped playing and was standing alone in the middle of the basketball court, staring at her. The game was going on all around him, youths scattering in one direction and then the other, racing from one end of the court and back again. Kramer seemed oblivious to them and to the game—to everything but her.

A tall boy bumped into him from behind and Kramer stumbled. Maryanne gasped, fearing he might fall, but he caught himself in time. Without a pause, he rejoined the game, racing down the court at breakneck speed. He stole the ball and made a slam dunk, coming down hard on the pavement.

Gloria ran back towards Maryanne and Katie. "I thought you said you and Mr Adams were just friends?" she teased. She was grinning in a way that suggested she wasn't about to be fooled again. "He nearly got creamed because he couldn't take his eyes off you."

With Katie on her lap, Maryanne sat beside the teenage girls watching the game. Together she and the three-year-old became Kramer's personal cheering squad, but whether or not he appreciated their efforts she didn't know. He didn't give a single indication he heard them.

When the game was finished, Kramer walked breathlessly off the court. His grey sweatshirt was ringed with perspiration, and his face was red and damp from the sheer physical exhaustion of keeping up with kids half his age.

For an anxious moment, Maryanne assumed he was planning to ignore her and simply walk away. But after he'd stopped at the water fountain, he walked over to the bench where she and Katie were sitting.

He slumped down beside her, dishevelled and still breathing hard. "What are you doing here?" he grumbled.

"I happened to be in the park," she answered, feeling self-conscious now and unsure. "You don't need to worry, Kramer. I didn't follow you."

"I didn't think you had."

"You look nice in blue," he said hoarsely, then cleared his throat as if he hadn't meant to say that, as if he wanted to withdraw the words.

"Thanks." The blue sweater was one of her favourites. She'd worn her long wool coat and was surprised he'd even noticed the periwinkle-blue sweater beneath.

"Hello, Katie."

Katie beamed, reaching out both arms for Kramer to lift her up, which he did. The little girl hugged him quickly, then leapt off the bench and ran to her sister, who stood talking to her boyfriend.

"You're good with children," Kramer said. His voice fell slightly, as though the fact surprised him.

"I do have a knack with them. I always have." She had been much-sought as a baby-sitter by her parents' friends and for a time had considered becoming a teacher. If she'd pursued that field of study she would have preferred to teach kindergarten. She found five-year-olds, with their eagerness to learn about the world, delightful. A couple of articles she'd written the week before were geared towards children's magazines. If only she'd hear something soon. It seemed to take so long.

"How many years of your life did you lose this time?" Maryanne asked teasingly.

"Another two or three, at least."

He smiled at her and it was that rare special smile he granted her only in those brief moments when his guard was lowered. His resistance to the attraction he felt to her was at its weakest point, and they both knew it.

Maryanne went still, almost afraid to move or speak for fear of ruining the moment. His eyes, so warm and gentle, continued to hold hers. When she tried to breathe, the air seemed to catch in her lungs.

"Maryanne." Her name was little more than a whisper.

"Yes?"

He raked his hand through his hair, then looked away. "Nothing. Never mind."

"What is it?" she pressed, unwilling to let the matter drop.

The muscles along the side of his jaw clenched. "I said it was nothing," he answered gruffly.

Maryanne gazed down at her hands, feeling an overwhelming sense of frustration and despair. The tension between them was so thick she could taste it, but nothing she could say or do would alter that. If anything, her efforts would only make it worse.

"Hey, Kramer," Eddie called out, loping toward them. "What's with you, man?" He laughed, tossing his basketball from one hand to the other. "You nearly lost that game because you couldn't take your eyes off your woman."

Kramer scowled at the youth. "You looking for a rematch?"

"Any time you want."

"Not today." Shaking his head, Kramer slowly pushed the sleeves of his sweatshirt past his elbows.

"Right," Eddie said with a knowing laugh. "I didn't think so, with your woman here and all."

"Maryanne isn't my woman," Kramer informed him curtly, his frown darkening.

"Right," Eddie responded. "Hey, dude, this is me, Eddie. Can't fool me! You practically went comatose when you saw her. I don't blame you, though. She ain't bad. So when are you two getting married?"

CHAPTER NINE

"I'VE CHANGED MY MIND," Barbara announced at closing time Monday evening.

Maryanne was busy refilling the salt and pepper shakers and reloading the napkin holders. "About what?" she asked absently, stuffing napkins into the small chrome canisters with practised ease.

"You and Kramer."

If Barbara hadn't had Maryanne's attention earlier, she did now. Kramer had left the restaurant about forty minutes earlier, after having his customary meal of chilli and coffee. He'd barely said two words to Maryanne the whole time he was there. He'd buried his face in the evening edition of the *Sun* and done a brilliant job of pretending he didn't know her.

"What about us?" Maryanne's expression might have remained aloof, but her heart was pounding furiously.

"Since the night of our pity party, I've had a change of heart. You're exactly the right kind of woman for Kramer. The two of you...balance each other. At first I agreed with Carol. My opinion of Kramer isn't as negative as hers, but you have to remember that those two work for rival papers. At any rate, I was concerned. You *are* really sweet."

Maryanne winced at the "sweet". It rather sounded as though friendship with her was like falling into a jar of honey.

"And now?"

"I don't know exactly what changed my mind. Partly it was watching Kramer when he was here. I got quite a kick out of him."

"How do you mean?"

Barbara's grin was broad as she continued to wipe the counter, her movements slow as if her thoughts were distracting her. "I swear that man couldn't keep his eyes off you."

Maryanne was puzzled. "What are you talking about? Kramer didn't look my way once."

"Oh, he'd scowl every time you were close, but behind that cross look of his was an intensity I can't ever remember seeing in him. It was like he had to come in and get his daily fix of you."

Maryanne's heart couldn't decide whether to lift with happiness or sink with doubt. "You're wrong. Other than ordering his meal, he didn't even speak to me. I might as well have been a robot."

"That's what he'd like you to believe."

"He was reading the paper," Maryanne countered. "The same way he reads it every time he comes here."

"Correction," Barbara said, and her face broke into a spontaneous smile. "He *pretended* to be reading the paper, but when you weren't looking his eyes were following you like a hawk."

"Oh, Barbara, did he really?" It seemed almost more than she dared hope for. He'd hardly spoken to her in the past few days, and he seemed to be avoiding her. The kids in the park had taken to teasing them about being sweethearts and asking pointed questions, and Kramer had practically fallen all over himself denying that they were anything more than friends.

"It's more than just the way he was watching you," Barbara said thoughtfully, slipping on to a stool. "Have you read his columns the past couple of weeks?"

Naturally Maryanne had, more impressed by his work every time she did. The range of his talent and the power of his writing were unmistakable. Within a few years, if not sooner, she expected his newspaper column to be picked up for syndication.

"Lately, I've noticed something unusual about his writing," Barbara continued, still clutching the dishrag. "That cynical edge of his—it isn't quite as sharp. His writing's less sarcastic now. I heard one of my customers comment earlier today that Kramer's going soft on us. I hadn't thought about it much until then, but Ernie's right. I don't know what's made the difference, but I figure it must be love. Oh, I doubt there's much in this life that's going to change Kramer Adams. He'll always be stubborn as a mule, headstrong and temperamental. That's just part of his nature. But mark my words, he's in love."

"But what you said earlier, about us being so different..."

"You are, with you so nice and all, and Kramer such a grouch. At least he likes to pretend he's one. You and I both know better, but most folks don't."

"And?" Maryanne probed.

"And, well, it seemed to me the two of you fit together perfectly. Like two pieces of a puzzle."

It seemed that way to Maryanne, too.

"You heard, didn't you?" Barbara muttered, abruptly changing the subject.

Maryanne nodded. Mom's Place was going to close the following month for remodelling.

"What are you going to do?"

Maryanne didn't know yet. "Find a temporary job, I suppose. What about you?" By then, she should have sold a few of the articles she'd submitted. At least she hadn't been rejected yet. She should be hearing any time.

"I'm not all that concerned about taking a month or so off work," Barbara returned, her look thoughtful. "I could use a vacation, especially over the holidays. I was thinking of staying home and baking Christmas gifts this year. My fudge is out of this world."

"I suppose I should start looking for another job now." Maryanne was already worried about meeting expenses. Mom's Place couldn't have chosen a worse time to close.

A HALF-HOUR LATER, she was waiting for the bus, her mind spinning with what Barbara had said. The diner's closing was a concern, but Barbara's comments about Kramer gladdened Maryanne's heart.

Kramer did feel something for her, something more powerful than he dared let on.

She supposed she should confront him with it, force him to acknowledge his feelings. A brief smile crossed her lips as she envisioned what would happen if she actually did such a thing. She nearly laughed out loud at the thought.

Kramer would deny it, of course, loudly and vehemently, and she'd have to counteract with a loud argument of her own. The smile appeared again. Her decision was made.

Feeling almost light-headed, Maryanne glanced down the street, eager for the bus to arrive so she could get home. The first thing she intended to do was march into Kramer's apartment and demand the truth. If he tried to ignore her, as he usually did, then she had the perfect solution.

She'd kiss him.

A kiss would silence his protests in the most effective way she could imagine. Maryanne felt herself almost melt at the thought. Being kissed by Kramer, being held in his arms, was like walking through the gates of an undiscovered paradise. Just remembering those moments made her feel faint with desire, weak with excitement. When they broke apart she was always left restless and impatient for something she couldn't quite identify. He seemed to experience the same regrets, Maryanne remembered hopefully.

Cheered by the thought, she nearly applauded when her bus arrived. The ride passed quickly and she hurried into the building, eager to see Kramer.

Consumed by her sense of purpose, she went directly to his apartment. She stood in front of his door, took several deep breaths, then knocked politely. No answer. She tried again, harder this time.

"Who is it?" Kramer growled from the other side.

"Maryanne. I want to talk to you."

"I'm busy."

She was only a little discouraged by his unfriendliness. "This'll just take a minute."

The door was yanked opened with excessive force. Kramer stood before her, dressed in a black tuxedo and white cummerbund, looking so devilishly handsome that he caught her completely by surprise. Her mouth sagged open.

"Yes?" he asked crossly.

"Hello, Kramer," she said, aware that her mission had been thwarted. Nothing he could have said or done would have affected her as profoundly as finding him dressed like this. Because it meant he was going out on a date.

"Hello," he said, tugging at the cuffs of his jacket, adjusting the fit. He frowned, apparently waiting for her to say something.

"Uh…" She tried to gather her scattered composure, and finally managed to squeak, "You're going out?"

He scowled. "I don't dress like this for a jaunt to the movies."

"No, I don't suppose you do."

"You wanted something?"

She'd been so confident, so sure she was doing the right thing. But now, seeing Kramer looking more dressed up and formal than he'd ever looked for her, she found herself speechless.

She couldn't help wondering where he was going—and with whom. The "with whom" part bothered her the most.

He glanced pointedly at his wristwatch. "How long is this going to take?" he asked coolly. "I'm supposed to pick up Prudence in fifteen minutes."

"Prudence?" His face, tight with impatience, drew her full attention. *Prudence,* her mind repeated. He'd tossed the name at her like a hand grenade. Who was this woman?

Then in a flash, Maryanne knew. It was all she could do not to laugh and inform him that his little plan just wasn't working. No imaginary date was going to make *her* jealous.

He wasn't seeing anyone named Prudence. Good grief, if he had to invent a name, the least he could have done was come up with something a little more plausible than Prudence.

In fact, now that she thought about it, Maryanne remembered Kramer casually mentioning a week or so earlier that he'd been asked to speak at a Chamber of Commerce banquet. There had also been a notice in the paper. Who did he think he was kidding?

Of course he intended her to believe he was dating another woman. That was supposed to discourage her, she guessed. Except that it didn't.

"It wasn't important…" she said, gesturing vaguely. "The radiators were giving me a little trouble this morning, but I'll manage. I was planning to go out tonight myself."

His eyes connected with hers. "Another pity party?"

"Not this time." She considered announcing she had a hot date herself, but that would have been carrying this farce a little too far. "Barbara and I will probably go to a movie."

"Sounds like fun."

"I'm sure it will be." She smiled up at him, past the square cut of his jaw to his incredibly dark eyes. "Have a good time with... Prudence," she said with a bright knowing smile.

Holding back a laugh, she returned to her own apartment. The rat. The low-down dirty rat! He was pretending to escort some imaginary woman to a fancy affair. Oh, he'd like nothing better than for Maryanne to think he considered her a pest. But she knew that wasn't quite the case.

Where was the man who'd rushed to her rescue when the pipes needed a little coaxing? Where was the man who'd nearly been run over on a basketball court when he saw her standing on the sidelines? Where was the man who'd tried to set her up with someone else he thought more suitable? Kramer Adams had just proved what she'd suspected all along. He was a coward—at least when it came to love.

Depressed, Maryanne slowly crossed the living-room and sank on to her sofa, trying to gather her wits. Ten minutes later, she still sat there, mulling things over and feeling sorry for herself, when she heard Kramer's door open and close. She immediately perked up, wondering if he'd had a change of heart. He seemed to pause for a moment outside her door, but any second thoughts he must be having didn't last long.

Barbara phoned soon after, full of apologies, to cancel their movie plans, so Maryanne spent the evening drowning her sorrows in television reruns and slices of cold pizza.

She must have fallen asleep because a harsh ringing jolted her awake a couple of hours later. She leapt off the sofa and stumbled dazedly around before she realized the sound came from the phone. She rushed across the room.

A greeting had barely left her lips when her father's booming voice assailed her.

"Where the hell are you?"

"Hello, Dad," Maryanne managed, her heart sinking. How like him to get to the subject at hand without anything in the way of preliminaries. "How are you, too?"

"I want to know where you're living and I want to know right now!"

"I beg your pardon?" she asked, stalling for time. Obviously her father had discovered her small deception.

"I talked to the managing editor of the *Seattle Review* this morning and he told me you haven't worked there in weeks. He said you'd quit. Now, I want to know what this craziness is you've been feeding your mother and me about a special assignment."

"Uh..." By now, Maryanne was awake enough to know her father wasn't in any mood to listen to excuses.

"You lied to us, girl."

"Not exactly..." She paused, searching for the right words. "It was more a case of omission, don't you think?"

"You've had us worried sick. We've been trying to get hold of you all afternoon. Where were you? And who the hell is Kramer Adams?"

"Kramer Adams?" she echoed, playing dumb, which at first point wasn't all that difficult.

"Your mother mentioned his name, and when I spoke to the paper, some woman named...Riverside, Carol Riverside, claimed this was his fault."

"Dad, listen, it's all rather complicated, so I think—"

"I don't want excuses, I want facts. You decided to work on the other side of the country. Against my better judgement, I arranged it for you with the promise I wouldn't intrude—and look where it's got me! To have you deceive us by—"

"Dad, please, just settle down."

He seemed to be making an effort to calm himself, but more than likely the effort was thanks to her mother. Maryanne could hear her arguing softly in the background.

"Can I explain?" she asked, waiting a moment or two for the tension to ease, although she wasn't sure what to say, what excuses she could possible offer.

"You can try to explain, but I doubt it'll do any good," he answered gruffly.

Now that she had the floor, Maryanne floundered.

"I take it this all revolves around that columnist friend of yours from the *Sun*?" her father asked. "That Kramer character?"

"Well, yes," Maryanne admitted reluctantly. But she didn't feel she could place the entire blame on him. "Leaving the paper was my decision—"

"Where are you living?"

That was one of several questions Maryanne was hoping to avoid. "I—I rented an apartment."

"You were in an apartment before. It doesn't make the least bit of sense for you to move. The Seattle has a reputation for excellence."

"Yes, Dad, I know, but moving was necessary." She didn't go on to explain why. She didn't want to mislead her father more than she had already. But at the same time, if she told him she couldn't afford to continue living at the Seattle, he'd certainly demand an explanation.

"That doesn't explain a damn thing," Samuel Simpson boomed.

Maryanne held the phone away from her ear and sighed heavily. This conversation couldn't have come at a worse time. She was groggy from her nap and discouraged by her relationship with Kramer. To complicate matters, she was truly in love for the first time in her life. Loving someone shouldn't be this difficult!

"I insist you tell me what's going on," her father said, in the tone of voice she remembered from childhood confrontations about missed curfews and other transgressions.

She tried again. "It's not that easy to explain."

"You have three seconds, young lady, to tell me why you've lied to your parents."

"I apologise for that. I've felt horrible about it, I really have, but I didn't want to say anything for fear you'd worry."

"Of course we'd worry! Now tell me exactly what it is we should be worrying about."

"Dad, honestly, I'm over twenty-one. I should be able to live and work where I please. You can't keep me your little girl forever.'' This conversation was not only reminiscent of several she'd had with Kramer, it was one she should have had with her father years ago.

''I demand to know why you quit the paper!''

Maryanne refused to be intimidated. ''I already explained that. I had another job.''

''Obviously you're doing something you're too ashamed to tell your parents.''

''I'm not ashamed! It's nothing illegal. Besides, I happen to like what I do, and I've managed to live entirely on what I make, which is no small feat. I'm happy, Dad, really happy.'' She tried to force some cheerful enthusiasm into her voice, but unfortunately she didn't entirely succeed. How she wished she could brag about selling her articles. Surely she'd receive word of one soon!

''If you're so pleased about this change in jobs, then why do you sound upset?'' her mother asked reasonably, joining the conversation from the extension line.

''I—I'm fine, really I am.''

''Somehow, sweetie, that just doesn't ring true.''

''I don't like the sound of this,'' her father interrupted impatiently. ''I made a mistake in arranging this Seattle assignment for you. It seems to me it'd be best if you quit whatever you're doing and move back to—''

''Dad, I refuse to quit now.''

''I want you to move back home. As far as I can see, you've got one hell of a lot of explaining to do.''

''It seems to me,'' Maryanne said after a moment of strained silence, ''that we should both take time to cool down and think this over before one of us says or does something we're all going to regret.''

''I'm calm.'' The voice that roared over the long-distance wires threatened to impair Maryanne's hearing.

''Daddy, I love you and Mom dearly, but I think it would be best if we both slept on this. I'm going to hang up now, not to be rude, but because I don't think this conversation is accomplishing anything. I'll call you first thing in the morning.''

"Maryanne…Maryanne, don't you dare—"

She didn't allow him to finish, knowing it would do no good to reason with him when he was in this frame of mind. Her heart was heavy with regret as she gently replaced the receiver. Knowing her father would immediately call again, she unplugged the phone.

Now that her family had discovered she wasn't working at the *Review,* everything was sure to change. And not for the better. Her father would hound her until she was forced to tell him she'd taken a job as a waitress. Once he discovered that, he'd hit the roof.

Still thinking about what had happened, she put on her flannel pyjamas and pulled out her bed. With the demanding physical schedule she kept, sleeping had never been a problem. Tonight, she missed the clatter of Kramer's typing. She'd grown accustomed to its comforting familiarity, in part because it was a sign of his presence. She often lay awake wondering how his mystery novel was developing. Some nights she even dreamed that he'd given her the manuscript to read, which to her represented the ultimate gesture of trust.

But Kramer wasn't at his typewriter this evening. He was giving a speech. Closing her eyes, she imagined him standing before the large dinner crowd. How she would have enjoyed being in the audience! She knew beyond a doubt that his eyes would have sought her out…

Instead she was spending the night alone. She lay with her eyes wide open; every time she started to drift off, some small noise would jerk her into wakefulness. She finally had to admit that she was waiting to hear the sounds of Kramer's return.

Some time in the early morning hours, Maryanne did eventually fall asleep. She woke at six to the familiar sound of Kramer pounding on his typewriter.

She threw on her robe, thrust her feet into the fuzzy slippers and began pacing, her mind whirling at hurricane force.

When she could stand it no longer, she banged on the wall separating their two apartments.

"Your typing woke me up!" Which, of course, wasn't fair or even particularly true. But she'd spent a fretful night thinking about him, and that was excuse enough.

Her family had found out she'd quit her job and all hell was about to break loose. Time was running out on her and Kramer. If she was going to do something—and it was clear she'd have to be the one—then she'd need to do it soon.

"Just go back to bed," Kramer shouted.

"Not on your life, Kramer Adams!" Without questioning how wise it was to confront him now, Maryanne stormed out of her apartment dressed as she was, and beat hard on his door.

Kramer opened it almost immediately, still wearing the tuxedo from the night before, sans jacket and cummerbund. The sleeves of his shirt were rolled past his elbows and the top three buttons were open. His dishevelment and the shadows under his eyes suggested he hadn't been to bed.

"What now?" he demanded. "Is my breathing too loud?"

"We need to talk," she stated calmly as she marched into his apartment.

Kramer remained standing at the door. "Why don't you come in and make yourself at home?" he muttered.

"I already have." She sat on the edge of his sofa and waited until he turned to face her. "So?" she asked with cheerful derision. "How'd your hot date go?"

"Fine." He smiled grimly. "Just fine."

"Where'd you go for dinner? The Four Seasons? Fullers?" She named two of the best restaurants in town. "By the way, do I know Prudence?"

"No," he answered with sharp impatience.

"I didn't think so."

"Maryanne—"

"I don't suppose you have coffee made?"

"It's made." But he didn't offer her any. The fact that he was still standing by the door suggested he wanted her out of his home. But when it came to dealing with Kramer, Maryanne had long since learned to ignore the obvious.

"Thanks, I'll get myself a cup." She walked into the kitchen and found two clean mugs in the dishwasher. "You want one?"

"I have some," he said pointedly, stationing himself in the kitchen doorway. He heaved a long-suffering sigh. "Maryanne, I'm busy, so if you could get on with—"

"My father knows," she said calmly, watching him closely for some sort of reaction. If she'd been looking for evidence of concern or regret, he gave neither. The only emotion she was able to discern was a brief flicker of what she could only assume was relief. That wasn't encouraging. He appeared all too willing to get her out of his life.

"Well?" she probed. "Say something."

"What the hell have you been telling him?"

"Nothing about you, so don't worry. I did mention you to my mother, but you don't need to worry about that, either. She thinks you and I... Never mind."

"*What* does your father know?" Kramer demanded.

She sipped from the edge of the mug and shrugged. "He found out I wasn't on special assignment for the paper."

"Special assignment? What does that have to do with anything?"

"That's what I told my mother when I moved."

"Why the hell would you say something like that?"

"She was expecting me to mail her my columns, and call every other day. I couldn't continue to do either of those things. I had to come up with some excuse."

He cocked an eyebrow. "You might have tried the truth."

Maryanne nodded her agreement. If she'd bungled any part of this arrangement, it had been with her parents. Unfortunately there wasn't time for regrets now.

"Dad learned I moved out of the Seattle. I didn't tell him where I was living, but that won't deter him. Knowing Dad, he'll have all the facts by noon today. To put it mildly, he isn't pleased. He wants me to return to the East Coast."

"Are you going?" Kramer's question was casual, as though her response was of little concern to him.

"No."

"Why not?" The impatient look returned. "For the love of heaven, Annie, will you kindly listen to reason? You don't belong here. You've proved your point. If you're waiting for me to admit I was wrong about you, then fine, I'll admit it, and gladly. You've managed far better than I ever dreamed you would, but it's time to get on with your life. It's time to move back into the world where you belong.''

''I can't do that now.''

''Why the hell not?''

''Because...I've fallen—''

''Good Lord, Annie, it's barely seven and I've got to get to work,'' he said brusquely, cutting her off. ''Shouldn't you be getting dressed? Walking around the hallway in your pyjamas isn't wise—people might think something.''

''Let them.''

He rubbed his face wearily, shaking his head.

''Kramer,'' Maryanne said softly, her heart in her throat. ''I know you didn't go out with anyone named Prudence. You made the whole thing up. This game of yours isn't going to work. It's too late. I'm...already in love with you.''

The whole world seemed to come to an abrupt halt. Maryanne hadn't intended to blurt out her feelings this way, but she didn't know how else to cut through the arguments and the denial.

For one wild-eyed moment Kramer didn't say anything. Then he raised his hand, as though fending off some kind of attack, and retreated from the kitchen.

''You can't be in love with me,'' he insisted, slowly sinking to the sofa, like a man in the final stages of exhaustion. ''I won't allow it.''

CHAPTER TEN

"UNFORTUNATELY IT'S TOO LATE," Maryanne told him again, no less calmly. "I'm already in love with you."

"Now just a minute," Kramer said, apparently regaining his composure. "You're a nice kid, and to be honest I've been impressed—"

"I am not a kid," she corrected with quiet authority, "and you know it. We both know it."

"Annie...Maryanne," he said, "listen to me. What you feel for me isn't love." His face revealed a bitterness she hadn't seen before. He walked towards her, gripped her shoulders and gazed down at her.

"That won't work, either," she said in the same quiet voice. She wasn't a poor little rich girl who'd only recently discovered who she was. Nor had she mistaken admiration for love. "I know what I feel."

She slipped her arms around his neck and stood on tiptoe, wanting to convince him of her sincerity with a kiss.

But before her mouth could meet his, Kramer abruptly jerked his head back, preventing the contact. He dropped his arms and none too gently pushed her away.

"Are you afraid to kiss me?"

"You're damn right I am," he said, burying his hands in his pockets as he hastily moved even farther away from her.

Maryanne smiled softly. "And with good reason. We both know what would happen if you did. You've done a good job of hiding your feelings, I'll grant you that much. I was nearly fooled."

"Naturally I'm flattered." His expression was darkening by the second. He stalked across the room, his shoulders hunched forward. He didn't say anything else, and Maryanne strongly suspected he was at a loss for words. Kramer was *never* at a loss for words. Words were his stock-in-trade.

But he was confronting emotions now, not words or concepts, and she knew him well enough to realise how uncomfortable that made him.

He'd hidden his feelings for her behind a mask of gruff annoyance, allowing her to believe she'd become a terrible nuisance in his life. He needed to disguise what he felt for her—to prevent her from learning what everyone else already knew.

Kramer was in love with her.

The mere thought thrilled her and gave her more courage than she'd ever possessed in her life.

"I fully expect you to be flattered," she said gently, "but I'm not telling you this to give your ego a boost. I honestly love you, and nothing my parents say is going to convince me to leave Seattle."

"Maryanne, please..."

He was prepared to push her away verbally, as he had so often. This time she wouldn't let him. This time she walked over to him, threw both arms around his waist and hugged him close.

He raised his hands to her shoulders, ready to ease her from him, but the moment they came to rest on her he seemed to lose his purpose.

"This is ridiculous," she heard him mumble. He held himself rigid for a moment or two, then with a muttered curse buried his face in her hair. A ragged sigh tore through his body.

Experiencing a small sense of triumph, Maryanne pressed her ear to his chest and smiled contentedly when she heard his racing uneven heartbeat.

"You shouldn't let me hold you like this." His voice was low and hushed. "Tell me not to," he breathed as his lips moved through her hair and then lower to the pulse point behind her ear and the tender slope of her neck.

"I don't want you to stop..." She turned her head, begging him to touch and kiss her.

"Annie, please."

"I want to be in your arms more than anywhere. More than anything."

"You don't know what you're saying..."

She lifted her head enough for their eyes to meet. Placing her fingers on his lips, she lightly shook her head. "I'm a woman, a grown woman, and there's no question of my not knowing what I want."

His hands gently grazed her neck, as though he was still hesitant and unsure. Kissing her was what he wanted—she could read it clearly in his dark eyes—but he was holding himself back, his face contorted with indecision.

"Go ahead, kiss me," she urged softly, wanting him so much her whole body seemed to ache. "I dare you to."

His breathing was laboured, and Maryanne could sense the forces raging within him. A fresh wave of tenderness filled her.

"You make it so hard to do what's right," he groaned.

"Loving each other is what's right."

"I'd like to believe that, but I can't." He laid his hand on her cheek and their eyes locked hungrily. He searched her face.

"I love you," she whispered, smiling up at him. She didn't want him to question her feelings. She'd say it a thousand times a day if that was what it took to convince him.

Flattening her hands against his hard chest, she leaned into his strength and offered him her mouth. Only moments earlier he'd pushed her away, but not now. His gaze gentled and he closed his eyes tightly. He was losing the battle.

It was while his eyes were closed that Maryanne claimed the advantage and kissed him. He moaned and seemed about to argue, but once their mouths met the urgency took hold and Kramer was rendered speechless.

To her delight, he responded with the full-fledged hunger she'd witnessed in his eyes. He slid his hands through her hair, his fingers tangling with the thick auburn mass as he angled her head to one side. Maryanne felt herself savouring the taste of his kiss. It was so long since he'd held her like this, so long since he'd done anything but keep her at arm's length. She wanted to cherish these moments, delight in the rush of sensations.

So many thoughts crowded her mind. So many ideas. Plans for their future.

He tore his mouth from hers and nestled his face in the hollow of her neck as he drew in several deep breaths. Maryanne clung to him, hugging him as close as humanly possible.

"Kramer—"

"It isn't going to work—you and me together...it isn't right," he whispered.

"It's more right than anything I've ever known."

"Oh, Annie, the things you do to me."

She smiled gently. "You know what I think?" She didn't give him the opportunity to answer. "I love you and you love me and when two people feel that way about each other, they usually—" she paused and swallowed once "—get married."

"What?" Kramer exploded, leaping away from her as though he'd suffered an electrical shock.

"You heard me," she said.

"You're a crazy woman. You know that, don't you? A certifiable loony." Kramer backed away from her, eyes narrowed. He began pacing rapidly in one direction, then another.

"Marriage was just a suggestion," she said mildly. "I am serious, though, and if you're at all interested we should move fast. Because once my father gets wind of it there'll be hell to pay."

"I have no intention of even considering the idea! In fact, I think it's time you left."

"Kramer, OK, I'm sorry. I shouldn't have mentioned marriage. I was just thinking, hoping actually, that it was something you wanted, too. There's no need to over-react." He had already ushered her across the living-room towards the door. She tried to redirect his efforts, turning in his arms, but he wouldn't allow it.

"We need to talk about this," she insisted.

"Oh, no, you don't," he said, opening the door and steering her into the hallway. "Your idea of talking doesn't seem to coincide with mine. Before I figure out how it happens, you're in my arms and we're—''

"Maryanne!" Her father's voice came like a high-intensity fog-horn from behind her.

Maryanne whirled around to discover both her parents standing in the hallway outside her apartment door. "Mom...Dad..." Frantic, she looked at Kramer, hoping he'd do the explaining part.

"Mr and Mrs Simpson," Kramer said formally, straightening. He removed his arms from around Maryanne, stepped forward and held out his hand to her father. "I'm Kramer Adams."

"How do you do?" Muriel Simpson said tightly as the two men exchanged brief handshakes. Her mother's troubled gaze moved from the men to Maryanne, surveying her attire with a single devastating look.

Until that moment, Maryanne had forgotten she was still in her pyjamas. She closed her eyes and groaned.

"Samuel," Muriel Simpson said in a shocked voice. "Maryanne's coming out of...his apartment."

"It's not what it looks like," Maryanne rushed to explain. "Mom and Dad, please, you've got to listen to me. I didn't spend the night at Kramer's, honest. We just happened to get into a tiff this morning and instead of shouting through the walls and—"

"Samuel." Her mother reached for her father's sleeve, gripping it hard. "I feel faint."

Samuel Simpson clamped his arm about his wife's waist and with Kramer's assistance led her through Kramer's open apartment door. Maryanne hurried ahead of them to rearrange pillows on the sofa.

Crouched in front of her mother, Maryanne gently patted her hand. Muriel wasn't given to fainting spells; clearly, she'd been worried sick about her daughter, which increased Maryanne's guilt a hundredfold.

"My little girl is safe, and that's all that matters," Muriel whispered.

"Listen here, young man," Maryanne's father said sternly to Kramer. "It seems you two have some explaining to do."

"Daddy, please." Jumping to her feet, Maryanne stood between her father and Kramer, loving them both so much and not knowing which one to confront first. She took a deep breath and blurted out, "I'm in love with Kramer."

"Sir, I realise the circumstances look bad, but I can assure you there's nothing between me and your daughter."

"What do you mean there's nothing between us?" Maryanne cried, furious with him. Good grief, she'd just finished spilling out her heart to the man. The least he could do was acknowledge what they shared, what they both felt. Well, if he wasn't so inclined, she was. "That's a bold-faced lie," she announced to her father, hearing Kramer groan behind her as she spoke.

Samuel Simpson, so tall and formidable, so distinguished and articulate, seemed to find himself at a loss for words. He slumped on to the sofa next to his wife and rested his face in both hands.

"Maryanne," Kramer said between gritted teeth. "Your parents appear to think the worst. Don't you agree it would be more appropriate to assure them that—"

"I don't care what they think. Well, I do, of course," she amended quickly, "but I'm more interested in settling matters between you and me."

Kramer's face tightened impatiently. "This is neither the time nor the place."

"I happen to think it is."

"Maryanne, please," her mother wailed, holding out one hand. "Your father and I have spent a long sleepless night flying across the country. We've been worried half to death about you."

"She didn't answer her phone," Samuel muttered in dire tones, his eyes narrowing suspiciously on the two of them. "If Maryanne had been at her apartment, the way she claims, then she would have picked up the receiver. We must have tried fifteen or twenty times to reach her. If she was home, why didn't she answer the phone?"

The question seemed to be directed at Kramer, but it was Maryanne who answered. "I unplugged it."

"Why would you do that?" Muriel inquired softly. "Surely you know we'd try to reach you. We're your parents. We love you!"

"That's it, young lady. You're moving back with us."

"You can't force me to leave Seattle. I refuse."

"This place..." Muriel was looking around as though the building was sure to be condemned any minute. "Why would you want to live here? Have you rejected everything we've given you?"

"The answer is obvious," her father bellowed. "She lives here to be close to *him.*"

"But why didn't her...friend move into her apartment building?"

"Isn't it obvious?" Samuel stood abruptly and stalked to the other side of the room. "Adams couldn't afford to live within a mile of the Seattle." He stopped short, then nodded apologetically at Kramer. "I didn't mean that in a derogatory way. You seem like a fine young man, but frankly..."

"I wouldn't care where Kramer lived," Maryanne informed them both, squaring her shoulders righteously. Any man she fell in love with didn't need to head a financial empire or be related to someone who did. "I'd live anywhere if it meant we could be together." Her eyes softened at her mother's shocked look.

"Don't you remember what it's like to be young and in love, Mom?" Maryanne asked her. "Remember all those things you told me about you and Dad? How you used to argue and everything? It's the same with Kramer and me. I'm crazy about him. He's so talented and—"

"That's enough," Kramer interrupted harshly. "If you're looking for someone to blame for Maryanne's living in this building and working at Mom's Place—"

"What's Mom's Place?"

"A very nice diner," Maryanne inserted quickly. "We do a brisk lunch trade and carry a limited dinner menu."

Her mother let out a small cry of dismay. "You're...you're working as a waitress?"

Miserable, Maryanne nodded. "But I'm doing lots of free-lance work. None of the feature articles I've written have sold yet, but it's too soon for that. I just found out the community newspaper's buying a couple of my shorter pieces, and I plan on selling them lots more."

"You might have warned me they didn't know about your being a waitress," Kramer muttered under his breath.

Samuel drew a hand across his eyes, as if that would erase the image of his daughter waiting on tables. "Why would you choose to quit the newspaper to work as a waitress?" Asking the question seemed to cause him difficulty.

"It's honest work, Dad. I don't understand why you're acting like this. You're making it sound like I'm doing something that'll bring disgrace to the family name."

"But your education is being wasted," her mother said, shaking her head. "You could have any job in publishing you wanted."

That much was true when it was her family doing the hiring, but when she was looking on her own her employers were more interested in her job skills than who her father was.

"I'm afraid I'm the one who started this," Kramer interrupted. "I wrote a column about Annie," he said bluntly. "It was unfortunate, because I was out of line in some of the things I said, but—"

"Kramer didn't write anything that wasn't true," Maryanne hastened to say. "He made me stop and think about certain aspects of my life, and I decided the time had come to prove I could make it on my own."

"By denouncing your family!"

"I never did that, Dad."

Samuel's shoulders sagged with defeat. The long hours her parents had spent travelling were telling on them both. They looked at her blankly, as though they couldn't quite believe even now what she'd been doing for the past month and a half.

"I did it for another reason, too." All three of them were staring at her as if they suspected she'd lost her mind. "I'd met Kramer and we'd had dinner together and I discovered how much I liked him." She glanced at the man in question and saw him frown, knitting his brow as if he was looking for a way to stop her. "I'm sorry, Mom and Dad. I hated lying to you, but I couldn't see any way around it. I didn't want to worry you," she said, stepping next to Kramer and wrapping her arm around his waist. "I belong here with Kramer." There, she'd said it! "I won't be returning to New York with you."

"Maryanne, sweetie, you can't continue living like this!"

"I have a wonderful life."

Her father was pacing again. "You're in love with this man?"

"Yes, Daddy. I love him so much—enough to defy you for the first time in my life."

Her father's eyes slowly moved from his only daughter to Kramer. "What about you, young man? How do you feel about my daughter?"

Kramer was quiet for so long it was all Maryanne could do not to answer for him. Finally she couldn't stand it any longer and did exactly that. "He loves me. He may not want to admit it, but he does—lock, stock and barrel."

Her father continued to look at Kramer. "Is that true?"

"Unfortunately," he said, gently removing Maryanne's arm, "I don't return her feelings. You've raised a wonderful daughter—but I don't love her, not the way she deserves to be loved."

"Kramer!" His name escaped on a cry of outrage. "Don't lie. Not now, not to my family."

He gripped her by the shoulders, his face pale and expressionless. She searched his eyes, looking for something, anything to ease the terrible pain his words had inflicted.

"You're sweet and talented, and one day you'll make some man very proud—but it won't be me."

"Kramer, stop this right now. You love me. You're intimidated because of who my father is. But don't you understand that money doesn't mean anything to me?"

"It rarely does to those who already have it. Find yourself a nice rich husband and be happy."

She found his words insulting. If she hadn't been so desperate to straighten out this mess, she would have confronted him with it. "I won't be happy without you. I refuse to be happy."

His face was beginning to show signs of strain. "Yes, you will. Now, I suggest you do as your family wants and leave with them."

Every word felt like a kick in the stomach, each more vicious than the one before.

"You don't mean that."

"Damn it, Maryanne," he said coldly, "don't make this any more difficult than it already is. We don't belong together. We never have.

I live in one world and you live in another. I've been telling you that from the first, but you wouldn't listen to me."

Maryanne was too stunned to answer. She stared up at him, hoping, praying, for some sign that he didn't mean what he was saying.

"Sweetie." Her mother tucked an arm around Maryanne's waist. "Please, come home with us. Your friend's right, you don't belong here."

"That's not true. I'm here now and I intend to stay."

"Maryanne, for the love of heaven, would you listen to your parents?" Kramer barked. "What do you intend to do once Mom's Place closes for remodelling?"

"Come home, sweetie," her mother pleaded.

Too numb to speak, Maryanne stared at Kramer. She wouldn't leave if he gave any indication he wanted her to stay. Anything. A flicker of his eye, a twitch of his hand, anything that would show her he didn't mean the things he'd said.

There was nothing. Nothing left for her. She couldn't go back to the newspaper, not now. Mom's Place was closing, but the real hardship, the real agony, came from the knowledge that Kramer didn't want her around. Kramer didn't love her.

She turned her back on him and walked to her own apartment. Her mother and father joined her there a few minutes later, obviously trying to hide their dismay at its bleakness.

"I won't need to give my notice," she told them, sorting through the stack of folded clothes for a fresh uniform. "But I'll stay until Mom's closes. I wouldn't want to leave them short-staffed."

"Yes, of course," her mother answered softly, then suggested, "If you like, I can stay with you here in Seattle."

Maryanne declined with a quick shake of her head, trying to conceal how badly Kramer's rejection had hurt. "I'll be fine." She paused, then turned to her family. "He really is a wonderful man. It's just that he's terribly afraid of falling in love—especially with someone like me. I have everything he doesn't—an education, wealth, and perhaps most importantly, parents who love me as much as you do."

MARYANNE HADN'T KNOWN it was possible for two weeks to drag by so slowly. But finally her last day of work arrived.

"The minute I set eyes on Kramer Adams again, I swear I'll give him a piece of my mind," Barbara declared, hands on her hips.

Kramer hadn't eaten at Mom's once in the past two weeks. That didn't surprise Maryanne; in fact, she would have been shocked if he had decided to show up.

"You be sure and write now, you hear? That Kramer Adams— he's got a lot to answer for," Barbara said, her eyes filling. "I'm gonna miss you, girl. Are you sure you have to leave?"

"I'm sure," Maryanne whispered, swallowing back her own tears.

"I suppose you're right. That's why I'm so furious with Kramer."

"It isn't all his fault." Maryanne hadn't told anyone the embarrassing details that had led to her leaving Seattle.

"Of course it is. He should stop you from going. I don't know what's got into that man, but I swear, for two cents I'd give him—"

"A piece of your mind," Maryanne finished for her.

They both laughed, and hugged each other one last time. Although they'd only worked together a short while, they'd become good friends. Maryanne would miss Barbara's down-to-earth philosophy and her reliable sense of humour.

When she arrived home, her apartment was dark and dismal. Cardboard boxes littered the floor. Her packing was finished, except for the bare essentials. She'd made arrangements with a shipping company to come for her things in the morning. Then she'd call a taxi to take her to Sea-Tac Airport in time to catch the noon flight for New York.

The next morning, dressed in jeans and a loose red sweatshirt, Maryanne was hauling boxes out of her living-room and stacking them in the hallway when she heard Kramer's door open. She quickly moved back into her own apartment.

"What are you doing?" he demanded, following her in. He was wearing the ever present beige raincoat, his mood as sour as his look.

"Moving," she responded flippantly. "That was what I thought you wanted."

"Then leave the work to the movers."

"I'm fine, Kramer." Which was a lie. How could she possibly be fine when her heart was well and truly broken?

"I guess this is goodbye, then," he said, glancing around the room, looking everywhere but at her.

"Yes. I'll be gone before you're back this afternoon." She forced a trembling smile to her lips as she brushed the dust from her palms. "It's been a pleasure knowing you."

"You, too," he said softly.

"Some day I'll be able to tell my children I knew the famous Kramer Adams when he was a columnist for the *Seattle Sun.*" But those children wouldn't be his...

"I wish you only the best." His eyes had dimmed slightly, but she was too angry to see any significance in that.

She didn't reply and the silence stretched, tense and awkward.

"So," she finally said, with a deep sigh, "you're really going to let me go."

"Yes." He spoke without hesitation, but she noticed that his mouth thinned, became taut.

"It may come as something of a surprise to learn you're not the only one with pride." She spoke as clearly and precisely as she could. "I'm going to do what you asked and leave Seattle. I'll walk away without looking back. Not once will I look back," she repeated, her throat constricting, making speech difficult. She waited a moment to compose herself. "Someday you'll regret this, Kramer. You'll think back to what happened and wish to hell you'd handled the situation differently. Don't you know it's not what you've done that will fill you with regret, but what you haven't done?"

"Annie—"

"No, let me finish. I've had this little talk planned for days and I'm going to deliver it. The least you can do is stand here and listen."

He closed his eyes and nodded.

"I've decided to haunt you."

"What?"

"That's right. You won't be able to go into a restaurant without believing you see me there. I'll be hiding behind every corner. I'll follow you down every street. And as for enjoying another bowl of chilli, you can forget that, as well.'' By now her voice was trembling.

''I never meant to hurt you.''

She abruptly turned away from him, brushing the tears from her cheeks with both hands.

''Be happy, Annie.''

She would try. There was nothing else to do.

CHAPTER ELEVEN

"HAVE YOU HAD A CHANCE to look over those brochures?" Muriel asked Maryanne two weeks later. They were sitting at the breakfast table, savouring the last of their coffee.

"I was thinking I should find myself another job." It was either that or spend the remainder of her life poring over cookbooks. Some people travelled to cure a broken heart, some worked—but not Maryanne. She hadn't written a word since she'd left Seattle. Not one word.

She'd planned to send out new queries, start researching new articles for specialty magazines. Somehow, that hadn't happened. Instead, she'd been baking up a storm. Cookies for the local day-care centre, cakes for the senior citizens' home, pies for the clergy. She figured she'd gone through enough flour in the past week to take care of the Midwest wheat crop. Since the holiday season was fast approaching, baking seemed the thing to do.

"But, sweetie, Europe this time of year is fabulous."

"I'm sorry, Mom, I don't mean to be ungrateful, but travelling just doesn't interest me right now."

Her mother's face softened with concern. "Apparently, baking does. Maryanne, you can't continue making cookies for the rest of your life."

"I know, I know. If I keep this up I'll look like the Goodyear blimp by Christmas."

Her mother laughed. "We both know that isn't true. If anything, you've been losing weight." She hesitated before adding, "And you've been so quiet."

When she was in pain, Maryanne always drew into herself, seeking what comfort she could in routine tasks. Such as baking. She was struggling to push every thought of Kramer from her mind. But as her mother said, she had to get out of the kitchen and rejoin the world. Soon she'd write again. Maybe there was a magazine for bakers—she could submit to that, she thought wryly. It would be a place to start, anyway, to regain her enthusiasm. Soon she'd find the strength to face her computer again. Even the sale of three articles hadn't cheered her. She'd stared at the checks and felt a vague sense of disappointment. If only they'd arrived before she left Seattle; then she might have considered staying.

"Is it still so painful?" Muriel asked unexpectedly. Kramer and Maryanne's time in Seattle were subjects they'd all avoided, and Maryanne appreciated the opportunity to talk about him.

"I wish you and Dad had known him the way I did," she said wistfully. "He's such a contradiction. Rough and surly on the outside, but mellow and gentle on the inside."

"It sounds as though you're describing your father."

She pondered her mother's words. "Kramer is a lot like Daddy. Principled and proud. Independent to a fault. I didn't realise that in the beginning, only later." She laughed softly. "No man could ever make me angrier than Kramer." Nor could any man hope to compete when it came to the feelings he evoked when he kissed her. She came to life in his arms, like a wildflower blossoming in spring.

"He drove me crazy with how stubborn he could be. At first all I could see was his defensiveness. He'd scowl at me and grumble—he always seemed to be grumbling, as if he couldn't wait to get me out of his hair. He used to look at me and insist I was nothing but trouble. Then he'd do these incredibly considerate things." She was thinking of the day she'd moved into the apartment and how he'd organised the neighbourhood teens to haul her boxes up four flights of stairs. How he'd later brought her dinner. The morning he'd fixed her radiator. Even the time he'd tried to find her a more "suitable" date.

"There's another man for you, sweetie, someone who'll love you as much as you love him."

A bittersweet smile crossed Maryanne's lips. That was the irony of it all.

"Kramer does love me. I know it now, in my heart. I believed him when he said he didn't, but he was lying. It's just that he was in love with someone else a long time ago and he was badly hurt,'' she said softly. "He's afraid to leave himself open to that kind of pain again. To complicate matters, I'm Samuel Simpson's daughter. If I weren't, he might have been able to let go of his insecurities and make a commitment.''

"He's the one who's losing out.''

Maryanne realised her mother's words were meant to comfort her, but they had the opposite effect. Kramer wasn't the only one who'd lost. "I realise that and I think in some sense he does, too, but it's not much help.''

Her mother was silent.

"You know, Mom,'' Maryanne said, surprising herself with a sudden streak of enthusiasm. "I may not feel up to flying off to Paris, but I think a shopping expedition at Macy's would do us both a world of good. We'll start at the top floor and work our way straight through to the basement.''

THE TWO SPENT a glorious afternoon Christmas shopping. They arrived home at dinner time, exhausted, yet rejuvenated.

"Where was everyone after school?'' Mark, the older of the Simpson boys, complained. At sixteen, he was already as tall as his father and his dark eyes shone brightly with the ardour of youth. "I had a rotten day.''

"What happened?''

Every eye was on him. Mark sighed expressively. "There's this girl—''

"Susie Johnson. Mark's bonkers over her,'' fourteen-year-old Sean supplied, grinning shrewdly at his older brother.

Mark ignored him. "I've been trying to get Susie's attention for a long time. At first I thought she'd notice me because of my brains.''

"What brains? Why would she do anything as dumb at that?''

Samuel tossed his son a threatening glare and Sean quickly returned to his meal.

"Some girls really go for that intelligent stuff. You, of course—'' he looked down his nose at Sean "—wouldn't know that, on account of only being in junior high. Which is probably where you'll stay for the rest of your life.''

Samuel frowned again.

"Go on," Maryanne urged Mark, not wanting the conversation to get sidetracked by her two brothers' trading insults.

"Unfortunately Susie didn't seem to be aware I was even in three of her classes, let alone that I was working my head off to impress her. So I tried out for the soccer team. I figured she'd have to notice me because she's a cheerleader.''

"Your skills have been developing nicely," Samuel said, grinning proudly at his eldest son.

"Susie hasn't noticed.''

"Don't be sure," Maryanne inserted.

"No, it's true." Mark signed melodramatically, as if the burden of his problem was too heavy to bear. "That was when I came up with the brilliant idea of paying someone—another girl, one I trust— to talk to Susie, ask her a few questions. I figured if I could find out what she really wants in life then I could go out of my way to—" he paused "—you know.''

"What you were hoping was that she'd say she wanted to date a guy who drove a red Camaro so you could borrow your mother's to take to school for the next week or so." Samuel didn't succeed in disguising his smile as he reached for the salad.

"Well, you needn't worry," Mark muttered, rolling his eyes in disgust. "Do you know what Susie Johnson wants most in this world?''

"To travel?" his mother suggested.

Mark shook his head.

"To date the captain of the football team?" Maryanne tried.

Mark shook his head again.

"What then?" Sean demanded.

"She wants thin thighs.''

Maryanne couldn't help it, she started to smile. Her eyes met her younger brother's, and the smile grew into a full-fledged laugh.

Soon they were all laughing.

The doorbell chimed and Maryanne's parents exchanged brief

glances. "Bennett will get it," Samuel said before the boys could vault to their feet.

Within a couple of minutes, Bennett appeared. He whispered something to Maryanne's father, who excused himself and hurried out of the dining-room.

Maryanne continued joking with her brothers until she heard raised voices coming from the front of the house. She paused as an unexpected chill shot down her spine. One of the voices sounded angry, even defensive. Nevertheless Maryanne had no difficulty recognising whose it was.

Kramer.

Her heart did a slow drumroll. Without hesitating, she tossed down her napkin and ran to the front door.

Kramer was standing just inside the entryway, wearing his raincoat. Everything about him, the way he stood, the way he spoke and moved, portrayed his irritation.

Maryanne went weak at the sight of him. She noticed things she never had before. Small things that made her realise how much she loved him, how empty her life had become without him.

"I've already explained that," her father was saying. Samuel managed to control his legendary temper, but obviously with some difficulty.

Kramer's expression showed flagrant disbelief. He looked tired, Maryanne noted, as if he'd been working nights instead of sleeping. His face was gaunt, his eyes shadowed. "You don't honestly expect me to believe that, do you?"

"You're damn right I do," Maryanne's father returned.

"What's going on here?" she asked, stepping forward, her voice little more than a whisper. She was having trouble dealing with the reality that he was here, in New York, in her family's home. But from the look of things, this wasn't a social call.

"My newspaper column has been picked up nationally," Kramer explained, his gaze narrowing on her. "Doesn't that tell you something? Because it damn well should!"

Maryanne couldn't conceal how thrilled she was. "But, Kramer, that's wonderful. What could possibly be wrong with that? I thought it was a goal you'd set for yourself.''

"Not for another several years.''

"Then you must be so pleased.''

"Not when it was arranged by your father.''

Before Maryanne could whirl around to confront her father, he vehemently denied it.

"I tell you, son, I had nothing to do with it.'' Samuel's eyes briefly met Maryanne's and the honesty she saw there convinced her that her father was telling the truth. She'd just opened her mouth to comment when Kramer went on.

"I don't suppose you had anything to do with the sale of my novel, either,'' he demanded sarcastically.

Samuel Simpson shook his head. "For heaven's sake, man, I didn't even know you were writing one.''

"Your novel sold?'' Maryanne shrieked. "Oh, Kramer, I knew it would. The little bit I read was fabulous. Your idea was wonderful. I can't tell you how difficult it was to force myself to put it down and not read any more.'' She had to restrain the impulse to throw her arms around his neck and rejoice with him.

"For more money than I ever thought to see in my life,'' he added, his voice hard with challenge. Although he was speaking to Samuel, his eyes rested on Maryanne—eyes that revealed a need and joy he couldn't disguise.

"Oh, Kramer, I couldn't be more pleased.'' Her heart was so full it felt ready to burst.

"Do you honestly expect me to believe you had nothing to do with that?'' Kramer asked again, more mildly this time.

"Yes,'' Samuel answered impatiently. "What possible reason would I have for furthering your career, young man?''

"Because of Maryanne, of course.''

"What?'' Maryanne couldn't believe what she was hearing. It was ridiculous. It made no sense.

"Your father's attempting to buy you a husband,'' Kramer growled. Then he turned to Samuel. "Frankly, that upsets me, because Maryanne doesn't need any help from you.''

Her father's eyes were stern, and he seemed about to demand that Kramer leave his home.

Maryanne stepped directly in front of Kramer, her hands on her hips. "Trust me, Kramer, if my father was going to buy me a husband, it wouldn't be you! Dad had nothing to do with your success. Even if he did, what would it matter? You've already made it clear you don't want anything to do with me."

His only response was silence.

"I may have spoken a bit...hastily about not loving you," Kramer said hoarsely.

Samuel cleared his throat, murmuring something about giving the two of them time to talk matters out for themselves, and promptly left the room.

Maryanne stood gazing up at Kramer, her heart shining through her eyes. Kramer *did* love her; she'd known that for a long time. Only he didn't love her enough to discard the burden of his self-doubts. The boy from the wrong side of the tracks. The self-educated, self-made newsman who feared he'd never fit in with the very people who were awed by his talent.

"You were right," he grumbled, the way he always grumbled, as if she'd done something to displease him.

"About what?"

His smile was almost bitter. "About everything. I love you. Heaven knows I tried not to."

Maryanne closed her eyes, savouring the words she'd never expected to hear from him. Her heart was pounding so furiously that her head spun. Only...only he didn't say he loved her as though it pleased him.

"Is that such a terrible thing?" she asked. "To love me?"

"No...yes."

He seemed trapped by indecision, dragged down by their differences, yet buoyed by the need to see her again, hear the sound of her voice, gaze at her freckle-dotted nose and run his fingers through her hair. Kramer didn't have to say the words for Maryanne to realise what he was thinking.

"When everything started happening in my life, I thought—I assumed—your father was somehow involved."

"Did you really?" she asked, her words echoing with doubt. The excuse was all too convenient.

Kramer lowered his gaze. "No, I guess I didn't believe he really had anything to do with the sale of my book. Having my columns picked up nationally came as something of a surprise. For a while I tried to convince myself your family had to be behind that, but I knew it wasn't true. What really happened is exactly what you said would happen. You haunted me, Annie. Every time I turned around I could've sworn you were there. I've never missed anyone in my life the way I've missed you."

Her eyes misted. "That's the most beautiful thing you've ever said to me."

Kramer's look was sheepish. "I tried to tell myself your father was out to buy you a husband. Namely me. Think about it, Annie. He got you that job with the *Review,* and for all I knew he could have made it his sole purpose in life to give you everything you want."

"I thought I'd proved otherwise," she said. "My parents went out of their way to make sure none of us was spoiled. I was hoping I'd convince you of that."

"You did." He slid his hands into the wide pockets of his raincoat. "I guess what I'm trying to say is that if your father was so willing to have me in the family, I'd be more than happy to take you off his hands."

"Willing to take me off his hands. How very kind of you," Maryanne snapped, crossing her arms in annoyance. She was looking for romance, declarations of love and words that came straight from his heart. Instead he was handing out insults.

"Don't get all bent out of shape," he said and the smile that stole across his lips was so devastating Maryanne's breath caught. "The way I figure it," he continued, "you need someone..."

Maryanne turned to walk away from him. Not any great distance, mind you, just far enough for him to know he wasn't getting anywhere with this argument.

"All right," he amended, catching her by the hand and urging her around to face him again. "I need someone."

"Someone?"

"You!" he concluded with a wide grin.

"You're improving. Go on."

"Nothing seemed right after you left. There was this giant hole inside me I couldn't seem to fill. Work didn't satisfy me any longer. Nothing did. Gloria and Eddie asked about you and I didn't know what to say. I was grateful Mom's Place was closed, because I couldn't have eaten there."

A part of her longed to hear all the romantic words a woman wanted to hear from the man she loved. But it wasn't too likely she'd get them from Kramer. He wasn't telling her he'd heard her name whispered in the wind or seen it written in his heart. Kramer never would say things like that.

"You want me to move back to Seattle so I'll quit haunting you," she finally said.

"No. I want you to come back because I love you."

"And need me?"

He nodded. "I still think you could do a hell of a lot better than marrying an ornery old cuss like me. I promise to be a good husband—that is, if you're willing to put up with me..." He let the rest fade. His eyes grew humble as he slowly, uncertainly, pulled her into his arms. "Would you...be willing?"

She smiled, and hot tears gathered in the corners of her eyes. She nodded jerkily. "Yes. Oh, you idiot. I could slap you for putting us through all of this."

"Wouldn't a kiss do just as well?"

"I suppose, only..."

But the thought was left unspoken. His kiss was long and thorough and said all the tender words, the fanciful phrases she'd never hear.

It was enough.

More than enough to last her a lifetime.

Harlequin Romance ®

EXTRA!!! The Times EXTRA!!!

Runaway Bride Seeks Affair To Remember!

Do you like stories that get
up close and personal?

Do you long to be loved *truly, madly, deeply?*

Ever wondered what Harry *really* thought of Sally?

**If you're looking for emotionally
intense, tantalizingly tender love stories,
stop searching and start reading:**

LIZ FIELDING
JESSICA HART
RENEE ROSZEL
SOPHIE WESTON

They're fresh, flirty and feel-good.

Look out for their latest novels,
coming soon to Harlequin Romance®.

HARLEQUIN®
Makes any time special ®

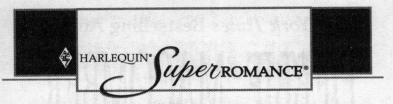

HARLEQUIN *Super*ROMANCE®

Welcome to Montana

BIG SKY COUNTRY

Home of the Rocky Mountains,
Yellowstone National Park,
slow-moving glaciers and
the spectacular Going
to the Sun Highway.

Set against this unforgettable background,
Harlequin Superromance introduces the
Maxwells of Montana—a family that's
lived and ranched here for generations.

You won't want to miss this brand-new trilogy—
three exciting romances by three of
your favorite authors.

MARRIED IN MONTANA
by Lynnette Kent on sale August 2001

A MONTANA FAMILY
by Roxanne Rustand on sale September 2001

MY MONTANA HOME
by Ellen James on sale October 2001

Available wherever Harlequin books are sold.

HARLEQUIN®
Makes any time special ®

Visit us at www.eHarlequin.com   HSRBSC-TR

New York Times Bestselling Author

DEBBIE MACOMBER

16 *Lighthouse Road*

Olivia Lockhart
16 Lighthouse Road
Cedar Cove, Washington

Dear Reader,

You don't know me yet, but in a few hours
that's going to change. You see, I'm inviting you to
my home and my town of Cedar Cove because I want
you to meet my family, friends and neighbors. Come and
hear their stories—maybe even their secrets!

Cedar Cove—people love it and sometimes they leave it,
but they never forget it!

See you soon...

Olivia

On sale September 2001 wherever paperbacks are sold!

Visit us at www.mirabooks.com   MDM830-TR

If you enjoyed what you just read, then we've got an offer you can't resist!

Take 2 bestselling novels FREE!
Plus get a FREE surprise gift!

Clip this page and mail it to The Best of the Best™

IN U.S.A.
3010 Walden Ave.
P.O. Box 1867
Buffalo, N.Y. 14240-1867

IN CANADA
P.O. Box 609
Fort Erie, Ontario
L2A 5X3

YES! Please send me 2 free Best of the Best™ novels and my free surprise gift. After receiving them, if I don't wish to receive anymore, I can return the shipping statement marked cancel. If I don't cancel, I will receive 4 brand-new novels every month, before they're available in stores! In the U.S.A., bill me at the bargain price of $4.24 plus 25¢ shipping and handling per book and applicable sales tax, if any*. In Canada, bill me at the bargain price of $4.74 plus 25¢ shipping and handling per book and applicable taxes**. That's the complete price and a savings of over 15% off the cover prices—what a great deal! I understand that accepting the 2 free books and gift places me under no obligation ever to buy any books. I can always return a shipment and cancel at any time. Even if I never buy another book from The Best of the Best™, the 2 free books and gift are mine to keep forever.

185 MEN DFNG
385 MEN DFNH

Name	(PLEASE PRINT)	
Address	Apt.#	
City	State/Prov.	Zip/Postal Code

* Terms and prices subject to change without notice. Sales tax applicable in N.Y.
** Canadian residents will be charged applicable provincial taxes and GST.
  All orders subject to approval. Offer limited to one per household and not valid to current Best of the Best™ subscribers.
  ® are registered trademarks of Harlequin Enterprises Limited.

BOB01-TR   ©1998 Harlequin Enterprises Limited